Devon ran down the steps, her hot tears mingling with the cold rain. She didn't look to see if Jordan followed. Why would he? He hated her.

Frozen inside and out, she dragged the duffel bag behind her and forced her leaden legs toward the bus stop. She would find a cheap hotel and regroup. All was not lost. She refused to believe that anything so precious to her could be lost.

She was so deep into her mental pep talk, the men were on her before she knew it. She yelped as a large hand grabbed her injured shoulder. Hands pulled at her bag, ripping it away.

Devon whirled around, instinct and years of training kicking in. Her foot flew out and caught the thief in the groin. He let go of the bag and dropped to the ground, gagging.

"Bitch!"

Fear surging, Devon took a running step. Another man wrenched her around. A fist slammed into her temple. Her last thought before she lost consciousness was the hatred in Jordan's eyes. That was something she would never forget.

RESCUE ME

A
NOVEL

CHRISTY REECE

BALLANTINE BOOKS • NEW YORK

A Ballantine Books Mass Market Original

4/35

Copyright © 2009 by Christy Reece
Excerpt from *Return to Me* copyright © 2009 by Christy Reece

Published in the United States by Ballantine Books, an imprint of The Random House Publishing Group, a division of Random House, Inc., New York.

BALLANTINE and colophon are registered trademarks of Random House, Inc.

This book contains an excerpt from the forthcoming book *Return to Me* by Christy Reece. This excerpt has been set for this edition only and may not reflect the final content of the forthcoming edition.

ISBN 978-0-345-50542-2

Cover design and illustration: Tony Greco

Printed in the United States of America

www.ballantinebooks.com

OPM 9 8 7 6 5 4 3 2 1

prologue

Chin in hand, Devon Winters crumbled the last of her blueberry muffin with her fingers. Sunshine flooded the area around the sparkling blue pool where Louisa set up breakfast every morning at six-thirty, as long as weather permitted. And somehow, except for a few months of winter, weather almost always permitted. Devon figured her mother controlled Washington, D.C., weather just as she controlled everything else in her life. The skies dare not rain on Alise Stevens's parade, or breakfast.

The one time Louisa defied her mother's edict, thinking it might rain, and had set up breakfast in the morning room, was a day Devon preferred not to think about. Having learned a painful lesson years ago, Devon worked hard not to put her mother into that kind of frenzied fury. Unfortunately, Louisa discovered the hard way, too, but at least she hadn't suffered the same punishment. Being screamed at was preferable to being locked in a dark closet.

"Devon, must you slump like a Neanderthal? By the time you graduate, you'll be humpbacked."

Without a glance at her mother, Devon automatically sat up straighter.

"Henry, don't forget, dinner tomorrow night at the Tollivers'. Though I'd much rather not go. That embarrassing incident with their daughter makes it so awkward. But the Tollivers are one of the oldest families in D.C. society. It could be damaging if we don't make an appearance."

Henry Stevens bent his morning paper ever so slightly, and his thin face peered over the edge. "The incident you refer to was tragic, not embarrassing. Their daughter died of a drug overdose."

Doing what she'd done for as long as Devon could remember, Alise ignored her husband's comment. "Also, the fund-raising event for Senator Mallard is set for a week from Tuesday. I've told Louisa three times to make sure your new tuxedo is cleaned. I do hope she can remember. It seems the older she gets, the more forgetful she is. Perhaps we should consider getting new help."

This time the paper came all the way down. Her stepfather rarely lost his temper, but Devon could tell an event was brewing. She held her breath.

"Louisa has been with me for years. Do not even think about letting her go. Do you understand?"

Alise waved a thin, elegant hand, not one bit intimidated by her husband's anger. "Really, Henry. You act as though I meant to kill her. I simply believe that—"

Henry turned his gaze to Devon. "Sweetheart, if you're through with breakfast, why don't you go get ready for school?"

Eager to miss the coming fireworks, Devon jumped to her feet. Unfortunately, Devon's movements distracted Alise, calling attention to the daughter who never pleased her.

Critical eyes skimmed over Devon's body. "I noticed yesterday that your school uniform is getting too tight. You do realize that you're not going to get a new one this year, don't you?"

"Yes, Mother."

"Then I suggest you stop stuffing yourself like a pig at every meal, or you'll soon look like one. Thankfully, your new school doesn't require uniforms. They can get so expensive."

The muffin Devon had consumed turned to lead in her stomach. "What do you mean, my new school?"

Her mother raised an eyebrow. "Just that. Next year, you'll be attending a boarding school in Boston."

The sound of Henry's newspaper being crumpled barely penetrated her shocked mind. They were sending her away?

Her stepfather's concerned face appeared in front of her. "We were going to tell you this weekend." He shot a loathing glance at his wife, then turned back to Devon. "I think you'll like it there. Meet new friends, see new places."

Devon could only stare up at him as bewildered hurt trampled over her heart. Henry had always been her champion against her mother. Why was he going along with this? "You don't want me anymore?"

Her mother huffed a loud, exasperated sigh. "Stop the dramatics, Devon. You'll do what we tell you to do. Now, go get ready for school. If you're late this morning, I won't write an excuse for you. You can just spend time in detention."

Henry pulled Devon to him in a hug, then released her and gave her one of his encouraging smiles. "We'll talk about it this weekend, sugar. But I promise it's not because I don't want you here. I just think you'd really enjoy it. And they're very excited you're coming. I told them how smart you are and how you pick up languages so easily. The headmistress can't wait to meet you. She's going to design a curriculum especially for you, with all of your favorite things."

"For heaven's sake, Henry, stop coddling her. It's the reason she needs to go away. You treat her like a baby. It's time she grew up."

Henry twisted his head around and snarled, "For God's sake, Alise. She's only thirteen years old. For once, please act like a real mother."

Fear whipped through Devon at the expression on her mother's face. Despite the hurt at being sent away, she couldn't prevent her legs from backing up as she saw her mother rise.

"You bastard, I am her mother. I could easily have aborted her or given her up for adoption. Instead, I've given her a home, and what credit do I get? None."

Looking as though he wanted to sit down and cry with Devon, Henry straightened. Nudging her gently with his hand, he whispered, "Go on, sweetie. We'll talk later."

Though tears flooded her eyes at her mother's cruel words, self-preservation had her nodding in agreement. She whirled around, took a running step, and slammed into a hard body. Her head jerked up; all breath left her lungs.

"Whoa there, squirt. You okay?" Jordan Montgomery looked down at her. Though his mouth lifted in a small smile, the sympathy and anger in his beautiful dark brown eyes told her he'd heard every humiliating word her mother had hurled at her.

Mortification and extreme delight created an odd jumble of emotions inside her. She worked hard at showing only the delight. Unfortunately, the tears rolling down her face spoiled her act.

Gentle, masculine fingers wiped a tear off her cheek. "You know, in another couple of years, Henry will be beating the boys back with a stick."

Even though a part of her knew he was only teasing, trying to make her feel better, the part that held her heart couldn't resist a shiver. Jordan thought she would be beautiful someday. Suddenly her day seemed brighter.

"Jordan, how delightful." Her mother stood right behind her, her voice lowered to a husky softness. "We didn't know you were coming."

Jordan's deep voice rumbled over Devon's head. "I'm on break from college, and thought I'd come by and say hello."

"Well, we're so pleased you did."

Devon frowned at the odd, purring sound in her mother's voice. Before she could wonder about it, fingers dug into her arm, pulling her away from Jordan. "I'm not going to tell you again. Get ready for school. Honestly, sometimes you are the most dense child."

Knowing her mother would only further humiliate her, Devon moved away from Jordan. How she wished she could stay home and just stare at him. Being around him always made her happy.

With one last glance in his direction, she headed toward the door. Jordan's deep voice stopped her. "Hey Dev, since I'm in town for a few days, how about a rematch on that chess game. Say tomorrow afternoon, around two?"

Life turned magnificently brighter. "You bet." Beaming, Devon ran into the house. She had a date tomorrow with Jordan Montgomery. Nothing could be better than that.

As she pulled on her snug uniform, she tried to forget her mother's cruel words. She'd known for years that her mother hated her. Nothing she said should be a surprise. Devon also tried to ignore the extreme worry that she would be going away to school next year. Henry would never send her away without a good reason. This school must be one of the best, because despite her mother's meanness, Henry would make sure she was all right.

Her gray eyes stared sightlessly at the mirror as she scooped curly blond locks into a ponytail holder. How lucky she was that Henry had married her mother. Not only was he a wonderful father, he'd brought Jordan into her life.

Jordan was Henry's godson. His parents had died years ago, and though he lived with his grandmother in Virginia, he often came to visit Henry. Since he'd started college, she hadn't seen him nearly as much. The rarity of his visits made them all the more precious.

Tall, dark, and *dreamy* were the only words to describe Jordan. He was always so nice to her, teasing her, making her laugh unlike anyone else. He played board games with her, told her jokes, and the last time he was here, she'd actually beat him in chess. She was definitely growing up. His comment today proved that. In a few years, she would be a woman.

He didn't know it yet, mostly because it was years too soon. But one day, when she was grown up and beautiful, and their age difference no longer mattered, she intended to marry Jordan Montgomery.

He was her dream come true.

As Jordan watched the young girl run into the house, his heart turned over. Poor kid. Hard to believe a sweet, sensitive girl like Devon belonged to the callous bitch standing in front of him, eating him with her eyes.

"I had hoped you'd come by, Jordan," Henry said. "Would you care for coffee?"

Jordan watched Henry's expression and knew the man was well aware of why he'd come. Sitting down for a coffee chitchat wasn't the reason. Especially with Henry's amoral wife salivating beside him like a hungry piranha.

"No thanks. I actually wanted to talk with you about a hunting trip I'm thinking of going on."

Henry's eyes flickered with knowledge, while Alise gave a huff of frustration. Jordan never changed his expression, but inside his mind he laughed. Though neither Henry nor Jordan was interested in hunting, they'd discovered long ago that this was one of the few things Alise wouldn't want to stay around to hear. Alise was a strict vegetarian and reviled hunting. Hard as hell to believe that someone who looked as though she could eat her young actually hated killing.

She gave Jordan one last once-over. "You boys and your guns. I'll leave you two alone." As she passed him, she paused and ran a teasing finger down his forearm. "Stop in my study before you go. I'd love to hear how your school year is going."

Forcing his face to remain impassive, Jordan didn't bother to acknowledge the invitation. She knew there was no way in hell he'd get caught alone with her again. Once had been enough. Though he'd escaped before she could get her claws into him, he wasn't stupid enough to give her another opportunity. He'd never committed violence against a woman, but Alise Stevens had come very close to receiving a punch in the face that day.

Seeing that he wasn't going to answer, Alise blew out a soft, feminine sigh as she went into the house. Jordan blew out his own sigh, wanting to get the stench of the woman out of his system.

"Let's go to my office." Henry's hard voice told Jordan he hadn't missed Alise's less than subtle advances.

Knowing that eyes and ears were all over the house, years ago Henry had built a small, soundproof office. Once a day, he meticulously searched for bugs. Some might consider Henry's paranoia odd. Since Jordan had known from an early age that Henry Stevens's quiet, cool demeanor hid a powerful, intelligent man, privy to much of the country's most secretive goings-on, he thought it more than appropriate.

The door closed behind them and Henry headed to his desk. For the first time ever, Jordan detected nervousness in the man. It confirmed what he'd greatly suspected. Henry knew about the visit Jordan had received from a mysterious stranger named Mr. Giles.

Jordan dropped into a chair across from Henry and stared hard at the man he'd known and trusted his entire life. "You want me to go first, or you want to go ahead and explain why I'm being recruited by a government agency only a handful of people know about?"

A small smile twitched at Henry's lips. "I knew you'd suspect me, but actually I fought against the recruitment."

"Why?"

Weary wisdom etched on his face, Henry said, "I'm your

godfather, Jordan. I was at the hospital when you were born. Your parents were my best friends. If I'd had a more stable life when they were killed, I would have insisted you live with me instead of that cold witch who raised you. I care about you and want you to have a normal life. You accept their terms, *normal* won't be in your vocabulary ever again."

"You're saying once I'm in, I can't get out?"

"No, I'm saying once you've done what they want you to do, you won't be able to live normally, even if you're out. The job will change you, harden you. The compassion and humanity I see in you now might cease to exist."

Jordan had already accepted that. If he chose to work for the government in this capacity, he would become a different man. He remembered little about his parents. They'd died when he was six, but Henry had worked hard to keep them alive for him. Myra and Jeffrey Montgomery had devoted their entire lives to service for their country. They had been true patriots. Could he do anything less?

Jordan couldn't deny another reason. The opportunity for adventure was appealing. Hell, he was twenty-one years old. What guy wouldn't be interested in traveling to exotic places, taking down evil men, and saving lives?

"Are you telling me I shouldn't do it?"

"Not at all. I just want you to understand the risks."

"If you didn't recommend me, how'd my name come up?"

Henry snorted. "Hell, son, you don't save a school bus load of kids from a deranged gunman and not hit somebody's radar."

Jordan shrugged, unwilling to discuss the event. He'd been seventeen years old and scared shitless. Kicking the gun out of the guy's hand and jumping him had been instinct. His brain had been frozen with pure terror.

"That's it?"

"That and the fact that you can speak seven languages fluently, already have a couple of black belts, and if I'm not mistaken, didn't you win a science award last year for creating some kind of nontoxic explosive?"

Jordan shifted in his chair, uncomfortable with the amount of information people he didn't know knew about him. Even allowing that most everything one did was up for public scrutiny, the knowledge that people had paid extra attention to him left him unsettled.

"What time frame did they give you?" Henry asked.

"Till the end of the semester."

Henry's grimace revealed his concern. "That's only a few weeks away."

Jordan nodded. "You say you didn't want them to contact me. Does that mean you're part of this agency?"

"Few people know everyone in the agency. I have knowledge of its existence and a few of the players. That's it."

Jordan stood. Henry had given him all the information he could. Now Jordan just needed to determine if he wanted to change his entire life. As a goal-oriented individual, he'd set several milestones for himself and achieved each one. Going undercover for an übersecretive agency hadn't been one of them, but that didn't mean he couldn't be flexible.

"Before you leave, I just wanted to thank you for your invitation to Devon tomorrow. God knows she doesn't get a lot of happy days around here."

"I heard Alise tell her about boarding school."

Henry blew out a long sigh. The sadness in his eyes was testament to his love for his stepdaughter and disgust for her mother. "I should have seen that coming and told Devon days ago. I just hadn't been able to come up with any words. I thought telling that sweet child I'm sending her away was going to kill me. Now that her mother's dropped the bomb, I need to figure out a way to pick up the pieces and reassure her it's not because I don't want her here."

"I thought most boarding schools had mile-long waiting lists. How'd you persuade them to take her so quickly?"

"Are you kidding? With her IQ and gift for languages, I had my pick of schools. Rossfield Academy had the best curriculum for the types of things Devon's interested in." His eyes brightened with affection and pride. "She's an exceptional child."

Jordan's admiration for Henry had always been great, but when he'd met Alise a few months after their wedding, he'd been shocked, thinking the man had made the biggest mistake of his life. At the beginning, it was apparent that Henry was besotted with his beautiful and much younger wife. That hadn't lasted long. What had grown and flourished was his love for his stepdaughter. Henry had blindly married Alise for her looks and sexual prowess, but stayed in the marriage for Devon.

"I guess it wouldn't do much good to tell her that going away to school will get her away from her mother."

Henry shook his head. "I doubt that Devon maintains any illusions that Alise cares for her, but I can't bear to tell her that's the reason I want her to leave. If she doesn't get out, though, Alise will destroy her. I've no doubt about that."

"I'm sorry, Henry."

"It's not all bad. I married Alise, not seeing what she was, but I can't regret the marriage. Even though Alise will never agree to let me adopt Devon legally, she's been everything I could have wanted in a daughter."

"When we're together tomorrow, I'll see what I can do to ease her fear."

"Thank you, Jordan."

"She's like a little sister to me." His mouth lifted in a grin. "I'm just glad as hell Alise isn't my mother."

Henry's dry chuckle was filled with understanding. "I don't blame you."

Leaving Henry in his office, Jordan strode through the foyer, then out the door. He had no intention of getting caught by Alise. Hopefully when he came to see Devon tomorrow, he could escape her attentions.

Poor kid had a tough life ahead of her. Learning that she was being sent away to school had crushed her tender feelings. Tomorrow he would concentrate on boosting her ego and getting her excited about her new adventure.

As for him, Jordan already knew the answer to his own quest for adventure. He would take on this new challenge. Making the world safer for kids like Devon was a more than worthy goal.

one

Eight Years Later

With world-weary cynicism, Jordan's sleep-deprived eyes roamed over the crowded ballroom. The young and not so innocent of Washington, D.C., society milled about, pretending to be all they could be and less than they were. They looked like kids. Or did he just feel so damned old? After the hell he'd just returned from, his twenty-nine years felt ancient and jaded.

A long swallow of his third Glenlivet on ice eased him, dimming the horrific memories of grown men screaming and body parts soaring through the air. He shouldn't have come, but he couldn't face the emptiness of his home. At least here there were people and some kind of normalcy. The music wasn't bad, the liquor was good, and the scenery downright delicious.

A vision in white caught his attention. Time suspended into endless moments of breathless anticipation as their eyes locked. A strong surge of lust swept through him, heating his blood and surprising the hell out of him. Immediate lust wasn't his usual style. Long past the days of admiring a woman just for her beauty, he valued intelligence, a quick wit, and honor even more.

So what made this woman different?

Gorgeous, yes. Above-average height, maybe five-eight. Slender, but curved in just the right places. Shiny, lustrous mahogany hair pulled back into a sophisticated twist framed a breathtakingly lovely face, worthy of a poet's dreams. The severe hairstyle emphasized her high cheek-bones, long, slender neck, and gently sloping shoulders. Creamy skin gleamed under the bright chandelier lights, giving her an almost ethereal glow.

Elegance, sensuality, and beauty combined into a mes-merizing temptation. His eyes riveted, Jordan made his way slowly toward her, almost afraid she'd disintegrate if he took his eyes off her or moved too fast.

She met him halfway, her gaze so bold and smoldering he briefly wondered if she was a hooker. These kinds of events usually drew several of the high-dollar ladies. This woman definitely possessed the beauty for it and made no secret she only had eyes for him.

Drawing closer, he changed his mind. *No.* There was nothing jaded or worldly about her. She was an intriguing mixture of sensuality and freshness, scorching desire and excited wonder.

They were within inches of each other, and the room siz-zled with their combined heat. Though surrounded by hun-dreds of people, Jordan paid little attention to them, his eyes fixed on the beauty before him. His groin tightened and a surprising tempo set up in his chest. Damned if he'd ever felt such instantaneous attraction.

"I've been watching you," Jordan murmured.

A cool smile lifted her full lips. "So I've noticed."

"You've been watching me, too."

"Yes."

"Why?"

"I would imagine the same reason you've been staring at me." Her confident tone and words washed over him like thick, warm honey, heating everything in its path.

"I've been staring at you because . . ."

She raised an elegant brow. "Because?"

"You remind me of someone."

A tiny wrinkle developed on her smooth forehead as an odd expression flickered across her beautiful face. "Who?"

"A goddess."

Startled, ocean-blue eyes blinked up at him and he got the strange sensation that he knew her. "Have we met?"

She backed away slightly and shook her head. "No . . . I . . . no, we've never met."

Grabbing her hand, he held it against his chest to keep her where she was. "You okay? You look a little pale."

"Yes."

His hand played with soft, slender fingers pressed against his chest. "Would you like to go outside . . . get some fresh air?"

"Yes."

"Is 'yes' all you can say?"

Another smile lifted her perfect mouth. "Do you require more?"

Desire, hot and potent, pounded through him. "No, not at this time." A sudden need to hold her in his arms had him growling, "Let's dance first." Ignoring her startled gasp, he drew her out onto the dance floor and wrapped his arms around her.

Jordan had been attracted to many women over the years, but none who had hit him as hard as this. His erection pressed against the zipper of his tuxedo trousers. The woman in his arms would soon feel that solid bulge against her. As they swayed to the music, he stared down at her. Would she draw away? His mind snarled no, but he wouldn't try to keep her if he'd frightened her. If she didn't want him, if this was just a light flirtation on her part, he would back away and say good night. To stay would be foolish because he would only try to change her mind.

Her eyes widened as she brushed up against him. There. She felt him. There was no mistaking the meaning. A slight flush darkened her face as a flicker of uncertainty entered her expression. Seconds later, passion flared, hot and intense, in the depths of her lovely eyes and Jordan hardened even more. Giving him her answer in a more direct way, she moved closer and pressed against him.

The relief was astonishing, the fierceness of his arousal staggering. He held her closer still, allowing himself the pleasure of having a beautiful woman in his arms. It had been too long . . . months since he'd held a woman or felt the hot pleasure of release inside a soft, giving body. The anticipation leading up to the culmination would only make it sweeter.

Her soft sigh washed over him as she nestled into his embrace. When she placed her head against his shoulder, it was all he could do not to lift her and fit himself against the warm, soft center of her sex. Muffled spurts of laughter and the distant sound of conversation barely penetrated the roar of lust and need in Jordan's head. They'd almost completely stopped dancing, holding each other tight, their bodies rubbing and caressing to the rhythm of sensual music only they could hear.

A distant cessation of sound told him the music had momentarily stopped. The beauty in his arms pulled away from him and visibly shivered as if dragging herself down from their lustful cloud. Damned if he wanted to come down.

She peeked up at him through thick, dark lashes. "Are you from D.C.?"

Hell. She wanted to make small talk and all he wanted was her under him. Talk could come later, everything could come later except one thing. He wanted to ease himself inside her beautiful, lush body and forget reality for a few hours. "Shall we go somewhere else?"

Her head tilted back as her eyes searched his. Jordan hid nothing. She needed to see what he wanted. He needed to see if she felt the same way.

Small white teeth worried her luscious lower lip. Jordan held back a groan, wanting to sweep down and join his mouth to hers, bite gently on that plump lip that glistened with moisture. When she whispered "Yes," he almost shuddered with relief.

Taking her hand, he led her through the crowded ballroom, unknowing and uncaring of the people surrounding them. Many of them he knew, but none of them mattered at the moment. The only person he cared about right now trembled with desire beside him. He had to find a place to ease both of them and soon.

She stopped suddenly, tugging loose of his hand. "Where are we going?"

"My house."

"Wait."

His heart thundered. Had she changed her mind? "Why?"

He was surprised at the quick look of unease that flashed across her expressive face. Was she reconsidering? Had he rushed her? Dammit. She'd seemed just as anxious as he had.

"I . . . just."

"What?"

Her eyes flickered strangely and then, surprising him, she reached up and kissed him softly on the cheek. "Okay."

At her whispered answer, relief made him careless, reckless. He grabbed her hand again. "This way."

She followed him down a flight of stairs, then out the door. Jordan handed the doorman a hefty tip to get a cab as soon as possible. Within seconds a taxi pulled up, and Jordan ushered her into the vehicle. He lived only a few blocks away, so the waiting wasn't as agonizing as it could have been. He glanced over to see if she was as anxious as he was to be alone and caught her biting that luscious lower lip again.

"You keep doing that and I'll have to kiss you right here."

She jerked as though startled. "What?"

Jordan lifted a finger to her bottom lip and rubbed the soft, moist spot with a fingertip. "Here. I'm going to have to kiss you right . . ." He leaned down and sipped lightly. "Here."

"Oh." The soft sigh went straight to his groin.

Dipping his head again, he traced her lips with his mouth, barely touching. . . . A tingling, like electricity, sparked in the scant space between their mouths. Her breath, sweet and moist, heated him and Jordan was surprised to find himself sweating. When was the last time he'd wanted a woman this bad?

"That'll be seven-fifty, buddy."

His head jerked up. Hell, he hadn't even been aware of where they were. He shoved a twenty at the driver, took the soft hand beside him, and helped her out of the car. Pulling her along with him, he walked up the short flight of steps and unlocked the door. With a slight nudge, he pushed her inside and slammed the door.

"You want a drink?" Jordan grimaced at the rough edge to his voice.

She shook her head as her gaze took in the foyer of his home. She seemed younger here, slightly awkward.

"You okay?"

"Yes." She swallowed and cleared her throat. "Yes, I'm fine."

"Good." He held out his hand again, a little amused at how she kept twisting her head around to look at his house as he led her upstairs to the bedroom. He'd give her a grand tour tomorrow. Right now, he had other priorities.

As he reached for the light switch to turn it on, her hand stopped him. "It's more romantic this way. Don't you think?"

Moonlight from the double window beside the bed cast the room in a soft, warm glow, giving them just enough light to see each other. At this point, she could have blind-folded him and he would have agreed. He slid his jacket off, undid his tie, and pulled her hands to his chest. "Un-dress me."

Her fingers fumbled at the first two buttons and then worked quickly to unbutton his shirt. Jordan pulled on his cuffs and almost ripped the shirt off. Warm, soft hands spread across his chest, moving delicately, slowly. Hot blood raced to his erection, surging toward explosion.

Teeth clenched for control, his hands dropped to her waist, caressing the soft curves as they moved up to her breasts. "Your nipples show through your dress. Did you know?"

"Only if I'm cold or excited."

"Which are you now?"

She gave a nervous half laugh, half gasp. "I'm certainly not cold."

"No. You're hot, flushed . . . burning."

He lowered his head and heard a soft hitch of breath as his mouth neared hers. Just before he touched her lips, he moved, whispering a soft kiss against the curve of her jaw. She smelled sweet, delicious, the scent so light he couldn't place it but knew he'd never forget it.

A quiver swept through her body and surged into his as he kissed, nibbled, and licked down her neck, to her shoulder. When his mouth reached the barrier of her dress, he flipped the button at the back of her neck, and the dress slid down her body, pooling at her feet. Jordan uttered an explosive, appreciative curse as his eyes roamed down her slender curves.

"Damn, you're beautiful." He took a step back. "Turn around."

"What?"

Her eyes widened like a startled, frightened doe. And why shouldn't she be afraid? Even to his own ears, his voice sounded deep and rumbling like a wild animal within seconds of taking down its prey. Desire throbbing and insistent, Jordan forced a smile, hoping it didn't look as feral as he felt. "I want to see all of you. . . . Will you turn around for me?"

There she went with those white teeth tugging at her lower lip. Before he could lean down and capture her mouth, she made a halting little turn and presented her back to him.

Breath caught in his throat. She was a beauty from any angle. A soft, slender back flowed down to the most delectable ass he'd ever seen. Unable to stop himself, his hands cupped the perfect cheeks.

He laughed softly at her surprised gasp. "You're beautiful everywhere. . . ." He licked at the small hummingbird tattoo on her right shoulder, tracing it with his tongue. "I like this, too."

"Thank you." Her answer, soft and low, sounded like a polite child thanking an adult for a gift, but there was nothing childlike about the soft, lovely curves before him.

Stifling the growl building in his chest, Jordan pulled her around to face him and lowered his head. Latching on to a perfect nipple, his mouth sucked hard, her soft cry of arousal shooting electric currents straight to his engorged penis. When her hands cupped his head, pressing him against her, he suckled harder, taking her nipple even deeper into his mouth, relishing her taste, sweet but spicy.

Oh dear God, what am I doing?

Her body quivered, inside and out. She needed to stop him . . . had to stop him. She needed to say the words *I'm Devon Winters*. But she didn't want him to stop . . . she wanted him to hold her forever. How many times had she lain awake in her bed, dreaming of this? Wanting this without really understanding what she wanted? This need, this overwhelming urgency went far beyond her fanciful imaginings.

If she said the words, he would stop. Everything would stop.

When she'd overheard Henry telling her mother that Jordan was back home and planned to attend this ball, she'd cooked up this plan. Finally, after years of waiting, she was going to see Jordan again. She'd gone into the charade with only one purpose . . . hoping, praying he would see her as an attractive, mature woman. Then, after a light, teasing flirtation, she would tell him the truth. They would have a good laugh and then he'd accept her as she was now and never look at her as the child she'd once been. Not in her wildest imaginings had she considered they'd end up in his bedroom.

Yes, she'd dreamed about him, fantasized about making love to him. But nothing had prepared her for the incredible intensity or rightness. Jordan Montgomery wanted her . . . Devon Winters. It was almost too good to be true.

For years, she had loved him . . . the prince charming of her childhood fantasies, the hero who rescued her from her nightmares. The love of her life. So many things in her life had changed, but the one thing that had remained constant was her love for Jordan. Not seeing him for years hadn't lessened her adoration. If anything, her love had only grown stronger.

He was still the most handsome man she'd ever met. Maturity and character had sharpened the once-smooth edges of his face. Dark velvet brown eyes held mystery and substance, as if he knew secrets the average person could never fathom. Whatever Jordan had been doing all these years, the experience had given him a sexy aloofness she found wildly attractive.

Warm breath caressed her as he moved away and then latched on to her other nipple. Hard calloused hands slid over her, fingers hooked the edge of her panties and pulled them down. She barely felt the silk land around her feet as

Jordan's hands cupped her butt and pressed her against his body. Devon held back a cry, partly of fear, mostly of the absolute beauty of the moment.

Hot clouds of desire washed over her, obliterating good sense and coherent thought. Nothing mattered. The truth could wait, everything could wait except the here and now. Devon closed her eyes on a sigh and surrendered to the glorious sensation of having her dreams come true. This was Jordan, and she loved him. Giving herself to him was natural and beautiful.

Consequences and reality vanished. With a small sob of need, Devon grasped his head and held him to her breast. The feel of him drawing her nipple deeper into the hot moist cavern of his mouth created a scorching heat. This was so much more than she anticipated. Her fantasies could never come close to the reality.

Pulling his mouth away from her breasts, he pressed soft kisses down her torso. Everything inside her was winding up and unraveling at the same time.

"Jordan," she groaned a tortured whisper.

He straightened and stared down at her. "How'd you know my name?"

Lost in the moment, it took Devon several seconds before she could come up with a reply. "I . . . I asked someone."

His sensuous mouth moved up into the beautiful smile she so loved. "You have me at a disadvantage then. You know my name, but I don't know yours."

"Mary." The name popped into her head and out of her mouth.

His smile dimmed. "I see." Brown eyes searched hers for several heart-pounding seconds. Had he somehow guessed her identity? Was he just playing a cruel game with her?

"You don't look like a Mary, but I can't call you Goddess all night long, can I?"

"No," she whispered, relieved he hadn't guessed the truth, but suddenly wanting to come clean and tell him everything. He might hate her for lying, but how much more would he hate her if they made love? As wonderful as this felt, she'd never intended to take her deception this far. "Jordan, I—"

His lips stopped her words. Devon opened her mouth on a gasp. Jordan took full advantage and swept his tongue inside. As his kisses threw her into a maelstrom of need, his hands slid down her body. One stopped at her breasts, the other went lower, stopping at the top of her sex.

Devon gasped under his mouth. Things were moving so fast! She pulled her mouth away and breathed, "Wait . . . I . . ."

"Shh. Open those beautiful legs and let me in. I'll make it good for you."

She gasped as a finger slid between her folds, and without conscious thought, she opened her legs and allowed him entrance.

He licked at her lips as his finger moved inside her. "Damn, you taste good . . . like butterscotch."

"My lip gloss."

"What?"

"My . . . my lip gloss. It's caramel flavored."

Muttering "delicious" and other words she couldn't make out, Jordan's mouth skimmed over her shoulders and neck. She heard a slight sound and knew he'd unzipped his pants. It was about to happen. . . . A small, lucid part of her brain told her to stop him before it was too late. Need and desire had already won the battle. . . . Devon shoved all rational thought aside.

When his body stiffened against her and he blew out a curse, she was sure her dream had ended.

Jordan pulled away and looked down at her. Devon had never imagined he could look at her with such need. "Condom."

The growling tone of his voice caused a throb deep inside. What had he said? Pulling herself out of depths she'd never experienced before, she asked dazedly, "What?"

"Protection." He grimaced as if in pain. "Need a—"

She closed her eyes on another throb and whispered, "I . . . that's . . . okay."

He gave a deep, sexy chuckle. "I should have known you'd be prepared." Holding on to her with one arm, he leaned over and slid open the drawer to his nightstand. "But I've got one right here."

Something in his words bothered her, but she told herself to worry about them later. She had a vague, cloudy thought that he was sliding on a condom, then the long, rigid length of his penis pressed against her. She was wet . . . pulsing with need. Though he felt enormous, surely she could take him . . . they were made to fit together. This was meant to be.

He hooked a hand under her right thigh, wrapped her leg around his waist, and plunged.

Devon bit her lip to keep from screaming at the steel-hard intrusion. She hadn't expected the pain, as if she'd been split in two.

Jordan groaned against her shoulder. "Damn, you're tight. You all right?"

"Yes, I . . . I think so." She hated how high and emotional her voice sounded. She wanted to be mature and sexy. Forcing herself to forget her pain, Devon moved against him and faked a pleasured moan. Even if she didn't enjoy it, this was still Jordan and that made it perfect.

Jordan evidently wasn't buying her feigned pleasure, and pulled out completely. Her world tilted as he picked her up. Laying her across the bed, he kneeled between her legs. Before she could fathom his intentions, his mouth was on her. This time Devon couldn't hold back a scream. But the scream was from pure pleasure. His tongue lapped at her, then thrust inside again and again. She hadn't expected this, didn't know how to deal with the acute ecstasy, the extreme buildup of something inside her, winding tighter and tighter. Panting, groaning, almost crying, Devon bucked up against his mouth. Jordan growled as he grabbed her hips to keep her still and continued his assault. With lightning speed, everything within her imploded, and Devon screamed his name.

Without giving her a chance to catch her breath or recover, Jordan slid inside. Within seconds he was pumping hard, pounding deep, and then with a low, raw growl, he stiffened and then collapsed on top of her. He lay over her for a few seconds, the harsh sounds of their heavy breathing the only noise in the too-quiet room. His silence and stillness scared her. What was he thinking?

Rolling away, he stared down at her, his eyes hard and searching.

Her body trembling with explosive emotions, she tried to curve her frozen mouth into a sexy, satisfied smile. Jordan's growl of "Stay there" stopped her. When he sprang from the bed, stalked to the bathroom, and slammed the door shut, alarm zoomed through her.

Sweet God in heaven, what had she done? Before she could give it any thought at all, she jumped from the bed, threw her dress over her head, and ran.

two

Worry and guilt weighing like a giant stone around her, Devon wearily pushed open the door to her house. Her mother stood beside it like a sentinel, her normally attractive face almost ugly with fury. "Where the hell have you been?"

Devon flinched but didn't back down. Tonight, with Jordan, she became something more than the obedient, helpless child her mother liked to think her. "Out," she replied and marched up the stairs. She made it to the second step.

A sharp tug on the back of her gown had Devon scrambling for a hold, her arms swinging out for balance. She fell backward and crashed onto the cold marble foyer, landing on her right shoulder. Agony . . . intense . . . burning seared her. Biting her lip, she blinked back tears, struggling not to pass out.

The woman who had given birth to her but had hated her from the time she slipped from her womb glared down at her. "I said, where have you been?"

Devon bit back the pain, her jaw so tight she had to force the words out. "I don't have to tell you where I go and what I do."

Glittering hazel eyes narrowed like an eagle. "You were at the ball."

"No, I wasn't—"

"You're a liar. Three different people called to tell me they saw you there. Saw you dance with Jordan Montgomery.

Said you were all over each other, practically having sex on the dance floor. Then you left with him."

Pain receded under a rush of fear. "No, I never—"

"Stop lying to me, dammit!" Her voice grew shriller with each accusation she hurled. "Were you with Jordan? Did you go with him? Did you screw him?"

Devon pulled herself to her knees, the pain in her shoulder agonizing, making her less clearheaded than normal. Why couldn't she laugh at Alise's accusation, tell her she was stupid to imply such a thing? Her mouth was dry, and her lips moved but she could form no words. Pushing to her feet, she swayed as the room swirled, nausea and dizziness hitting simultaneously.

Alise grabbed her injured shoulder, her hand biting into the damaged muscle. "Answer me. Did you?"

Devon held back a sob. "Stop. Please . . . my shoulder . . ."

"Look at your face. Lipstick smeared all over you, mascara smudged. You look like a whore."

"What's going on down there?"

Both women looked up at the top of the stairs where Henry stood, his sparse head of hair standing on end, blinking owlishly down at them.

"Your little slut of a stepdaughter went and got herself laid."

"What?!"

"You heard me." She glared, fury and jealousy rivals in her gleaming eyes. "But it wasn't just any man, was it, Dev? It was Jordan Montgomery."

Henry ambled down the stairs, his bones popping noisily as he approached them. "Jordan? No, he would never do anything—"

Alise's wild gaze never left Devon's face. "He didn't know who she was, you old fool. Did he, Devon? The way you've changed your looks, changed your hair. He hasn't seen you in years, and I'm sure you didn't tell him who you were. There's no way in hell he'd sleep with you if he knew it was you."

Devon shook her head. "Stop it! Just stop it. It wasn't anything like—"

"Come on, Devon. You've had the hots for him since you were a kid. Don't you think I know? Don't you think he knows? Jordan and I used to laugh at your puppy-love expressions every time you looked at him. The only way he'd ever sleep with you or be attracted to you was if he thought you were someone else. Do you honestly think a child like yourself could attract such a man, much less hang on to him?" She shook her head with disgust. "You're even stupider than your father, and he was an idiot."

Before Devon could digest this heart-wrenching statement, her stepfather snapped, "Shut up, Alise."

Alise whirled her head around to her husband. "Oh dry up, Henry. You're just upset it wasn't you who got to her first."

Devon's stomach heaved. Oh God, what kind of family said things like this to one another?

Henry drew himself up to his five-foot-six stature. "That's disgusting. I've never—"

Alise's shrill laughter blended with the horror of her words. "From the time Devon turned fifteen, you've sniffed at her like a stray dog after a bitch in heat."

Devon's head shook in denial. Unable to listen anymore, she took a running step to the half bath in the hallway.

Alise grabbed the strap of her gown, ripping it from the seam. "Come back here, you little tramp. You haven't answered my questions."

"Leave me alone."

Alise grabbed at her again, but Devon jerked away and rushed to the bathroom. She slammed the door and locked it. Their arguing continued, Alise spurting her venom, Henry making angry denials.

Devon closed the lid on the toilet and sat down. Bending her head, she took deep, controlled breaths to hold back the panic and the pain. She had no choice but to leave. She had a little money . . . not a lot, but it would get her back to school. She would never come home again.

Taking one last bracing breath, Devon opened the door. Alise was gone, but Henry sat on the bottom step of the stairway. Her chest tightened as she took in the slumped posture of a defeated man. Henry had never done or said anything inappropriate and she loved him like a father. How could Alise treat him so cruelly?

Henry raised his head as he heard her approach. "I'm sorry, Devon."

"Why do you stay with her?"

A sad smile pulled at his mouth, making him look like a basset hound. "For a lot of reasons you'd never understand."

Devon shook her head, unable to understand any reason valid enough to stay with a woman like her mother. "I think it's best I leave."

"Devon, what Alise said . . . it's not true. I hope you know that."

Devon bent down and kissed his cheek, never doubting him. "I know, Henry. You've been a wonderful father. I love you and thank you for that."

"About you and Jordan . . ." The furrows in his forehead grew deeper with worry. "He's too old for you, sweetheart. Not only in age, but in experience. He's seen things . . . done things you'd never understand."

Devon drew a shaky breath. Talking with Henry about Jordan wasn't something she was prepared to do. Explaining how she'd deceived him would only get her a lecture. Knowing she deserved one didn't help.

Besides, Jordan was the one who deserved an explanation.

Devon swallowed hard to clear her throat of the giant lump of emotion. "I can't really talk about it right now."

The understanding look in his eyes was almost her undoing. When she was a split second away from sitting down with him and spilling her guts, he said, "I'm here when you're ready."

Planting one last kiss of appreciation and affection on his cheek, Devon took a deep breath and stepped around him. Feet almost dragging from weariness and pain, she made her way up the stairway to her bedroom. Her shoulder throbbed, her stomach felt like a giant twisted knot, and her heart thudded against her chest with a slow pound of impending doom.

She took her duffel bag from the closet and gazed around. This room had ceased to be hers once she went away to boarding school. It had become a place she slept on her infrequent visits home. Since she never intended returning, her eyes searched for mementos she wanted to keep. There was nothing. Her mother had redecorated years ago, turning her pretty, feminine bedroom into a cold, elegant guest room. There was nothing left of Devon in it. She grabbed the few items of clothing she'd brought with her from school and stuffed them in the bag.

The beautiful white gown she'd selected with such care and anticipation pooled on the floor as she stepped out of it. A mocking reminder of the excitement and hope she'd felt earlier. Turning her back to it, Devon slid into a pair of jeans. Her arms lifted to pull a sweater over her head but stopped at the wrenching pain in her shoulder. Fighting tears, she settled for a soft cotton long-sleeved shirt. Her fingers trembled as she struggled to button it.

Looking neither left nor right, she marched down the stairway, through the door, and into the night. At some point she would see Henry again, but never her mother. What little affection she'd had for the woman was completely destroyed.

The temperature was freezing and a light mist shrouded the darkness with a haunting, eerie quality. At the corner, relief made her stumble when she saw a taxi heading toward her. Since it was just a little before dawn and taxis were scarce this time of night, her spirits lifted slightly. Maybe her luck was changing.

Though sick dread filled her at the thought, she had to see Jordan. Alise would call him . . . turn into something dirty what had been the most wonderful experience of her life. She prayed that at least a couple of hours would go by before her mother went on the attack again.

He had to know what happened hadn't been planned. The deception, yes, but not the other. The experience had been special, too wonderful to be premeditated.

Huddled in the backseat of the cab, she shivered under the thin, wet shirt. Why hadn't she remembered to get her coat from the hall closet? There were sweaters in her duffel, but her shoulder hurt too much for her to make the effort to try to find them.

Traffic was light, so the taxi flew down Grayson Street, and all the while, panic built. The closer she came to Jordan's house, the harder it was to control the dread. She fought it back, but didn't try to lie to herself. He would be angry—that was a given. A man as proud and honorable as Jordan would feel duped and betrayed. She had to make him realize not only that had she loved him for years, but that this had been the only way she could think to make him see her as a woman. The reckless plan hadn't included making love to him, but she couldn't regret it.

His anger didn't worry her. Hadn't she heard Henry say on more than one occasion that Jordan Montgomery never lost his cool? That he was the most calm, controlled man he'd ever seen? No, it was the hurt and betrayal Jordan would feel that tore her insides to pieces. She had to make him understand she never meant to hurt him.

Jordan had always been so kind to her. Made her feel

important . . . special. She knew he hadn't seen her as anything but a child. But even then she'd known for years he was the love of her life. That was why she had to deceive him, to show him she was an adult now. He had to understand.

The cab pulled up to the elegant brownstone she'd left only a little while before. Devon paid the driver, wincing as she realized her funds were going to go faster than anticipated if she had to take a taxi everywhere. Good thing her plane ticket back to school was already purchased.

A fresh wave of pain washed over her as she stood in front of his door. After she and Jordan settled their differences, she would probably need to go to the doctor. Her shoulder was either dislocated or badly bruised. Either way, she needed X-rays and at least a sling.

Devon closed her eyes and took a bracing breath. Trying not to panic, trying not to cry, she pressed the doorbell.

The door jerked open and Jordan stood before her. The dark, beautiful eyes that had looked at her with such heat and desire glared at her with contempt.

He knew.

Jordan stared at the woman who only hours ago had been in his bed. Little Devon . . . all grown up. A little more grown-up today than she'd been this time yesterday. But wasn't that what she had planned?

Disgusting pieces of Alise Stevens's phone call only minutes before resounded in his head. *"She thinks she's in love with you. Devon tried to seduce two other of our friends last year. She's been seeing a psychiatrist. She's sick . . . delusional. Convinces herself she's in love and then tries to seduce men into bed. I just can't believe you, of all people, fell for her act. My God, Jordan, she's just a child."*

"Hello, Jordan. May I come in?"

Rage, disappointment, embarrassment, and betrayal barreled through him. Grabbing her arm, he pulled her into the house, ignoring her hiss of pretended pain. He hadn't hurt her and he knew the bitch was a liar.

Eyes narrowed, he inspected her, trying to see what he had missed before. No. Even without the contact lenses, he wouldn't have recognized her. A person could change a hell of a lot in eight years. Devon had changed more than most.

Adolescent plumpness had given way to sleek curves. Elegant, high cheekbones had replaced a round, cherubic face. Once-blond curls had been colored to a dark, gleaming mahogany. She was at least five inches taller.

Last time he'd talked to Henry, he'd mentioned that Devon was growing into a lovely young woman. Unfortunately, Henry had failed to mention she was also a little liar.

"Are you . . . can I . . ." She blew out a ragged sigh. "May I sit down? I'm a little tired."

Jordan jerked his head toward the sitting room. He watched as she dropped her duffel bag on the floor and made slow, careful steps across the foyer into the room, holding her right arm carefully to her side.

What was she faking now? Her lips were blue and she was shivering, so he at least believed she was cold. Before she left his house, he'd give her something to be cold about.

Fists clenched, jaw tight, Jordan worked to contain his anger—much of which was self-directed. Hell, he'd seen signs of innocence and inexperience. Instead of questioning them, he'd ignored them. For the first time in his life, he'd allowed lust to override his instincts. Disgust with himself and fury at her mingled with an astonishing disappointment he refused to even contemplate. Dammit, this was Devon. A girl he'd known forever.

Devon fought against tears as she stood in front of the cheerfully roaring fire. Ice-cold despair washed over her, followed by an all-consuming weariness. The ache in her shoulder, blended with the excruciating pain in her heart, made coherent thought almost impossible. What could she say that would make what she'd done right? *Nothing*.

He knew—there was no doubt about that. When he'd opened the door, his face had been full of disdain, his eyes brimming with revulsion.

Alise. Her mother would have put the worst possible spin on the situation. Devon took in a shaky breath. Well, she was here now and Alise wasn't. She would make him see, make him understand.

"Sit before you fall down."

Devon winced at the white-hot fury in his tone. Yes, he may be a calm, controlled man, but he felt betrayed. What proud man wouldn't be angry and want to lash out?

"I said, sit."

Devon collapsed onto the sofa and held her hands toward the fire to warm them. She should speak. Needed to begin her explanations. For the life of her, she couldn't seem to think of a thing to say.

"Well, *Devon*? Did you come to just sit by my fire or was there perhaps another reason for your visit? Did you come here to get fucked again?"

As his voice lashed out at her, she jerked, then bit back a whimper as agony ripped through her shoulder. Of all times to be in so much pain, she could barely think straight. Jordan stood within feet of her, waiting for the reason for her deception, and the only thing she could think to say was "Do you think I could have some water and aspirin?"

Furious brown eyes glared at her for interminable seconds before he whipped around and stalked out of the room. When the door slammed shut, Devon leaned back against the sofa and let pain wash over her.

He hated her. And why shouldn't he? In his mind, her behavior was pure deception and betrayal. Nothing more. How could she convince a man who now despised her that she had given herself to him because she loved him? He would laugh at her, of course. Reject her love . . . spurn her feelings. And he would deny any feelings himself. Why hadn't she thought about what she would say when she'd planned this? Even though she'd never intended for things to go as far as they had, she still should have come up with something. She had just assumed he would feel the same things she did. God, she was so stupid.

The door opened and Jordan returned, carrying a glass of water and an aspirin bottle. He slammed the glass onto the table in front of her, water sloshing over the sides, then thrust the bottle of aspirin at her. "Now, is there anything else I can do for you?"

Devon tugged at the childproof cap.

With a vile curse, Jordan took the bottle from her, opened it, and slapped two aspirin in her palm.

"Thank you."

Devon took the aspirin and drank the water, hoping the cool liquid would loosen her tongue.

"I'm waiting."

She took a deep breath and looked up into the scornful eyes of the man she'd loved more than half her life. "I'm sorry."

"That's it? You're sorry? You purposely led me to believe you were someone else. Let me screw you silly. When all the while, if I had known it was you, I would have vomited before I touched you?"

Oh God. Please. Don't let him have said that. Please. Please.

"Are you going to tell me you did it because you love me? Is that the excuse you're going to use for having lied?"

"Jordan. Please . . . I . . ."

"You. Little. Slut. That's exactly what you were going to do, wasn't it?"

Shaking her head in denial, Devon stood without conscious thought. He had to stop saying these things. He didn't mean them. Jordan was heroic and funny, brilliant and astute. Kind. He had to see that what they'd shared was more than sex. It had been beautiful and magical.

She drew in a deep, controlled breath. She had to tell him before he completely destroyed the most wonderful experience of her life. "I know you're angry with me and you have every right to be. But I knew if you knew who I was, you would never have seen me as a woman."

"That's why you let me fuck you?"

"Stop it. Just stop saying that. It wasn't like that. I . . . never planned to . . ." Desperation turned to bubbling panic. "I never planned for it to go that far. I wanted you to see me as a woman and then realize what we had together. It was—"

"It was sex," he said flatly. "And not even good sex."

She flinched but shook her head. "No, it was more than sex. You know it was. We shared more than our bodies."

He snorted and shook his head. "We almost did. That's the only smart thing I did last night." His accusing eyes seared her. "Tell me, if I hadn't used a condom, would I have found out in a few weeks that you're pregnant? Is that what you planned all along?"

Pain stabbed through her. "No! I would never—"

"Yeah, like I'm going to believe a lunatic."

The hurt consuming and overwhelming, she put her hand out in protest. "Jordan, please . . . please stop saying these things."

"Do you deny you've been seeing a psychiatrist?"

Devon couldn't control the shocked gasp. "How did you . . . ?" She closed her eyes. "Mother, of course."

"Well, what about it, Dev? You've obviously got some mental problems."

Her mouth was frozen, no words would come. What could she say anyway? Nothing she said would make it right.

This was so much worse than what she ever could have believed. Alise had poisoned his mind and there was no way to convince him otherwise. The fact that she'd been seeing Dr. Reynolds for several years added a final nail to her already tightly covered coffin. Explaining why she saw a psychiatrist wouldn't help her case, even if he believed her.

She turned toward the door, the defeated, shuffling sound of her feet distant and vague under the roaring in her head.

"Where the hell do you think you're going?"

Unable to take the hatred in his expression any longer, Devon avoided looking at him as she trudged to the door. Digging deep, she found a small spurt of courage, and muttered, "You're not willing to listen to any explanation I have, and quite frankly, I'm tired of being called a slut and a lunatic. Maybe after you have some time to think about things, you'll—"

A sharp burst of laughter erupted from him. "What? You think last night was so damn special, I'm going to wake up one morning and realize how wonderful you are? You really do live in a fantasy world, don't you?"

Tears seeped out before she could stop them. With a soft sob, Devon ran from the room.

"Shit! Devon, wait."

Grabbing her duffel, she dashed to the door. As she jerked it open, the door flew back, slammed against the wall.

"Devon, wait . . . don't—"

She whirled around to face him, tears blurring her vision. "Believe what you want. I gave my body to you because I love you. I have for years. Whatever my mother told you isn't the truth, but I'll leave that up to you to figure out."

She looked out at the drizzling rain and then back at the man she would always love but never have again. "You've always been my hero, Jordan. I'm just sorry I couldn't be yours."

Devon ran down the steps, her hot tears mingling with the cold rain. She didn't look to see if Jordan followed. Why would he? He hated her.

Frozen inside and out, she dragged the duffel bag behind her and forced her leaden legs toward the bus stop. She would find a cheap hotel and regroup. All was not lost. She refused to believe that anything so precious to her could be lost.

She was so deep into her mental pep talk, the men were on her before she knew it. She yelped as a large hand grabbed her injured shoulder. Hands pulled at her bag, ripping it away.

Devon whirled around, instinct and years of training kicking in. Her foot flew out and caught the thief in the groin. He let go of the bag and dropped to the ground, gagging.

"Bitch!"

Fear surging, Devon took a running step. Another man wrenched her around. A fist slammed into her temple. Her last thought before she lost consciousness was the hatred in Jordan's eyes. That was something she would never forget.

three

Darkness was her friend. Born into pain, she remembered nothing of what she was, what had been. Pain was her only knowledge, her only companion. Consuming. Overwhelming. Total. Until he came. He whispered to her, infuriated her, made her fight, gave her comfort. She knew him, yet she didn't. Father, brother, confessor, and creator. He gave her life, purpose . . . a reason to exist.

With lightning speed, pain attacked, immense in heat, its overwhelming entirety. In furious silence, she fought as it tried to weaken her, tried to destroy what they had built. She battled against it even as it suffocated her. A whirling vortex of despair coated her lungs, drowning, choking, obliterating all hope.

A gasping cry penetrated the smothering blackness, waking her. She jackknifed and flew out of bed, landing on her feet with a soft, soundless thump. She crouched low, tiny, frantic pants of air escaping as her wild-eyed gaze surveyed the dimly lit room. The threat—imminent, dark, and forbidding—held the stench of defeat as it clung, then dug deep, piercing the sanity for which she'd fought so hard. Her mind and soul clawed toward consciousness and reason.

Icy-cold remnants of fear still pounding in her blood, she straightened like a pointed arrow as realization hit. Her eyes absorbed the cool, sea-green walls, the flutter of light camel-colored drapes at the open window, the soft, plush carpet under her bare feet. The quiet, peaceful normalcy of her bedroom surrounded her.

With bitter disdain, she beat back the bubbling panic. *The dream again.* It always came around this time of year. She should have expected it. Been ready for it. But this time, the dream had been more real—as if whatever threatened loomed closer than ever.

She didn't believe in visions or psychic abilities— mumbo jumbo, elusive vague bullshit. She believed in cold, hard facts. A dream, nothing more. The fact that it felt more realistic than at any other time didn't mean squat.

Pure hot fury clenched into her system . . . cleansing and cauterizing, replacing any hint of vulnerability. She didn't have time for this crap. She was on assignment. The meeting tomorrow would require her total concentration.

Deep, even breaths expanded her lungs, forced out all thoughts but her mission. She locked any remaining fears into the tiny tight compartment only she was aware of— one only she had the key to. That door stayed locked. Always.

Refusing to allow the dream any more credence, she pulled on shorts, sports bra, and running shoes, tied her long hair out of the way, and marched into the second bedroom, which she'd converted into a gym. At the door, she stopped and took a deep breath of renewal. *Focus. Forget.*

The dream disappeared into oblivion as she pummeled, kicked, punched, and tumbled it into submission. Sweat poured from her in rivulets, and she relished the deep cleansing. Whirling from her boxing bag, she set the treadmill to a breakneck speed. Feet pounding in rhythmic pace with her heart, she raced away from any remaining demons.

Self-punishment, Noah would have called it. "When

you're angry, perceive any kind of vulnerability in yourself, you beat yourself to a pulp."

As she'd told him more than once, "Noah, you don't know shit." He'd just give her that calm smile of superiority he'd perfected over the years, pissing her off even more.

Her feet pounded faster. Noah was wrong. She had no vulnerabilities or weaknesses. Not when it came to emotions. Nothing fazed her. She liked it that way. She took care of problems, removed obstacles. But it was all done with cold, controlled, emotionless emptiness.

Noah McCall had taught her that.

Life had taught her that.

A stomach rumble forced her to stop. The need for sustenance vied for supremacy and won over the rush of adrenaline pumping through her body. Wiping her face and body down with a fresh towel, she headed for her utilitarian kitchen.

Within minutes, she'd prepared and demolished scrambled eggs, toast, and coffee. Easy and digestible were her only requirements. Food was fuel—nothing more. She neither enjoyed nor craved it, but she couldn't survive without it and if she'd learned anything, she'd learned how to survive.

After the food came her favorite part. She entered her bathroom and allowed herself for the first time since rising to slow down and almost enjoy the ritual. Stripping, she stood under the pulsing water, allowing the hot, cleansing spray to obliterate and drown any concerns. As wet hands glided over her soapy body, she closed her eyes in almost sensual enjoyment.

Stepping out of the shower, she towel-dried her strawberry blond hair, barely noticing it wasn't her natural color. Changing her hair and eye color was as normal as changing shoes. She blow-dried the mass of hair and allowed it to flow down her back. When she completed her assignment, she'd go back to her white-blond mane, which she preferred.

Research had revealed that her mark favored this color in his women. And since she definitely wanted to please him, it was a necessity.

The porcelain flawlessness of her face, carved into perfection by a top plastic surgeon's masterful hands, took little time to enhance . . . light foundation, a soft glow of blush to emphasize high, exotic cheekbones, and a tinge of mascara to lengthen long, lush lashes. She outlined her full lips with a soft, subtle pink and in an odd flash of whimsy, touched her tongue to the corner of her mouth, thinking of the cotton candy she'd enjoyed as a child. Her lips twisted as the bitter flavor hit her taste buds. How appropriate.

A quick glance at her nails reassured her that the manicure she'd had yesterday was still intact. Cloaked with the all-important sensuality and femininity that made her one of the best undercover operatives in the business, she strolled to the bedroom and threw open the closet door. Though she would only be seeing Noah today to review some details of her latest assignment, she was on duty at all times, which meant performing her role.

She slid her sleek, hard body into an understated but elegant green sleeveless dress, knowing it would emphasize her eye color choice of new spring grass. Slipping her feet into Manolo Blahniks, she surveyed the woman in the full-length mirror. Beautiful, poised perfection. Artists wept to paint her, photographers begged to capture her image, and men would die to sleep with her.

A slight smile of satisfaction softened her face, altering her looks. Anyone who looked at her now would see something otherworldly and ethereal—almost angelic. But if they drew closer . . . close enough to gaze into the stormy depths of her eyes, they would see nothing . . . a soul stripped bare. A beautiful shell, unfathomable . . . cold, empty.

All traces of vulnerability gone, Eden St. Claire stepped out of her apartment and quietly closed the door. Purpose and goal clear and resolute once more. Dreams became nonexistent vapors of bad karma floating into empty air. Nothing and no one could touch her . . . or hurt her, ever again.

Eden glided into the nondescript building that housed the Paris office of Last Chance Rescue Enterprises. Nestled between a small insurance company and a mediocre pastry shop, LCR looked to be an ill-kept, not very successful travel agency. It boasted two full-time employees, and any unfortunate person who walked through the shabby, paint-chipped doors looking for help with their travel destination left quickly, disappointed and usually annoyed. The employees appeared to be unmotivated, barely competent, and slightly belligerent. They were as deceptive as the building itself. On the tenth floor, behind a locked, hidden door, were some of the best-trained mercenaries in the world.

The Paris LCR location was the home office. There were six branch offices throughout the world. Each employed between ten and twenty-five lethal and highly motivated people whose sole purpose was to rescue victims.

LCR had few restrictions on rescue other than absolute secrecy, no police or government involvement, and no retaliation against the kidnapper unless warranted by the operative responsible for the mission. LCR was not in the revenge business. Rescue was their one and only priority, with few exceptions. But if the opportunity arose, they gladly put those people or organizations out of commission.

Eden nodded toward the overtattooed young woman sitting at the desk, filing her nails and chewing a giant wad of gum. Pressing her hand against a panel that immediately recognized her fingerprints, Eden barely noticed the normal routine of shades drawing closed and the click of the front door locking behind her. When an opening appeared in the wall, she slipped through and into the elevator, throwing over her shoulder, "See you later, Angela."

Seconds later, the door slid open and Eden stepped out. Thick, coffee cream carpet cushioned her footsteps as she approached Noah's office. No expense was spared for any LCR branch, though she thought this one was the nicest. With its arched windows, abundance of lush, green plants, and collection of Asian artwork, the décor was stylish but unpretentious.

She knocked briefly before opening the office door.

Noah sat in his usual slumped position in his chair, staring at three different monitors on his gargantuan cherry desk. Eden often joked that from here, he manipulated and ran the world to suit him. Sometimes she wasn't sure that wasn't the truth. The man often knew things well before they happened, making him either clairvoyant or having more control than any one person should have. She could only be grateful they fought on the same side. Having Noah on the opposite side was not something she cared to contemplate.

"Darlin', you look like something the cats gnawed on all night long and spit out this morning."

She rolled her eyes as she perched on the leather chair in front of him. "Noah, using your good-old-boy southern drawl doesn't make your insults any less insulting."

A small smile played around his stern mouth and Eden once again marveled how she could look at this movie-star-handsome man and feel no attraction whatsoever. Another reinforcement that those kinds of feelings had been destroyed long ago.

"When's the last time you had a full night's sleep?"

Denying vulnerability came as natural to her as breathing. "I don't know what you're talking about."

Without moving a muscle or even looking directly at

her, she sensed his tension. He knew she was lying and if there was one thing her boss hated, it was lies. Though they both did their fair share of lying when appropriate, doing it to each other was taboo.

Settling deeper into the comfortable chair, she blew out a small sigh. "Fine. I had a few disturbing dreams. You know I always do this time of year. They'll be gone in a few days and everything will be back to normal."

"Not nightmares?"

"You know I don't have nightmares." Dreams happened during sleep; nightmares occurred when a person was wide-awake, so they were able to fully appreciate the experience.

He granted her a small reprieve by giving a nod of acknowledgment and not pursuing the discussion. Why should he when Noah knew better than anyone what those dreams were about and what triggered them?

"You ready for your lunch with Georges tomorrow?" Noah asked.

Eden watched with curious eyes as he fiddled with a pen on his desk. For some reason, she got the idea he was nervous. Ridiculous. Noah wasn't any more human than she was when it came to those kinds of emotions.

"More than ready. I'm just hoping he doesn't blow me off again. I just knew I was going to get an invitation from him last week, and then his father called him in for a family meeting. Hopefully the meeting included big brother Marc. If the bastard's concentrating on family business, at least he's not raping a child somewhere."

Noah's mouth flattened in a grim line. "It's been over a month since Christina was kidnapped."

"Yes, and she would already be at home, safe and sound, getting the help she needs if her father hadn't tried to handle this on his own. Thank heaven her mother came to us."

Pushing his chair back, Noah stood and stretched his big body. There was no telling how long he'd been at his desk.

With ten operatives under his wing, not to mention all the other branches, it was a wonder he got away from his desk at all. Today, for some reason, he seemed more tense than usual.

"I'll get her back, Noah. From what her mother told me, Christina's a fighter. She'll do what she has to do to survive until I can get to her. She won't be the innocent child she once was, but she'll be alive and she'll learn how to function."

As her friend and mentor walked around his office, stretching out stiff muscles, Eden couldn't help but admire him. Though she felt no attraction, she was still woman enough to appreciate exquisite craftsmanship. And Noah McCall was a superb specimen.

Standing well over six feet tall, shoulders NFL-broad, with slender hips that might be the envy of many a woman, and long, muscular legs that could be considered lethal weapons. She should know. How many times had he wrapped them around her and tried to squeeze the life out of her in a training exercise? There was little about Noah that wasn't lethal. And all those solid steel muscles were covered in a swarthy darkness. In another lifetime, Noah would have been a pirate . . . ruthless, invincible, and deadly. Not really different than he was today.

"What time's your meeting with Georges?"

"One o'clock. I'm hoping to at least get him to talk about some locations we can check out. He's been frustratingly closed-mouth, but if I can get him to boast about his family's wealth, perhaps he'll give us something we can use. What I really want is an invitation . . . something I can sink my teeth into."

A small smile lifted Noah's lips again. "Just don't bite off more than you can chew."

Eden turned up her nose at the thought of having to put her mouth anywhere on Georges's body. "Trust me, I'd spit him out before I became infected."

She stood and bent her head back and forth, wincing at the small pop from her stiff neck. Her poor night's sleep was beginning to make her feel itchy and out of sorts. "If you've got no more words of wisdom, I think I'll head back home and regroup before my meeting tomorrow. I don't mind looking a little peaked, since Georges can be so protective, but neither do I want to look like a zombie."

"Actually, I have a couple of new cases to discuss with you, but I need to do a little more research before bringing you in."

Eden nodded, trusting that when the time was right, Noah would brief her. She'd trusted the man with her life, so she rarely second-guessed him on his decisions. She had more than enough to occupy her until her next assignment.

Not until Eden blew a kiss and walked out the door did Noah allow the tension in his body to relax. He hadn't been wrong in his assessment. She did look rough and worn-out . . . or at least as rough as Eden could look. With beauty like that, even exhaustion looked good on her. She was right, Georges would eat up that kind of fragility.

Fragile. Exactly what she didn't need to be. Extracting Christina Clement would take her full concentration. She could afford no weakness. Unfortunately, this time of year always brought any remaining weakness in Eden to light. The anniversary of her worst nightmare was on the horizon and with it came the requisite torturous dreams.

And if what he believed he'd set into place weeks ago was about to happen, then those dreams would become even more real.

Returning to his desk, Noah clicked a couple of keys on the keyboard. As the familiar image appeared on the monitor, he stared hard at the strong, masculine features of the man who could very well destroy one of the bravest

women he'd ever known. And if that happened, it would
be Noah's fault. But he hadn't seen any other way.

Eden was twenty-eight years old now. Seven years ago
she'd gone through one of the most horrific events any
person, woman or man, could face. She'd triumphed and
become more than she ever thought she could be. She'd
even surprised him and he was hard to surprise. But the
decision he'd made all those years ago was beginning to
nag at him. Noah was well aware of his tendency to play
God with people's lives. He rarely regretted it because he
was really quite good at it.

On her last birthday . . . or the date they always acknowledged as her birthday, which was her first day as an
LCR operative . . . he realized that unless things changed,
Eden would remain with LCR for decades. Which wouldn't
be bad for LCR. She was one of the best he'd ever had. But
it also meant, at some point, she would either get herself
killed or burn out. He wanted neither of them for her.

She had no friends other than him, no social life. The
few times he'd urged her to take time off, she'd scoffed
and refused. Once, after being forced to take out two vile,
evil creatures who'd stolen a child from a playground, he
insisted she take a small vacation. She reluctantly agreed,
but then returned the very next day, insisting she just
couldn't do it.

The man about to come back into her life would either
give her absolution and peace or harden her even more.
Noah was willing to take the risk . . . he had to take the
risk. This man had been looking for Eden for seven years
and Noah had personally seen to it he wouldn't find her.
That decision should never have been his. Eden deserved
the chance to put her past to rest.

He only hoped it wasn't too late.

Pushing aside her half-eaten meal, Eden stretched a
slender hand across the elegant white tablecloth and

touched the manicured, masculine hand. "It's so wonderful to see you again."

Georges Larue brought her hand to his mouth. "My darling Claire, how I've missed you. Please tell me the truth. . . . How are you, really?"

Her fingertips caressed Georges's too-soft skin as she pulled away. Settling back into her chair, she flipped her hair over her shoulder. Triumph hit her as his hot gaze followed the feminine movement, desire darkening his eyes.

"Last week was difficult, but we survived. Jacques seemed to be in such pain, but the doctors assured me his condition hasn't changed. Of course, my Jacques is so strong, so courageous, he would never tell me if he was truly hurting." Tears welled in her eyes. Just a small amount to make them glisten, appear more luminous.

"Oh my sweet, I wish I could have been here for you."

Her mouth formed into a brave smile, the bottom lip quivering just a bit. "It is no matter. I knew you were busy and things are better this week. He seems to be resting more comfortably."

"I'm so glad for you. I worried all week." His light blue eyes gleamed with a mixture of affection, adoration, and lust.

A wicked, teasing gleam entered her expression as her mouth puckered into a moue to draw attention to full, luscious lips. "Now tell me, what was so important to drag my Georges away from me last week."

His broad shoulders lifted in a careless shrug. "Business . . . boring business."

"But Georges, it had to be more than just business. Please say it was. . . . I couldn't bear it if you left me in such need when only business called you away."

"Ah darling, business for me is so often a family obligation. One I can't always escape."

She shook her head, all sympathy. "My poor Georges. Your father is such a slave driver."

"That he is."

"Would mademoiselle care for more wine?"

Eden tore her attention from Georges's adoring face to glance at the attentive waiter. Dammit, she didn't need a distraction right now. "No, thank you."

"Nonsense, darling, have another glass."

"I can't. You know I have to return to Jacques soon."

"Of course, my sweet. What was I thinking?" Georges tossed an arrogant glance at the waiter. "Our check, if you please."

Eden forced herself not to slump in her chair. She wasn't ready to end their meeting, having learned almost nothing, other than that he'd had to take care of urgent family business.

"Come back to my hotel room with me, *chérie*, and I'll make that little frown disappear forever."

She struggled not to shudder. His kiss on her hand was almost more than she could bear. Taking it any further would be the ultimate in revulsion, though if it would get her the information she needed, Eden would allow that and more to accomplish her goal, no matter her distaste. Not that Georges wasn't attractive. Most women would look at him and see only his model good looks. Wavy blond hair, sky-blue eyes, high cheekbones, and square jawline. At six feet of sleek slenderness, he was probably many women's and some men's idea of a wet dream. To Eden, who knew way too much about what he and his family dealt in, he was the slime of the earth.

"You know I cannot betray Jacques in this way."

Georges nodded sadly and blew out a long sigh.

It never failed to amuse her that evil people actually had ethics. While the entire Larue clan had murdered, raped, kidnapped, stolen millions of dollars, and God only knew what else over the years, they had a surprising moral code when it came to certain things.

His father, Alfred, was known to be totally devoted to his

wife of forty years. Georges had somehow inherited that small amount of honor. As much as he desired Claire, he respected her refusal to cheat on an invalid husband. Faithfulness in a spouse was something he greatly admired. Before arranging her chance meeting with Georges, she'd studied the family extensively. Georges's profile had yielded this valuable tidbit. And Eden used it with skillful glee.

Though his brother, Marc, was the real person she wanted to reach, he had been impossible to attract. Unfortunately only young girls, ten to fifteen years of age, appealed to the scum-sucking Marc. She'd passed looking like a fifteen-year-old years ago. The best she'd been able to do was make contact with his brother. Hopefully . . . soon . . . she would get an invitation to meet more of the family. Specifically, his pedophile brother.

"So, your demanding father needed you. This problem was solved to his satisfaction?"

"It involved my niece. She is turning eighteen in a few weeks and insisting to live on her own. She no longer listens to Marc, her father. My family thought I could talk sense into her."

Eden refused to consider why Marc's daughter no longer listened to her father. Marc Larue had five children, three of them girls. He'd probably molested them all. Though it sickened her, that was not her mission. However, if something happened to Marc during the course of her mission, something fatal perhaps, it would be no loss to anyone.

"Eighteen. What a wonderful age. Were you able to help her?"

For the first time ever, she saw a flicker of what looked like shame in his eyes. So he knew what his brother was, might not condone it, but hadn't bothered to stop it, either. Most likely his entire family knew about Marc's twisted obsession. How could they allow his sickness to go unchecked?

"I agreed to discuss it again with my brother if she

would remain with the family six more months." His expression lightened as he chuckled. "Of course, the little minx coaxed a larger birthday party than what we'd planned. Now it's going to be a three-day weekend at my brother's vacation home."

Ears perking up, Eden allowed no excitement or anticipation to show, but did allow a small tinkling laugh to escape. "Well, you only turn eighteen once. How wonderful to have such an amazing party." She said the last part somewhat wistfully. When his eyes darkened further, she worried she'd overplayed her hand.

"Why don't you come with me, as my guest?"

Though relieved at his words, she drew away and sighed, regret shadowing her expression. "Oh, how I would love to, but I can't leave Jacques for that amount of time."

"But didn't you tell me last week, before I left, that he encouraged you to take a trip, relieve some of the pressure of caring for him?"

Satisfaction made her toes tingle. So he had remembered. She'd let that little comment drop last week, in hopes he'd take the hint and offer to take her to one of his family's many houses. Though her chances of finding any information were slim, it would have given her an opportunity to snoop. If anything was to be found there, she would find it. But this was so much better. To be in the midst of the entire Larue clan, at Marc's home. She kept her excitement buried and admitted haltingly, "Yes . . . he did . . . but . . ."

"But nothing, my darling. It will give you a much-needed rest and me the opportunity to be with you. You'll also get to meet my family, and I know you will love them as I do."

Since loving pedophiles and murderers was not her cup of tea, she doubted it. "Oh Georges, that does sound wonderful." She allowed her gaze to drop slightly as if she were torn. Then, seeming to come to a difficult decision, she lifted her head and said, "I'll do it."

"Excellent, darling, I'll—"

"Devon? My God, is it you?"

The gravel-rich masculinity of that voice could never be forgotten. Years ago, it filled her innocent dreams with delight. Later, it filled her nightmares. Now, today, her insides shredded to pieces.

Everything within her froze. Time stopped. Breath stopped. Her heart stopped. Barely a second later, life resumed. She lifted a cool gaze to the man standing in front of her. *"Je crois que vous vous trompez."* (I'm afraid you are mistaken.)

four

Jordan stared down at the beautiful woman shooting sparks of irritation at him from vibrant green eyes. She looked nothing like Devon. How ridiculous to have thought otherwise. This woman, though stunning, could never have the pure innocent loveliness of Devon.

With long, reddish-blond hair, eyes like clear green glass, aristocratic nose, and softly pointed chin, this exquisite creature screamed maturity, aloofness, and experience. Nothing like the lovely woman/child Jordan had known all those years ago.

"Excusez-moi. Je me trompe. Pardonnez-moi s'il vous plaît." (Excuse me, I am mistaken. Your pardon.) Backing away, Jordan returned to his table.

He noticed the woman never missed a beat as she resumed an animated conversation with her companion, her lovely shoulders twitching as she laughed. Her shoulders . . . that's what had drawn his attention. Rather her right shoulder. Bare and gloriously creamy looking, it sported a small, vivid tattoo—a hummingbird. The same kind of tattoo Devon had, and it was on her right shoulder, as Devon's had been.

But this woman wasn't Devon. Had nothing in common with her other than the tattoo.

Jordan stared morosely at the meal he'd been enjoying. He hadn't made a mistake like that in years. When Devon first disappeared, he'd seen her everywhere. On every street corner, in every restaurant, in every bar. It became an obsession.

When he realized the police were never going to find her, he took a leave of absence from his job. With his experience and contacts, finding one young woman should have been a cakewalk. Six months later, after exhausting every lead, he'd come to the same conclusion as the police. Devon Winters could not be found.

Whether something nefarious had happened to her or she'd somehow evaded the hundreds of people searching, he didn't know. Jordan finally concluded she either didn't want to be found or she was dead. The first scenario angered him and the second one filled him with anguished guilt.

He remembered clearly the things he'd said to her, the agony on her face. His fury immense, the words that spewed from his mouth surprised even him. Known for his control, few things ever drew a sharp word from him, much less the pure rage that erupted that day.

He shook his head, refusing to go down that path again. If allowed to go back in time and change one event in his life, that would be the one he'd change. But he couldn't. He might never know what happened to Devon, and he lived with the knowledge that whatever had happened, it was his fault.

He could blame Alise. God knew Devon's mother had been one of the worst mothers in the history of motherhood. The lies she'd spouted had fanned his fury, leading him to treat Devon with unparalleled cruelty.

No one was innocent. Even Devon. She'd set out to deceive him. Her immaturity and tender heart led her to believe she was in love with him. A small part of him still felt the anger. He'd been deceiving people for years. Hell, he lived in Washington, D.C., where lies were told with every breath. The fact that an inexperienced twenty-one-year-old schoolgirl had seduced him not only infuriated him but also shamed him.

How had he not seen through her disguise? Jordan knew the answer, though he would have liked to deny it. He hadn't seen through Devon's disguise because he hadn't wanted to see anything other than a beautiful, sensuous woman. The alcohol he'd consumed, along with his exhaustion, had blurred his judgment and weakened his instincts. Even the somewhat startled looks she gave him when he said something explicitly sexual hadn't dented his radar. He'd been intent on getting her into bed, not discovering her secrets.

He'd been protecting innocents most of his adult life, but the one night he let his guard down, Devon paid the price. No, she wasn't to blame. She'd been a child, however misguided, and trusted him to take care of her. He'd failed miserably.

A movement in his peripheral vision caught his attention. The woman was getting up from her table. All slender elegance, like a ballet in slow motion, she tugged a thin sweater over her gleaming shoulders, placed a quick kiss on her companion's cheek, and floated out the door.

Jordan stood, threw a handful of francs on the table to cover his meal, and followed her. The least he could do is apologize again.

A taxi. She needed a taxi. *Sweet God above, please get me a taxi.* Breaths sawed and shuddered through her. Once she was safely ensconced in one—alone, away from here, away from him—she would be able to take a normal breath.

"Excusez-moi, je voudrais faire des excuses encore pour interrompre votre déjeuner." (Excuse me. I wanted to apologize once more for interrupting your lunch.)

No. This can't be happening.

You're a professional. Act like one. The furious voice penetrated her frozen brain, jerking her out of her misery.

Eden turned and pulled from her arsenal of charm and wit. *"Pas du tout, Monsieur. J'espère que vous avez apprécié votre repas. Oui?"* (Not at all, monsieur. I hope you enjoyed your meal. Yes?)

"Oui, c'est l'un de mes restaurants préférés à Paris." (Yes, this is one of my favorite restaurants to eat at when I come to Paris.)

"Vous n'êtes pas d'ici?" (You are not from here?)

"Non." (No.) He grinned in a charming, boyish manner she remembered well. *"Non. Je suis Américain—des Etats-Unis. La Virginie, spécifiquement."* (Born and bred in the U.S.A. Virginia to be exact.)

Without conscious thought, she responded in English. "I have heard of Virginia. That it is beautiful."

He looked delighted that she spoke English. She had no worry he would recognize her voice or indeed anything about her, other than the damned tattoo. It was the only thing that hadn't changed.

"Yes, Virginia is beautiful."

A taxi drew up in front of her and she fought the overwhelming urge to grab the door handle and throw herself into the vehicle. Playing it cool, staying calm, was her only option. "If you'll excuse me, I have an appointment I must keep. I hope you enjoy your stay in Paris."

"Wait." A warm, calloused hand grabbed her wrist. He didn't hurt her, but pain as she'd not known in years swept through her. Sweet heavens, she had to get away from him.

She turned to look up at him, allowing only surprised curiosity to enter her eyes. "Yes?"

"I'd like to see you. Perhaps for dinner. Would you consider this?"

She swallowed a hysterical laugh and wondered what he would do if she bent over and threw up her excellent lunch onto his shiny, expensive shoes? "No, I'm afraid that's not possible. I am a married woman."

"But not to the man you had lunch with."

He couldn't know this, it was an educated guess, but the anger she felt at his comment grounded her. "I fail to see that is any of your business."

He released her arm and stood back. "I have offended you. I apologize again."

She gave a small nod of acknowledgment for his apology as she went to open the door to the taxi. Jordan's hand was there before she could touch it. "Allow me."

Eden slid into the cab, her relief to be escaping from him so immense, a small wave of dizziness attacked her senses, disorienting her. Before she could close the door, he stooped down, his dark brown eyes piercing her soul. *"Bonne journée, mademoiselle."*

"Au revoir, monsieur," she whispered.

He closed the door and the taxi sped away, giving Eden her escape, her breath, and a brand-new nightmare.

God in heaven, how had he found her?

Staring blindly at the back of the taxi driver's head, she kept her mind carefully blank, frozen. If she moved, blinked . . . allowed herself to feel anything, all would be lost.

At last in front of her apartment building, Eden dropped a wad of francs on the front seat before the driver could speak. Shoving the door open, she dashed toward her apartment.

The shaking started just as she opened her door. She had the presence of mind to slam the door shut, knowing it would lock automatically. Her hand released the death grip on her purse. She heard a distant thud as it fell to the floor, and then she ran, stumbling to the bathroom. A sob built inside, exploding, imploding. Myriad emotions blended together into a mishmash of boiling anguish and fear.

She made it to the toilet in time to throw up breakfast and lunch. Gagging and then gasping for breath, she closed her mind to the memories bombarding her. No. She wouldn't allow them to return. She remembered little, wanted to remember nothing. She knew how to shut them out. Had been taught how to kill them.

Forcing herself to her feet, Eden flushed the toilet and stumbled to the sink. Unable to face the horror she would see in her face, she kept her eyes from the mirror as she rinsed the vile taste from her mouth. Her hand gripping the sink for balance, she pushed away from it and tried to focus on her bed, only a few feet away. Darkness was coming, closing in on her. Her mind screamed a warning. Told her to hold it together, she could get through this. *Just hold it together.*

She made it to the middle of her bedroom and then everything within her collapsed. Darkness tunneled . . . her arms stretched forward, tried to reach her bed. Heard a distant, hard thud . . . felt a vague, jarring impact to her numb body as she fell to the floor. Horrific and vivid images flashed through her. Brilliant, hideous memories of exquisite pain, anguish, despair, wild, sobbing screams. A hoarse voice begging, pleading, for them to stop. Hers. All hers. Eden curled into a tight ball, covered her head with her arms, and allowed everything to crash down upon her, smother her, destroy her.

Knives slashed, fists cracked bones. In a dim part of her mind, she felt the painful intrusions . . . harsh laughter, hideous grunting, disgusting language . . .

Then sweet, blessed nothingness.

Noah breathed out a harsh curse as he lifted an unconscious Eden from the floor. What the hell had happened? She was a dead weight in his arms. Face pale and still, skin cold as death. He laid her on the bed and pressed his fingers on the pulse at her neck. Steady, normal.

"Eden, wake up." He kept his voice harsh, devoid of emotion. It wasn't emotion she needed. Lightly tapping her cheek, he snapped, "Wake. Up."

Her eyes flickered open. She mumbled, "For heaven's sake, Noah. Is there any reason for you to yell at me?"

Relief washed through him. "You want to tell me what you were doing lying on your floor . . . unconscious?"

"Needed a nap. Why else?"

Her nonchalant words didn't fool him for an instant. He hadn't seen this kind of emotion in her eyes in almost seven years. Part of him gloried in its return. He hadn't been sure he'd ever see it again. Another part of him wanted to shut it down again. Emotions caused mistakes, cost lives. She couldn't afford them, and he couldn't allow them.

"What happened?"

A sad little smile tilted her lips. So sad, it would have fractured his heart if he had one. Eden had told him on more than one occasion he was one of the few fortunate people in the world who would never have to worry about a heart attack. Can't have a heart attack without a heart. He'd always laughed at her, but knew it to be true.

"I'm not going to ask again . . . *Devon*."

She crumpled. He'd used the name to get a response. This wasn't the response he expected. The woman who'd seen hell, lived and breathed it, and come out of hell a strong, secure, hard-as-nails bitch, collapsed into his arms as if she were a frightened child.

What the hell?

Without a second thought, Noah broke one of his biggest rules. He crawled into the bed, wrapped his arms around her, and let her escape in tears.

For what seemed like a lifetime, but was probably only about five minutes, he held her. He didn't bother murmuring platitudes. They both knew he wouldn't mean them . . . if he even knew any. When the sobs slowed to shudders, he pulled away and sat up. She blinked up at him, eyes swollen and red, nose running and mouth trembling. She looked like she'd been through the wrong end of a tornado, and the hell of it was, she was still beautiful.

"You ready to stop sniveling like a coward and tell me what happened?"

A transformation took place. One he expected, but could still amaze him. She lifted her chin as swollen, bloodshot eyes shot sparks of haughty anger. A deep, rasping breath shuddered through her, then she lifted herself up to sit on the bed beside him.

"I've had a somewhat trying day."

He grimaced at the hoarse raspiness of her voice, though the thread of steel running through it gave him the answer he needed. Noah stood, allowing her to rise. She needed to get her feet back on firm ground and feel that control again.

And as always, his admiration surged as she rose gracefully, stretched out the kinks, and then gave a small jerk, as if she could literally throw off her heartache. He only hoped it was that simple this time.

She glided out of the bedroom and Noah followed. Her living room, elegantly understated, suited her personality. Splashes of wild colors blended with tranquil pastels, creating a comfortable and eclectic atmosphere.

Dropping gracefully into an overstuffed chair she knew was his favorite, she arched an elegant brow. "So, why are you here?"

"We had an appointment. You missed it."

Without a flicker of emotion or apology, she said, "I was delayed."

Relaxing, Noah dropped onto the sofa, a little surprised his limbs felt somewhat weak. He hadn't been sure he could get her back so soon.

"And that delay was . . . ?"

An infinitesimal shrug. "An old acquaintance."

His gut sank, already knowing. "Who?"

"Jordan Montgomery."

Good God, out of the blue, with no warning. No wonder she'd had a meltdown. He smothered any guilt he might have felt for not warning her ahead of time. It was done. Now he needed to determine the consequences. "Did you speak to him?"

Her laugh, cool and low, held mild amusement. "Oh yes, we had an intriguing conversation."

"Such as . . . ?"

"He recognized me."

Noah shot out of his chair. "That's not possible."

"Relax. He realized his mistake immediately."

Noah dropped back onto the sofa. "Why would he think you were the other woman?"

Eden stood and tugged her thin sweater off her arms, revealing bare, luminous shoulders. A slender finger pointed to the small hummingbird tattoo on her right shoulder. "This, I would imagine."

"I told you we needed to have that thing removed."

Slender shoulder lifted in a nonchalant shrug, she returned to her chair. "I need the reminder."

A statement he couldn't argue with. She did need the reminder, small though it was, of what had been and would never be again. She had been young and fragile, an innocent, easily broken. The reminder of what had been an excellent contrast to the woman she was now.

"So what happened?"

"He interrupted an invitation from Georges. Fortunately, I was able to get him back on track. I don't need Georges thinking I may be something I'm not. When Jordan acknowledged his mistake and left, we were able to pick up where we left off."

"And the invitation was . . . ?"

"A three-day birthday celebration for his niece at Marc's home in the Greek islands."

Noah nodded his approval. "Good. I was beginning to think we were going to have to go after Marc after all."

Eden's brow arched at this comment. Not because she felt insulted. The woman was almost impossible to insult.

No, he knew what she questioned was his willingness to find a young woman savvy enough to fool Marc into believing she was a fifteen-year-old girl.

"Did you have someone in mind?"

Noah hid a satisfied smile. The threat to a child was one of the few things that touched her emotions, though those emotions were well hidden. Few people saw the fury inside as she calmly rescued those children and sometimes and without remorse, when she had no other choice, punished those people who preyed on children. His Eden wasn't a killer, but she would kill. He liked that in a woman.

Her cool eyes demanding an answer, Noah shook his head. "No, I had no one."

"Good, because it's not necessary. The party is next weekend."

"You know once Alfred Larue hears about the invitation, his investigation will go deeper."

Another arched brow, and this time he couldn't contain his smile. Eden couldn't be insulted, but she was reassuringly vain about some things. Her ability to create an impenetrable cover was one of her greatest prides and best talents. Eden was an excellent liar. He liked that in a woman, too.

Her voice, soft and emotionless, held no tinge of outrage at his statement. "I don't think I need to answer that, do I?"

"No, you don't." Noah drew a breath. "You do, however, owe me an answer for your earlier behavior."

He watched her closely. If she gave even a microscopic clue that his challenge bothered her or a memory still lingered, he would have no choice but to act.

"Therapy." Her voice, cool, arrogant, and somewhat amused, hung in the air.

Noah locked his eyes with hers, searching. Eden would know any flicker of uncertainty or doubt would be met with a challenge. Weakness of any kind was an unacceptable risk. He saw nothing. No emotion, movement, or even aura to indicate that ten minutes ago she'd been a basket case.

"And will any further therapy be required?"

"Not that particular therapy—no. However, I do believe another one is required."

Noah stood, removed his leather jacket, and proceeded to unbutton his shirt. "I couldn't agree more."

Sweat poured from the man standing in front of her, though his breathing had barely increased and his pulse was probably still normal. Ah yes, Noah was a worthy adversary.

Knees slightly bent, Eden circled her opponent, looking for that vulnerable spot. In more than six years of training, she'd yet to find it, but that would never stop her from trying.

After her earlier weakness, she needed to convince him, but most of all herself, it had been a mirage. A brief weakness that would never and could never return. They'd both known the day might come, and she would be confronted with her past. The way she handled it wouldn't have been her choice, but the tears had been cathartic—tears she hadn't shed when she needed them all those years ago. Now they no longer threatened, no longer existed.

"What about it, baby? You just going to circle me all day like a—*oof!*"

With a sharp sweep of her leg, Noah's feet went out from under him, and the next instant he was on his ass. Half a second later, he bounced back and came at her like a Mack truck.

With swift, easy movements, Eden dodged every blow, until they became quicker and meaner. The blows he scored stunned, then burned, but she wouldn't stop.

Evidently deciding he'd punished her enough, he landed one last blow to her head. Eden felt herself flying through the air and knew a fury she hadn't felt in years. *Like hell.*

She landed on her butt, jackknifed to her feet, and went after him full force. A brief flicker of surprise hit his face just before her fist slammed into his jaw. Without a word, Noah smacked against the wall and then slid down.

He worked his jaw as he looked up at her, admiration and pride filling his eyes. "Damn, baby, that was good."

Laughing with delight, feeling almost normal for the first time in hours, she held out her hand and pulled him to his feet. "Come on into the kitchen. I think I have a bag of frozen peas for your jaw. They'll go nicely with the steak I'm grilling for dinner."

Hours later, Noah was gone, and the silent whispering of the clock beside her bed filled the night. In rhythmic tick-tocks, it whispered, "He's here . . . he's here . . . he's here."

Eden rolled over in the darkness. Burying her head under the pillow, she wished she could as easily bury her memories of what had happened earlier. *Jordan.* It had been seven years. Seven brutal, torturous years and still she could look at him and get lost in those unfathomable, velvet brown eyes. His hair, black as a moonless, midnight sky, was longer than she remembered. He would be about thirty-six now, but she saw no sign of graying.

The biggest difference between now and seven years ago were the lines around his eyes and mouth. They were deeper, making him even more ruggedly handsome. Time might have marched across Jordan's face, but he still could make her heart thud like a herd of thundering buffalo. No other man had ever been able to do that. And in the deepest part of her soul, she knew no other man would ever be able to do that.

Why? Hadn't he hurt her enough? Hadn't she suffered enough because of him?

She shot up from the bed and threw her pillow across the room. *Because of him?* Who was she kidding? She was the one who instigated that little charade all those years ago. He'd done nothing other than what any red-blooded heterosexual single male would have done.

How she wished she could blame someone else. It would be so easy to say it was his fault because he hadn't seen beneath her façade of sophistication to the romantic idiot underneath. Or even the fault of her mother, who'd fed him her venom.

No. She'd learned long ago to stop the blame game. When shit happened, it happened. It didn't matter where, when, how, or who. The point was to live through it, get to the other side, and survive.

She might not have planned to have sex with him that night, but in the end, she hadn't stopped him. If she'd blurted out the truth, no matter how far they'd gone, he would have stopped. But she'd been so carried away with passion, with what she thought was love, nothing mattered other than to be with him in the way she'd dreamed about forever.

No, there was no one else responsible but herself.

Eden pushed herself out of bed. She couldn't sleep, might as well get in some training. Having Noah almost beat the crap out of her earlier should have been enough to exhaust her, but she was too wired to sleep. She rarely drank, never took drugs, so no getting help from that end.

Pulling on her workout clothes, she forced herself into her gym. If she beat the hell out of the boxing bag, maybe she'd sleep for a few hours. Noah had called her in for a consult on another case. She needed at least three hours sleep to function. The case sounded a little more unusual than their normal rescue. Even as tired as she was, she couldn't help but be intrigued. This was what she lived for, what she'd worked for. This was her calling, her passion, her life.

five

"I miss you. When will you be home?"

His head pressed against the cushion of the chair, Jordan closed his gritty eyes, fighting the urge to growl at the woman on the other end of the phone. She'd done nothing to deserve his irritation. "Couple of weeks, maybe less."

"I know you've only been gone a few days, but I feel as though it's been forever."

Familiar guilt hit him. He didn't feel the same. He wished he could love her, as she deserved to be loved. Samara Lyons was exactly the kind of woman a sane man dreams to settle down with. Beautiful, talented, gentle, and spirited. She was perfect. In his way, he loved her as much as he'd ever been able to love another living being. But he wasn't in love with her, had grave doubts he was even capable of such a nebulous emotion.

They'd been talking about marriage the past few weeks. Mostly in generalities, but he'd seen the knowledge in her eyes. She knew he was considering proposing. And when he did, they both knew her answer would be yes. Marrying Samara just made sense.

"Jordan . . . you there?

"Yeah . . . sorry. How was your day?"

As her soft voice flowed over him, he saw her beautiful face and kind eyes, and was again reminded of the reasons he'd existed in the shadows for so many years. Innocence and goodness still existed and he'd worked long and hard at his chosen occupation to preserve it.

Several months back, he'd come to the realization he needed a change. He'd taken enough bad guys down to fill a few prisons. Didn't he deserve a rest? He'd be thirty-seven his next birthday. What once he'd sworn never to consider, a wife and a family, he now longed for with a need he found surprising.

He wanted the fairy tale, after all. Or at least a reasonable facsimile.

Not long after coming to that astonishing realization, he'd met Samara and a whole new world opened up for him. From a large family, Samara didn't know the meaning of secrecy. Oh, she had plenty of confidential information she kept with her job as a social worker, but emotional secrecy just wasn't part of her makeup. She was an open book, honest, sweet, and giving. How had he gotten so lucky and why the hell didn't he appreciate it more?

"Jordan, you still there?"

Well, so much for changing his ways. She'd been talking a full five minutes and he had no idea what she said. "Sorry. Had a difficult day. I saw a woman today, thought she was Devon."

"Oh my gosh, Jordan. What happened?"

Jordan had kept nothing from Samara. He figured if she was going to get mixed up with the likes of him, she needed to know how badly he'd screwed up. And in his opinion, he'd never screwed up anything as badly as he had with Devon.

"She had a hummingbird tattoo on her shoulder. Before I knew it, I was on my feet, asking her if she was Devon. The instant I saw her face, I knew it wasn't her."

"I know that must have been difficult. Are you going to contact those people you told me about?"

"Hell, what's the point? They couldn't help me years ago, when she first disappeared. Devon's been gone seven years now. The trail's even colder. She's either dead or doesn't want to be found. Is there any reason to go looking for her . . . another wild goose chase?"

Though thousands of miles away, the compassion in her voice reached through to him. "Finding Devon for her sake might be pointless. Finding her for your sake isn't. If you don't exhaust this one last avenue, will you ever be able to let it go?"

He rubbed the knot of nerves at the back of his neck. She was right. He'd never be able to let this go without exhausting every opportunity, no matter how remote. "After my business is complete, I'll make the contact. If it looks like this Noah McCall might be able to help, I'll go from there."

"I'm glad. Jordan?"

"Yes?"

"You're sure there's nothing dangerous about this job?"

Though he could tell her almost nothing about this assignment and little of his career, he could reassure her. "The most dangerous thing I'll be doing is eating too many pastries and having to run extra miles to work off the calories. Everything else is a piece of cake."

She laughed, as he knew she would. Laughter came easy to Samara.

"I'd better get off here. I've got an early case-file meeting and I still need to read over my new cases."

"Sleep well, Samara."

He stared at the phone in his hand long after he heard the click of her hanging up. A part of him wished she was there with him, another part was glad she wasn't. If he went to LCR for one more opportunity to find Devon and they told him there was no chance, he expected the gremlins to come out of the closet and play with his guts for a while. Samara didn't need to see that no matter what happened, no matter what anyone said, he'd never get over not finding Devon.

Standing, Jordan pulled his clothes off, dropped them on the floor, and fell across the bed. Tired, weary eyes stared sightlessly at the stark white ceiling of the hotel room. Seeing the woman with the tattoo today brought back memories he'd successfully shut out for years. Now they flooded through his mind like a torrential rain of fire . . . Devon's beauty and innocence, his monumental error in judgment, and then his supreme cruelty. Jordan closed his eyes as images both sweet and bitter danced inside his head. For the first time in years, he gave in and allowed himself to remember the magic and then the misery.

"I understand this will be your last assignment."

Clicking the briefcase shut, Jordan jerked his head in a curt nod. Starting up a friendly conversation with a man who brokered terror information as if he were a shoe salesman wasn't something he felt obligated to do. Get the information, dump the money, and get out. Playing pretty wasn't in his job description.

The man crossed his lanky legs and settled more comfortably onto the leather sofa, as if he had all day. "You're leaving the team?" An almost fatherly smile twisted his thin lips.

Though on edge at the unusual path this transaction had taken, Jordan had trouble holding back a humorless laugh. *Team?* Amazing how the agency called itself a team when each assignment was always an individual effort. And if that individual suddenly found himself in trouble? The *team* didn't exist. No white knights would come riding to the rescue.

He'd lived with that knowledge for years. Accepted it as a risk worth taking. The work he did too important not to take. Having met few of his team members, he'd never really concerned himself about them. They knew the risk, just as he did, and accepted it as such.

Years ago, Henry Stevens had warned him of the risks of becoming an undercover operative. Though Jordan had heard his advice, the excitement and danger had been too tempting to pass up. How incredibly naïve he'd been, but had doggedly stuck to his commitment.

One day last year, his tolerance of that risk punched him in the gut and left a gaping hole. One of the few team members he'd met found herself in deep shit.

On assignment in Austria, Jordan only learned of it later, after it was over.

A female operative—and, from what he remembered, intelligent and talented—had been betrayed by her informant. Unable to explain her presence and reasons for being in the extremely anti-American country, the radical and soulless government decided to make an example of her. Though having her rescued would have caused only a slight diplomatic problem, if that, their *team* leader chose to let her go. Jordan's sources informed him she'd been executed, after severe torture. And the *team* didn't give a fuck.

Jordan decided then that his time with the *team* was at an end.

"I'm sure your talents will be missed."

Yeah, right. Making the assessment that the creature across from him might be feeling somewhat sentimental since they'd worked together in the past, Jordan stood, wanting to end a conversation he hadn't wanted in the first place. He held out his hand and touched the elegant, somewhat effeminate hand, reflecting on how much scum of the earth he'd dealt with in his career as an operative for a nonexistent government agency. This would be his last. The information Bill Smith—a lame-ass fake name the guy had used for years—sold to the United States could very well stop a major terrorist attack against several embassies.

These kinds of meetings usually held minimal threat but optimum benefit. Jordan didn't mind paying millions of dollars for what could possibly save thousands of lives. As long as he was certain the money wasn't going to fund any other terror group or event, he'd dole out money to scumbag moles all day long.

He never questioned where the money came from, though he figured it was diverted money from special interest groups, dummy organizations, and Uncle Sam's contribution. If it saved lives, he didn't care if it was counterfeited in someone's basement. The results were what mattered and his results always delivered.

He offered Bill a grim nod and walked out the door. This might be his last assignment but for some reason, he felt no relief. Long strides carried him through the lobby of one of Paris's finest hotels. Though always aware of his surroundings, he paid little attention to the subtle signs of wealth in the people he passed or the understated opulence of the hotel's interior. Before the doorman could reach him, Jordan pushed the door open, walked down the concrete steps and onto the narrow sidewalk.

Inhaling deeply, he absorbed the sights and scents of one of the great, unique cities in the world. He caught a glimpse of the top of the Eiffel Tower through the trees and stopped abruptly, ignoring the cursing bicyclist who swerved around him.

How long had it been since he'd played a tourist in Paris? This city had always been one of his favorites. A small part of him wanted to take a few days and just enjoy the flavor and unique quality he'd only ever found here, but he was just putting off the inevitable. He would arrange for the transfer of the information he'd just purchased, and tomorrow he'd make an appointment to see Noah McCall.

Research had yielded little information on the powerful but shadowy organization and even less on its mysterious founder.

He knew LCR had been in existence for at least ten years. Unofficial reports indicated they employed well over one hundred people, though some speculated it was much more.

There were numerous rumors but none he could substantiate about McCall. Some said he came from a Mafia family and, having decided he'd had enough of his family's bad business, had chosen to do good instead. Other reports indicated he was a rogue former government agent who got tired of having to abide by the rules.

Jordan did know that LCR's success rate of finding kidnap victims, runaways, and missing persons was nothing short of phenomenal. They were so successful that law enforcement officials and even some government agencies turned a blind eye when they went beyond legal means to accomplish their goals.

LCR's goal wasn't to punish the wrongdoer but the perps rarely got away, and that was one of the many reasons the local law let them have their way. If the bad guy was caught, the law was called and given full credit for the arrest. Hard to resent that kind of assistance.

Within months of Devon's disappearance, Jordan contacted the D.C. branch of LCR. After a few weeks, he'd been told the trail was too cold. They couldn't find her. Since Jordan used his considerable contacts and netted the same results, he'd been disappointed but not surprised.

He'd never considered trying them again. Then, a few weeks ago, an acquaintance happened to mention that LCR's main headquarters was in Paris. That started him thinking. Even though Paris was thousands of miles from where Devon was last seen, and it had been seven years, what if he went directly to the head of LCR? Would that make a difference? Would McCall be willing to take on such an old case?

Was one last chance even possible?

"Ah Eden, glad you're here. I'd like you to meet Amelia Beard."

As Eden drew deeper into the hotel suite, her eyes were drawn immediately to the short, middle-aged woman standing between what looked like two giant oak trees, somber and solid. Whoever this woman was, she'd come with some impressive protection.

Mrs. Beard's faded blue eyes held an unbelievable sadness; her double chin wobbled slightly as her mouth lifted in a small, twisted parody of a smile. "How do you do?"

Eden shook the older woman's soft, wrinkled hand. Late forties, early fifties, privileged upbringing, but a demeanor of calm, kind dignity. The soft yellow pantsuit she wore was expensive, but not designer made.

Without glancing at the giants beside her, Eden sensed their eyes were focused on the woman, ready to deter and deal with anything that threatened her.

She raised a brow at Noah and he shrugged. "Mrs. Beard's bodyguards. They go where she goes."

Deciding to ignore their presence for the time being, she crossed over to one of the sofas and made herself comfortable.

Mrs. Beard's face flickered with uncertainty at Noah, as if she weren't sure she should sit unless invited.

Noah threw out his hand at a chair. "Please have a seat and we'll begin. Would you care for something to drink before we get started?"

Mrs. Beard answered with a tight smile and a quick shake of her head, then settled herself on the edge of a chair across from Eden.

Noah, always the one to put people at ease while Eden silently dissected them, sprawled into a chair beside Mrs. Beard and smiled his famous "you can trust me with your soul" smile. "Tell me, Mrs. Beard, what brings you to Last Chance Rescue?"

Mrs. Beard drew herself up and Eden was impressed by the way she changed from a cowering, defeated woman into someone with purpose. Ah yes . . . amazing what purpose could do to transform a person's life.

"We live in a small village, on the outskirts of Madrid. My daughter, Risa, was kidnapped from her school. . . . She was gone for eight days."

Noah leaned forward slightly, his attention caught, as was Eden's, by the strange wording. "Since you said eight days, I'm assuming she's been found?"

Mrs. Beard's lips and chin trembled slightly, the only indication of her emotions. "Yes, my husband, Marisa's father, was able to have her safely returned."

"When was she taken?"

"Almost two months ago."

"And a ransom was paid?"

"Yes."

"I'm a little confused. Your daughter was returned. You know LCR's mission is to rescue individuals, not go after the perpetrators of the crimes?"

"Yes, I do know this."

Noah's normally smooth brow was slightly furrowed. "Then why . . . ?"

Mrs. Beard cast an anxious eye over to one of the shadows in the corner, as if looking for reassurance. By no movement or expression did the man in the shadows give out any signals, but for some reason the older woman seemed to relax. She released a heavy sigh and whispered, "There are others."

"Others?"

As if unplugging a dam, information gushed forth. "My Risa was taken by men who do this for a living. They kidnap people, mostly children. Some are babies, others in their teens. There are two different parts of this organization. One takes these children and ransoms them. Often the families are not able to pay the ransom, so they go to the other area."

When she paused to catch her breath, Eden shot a quick glance at Noah. He was sitting on the edge of his chair, just as she was. Why had they never heard of this organization?

"What's the other area?" Noah asked softly.

"It is strictly a sell to the highest bidder."

"How do you know all this?"

"My husband paid the ransom but only after being told"—her voice thickened—"my Risa would be sold."

"How do you know this wasn't just a threat to push you into paying?"

"My daughter has been deaf since the age of five. People often talk in front of her, saying things they wouldn't normally say, because of her disability. But people fail to realize how easy it is for some people to read lips. Risa had learned this to perfection. This was how she learned other children are sold to individuals for all different reasons."

"Why are you just now coming to us?"

"We were threatened. If we told anyone about the kidnapping, Risa would be taken again, and this time she would be immediately sold. We couldn't take the risk."

"What's changed?"

Mrs. Beard looked down at her hands and shuddered violently. Again the shadow in the corner made no motion toward her, but for some reason, Eden could almost feel waves of support and sympathy coming from his direction.

Finally gathering her composure, she whispered, "My Risa was killed in an automobile accident two days ago. I have no other children. They cannot hurt me any more than I've already been hurt."

"I'm sorry for your loss, but how can we know where—"

"There are houses."

Noah stiffened. "Houses?"

"Where they keep the children until they sell them."

"You know where the houses are located?"

"I know where two are. I'm sure there are more." Though her voice was soft, a new strength seemed to come from her. Amelia Beard was a determined woman.

"Did you go to the authorities with this information?"

Again she looked over at the shadow and this time, the shadow nodded. She looked back at Noah. "Yes, but they seemed uninterested."

Eden caught Noah's quick glance at her. When local authorities seemed uninterested in something like this, it usually meant one thing: They'd been bought off to ignore the criminal activities.

Noah leaned forward. "Mrs. Beard, did your daughter ever learn any names, first or last, that we might be able to—"

"Yes." Mrs. Beard nodded emphatically. "She was able to remember several different names." Unzipping her purse, she pulled a piece of paper from it and handed it to Noah. "I've listed all the ones she could give us."

Noah was a difficult man to read. Only by watching him closely did Eden understand that something on the paper disturbed him. A tic in his jaw and the flex of his right hand on the arm of his chair her only clue that something was very wrong.

Knowing whatever troubled him wouldn't be revealed until Mrs. Beard and her bodyguards left, Eden forced herself to concentrate on the remaining information Mrs. Beard gave them. As she listened, everything within her tightened. This operation would be huge . . . bigger than anything they'd handled since she'd come on board. It would take everything LCR had to pull this off.

She watched Noah's face. His expression remained bland, almost pleasant, but the cold determination in his eyes blazed like a beacon. No matter the cost, they would definitely be shutting these bastards down.

Never long on patience, Eden waited as long as she could and then burst out, "How long are you going to keep me in suspense?"

Mrs. Beard and her shadows were gone. The instant the door closed behind them, Noah erupted from his chair and headed to the bar. Eden watched him fill two glasses with orange juice. His silence, along with the set of his shoulders, told her something was definitely off.

"This'll be the biggest operation we've taken on." Noah's voice rumbled across the room.

"I don't care if it's just a one-woman mission. It's got to be done."

Handing her a glass of juice, Noah slumped into the chair he'd sat in earlier. "You being that woman, I assume?"

Eden shrugged. "If the high heel fits." She narrowed her gaze at him. "Why? Don't you think I'm up to it?"

Leaning forward, Noah handed her the list Mrs. Beard had supplied. "Take a look."

Eden read through the list of names, none of them sounding familiar, until she came to a too-familiar name near the bottom. Breath left her. The juice almost fell from her hand. Raising her eyes to Noah's furious face, she whispered, "Holy hell, how did we not know this?"

A slow shake of his head told Eden he was still struggling with the knowledge. "Based on Alfred's taunting of the Clements, we knew he gave Christina to Marc. And we knew Marc was getting fresh victims from someone. How we didn't know that his father is his main supplier is beyond my comprehension."

Eden jumped to her feet and began pacing as ideas and scenarios exploded through her head. "We know now. . . . We have to shut them down."

He gave a sharp nod of his head. They both knew they couldn't let Larue's operation continue. Not when they had the power to stop it. Yes, it would be complicated and might cost them their lives, but what they did was worth their lives. Eden learned that long ago.

"Christina has to come first."

Eden couldn't argue with his logic. She'd made this connection with Georges to retrieve the young girl and would have to complete her mission before making headway against Alfred Larue.

"In the meantime, I'll do more digging. Somehow this dirty secret of Alfred Larue's has escaped our investigation, which makes me think he's keeping it separate from the family business. If this operation's as large as it sounds, we'll need to call everyone in on this. It'll take all we've got and then some."

Energy she hadn't felt since seeing Jordan surged through her. This was what she lived for, what she was good at. Everything she'd ever done or experienced had led her to Last Chance Rescue and the work she did. That horrific event seven years ago might have been the catalyst, but LCR was her destiny.

six

With a long sigh of contentment, Alfred Larue allowed his heavy bulk to sink into the sumptuous leather sofa. Soft music flowed through the room from hidden speakers. A small, comforting fire erased the slight chill from the air. Though his home was a comfortable size, with eighteen bedrooms and twenty-two baths, this cozy room off the master suite was his favorite. He took a swallow of brandy as he waited for Inez, his wife of forty years, to join him.

They led busy lives. Visiting an hour before retiring for the night was a treasured tradition. Wrapped in each other's arms, they would share news of the day and discuss any family issues that had arisen over the last twenty-four hours. They'd worked hard over the years to create their vast empire and kept nothing from each other.

One of the issues he planned to discuss with Inez tonight had him reflecting on the meeting he'd had earlier today with his cousin-in-law Thomas Bennett. Their business relationship was based upon mutual greed and the single-minded purpose of fulfilling a need few people could or would. They'd made an enormous amount of money performing a beneficial service.

Word had come to him last week that some of the merchandise on a recent shipment had come in damaged. He'd called Bennett in for an explanation.

Thomas was a singularly unimpressive man in appearance. Average height, pale, pockmarked skin, thinning brown hair, and somewhat beady eyes, he was the kind of man most people passed on the streets without seeing. A sharp intellect, skewed morals, and relentless greed made him an excellent business partner.

"I'm assuming the merchandise will not be damaged in the future?" Alfred had asked.

Thomas's thin lips curled up into a skinny, zigzagged grimace. "The employee and problem have been eliminated. A messy but necessary demonstration of our commitment to quality. The rest of the staff witnessed what happens when orders are disregarded. Nothing like a little show-and-tell to convince people. We won't have another problem."

"Good. I don't have to tell you that our customers require fresh, unmarked merchandise, Thomas."

"It won't happen again."

Alfred nodded. "I knew I could count on you."

"Your son's gift will be delivered tomorrow at the usual place."

"Marcus was pleased with the appearance of your last delivery, but the quality hasn't held up to his exacting standards. He's more than ready for a replacement."

"I believe this particular piece is sturdier and will last him longer," Thomas said.

Familiar with his son's specific taste, he said, "Blond and attractive though, yes?"

An interesting light glinted in Thomas's eyes. "Blond. And yes, extremely attractive."

"Excellent. Anything else?"

"I'm assuming the Clement problem is being taken care of?"

"Yes, but not as quickly as it could be. Hector still hasn't agreed to all of my demands. Until that happens, his daughter will remain a guest of my son."

"Will we dispose of her in the usual way?"

"No, I'm a man of my word. Once Hector relinquishes

control of his South American interests, I'll return his daughter as promised."

"It's very generous of you . . . much more than he deserves."

"I may be a businessman, but I'm a family man at heart. I understand the devotion a father has for his loved ones. There's nothing I wouldn't do for mine. Hector knows all of this is his fault and the sooner he gives in, the sooner his daughter can go home to her family."

Nodding his agreement, Bennett had risen to his feet. "I'm headed back home in a few hours, but I'll be back in time for the next shipment."

Alfred took another sip of brandy to ward off the uneasy chill. A visit from Thomas Bennett always put him on edge. There was just something creepy about the man, though he was a damned fine business partner. When he'd asked his cousin Celia to marry Thomas as a favor to the family, it had paid off well. They had two daughters and now a grandson. More important, the marriage established Thomas as a member of the family. No one dare betray the family.

A sound caught his attention. Inez came into the room, looking as lovely as she did when she was a mere child of sixteen and had given her hand to him in marriage. Blond hair, cut into a flattering, casual wave of curls, surrounded a beautiful, aristocratic face. Medium height and slender in stature, her beauty had caught his attention all those years ago, but it was her strong will and love for family that had kept him from straying. Like him, there was nothing that his Inez wouldn't do for their family. Their shared beliefs made their marriage strong and unshakable.

Alfred patted the couch. "Come, my darling, and tell me how your day has been."

Sitting next to him, she kissed his cheek, then cuddled beside him. "Exhausting but productive. We had to halt production at two of our plants due to some unusual police activity. Philippe is handling the matter, and we anticipate reopening next week."

"Any idea why the extra attention?"

"Philippe believes our protection sources are wanting an increase in salary. He will make sure they understand this isn't the proper way to request a raise."

Chuckling at her dry humor, Alfred hugged her to his side. No business partner could rival his wife for loyalty, determination, or clearheaded decisions. He knew he had a tendency to get emotional when it came to certain disturbances, but not so his Inez. She could handle any situation with the minimum of fuss or emotion. What a treasure she was.

"I did have a somewhat disturbing conversation with Georges earlier, though," Inez said.

"Such as?"

"He will be here in a moment. I'll let him tell you himself."

Alfred shook his head, his smile indulgent. "Since it involves Georges, I can only assume it involves a young woman."

"Yes, but not just any young woman," Georges replied.

Alfred's smile grew wider as Georges entered the room. Parents should have no favorites, but he couldn't deny a special fondness for his youngest son. A masculine version of his beloved Inez, Georges shared his parent's fierce emotions when it came to family and embodied the best of him and Inez.

"Come in and tell me what makes this particular young woman so special."

Alfred eyed his son with some concern as he settled across from them. Georges did appear to be tired and somewhat distraught.

"Her name is Claire Marchand. I met her at a party last month. She's beautiful," Georges said.

Alfred couldn't suppress a small chuckle. "Of course she

is. But why is this woman different than the multitude of other beautiful women you've courted?"

"She just is, Papa. She's kind and fun to be with."

"Are you in love with her?" Inez asked.

"I believe so, Mama."

"Does she return your feelings?"

"She would if there weren't obstacles."

An alarm clanged in Alfred's head. "What obstacles?"

"She is married."

Alfred shook his head with regret. "You cannot break up a marriage. Have we not taught you better?"

"But it's not a real marriage, Papa. Her husband is an invalid. Claire only stays with him out of loyalty and duty."

"That is her choice, Georges," Alfred said.

"Only because she doesn't feel she has any other choice."

"What does that mean?" Inez asked sharply.

Georges's eyes skittered nervously away and then back. "You arranged an accident for Lisa's husband's first wife so he would be free to marry her."

Alfred ignored Inez's gasp. It wasn't because she didn't know about the situation. However, neither of them was aware that anyone else in the family knew what they'd done for their oldest daughter.

"That was a different circumstance, Georges," Alfred said.

Georges crossed his arms; his mouth crimped in a mutinous line. "How was it different?"

"Your sister was distraught, almost suicidal. We had no choice but to help her."

Tears filled his son's beautiful eyes. "I am distraught. My heart is breaking for her. Claire is young and so very brave, but her spirit will soon be broken. I love her enough to handle things on my own, but had hoped for your help and support."

Inez went to her son and wrapped a comforting arm around his shoulders. "Georges, you cannot do this your-

self. You have no experience taking care of such matters."
She turned pleading eyes to Alfred. "We can't allow him
to handle this on his own."

Alfred's heart turned over. Inez rarely became emotional, but with their children she was often a mother hen.
She was also correct. Georges had no experience eliminating obstacles. He would most likely mess things up
and get caught.

"I want to meet your friend before I make a decision.
Can this be arranged?"

A brilliant smile brightened his son's face. "Thank you,
Papa. And yes, I've invited Claire to Marc's next weekend.
You'll be able to see for yourself how special she is."

"Excellent. We look forward to meeting her, don't we,
Inez?"

Still biting her lip in worry, she nodded and smiled. "Yes,
that's sounds like a fine idea. I'm sure she's a wonderful
young woman."

Like a child who'd just received an expensive toy he'd
been asking for, Georges jumped to his feet. "Thank you,
Mama and Papa."

Alfred waited until his son closed the door before looking at his wife. "How did he know about the assistance
we gave his sister?"

"I'm not sure unless she confided in him." Returning to
his side, she cuddled against him again. "It is no matter.
We can't allow him to take care of this himself."

"You're right about that. Our Georges is an innocent
in affairs such as this. However, I'm not willing to make
these arrangements until we're both assured that this is
what should be done. The young woman may be playing
upon Georges's tender heart."

Inez nodded. "If it appears she is indeed what she seems
to be, I think we should oblige him. He asks for so little."

Alfred couldn't help but agree. All of his children were
precious, but Georges was the only one who never asked

for more than money. Smoothing the rough paths for their children was a parent's responsibility. Georges had been the least demanding of their offspring and most certainly deserved assistance.

Alfred would reserve judgment until he met this Claire Marchand. If Georges truly loved her, then he would make the arrangements for Claire to become available and able to marry his son.

Eden sipped ice-cold champagne and tried to tap down her excitement. Finally, hopefully, she was moving toward success. The Larues' private jet, heading toward the Greek isles, held only two pilots; one lovely, well-endowed flight attendant, who gave Eden the evil eye whenever she was sure Georges wasn't looking; Georges; and herself.

She glanced over at the man across from her. How handsome and charming he was. Amazing how some people could put on the most charming façade and underneath be the most heinous creatures on earth.

Not that Georges was the creep his brother or father was. From what she knew, Georges was just an average, ordinary womanizer, with no real proclivities other than an apparently high sex drive and little ambition other than to sleep with as many attractive women as he could.

However harmless he was in his personal life, he knew of his brother's predilection for young girls and did nothing to stop it. In her opinion, that was indefensible. Allowing it to happen was almost as bad as committing the deed. Years ago, Eden had learned there were shades of gray to almost everything. This wasn't one of them.

Did he know about his father's side business of human trafficking? Noah seemed to think not, but she was reserving judgment. Every time she thought the Larues' consciencelessness and twisted morals had reached their limit, they surprised her with new heights of depravity.

Still, she had no plans to physically hurt any of the

Larues. Punishing the bad guy would never be her mission, though on occasion, it had been unavoidable. Right now, recovering the daughter of Hector Clement was her only purpose. That Hector was part of an organized crime ring, which dealt in drugs, prostitution, and gambling, made no difference to her or LCR.

Alfred Larue had kidnapped Hector's twelve-year-old daughter. The kidnapping was in part revenge for Clement stealing business from the Larues. The other part was because of his son's sick need for fresh teenage flesh. Apparently, what Marc wanted, no matter how sick, Alfred provided.

Christina Clement was an innocent victim, caught in the middle of some very evil men. She needed a champion. And Eden was determined it would be her.

"What did you tell your husband about this weekend?"

Slipping back into her role as Claire Marchand was as easy as taking a breath. Her fingers pressed against her lips as if to stop them from trembling, and tears welled in her eyes. "My Jacques is such an understanding man. I simply told him I needed to get away for a few days with a friend. He knows I would never betray him and has total confidence in me."

Georges smiled in seeming sympathy, but was unable to hide the predatory gleam in his eyes. Eden knew he had every intention she would indeed betray her fake husband this weekend. That didn't concern her. She would handle Georges when the time came. If he became too amorous before she could accomplish her mission, she had a few tricks up her sleeve—rather, in her cosmetic case, disguised as makeup—that would take care of Georges. No, she wouldn't kill the bastard, but she'd make sure he suffered, if only temporarily.

Perhaps, if the timing worked out, she'd be able to treat more than one Larue. The bastards would be too sick to concern themselves with kidnapping or anything else for

several weeks. One of her little "bugs" could make havoc
with a person's intestines, turning the strongest of men
into whimpering, vomiting creatures of retching pain. A
small smile lifted her lips.

"What are you smiling about, my love?"

A slender shoulder lifted. "Just thinking that this weekend is exactly what I need."

Georges leaned over and grasped her hand. "I'll make
sure it is, darling."

Eden's smile grew brighter. Yes, there were definite
perks to her job. Creating chaos in the lives and bellies of
some of the most reprehensible people in the world was
without doubt one of them.

Though Christina was her priority, Eden would take the
opportunity to snoop around for information. If Noah
was correct and Alfred kept this part of the business to
himself, she most likely wouldn't find anything, but she
had to try.

Jordan held out his hand to Noah McCall. "I appreciate you seeing me on such short notice."

The founder of Last Chance Rescue didn't look anything
like what he'd expected. Ink-black hair, shorn to almost
military standard, brown, almost black eyes, hawkish nose,
and firm, determined jaw, he looked less like a Mafia hit
man and more like a D.C. lawyer.

"Not at all," McCall said. "The information you gave
me sounded intriguing. Why don't you come in and tell
me what you can."

Jordan entered the nondescript hotel room, identical to
the hundreds of hotel rooms he'd done business in during
his career. He seated himself in a comfortable, overstuffed
fake leather chair and watched McCall amble to the bar.
"Would you care for something to drink?"

"Water."

Returning with a glass filled with ice and sparkling water, he handed it to Jordan, then sat across from him and folded his hands, waiting for Jordan to start.

Pulling a thick file from his briefcase, Jordan slid it across the table. It contained every detail, no matter how small, on his investigation of Devon's disappearance.

"Devon Winters disappeared seven years ago last April in Washington, D.C. I believe I was the last person who saw her before she disappeared. She was twenty-one and emotionally distraught at the time. I'm sure that had something to do with her disappearance."

McCall's eyes flickered down briefly at the file and then back at Jordan. "What happened to upset her?"

Jordan blew out a deeply held breath. He'd known he would have to spill his guts today, hold nothing back. Though remembering that time always twisted his insides into knots of fire, if this was his last chance to find Devon, he'd spare himself nothing to accomplish that goal.

After a long swallow of water, Jordan replaced the glass on the table. "I've known Devon and her family for years. Her stepfather was my godfather. I saw her often, whenever I stopped in to see Henry. She was a sweet, innocent kid. She went off to boarding school. I got involved in my career. Whenever she came home for visits, I was out of town. Years passed."

In his mind, he saw that young girl. Curly, golden blond hair framed a round, dimpled face, and even with a mouth filled with metal braces, her smile could light up the hardest of hearts. She had clear gray, guileless eyes, a cute little button nose, a quick, intelligent mind, and a delightful slant on life that brought him to laughter more than once.

"And then?"

Jordan looked at Noah McCall, knowing full well the

man had an excellent idea of what happened, without Jordan spilling his guts. It didn't matter. Jordan would do it anyway.

"I was at a party . . . ball, actually. Shouldn't have been there. I'd just got back to the States from a . . . job. It hadn't gone well. I was running on almost no sleep . . . in a lousy frame of mind, and I'd had too much to drink." He rubbed a weary hand down his face. There he went, making excuses for himself, when there were none. "And then, there she was . . . like a beautiful goddess."

"And by she, I can only assume you mean Devon and that she had grown up?"

"Yes . . . but more than that. She'd changed so much, I didn't recognize her. I saw a beautiful, mature woman . . . not an innocent, inexperienced child."

McCall's forehead wrinkled. "I thought you said she was twenty-one."

"It doesn't matter. I was eight years older, in age and experience. I should have seen behind her act."

"So you didn't recognize her and Devon decided to keep her identity a secret?"

"Yes, apparently she'd had a crush on me for years, something I never knew. She saw me at the ball and decided to test her newfound maturity."

"I'm assuming you slept with her?"

Jordan held back a humorless laugh. Twenty minutes of the most intense sexual experience of his life couldn't really be summed up in such a common, unemotional way. He wasn't sure there were words for what had happened, though when he'd learned the truth of her identity, the only words to describe his behavior were *reprehensible, disgusting,* and *vile.*

Suddenly wanting to get it all out, Jordan spit the words as if they were bullets. "After it was over, she disappeared. I still didn't know it was Devon. . . . She told me her name was Mary. An hour or so later, Devon's mother called me. She somehow discovered what Devon had done. Told me a bunch of lies I was stupid enough to believe. A few minutes after that phone call, Devon came back to my house and I tore into her as if she'd committed a major crime."

"Can you tell me what you said?" When Jordan glared at him, McCall shrugged. "It might help, but if you don't want . . ."

Without even trying, his mind zoomed straight to the one event he regretted more than anything else in his life. "Alise, Devon's mother, told me Devon tried to seduce two other of their friends, that she was seeing a psychiatrist for her problems. I believed her, and I accused Devon of setting everything up, seducing me."

"Well, wasn't that what she did?"

Jordan shook his head emphatically. "If anything, I seduced her. I ignored all the signs of innocence, uncertainty, fear . . . and took what I wanted."

"Why are you avoiding telling me what you said to her?"

Irrationally angry at McCall's persistence, self-loathing tinged his bitter words. "Because I called her a slut. Told her if I'd known who she was, I would have vomited before I touched her. I asked her if I hadn't used protection, would I have found out in a few months that I'd fathered a child with a lunatic."

His guts churning, Jordan glared at the man across from him. "That's why, McCall. This sweet, innocent girl I practically seduced was verbally raped by the man she thought her hero."

McCall's face remained impassive, his eyes empty. What had he expected? Exoneration? Understanding? This man's opinion didn't matter. What he needed was to find Devon . . . to know she still lived.

"What happened after that?"

"She ran out the door, but not before she apologized for about the tenth time, told me she loved me, that I'd always been her hero and she wished she could have been mine."

"And that was the last time you saw her?"

Jordan nodded. "I went after her a few seconds later. It was pouring rain. . . . I walked up and down the street but couldn't find her. I assumed she caught a taxi."

Unable to sit still any longer, Jordan stood and started to pace. He'd never repeated those shameful words to anyone. Saying them again caused an ache deep inside.

"I got called out of the country a few hours later. It never crossed my mind that she hadn't returned home. I figured when I got back, I'd be less angry and more inclined to listen to her. It was a couple of months before I could get back. I went to her parents' house. That's when I found out she'd been missing since that day."

"I'm surprised her parents or the police didn't contact you."

"I was on a project few people were aware of . . . no one could contact me."

He went on to detail his conversations with the police, his own inept investigation, and the number of private detectives he'd had working on her case for years. He briefly mentioned he had many contacts in the government and used every one of them in his effort to find Devon, all to no avail.

While Jordan Montgomery spilled his verbal guts, Noah took careful measure of the man he'd known for years, yet had never met. The photos he'd seen didn't do him justice. Attractive, mid-thirties, thick dark hair, and chocolate-brown eyes. Looked to be in excellent shape, well over six feet tall with a commanding presence that would entice many women. Noah could easily see how a young, innocent woman could be so fascinated by him.

Exuding self-confidence, cool sophistication, and danger, Jordan Montgomery would draw women to him like bees to honey.

Noah was more than a little shocked by his own anger toward Montgomery. After hearing the things this man said to a young, innocent Devon, he had the overwhelming urge to slam his fist into Montgomery's gut until he gagged. Profound guilt might have eaten at the man for seven years and the mistakes he'd made stemmed from anger and betrayal, but what Montgomery inadvertently set in motion made his crimes much worse.

But it wasn't Noah's place to pin blame or offer pardon. All of this would be left up to Eden. What would she think when she discovered Jordan continued to search, even after all these years?

Montgomery dropped back into his chair. "What do you think the chances are of LCR finding her?"

Noah would reveal nothing. This would be Eden's decision. If she chose to expose herself, he was almost certain to lose her as an operative. She had buried her trauma, but bringing it back out into the open, having her reveal that trauma to the man who'd unknowingly been responsible for it, wasn't something he figured she'd be able to handle and come away from not changed in some way.

Eden's coolheaded, emotionless persona was a far cry from the overemotional, damaged, and weak Devon Winters found in the alley all those years ago. If she returned to any part of that person, LCR would no longer be a fit for her. She'd be a real person instead of the hardened, detached mercenary he'd trained.

Noah shook off his disquiet and regret. He'd set this into play. He wouldn't back out now.

"You don't look very optimistic."

Noah jerked himself out of his introspection. The last thing he needed was Montgomery wondering what was going on in his head. "Just giving careful thought to what you've told me." He eyed Jordan speculatively. "You went to our D.C. office years ago and we weren't able to help. I read our file. You and her stepfather offered a huge reward. Her face was plastered all over the world. The story got local and national attention. Nothing came from all of that. Why do you think that years later, this will be any different?"

"As your name implies, this is my last chance. I had to come here on business and I knew the founder of LCR was here in Paris. It's a long shot, but I have to give it one more try. My job has afforded me the ability to search for Devon on my own and I always believed at some point, I'd come across some kind of clue."

"What's changed?"

"Nothing yet, but it soon will. I've left my job. And I'm . . . getting married. I guess you could say I want to give finding her one final try before I give up completely and decide there's nothing more I can do."

"Will you ever truly give up?" Noah asked quietly.

"You mean will I stop looking at every tall, slender, blond woman and wonder if it's her?" Montgomery shrugged with a restrained weariness. "Probably not."

"I'll be honest with you. Seven years is a lot of time and mileage to cover. Most of the things you've done, we would have done, too. It could be Devon is dead, which I assume is your greatest fear. But it could also be she doesn't want to be found. She may have left that part of her life behind her. It doesn't sound like she had a lot of support or love surrounding her and may have just decided to make a new life for herself."

Montgomery leaned forward, his eyes haunted. "If that's the case, that's fine. I don't even have to know where she is . . . won't even try to see her. I just need to know if she's safe . . . alive."

Noah stood, indicating the interview was over. "Let me

give it some thought and see what kind of headway I can make based upon what you've told me and the file you brought."

Montgomery rose and held out his hand. "I'd appreciate any help you could offer."

As they made their way to the door, Noah couldn't help but ask a question. "Do you think Devon's mother will be of any help if we contact her?"

An expression of bitter hatred appeared on the other man's face. "Alise wouldn't cross the road to save her daughter, so no, I don't expect you'll get any help from her. But if you think you can, then by all means, go ahead. Once you talk with her, you'll better understand Devon's disappearance."

So Montgomery didn't know Devon had contacted her mother a few months after she was released from the hospital. Devon had been told not to call back and she hadn't. The conversation, brief and cruel beyond Noah's comprehension, had solidified his decision to help her disappear completely. Evidently Alise never told anyone.

The woman was indeed the bitch from hell.

Eden wouldn't know about any of this until her assignment was finished. She didn't need the distraction. In the meantime, he planned to get even more information about Jordan Montgomery. He knew quite a bit already, but based on some of the things Montgomery had told him, Noah got the impression there was much more to the man than what he revealed. He suspected Montgomery might work with or for the government in a capacity other than as the CIA analyst his file indicated. If so, he'd probably figure out Eden's identity at some point, so she would need to make a decision pretty quickly on what she wanted to do.

Also, though he knew Eden wouldn't like it and he wasn't sure it was the best idea he'd ever had, if Jordan Montgomery was as sharp and tough as he appeared to be, Noah wondered how he could be used. Noah had no compunction about using people for his own needs. What he and LCR did went beyond a single person. Using people to achieve his goals was as normal to him as breathing. If Montgomery could offer assistance with their new project, then he'd use him, despite Eden. She wouldn't like it, but she would understand.

First things first, though. Just who exactly was Jordan Montgomery?

seven

Marc Larue's stone and brick mansion neither daunted nor impressed her. It might be a summer cottage to these people, but it boasted twelve bedrooms just in the main house. According to Georges, there were several other cottages on the compound. Selling and ransoming human beings, along with a multitude of other illegal activities, had paid off well for the Larues.

Eden closed the door on the last bedroom to check and turned to head back to the east wing and her bedroom suite. She didn't expect Marc to house his victim with his family. Nor did she expect to find information on Alfred Larue's human trafficking business. Nevertheless, she could leave no stone unturned. There was a surprising lack of security in the house. Evidently the family believed whoever made it inside their doors was either worthy of their trust or not worthy of their distrust. As usual, her fake background checked out perfectly.

Tonight, if all went as planned, she'd check the rest of the compound. If Christina was on the island, Eden would find her.

Once his daughter was safe, Hector Clement would no doubt seek retribution against the Larue family. She had no feelings one way or the other on what might happen to the adults in this family. They deserved punishment. The children, however, were a different matter. Noah had made it clear to Clement that if anything happened to any of the Larue children, Clement would pay dearly. Noah could be very convincing.

"There you are. I've been looking all over for you," Georges said.

The coy but sexy smile she flashed was calculated to get him to concentrate on her, not her location. Eden slid her hand into the hidden pocket of her skirt, hiding the small tool she used to open locked doors. "I was just wandering around, enjoying the beauty of your brother's magnificent home."

Georges's indulgent expression relieved a small spurt of tension.

"Tomorrow, I'll show you around the island. You've yet to see the grandest part of all. I'll take you to the top of the mountain and we'll watch the sunrise together."

Eden held out her hand to him to lead him away from the rooms she'd just checked. "Imagine, having your very own mountain."

Georges took her hand. "I could give you a mountain and so much more if you would but let me." He turned her hand over, and kissed her palm, inserting his tongue between her middle two fingers.

An appropriate and expected shiver of arousal shuddered through her. Georges need never know it was actually revulsion. "Georges . . . please. You know I cannot betray Jacques."

"But Claire, my love, your husband cannot give you the satisfaction I know your body cries out for. Let me at least give you that."

Eden pulled her hand away. "I can't ask that of you, and whether Jacques can give me physical pleasure is not important. I made my vows to him, to keep myself only to him."

A glimmer of anger flickered in his eyes before he quickly banked it. A small alarm clicked on inside her. If Georges became impatient, if he forced the issue, she would have a choice to make. She wouldn't leave without finding the child or some clue to where she might be. If she used her little viral bug, Georges would become violently sick, but she stood the chance of being removed from the island if they insisted on taking him to a hospital.

Another option was the knockout drug she always carried with her. Of course, that would involve allowing him a sexual favor or two. Though it made her skin crawl and her stomach roil, Eden had been prepared for that from the beginning. In every assignment, she knew there were such risks.

Saving the child was the objective. Any sexual act would be put out of her mind, just as anything else she did that might bother an ordinary person. Eden no longer made the claim of ordinariness . . . it had been beaten out of her years ago. She was a survivor and would do what was necessary, no matter how distasteful.

Georges continued to stare at her for what seemed like endless seconds, as if the sheer power of his eyes would compel her to change her mind and agree to go to bed with him. Since that wouldn't happen until she knew there was no other option, she returned his stare until he had the grace to look slightly ashamed. Some small, decent part of him still admired her loyalty to her husband and she planned to play on that as long as possible.

"Come, my love, it's time for dinner."

Allowing him to take her hand, Eden followed Georges down the stairs to the large dining room. She had met many of the family members throughout the day. Georges's mother had been the biggest surprise. Gracious and kind, she'd welcomed Eden into her home as if she were a long-lost daughter. An attractive woman in her mid-fifties, Inez Larue appeared to be a warm, loving woman who doted on her children and grandchildren. If Eden hadn't known for certain that she was responsible for some of the most heinous acts of the Larue family, she'd believe Inez was the epitome of motherhood. Too bad these people were criminals. With their acting abilities, they'd make great LCR operatives.

Marc, on the other hand, was how she'd pictured him. Handsome on the surface, but with something in his blue eyes that revealed the slimy pervert inside. Though he did his best to hide it behind a charming smile, Eden had no problem recognizing evil.

She'd yet to meet Alfred Larue, but he was due later in the evening.

Though polite, the rest of Larue family wasn't overly cordial. She got the distinct impression that Georges brought women to family events on a regular basis and she was considered just one more. Fine with her. If they thought of her as just another bimbo Georges was sleeping with, their scrutiny and questions would be much less intrusive.

She put on her most winning smile and headed toward the mass of laughing and apparently happy people gathered in the enormous living room. Funny, they all seemed nice and normal, giving no indication they were aware of the child rapist in their midst or that their wealth had been gained through the misery and suffering of others.

Georges warned her that even more of the family would arrive tomorrow. Meeting and lying to all of them wasn't a problem. Escaping so many eyes might be.

"Claire, my love. Let me introduce you to my father."

Turning from a discussion of current fashion trends with one of Georges's sisters, Eden looked up into faded blue eyes. Tall, with an impressive paunch and balding blond hair, Alfred Larue looked like an ordinary businessman and grandfather. Eden looked hard, surprised that his eyes held only a warm, friendly welcome.

"Madam Marchand." Alfred took the hand Eden extended and kissed it with a charming ease. "It's a pleasure to meet you. Our Georges has become enamored of you and I can see why. You are beyond lovely."

Her lips curved with sweet innocence. "How do you do, Monsieur Larue. Please, call me Claire."

"Very well. And you must call me Alfred." He beamed at his son. "She's as charming and beautiful as you said, Georges."

"I knew you would think so, Papa."

Alfred turned and caught his wife's attention. Eden watched as the two exchanged a look of understanding. A strange tension zipped through her. Something was going on here and it involved her. Had they discovered her identity? Was she about to become another victim of the Larues? Her spine stiffened. *Like hell.*

"Come, my love, I believe my mother and father want to get to know you better."

Adrenaline pumping through her, she pasted a bland, pleasant expression on her face and allowed Georges to lead her from the room. Her eyes assessed her chances of escape. Not good. Two exits. The patio door, blocked by two oversized goons whose dinner jackets didn't hide their impressive weaponry underneath, was on the other side of the massive living room. The other exit was the one she was going through with Georges, his mother, father, and two more goons. She could probably handle two, maybe three of them. But if they chose to shoot her, she had little chance of surviving. Her silver cocktail dress wasn't made of Kevlar.

Georges led her through an arched doorway of heavy oak into a small room with comfortable-looking furniture and a small, cozy fire. Alfred and Inez headed to a sofa. Georges led her to an opposite sofa and sat beside her. The two goons didn't enter the room. Faces hard and expressionless, they closed the door and Eden knew they were guarding it on the outside. To keep people out or keep her in? She would soon find out.

The smile Inez Larue flashed her was one of reassurance. "Tell us about yourself, Claire."

Comprehension came quickly and with it, a different kind of unease. These people didn't suspect her of wanting to rescue their son's latest victim or bring down their organization. They were concerned parents wanting to get to know a woman their son was enamored of. Other members of the family might have looked at her as if she were just another woman in Georges's bed, but apparently his parents believed otherwise. Had she underestimated Georges's feelings? Was he in love with her and she'd missed the signs?

Before answering, she turned to Georges with a vulnerable, questioning expression. The avid desire in his eyes reassured her. No, Georges wasn't in love with her. He was in lust. Big difference, but would his parents see that?

Alfred studied the young woman Georges claimed to be unable to live without. She was beautiful, but he had expected that. His youngest son's taste in women was as predictable as sunrise. What he hadn't expected was the character and strength he saw in her eyes. This woman was different from any other Georges had brought home. Based upon her answers to Inez's questions, they would determine if she would become a member of their family.

In a soft, melodic tone, she said, "I was raised in the outskirts of Marseilles. My papa died when I was six. Mama worked at a fabric mill to support us."

"Are you an only child?"

"Yes."

"And your mother?"

"Mama passed away a few months after I graduated from school."

"So you are alone in the world?"

"Yes, except for my Jacques, of course."

"Ah yes, your husband. So sad that he is an invalid."

"Yes. The stroke hit him early in life, taking us by surprise."

Inez nodded in sympathy. "Tell us about him."

Looking somewhat flustered by all the attention, young Claire shifted in her seat. Alfred watched her carefully. Yes, she moved toward Georges, no doubt looking to him for support and comfort. A good sign.

"I met Jacques when I was working in a restaurant. We were immediately attracted to each other. A friendship began and then we fell in love."

"He is much older than you, is he not?"

She lifted a slender shoulder. "Love knows nothing of age."

"And do you still have this love for your Jacques?"

Innocent eyes rounded with shock at the question. "But of course, he is my husband."

"And he doesn't mind that you've left him for a few days? Who is caring for him while you're here?"

"Fortunately Jacques is a very wealthy man. We are able to afford excellent care for him. And Jacques knows how much I love him. He need never doubt my faithfulness and devotion."

Alfred glanced at his wife as she nodded in approval. Georges had chosen well. Claire's love for her husband continued despite his infirmity. Loyalty such as this was hard to find. She would make a fine wife for Georges and an excellent addition to the Larue family.

Crystal chandeliers glowed, highlighting the enormous dining room. By anyone's standards, Maria Larue's birthday party was a rousing success. Well over fifty people sat around the gigantic, food-laden table. Laughing and boisterous, the Larues certainly knew how to enjoy themselves. Eden had never seen so much food or wine in her life.

Despite her knowledge of how they'd achieved most of their wealth, she couldn't help but be intrigued by their closeness. As an only child, with no known relatives other than her mother and stepfather, any meals they'd taken together were quiet other than silverware clanking against plates, or a stinging lecture from her mother on some issue that hadn't pleased her. More often than not, Eden had gotten up from the table with a stomach filled with knots of nerves instead of food.

Eden slammed the door on those thoughts. She hadn't given any thought to her past in years and doing so while on a mission was beyond stupid. Seeing Jordan again had most likely prompted them, but allowing personal reflections, especially painful ones, while on a job was a distraction she couldn't allow.

Georges whispered an inane compliment in her ear, bringing her back on point. A small nervous smile curved her mouth, showing her appreciation for his compliment but that she was still not comfortable with his ardor. Georges's disintegrating ethics regarding her faithfulness to her husband were becoming a reality. They'd spent the entire day together and his conduct had been that of an ardent but restrained lover.

Last night, after his parents' polite inquisition, she retired to her room, claiming exhaustion. When the mansion grew quiet, she'd crept out of her bedroom to explore, but had to rush back inside at the sound of approaching footsteps. After more than a dozen attempts throughout the night, she'd given up.

A slender, masculine hand ran up and down her forearm. "Claire, my love, do you not like the meal?"

Ignoring the curious glances of people surrounding her, she lifted guileless eyes to Georges. "It's delicious, truly." Her voice lowered to a whisper: "I think perhaps I'm just a little nervous around so many people. Jacques and I lead such a simple, quiet life that I'm feeling a bit overwhelmed."

Her somewhat simplistic plan was to ask for Georges's

understanding, plead a tension headache, and be allowed
to go to her room. Having the family distracted with their
grand dinner would give her the opportunity to search for
Christina. Today's island tour with Georges had given her
an excellent location to search. But first, she had to ditch
Georges.

In an instant, she sensed that her plan had backfired
miserably. His smile leering, Georges raised his hand for
a servant. The attentive man leaned down and Georges
whispered something in his ear. Tilting her head slightly,
she overheard the word *immediately*. Before she compre-
hended his intent, Georges pulled her from the chair. His
arm draped over her shoulders, he addressed the fifty-plus
people chatting and eating around them. "Mama, Papa,
everyone. Claire and I need some time to ourselves."

She barely got out a breathless "Good night" before
Georges pulled her from the room and into the giant foyer.
Pulling at the hand gripping her arm, she said, "Georges,
no . . . You should stay with your family. I'm really quite
tired and my head is—"

"Nonsense. I see my family almost every day. You, my
love, I see much too infrequently."

His hold firm, Georges led her up the stairs, down a
long carpeted hallway, and into what looked to be a sitting room. A table sat in front of a small fire and two
solemn female servants were hastily setting the table, as
another servant rushed in with plates filled with some of
the delicacies from dinner.

Candles glowed, and soft music played through invisi-
ble speakers. It was a less than subtle setup for seduction.

Biting the inside of her cheek, Eden peeked up at
Georges. His adoring, lust-filled eyes told the story. The
man was intent on romance. With a small inner sigh, Eden
knew she had no recourse but to pretend to be pleased
with his romantic efforts.

"Oh . . . my. You are too kind and sweet." Leaving his

side, in case he decided to start groping, she drifted to the table, picked up a grape, and nibbled delicately.

"Come . . . you can do better than that." Georges pulled out a chair for Eden and she sat down abruptly, her mind whirling on exactly how she was going to get herself out of this situation. Always prepared to do what was necessary to ensure a successful mission, she nevertheless would put off the inevitable until she no longer had a choice.

Over the next half hour, Eden dined on what she was sure was succulent lobster, mouthwatering pastries, and ultraexpensive wine, but she tasted nothing. She giggled and simpered like an imbecile, hoping Georges might possibly become disgusted by such inanity. God knew she was.

When she suddenly found her hand clasped in his while he sucked butter from her fingers, she knew she wasn't going to get out of this as smoothly as she had on other occasions.

Nevertheless, she would try.

"Georges, you know I cannot betray my marriage vows. Why must you torture me?"

"Now, now, my love, you knew when you accepted my invitation what would happen. You've put me off much too long. Tonight, you will become mine."

If she hadn't had to stay in her role as the silly and naïve Claire Marchand, Eden would have rolled her eyes at such drivel. But since she couldn't be herself, she did what she thought any young woman should do when presented with a man who was basically telling her she was going to sleep with him whether she wanted to or not. She became indignant.

Spine straight, eyes flashing, she snapped, "That is not true, Georges. I thought you were my friend, that you understood—"

Moving quicker than she'd ever seen him, he jumped to

his feet and pulled her into his arms. Before she could protest, his mouth was on hers. Since he outweighed her by at least a hundred pounds and had wrapped her in a tight embrace, she had no choice but to pretend to welcome his kiss. She blanked out everything but what she needed to do.

Pressing her body against his, she took his tongue into her mouth and moaned, rubbing against him with sensual intent. At her submission, he loosened his hold. Eden took advantage and pulled away. Gasping breathlessly against his shoulder, she put as much emotion as she could into her voice. "You're right, my darling. I do want you . . . but please, not here, where servants are around. Come to my room."

Georges drew away, his eyes glinting with triumph and lust. "I will make you happy, Claire. I promise."

With a tremulous smile, she took her purse in one hand and held out her other hand to lead him out the door. It should have taken them less than a minute to reach her bedroom. However, now that Georges believed he had free rein with her body, he stopped frequently to kiss and paw her every few feet.

By the time they made it to her room, Eden was not only breathless, she was furious. She hadn't worked this hard in a long time and was determined this would be the last time Georges Larue touched her. The door swung open and Georges suddenly decided to show his romantic side by sweeping her into his arms and carrying her over the threshold.

Really, this was just too much. Giggling like a besotted idiot, she planted a loud kiss on his cheek and whispered, "Let me go for a second. I have a special surprise for you."

At last, Georges dropped her legs, allowing her to stand. Purse in hand, Eden floated toward the bathroom. "I'll be right back. . . . I think you'll be happy with my surprise."

She closed the door just as Georges was pulling his shirt over his head, his gleam of anticipation making her dread the next few minutes, though she looked forward to the outcome.

Withdrawing a cosmetic pouch from her purse, she pulled out a small perfume bottle and from a hidden zippered compartment, a tiny hypodermic needle.

Her cellphone vibrated just as she lifted the bottle to fill the syringe. Knowing only one person could be calling, Eden set her materials aside and held the phone to her ear.

"Get out." The urgency in Noah's voice told her more than his words.

"What?"

"Your cover's been blown. Two men just showed up at the address you gave Georges, looking for Jacques Marchand . . . with some damn impressive firepower. We handled them, but others are sure to come. I'm picking you up at the designated spot in fifteen minutes."

Eden kept her voice to a whisper. "I can't leave. I'm certain she's here. I'm not going—"

"Dammit, Eden, that's a direct order. You're dead if they—"

"I'm not leaving. I'll contact you as soon as I locate her."

"Eden, you can't—"

"I'm her last chance, Noah. You know that. When Larue finds out about me, Christina will be in even more jeopardy. They'll either take her deeper or kill her. We can't let that happen."

A long, taut pause, then Noah sighed. "Call the second you find her."

She closed the cellphone. An abrupt knock on the door startled her, causing the perfume bottle to fall into the sink and clatter toward the drain.

"Claire, darling. Are you all right?"

Grabbing the bottle, she replied with just the right

amount of sugary sweetness. "I'm fine, Georges. Give me one more minute. I promise you won't be disappointed."

"My darling, I'll make sure neither of us is disappointed."

Resisting the urge to roll her eyes, Eden prepared the needle. She tapped down the revulsion of the coming event . . . getting Christina her only focus. Fortunately his family would think they were occupied, which should give her enough time to do her job.

"I'm giving you until the count of ten and then I'm coming in after you."

Taking him at his word, Eden pumped the last of the liquid from the bottle into the tiny syringe and pushed out the air. Without blinking an eye, she pulled her dress over her head, unhooked her bra, and slipped her panties off, just as a naked Georges pushed open the door.

As his gaze settled on Eden's nude body, his eyes widened to almost saucerlike proportion, making him look like a cartoon version of himself.

Flashing a seductive "Come and get me" smile, she put her left hand behind her back to hide her little "gift." Her right hand pushed her hair over a shoulder, and began a slow, sensual caress, starting at her neck, over her breast, trailing lower.

Georges focused on her hand, seemingly mesmerized.

Eden approached him slowly, pleased to see him back up . . . ah yes, now the kitten stalks the tiger.

Georges backed all the way into the room and then stopped as if rooted to the floor. Her smile promising him every sexual, secret delight in the universe, she pressed a finger against his chest, until he began to back up again, finally reaching the bed. When he tried to grab her, Eden jumped back, drew her mouth into a pouty bow, and wagged her finger at him. "No . . . no . . . no. Let Claire show you how much she wants you."

Her hand flat against his chest, she pushed hard until he

fell onto the bed. Eden came over him, straddling his legs. She tried to ignore the erection he sported. Had yet to even look at it, and fervently hoped this little trick worked so she wouldn't have to touch it. Leaning over him, she pressed tiny kisses all over his face, then his neck.

Georges grasped her shoulders to pull her down and Eden settled over him, trying without much success to avoid his penis. His hands caressed her back, slid down to her buttocks, kneaded and pinched. When one hand headed in a direction she definitely didn't want him to go, she knew it was now or never. Moaning loudly, as if she'd never tasted anything more delicious, she licked the side of his neck. Then, in a pretense of caressing the other side with her hand, she brought the needle up and injected it beneath his skin.

"Ow! Claire . . . Did you bite me?" His voice slurred. "Wha di . . . ?"

Eden jumped from the bed and threw a blanket over an unconscious Georges. With the swiftness of a speed dresser, she pulled on clothes she'd set out earlier. Grabbing the few items she wouldn't leave the island without, she turned off the lights and exited the room. The drug should keep him out most of the night. However, if Larue's men were supposed to report in at a certain time and didn't, an alarm would go up. Others would soon be searching the entire island for her.

Every second counted.

Under the cover of darkness, Eden crouched behind one of the few trees on the island. Georges had taken her on a tour of the entire area earlier in the day and she'd asked seemingly innocent questions to determine camera locations and where security roamed.

As Georges had showed her the sights he thought she might be interested or impressed with, she'd become concerned. There seemed to be no secret places he wanted to steer clear of showing her. They'd almost finished their excursion when she spotted a two-story house on top of a small hill overlooking the water and pointed to it. "What's that lonely-looking house up there?"

His mouth grim, there was a slight hesitation before he shrugged and said, "It's empty. My great-aunt lived there and died just recently. We will probably renovate it at some point, but we miss her so much, none of us have had the heart to do anything to it."

She offered condolences, though warning bells rang in her head. What better place for Marc to keep his victims? The house was far enough away from the rest of the buildings where no one would be bothered by their cries or screams. Despite herself, a shiver of revulsion had run through her, prompting Georges to become concerned she was catching a chill and end their tour.

Eden stayed in the shadows as she crept up the path toward the house she suspected never held the Larues' aunt. Dressed in a long-sleeved black turtleneck shirt and jeans, she'd covered her hair with a black knit cap. A utility belt around her waist held the small but necessary tools of her trade, and in her pant leg she had hidden one of her favorite weapons. She didn't plan on getting caught, but if she did, she felt reasonably prepared.

The reason behind Larue's men showing up at her fake address in search of Jacques Marchand wasn't lost on her. Apparently Georges had asked his father to ease his way into her bed by eliminating the competition. Sleeping with a married woman went against his ethics. Having her husband murdered was not a problem. Thankfully she and Noah had anticipated such a move and had LCR people waiting. But now, speed was even more critical.

A blast of light slammed inches in front of her feet. Dropping to her knees, Eden scrambled behind a giant bush. Dammit, she hadn't known about the spotlights. Her face lowered to the ground. The light could pick up nothing other than pale skin. When the glow disappeared, she dashed up the hill, her legs eating up the distance like a track star.

At the top, she jogged the last few steps to the house and stopped. Crouched low, she took a few seconds to survey the area. Other than the distant sound of waves hitting the shore and muted music from the main house, she heard nothing. She slid a slender knife from a holder sewn into her pant leg. Just because she saw no one, didn't mean the place wasn't guarded. After learning the hard way one too many times, she knew to be prepared for any eventuality.

Bent low, she moved at a quick pace around the house. One small light shone from a second-floor window. A slight smile curved her lips as anticipation and excitement zoomed. The window was opened slightly. If she couldn't go through the door, this would be an easy entrance.

The rest of the residence sat in quiet, somber darkness. With the moon hidden behind the clouds, it was hard as hell to see, but using her small flashlight was out of the question.

About to stand on her toes to peer in a low window, light flooded the front of the house. Eden dropped to the ground and held her breath. Cold fury flashed through her. Marc Larue stepped out of the house, a cruel smirk of satisfaction on his Lucifer-handsome face. He looked supremely pleased and that could only mean one thing. Someone inside the house had fulfilled his perversions.

The knowledge that only a few yards away his daughter was in the midst of celebrating her birthday while he was performing vile acts against a child was almost more than Eden could comprehend. Did the bastard have no limits or control over his blatant wickedness?

Though she wanted nothing more than to leap up on the porch and take him out of this world so he could begin his punishment in hell quicker, she wouldn't. Christina was the mission. The pervert would get his just deserts soon enough.

As Marc swaggered down the hill to the main house, Eden took advantage of the light he'd left on. Jumping over a bush, she ran to the back door and tugged. Locked. A quick glance at the locks told her she could get in with her handy little tool, but it could take several minutes. Minutes she didn't have.

Not taking a chance with the front door, she backed up and threw a rope up to the metal railing of the second-floor balcony and yanked. Hooking the clip to the small harness at her waist, she scampered up the wall and jumped over the side. A jerk on the balcony door—locked. A glance through the glass showed nothing but darkness.

The opened window was her only option.

Eden jumped back up the balcony railing and held tight to the iron rails as she scuttled to the ledge. Thankful for years of ballet and gymnastics classes, she put a foot out on the ledge, bounced a couple of times to test its strength. Her thoughts on her goal, she ignored the hard ground twenty feet below. The ledge, about four inches wide, seemed sturdy enough. Her left hand pressed against the wall, she held her right arm out for balance as she inched heel to toe along the ledge. Halfway to the open window, she heard a creak. Froze. Heard nothing more. She took another step and heard a crack. The ledge was giving way. Adrenaline surged. With a flying leap, she threw herself at the window just as the ledge beneath her feet disappeared. Her hands caught and gripped the windowsill. Body swinging crazily back and forth, her arms strained with the weight. Taking a deep breath to steady herself, she pushed up and through the window.

Landing on her butt with a hard thud, she ignored the breath rasping from her lungs. Rest could come later. There was no time to waste. One distinct sound caused a painful tug to her heart and had her up on her feet in an instant, running toward the soft sobs.

With such easy access and no apparent security system, Marc obviously had full faith in his ability to keep his prey incarcerated. And no wonder.

At the entrance to an oversized bedroom, Eden gripped the doorjamb and trembled with a familiar but controlled rage. Pale moonlight filtered through the large window, revealing a horror no one, especially a child, should ever know. The room held two queen-sized beds. A girl lay on each bed, nude and chained to the iron posts. Both were quietly crying. One she recognized as Christina. The other she didn't have a clue. But they were both leaving with her.

With slow, careful steps, she backed out the door before either girl saw her, wanting to contact Noah prior to announcing her arrival. Extraction would be from the water. He and four others were sitting in a boat, a mile from shore, ready to respond.

After a brief conversation with Noah, confirming location, Eden returned to the bedroom.

"Christina?"

Head jerking up, a thin, hoarse voice whispered, "Yes."

Hands at her side in a nonthreatening stance, Eden said, "Your parents sent me to bring you home."

A harsh sob was her answer.

Taking a tool from her pouch, she unlocked Christina's cuffs and then turned to the other girl. As she twisted the lock on her handcuffs, she asked, "What's your name, honey?"

In a voice so low Eden had to lean close to hear, she whispered, "Amanda."

"I'm taking you, too, Amanda."

Though the room was dim, the gleam of hope in her eyes was unmistakable.

Ignoring the obvious signs and scents of sexual abuse, Eden concentrated on the most important factor: speed. She

opened a closet, relieved to see several items of clothing.
Throwing the clothes toward them, she whispered, "Put
these on—quick."

She turned and stood at the window to keep an eye out.
Any minute now, Larue's men could be headed their way.

A quick look back reassured her that Christina had
dressed and was now assisting the other girl with her
clothes. Mrs. Clement was right. Christina was a fighter.

Once both girls were dressed, Eden held up her hand for
them to follow her. Knife in one hand, flashlight in the
other, she led them down the stairs and to the back door.
Flipping the locks, she eased the door open. Peered out . . .
still clear.

Eden shot a quick glance back at the shivering, trauma-
tized young girls, willing them strength for the journey
ahead. "We're going down the hill, to the shoreline. A
boat will be waiting for us. It rained this morning, so it'll
be slippery. Hold on to each other."

At their nod, Eden stepped out the door and froze. The
moon cast a soft glow on the grounds below them, revealing that Marc Larue stood only a few feet away. The
menace on his wicked face didn't faze her; she knew she
could handle the man. It was the revolver in his right
hand that gave her pause.

*How the hell did he . . . ? Dammit . . . motion censors.
Why the hell didn't I check?*

"Going somewhere, bitch?"

Blocking his view of the girls, Eden marched down the
steps toward him. Hands at her side, she wished for her
own gun, a .38 Smith & Wesson Airlight she was rarely
without. Since she hadn't known if she'd be searched, she
hadn't taken the chance on bringing it with her. Knives and
small innocuous tools were much easier to hide or explain.

Pulling in a breath to center herself, she kept the knife
hidden against her right palm and wrist. "Stand back,
Marc. We're leaving."

"Oh, I don't think so." The charming man she'd met the day before had disappeared. In his place stood the real Marc Larue, evil personified. "I knew Georges couldn't get a woman like you."

He shifted his head to flash a smile at the girls cowering behind her. Eden's skin crawled at the loving expression. "Chrissie, you and Mandy, go on back in the house."

Her tone firm and commanding, she said, "Christina and Amanda, stay right where you are."

"You really think you can handle me?"

Her snort of laughter held pure contempt. "A slimy, perverted child molester? Yeah, I can whip your ass, no problem."

An ice-cold mask covered his face as his eyes roamed over her body. "I prefer them younger, but I might just make an exception with you."

Though the weapon in his hand could be deadly, the awkward and stiff way he held it from his body told her he had little experience with guns.

Advantage, Eden.

In one simultaneous motion, Eden tossed the flashlight behind her and let the knife fly, aiming at the arm holding the gun. Just as the knife sliced into Marc's upper arm, she whipped her foot up in a front kick, knocking the gun from his hand.

With a yelp, Marc grabbed his injured arm. Looking down at the blood seeping through his fingers, he snarled, "You bitch, you'll pay for that." With a roar, he lunged.

An instant before he reached her, Eden swooped left and dodged him. Marc landed a few feet behind her. Eden whirled and, taking advantage of Marc's teetering balance, kicked his ass hard. He fell face-first onto the walkway with a loud, satisfying crunch. The bastard had broken his nose. Giving him no time to recover, Eden leaped on top of him, knees digging deep into his shoulder blades. Without turning, she addressed the girls: "Christina, take my flashlight.

You and Amanda head down the hillside, toward the water. Don't stop for any reason. I'll be right behind you."

The patter of footsteps moving away told her they'd obeyed. She bent over the cursing, bucking man beneath her. "You perverted piece of shit, I'd like nothing better than to cut off that pathetic piece of meat between your legs. Sadly, I don't have time." Grinding her knees deeper into his shoulders, Eden pressed hard into a pressure point under his arm, Marc's muffled squeal of agony an assurance she'd hit the right spot. Then, with one last sob, he relaxed into unconsciousness.

Eden leaped to her feet. Grabbing her knife, she slid it into her tool belt and then took Marc's gun. Without a backward glance, she took off after the girls. Christina and Amanda were her priority no matter how much she'd like to kill the creep.

Thankful for the moonlight, she held on to moss-covered boulders as she made her way down the hillside toward the water. Reaching a giant, craggy rock, she paused to check the girls' location. Relief flooded through her when she caught sight of them at the edge of the sandy beach. Freedom was in sight.

She took half a step forward. *Craack*. Rock splintered inches from her face. Eden ducked and ran as bullets pinged and zoomed around her. Slipping and sliding on the wet boulders, she ignored the jagged edges of the rocks cutting into her palms as she propelled herself downward.

The rumble of the speedboat racing toward the beach was a beautiful sound. Seeing the girls hesitate and look up at her, Eden shouted, "Keep going!"

They nodded and ran toward the boat. Eden raced toward them. Noah and two others jumped into the shallow water. Guns in hand, they laid down fire cover as the girls were pulled onto the boat. Eden took a flying leap and landed on the deck.

Breath wheezing from overtaxed lungs, she lay on her

back and listened as a torrent of shots were exchanged. A thump had her twisting her head sideways to see that Noah had jumped on board. At his shout of "Let's go," her eyes closed in relief.

Pounding heart and aching lungs now eased, Eden sat up. Wind whipped water spray into her face as the boat raced toward their waiting yacht. Her heart clutched to see the young girls huddled together on a bench, blankets covering their shoulders. They looked shell-shocked and dazed. But they were alive. Now the healing could begin.

She felt a hand on her shoulder. She looked up as a grinning Noah offered her a cup of coffee and shouted over the roar of the motor, "You okay?"

Nodding, Eden gratefully accepted the steaming liquid and took a long swallow of sugar-laced caffeine. As she watched the shoreline disappear, extreme satisfaction banished exhaustion. Oh to be a fly on the wall at the Larue mansion.

Damn, she loved her job.

eight

Three Days Later

Noah gazed out over the city that had become his home. He'd been here so long, sometimes it was hard to remember the tiny Mississippi community where he'd grown up. He'd been wilder than a feral cat and meaner than a junkyard dog—at least that's what his part-time preacher, full-time alcoholic father shouted as they'd dragged Noah away that day. The years he'd spent in prison had taken much of the wildness and meanness out of him. Unfortunately they'd also left a cold, detached bastard in his place.

That's what Eden would accuse him of when she discovered he'd asked Jordan Montgomery to work for LCR on the Larue project. It took a lot to impress Noah. He could count on one hand the number of people who'd managed to do that. Eden wouldn't be surprised she was one of them; she might be surprised Jordan was also. The man had a mighty impressive background.

Working for an ultrasecret government agency, whose employee turnover rate rivaled a fast-food restaurant due to its lack of support if an agent found himself in trouble, was impressive enough. Finding out Jordan spent fifteen years with said agency told him a lot more. Jordan Montgomery found his own way out of problems and knew how to take care of himself. Noah needed that kind of person working for LCR. It was the only kind he hired.

Eden had completed her assignment. Christina Clement and Amanda Blackburn were back with their families. They would receive the counseling they needed to help them move on and someday go on to lead productive lives. Another LCR mission accomplished.

An unsurprising incident occurred a few days after Christina returned to her family. Marc Larue's Mercedes was blown to hell . . . with Marc inside, speeding straight toward his reward in the fiery pit. Marc had a new and permanent home and the devil was his new playmate.

Hector Clement had fittingly punished the man who'd raped and tortured his daughter.

Sources revealed that Alfred Larue was now out for vengeance. Since neither Claire nor Jacques Marchand existed, his search for them would be fruitless and any revenge plans pointless. Albert might link Claire to LCR, but that wasn't a concern, either. LCR employees and locations existed in full anonymity.

At the sound of a soft buzz, he turned. Montgomery was on his way up. They'd have a few minutes to chat before Eden arrived. She knew nothing about Montgomery's involvement or his search for Devon. She thought the meeting was to give a final report on the Larue mission and then to discuss her next assignment. And that was correct. She just had no knowledge she would have a partner.

Noah felt a slight tug in the area where his heart should be. He ignored it. Eden had known from the beginning that to toughen yourself up, you had to expect the unexpected in sometimes a truly horrific forum. Having Montgomery here when she arrived would either blast her to pieces or toughen her defenses. If it did the first, she didn't belong with LCR. If it toughened her even further, then there was an added benefit to inviting Montgomery into their realm.

The door opened and Jordan Montgomery walked in. Noah sensed immediately that not only had he been checked out, Montgomery was on high alert. The man now knew how powerful Noah was and was wondering if this was set up. Montgomery had excellent instincts. Those instincts probably saved his life numerous times and would be an asset to LCR. For Noah, the small bite of conscience of manipulating people to do his will disappeared. All operatives of LCR were expendable. It was something both Eden and Montgomery were used to and expected. Noah would make no excuses for doing what he had to do to get the job done.

With professional wariness, Jordan entered Noah McCall's office and took careful note of his surroundings. The room reeked of elegance and wealth. A massive desk in the center of the room held three monitors. A giant flat-screen TV covered one wall and a large wet bar covered another. Hell, the view alone behind McCall's desk, over-looking the Pyramide du Louvre, would be worth millions.

LCR might do damned good work, but it was obvious they were well paid for it. Not that Jordan had a problem with that. If they found Devon, he'd gladly give his savings. Most people who approached LCR probably felt the same way.

He settled himself into the leather chair McCall indicated with a nod of his head. After McCall contacted him about working with LCR, Jordan had called in some favors from his many sources. It had taken extensive digging, but he'd found out a little more about the head of LCR. Noah McCall had more power than was good for any one individual. That kind of power, when owned by the wrong person, could destroy lives and wreak untold havoc. Jordan trusted few people and McCall had just gone to the top of the list of people he trusted least of all.

It wasn't that the man didn't do good with his power. He'd saved a lot of people over the years. But the number of people who owed him something was downright scary.

McCall leaned back against the couch and lifted his mouth in a small, enigmatic smile. "I'm assuming the things you found out about me were to your satisfaction?"

Jordan raised a brow at the other man's arrogance. "My satisfaction? No. But I learned enough to know the good you've done outweighs the bad. That's enough for me. At least for now."

Though his expression didn't change, Jordan sensed an ease he hadn't felt before. Was it because he'd given his approval of McCall's methods or because he'd missed something in his investigation? Jordan didn't know, but as always, he would be on watch. If McCall wasn't on the up-and-up, he'd know soon enough.

"Tell me about this mission you mentioned. From what you've said, everyone in your organization will be involved."

"That's true. But I'd like to wait a few minutes. Your new partner will be here soon and I'd like to discuss the operation with both of you present."

"My partner?" Jordan had trouble keeping the disbelief from his voice. He hadn't counted on working with anyone, but held back from voicing his reservations. Just because in his previous line of work he'd never relied on anyone but himself didn't mean he couldn't play well with others.

McCall's arched brow told Jordan he was well aware of his reservations. "In a case like this, working with a partner is imperative."

A small buzz sounded and though his expression didn't change, Jordan sensed a new tension in the other man.

"Looks like your new partner has arrived."

Jordan stood at a soft knock. The door swung open. Everything within him stilled. *What the . . . ?* It was the woman from the restaurant. The one he'd mistaken for Devon. She'd changed the color of her hair to a soft white-blond and her eyes were cobalt blue instead of the light green he remembered. Nonetheless, she was the same woman. What was she doing here?

"Eden, come in. I'd like you to meet your partner."

The woman stood stiffly for a second, and then, with a graceful confidence he remembered well, she glided into the room. Did she remember him?

Her smile was somewhat cool at first and then he could almost see her body change, relax. But she couldn't hide the fact that she'd been just as surprised to see him, maybe even more.

"Jordan, allow me to introduce Eden St. Claire. Eden, this is Jordan Montgomery."

Without acknowledging the man who'd made the introductions, Eden St. Claire held out a hand to Jordan. "But we've already met, haven't we, Mr. Montgomery?"

Her sultry voice, low and melodic, hummed along his senses like a musical caress. He'd forgotten how enchanting he'd found that husky, sensual tone. Something else that struck him as he drew closer to shake her hand . . . she was angry. Though showing him nothing but a cool, pleasant smile, Jordan could feel vibrations of displeasure bouncing from her and he got the distinct impression those feelings were all targeted toward Noah McCall.

"Already met?" McCall asked.

Jordan slowly drew his gaze from the lovely Ms. St. Claire as he answered, "Yes, in a restaurant, a couple of weeks ago."

Jordan looked back at the beautiful woman who sat across from him. She leaned back into her chair and crossed long, elegant legs. He ignored the gut punch of attraction. Damned if he needed that kind of complication.

Eden had learned long ago to compartmentalize. It had saved her life on more than one occasion. Today it saved her sanity. If she allowed herself to dwell for one second on the fact that Jordan Montgomery sat across from her, she wouldn't be able to function. Just knowing Jordan might still be in Paris had been making her crazy. She'd been eager to jump into their new project, not only for the anticipation of destroying Alfred Larue's organization, but also because of the constant worry of bumping into Jordan again. Paris was a big city and the chances of that happening again were small.

She hadn't counted on Noah, though.

How stupid not to see this coming. Noah had allowed her to get away with a small breakdown with very little comment. In his cold, unemotional mind, he would see this as a test. One she would either pass or fail. If she passed, it was what he expected from her. If she failed, she'd be out on her ass. She held no illusions on that. Noah might have saved her life, but that didn't mean he expected less of her than he would of himself or anyone else. She had a job to do. If she couldn't handle it, he needed to know.

Though furious emotions raged inside, she put them where they belonged. As she listened to Noah describing their mission, she forced everything away except her role as a well-trained, highly skilled LCR operative.

Noah sat sprawled in his chair as if he didn't have a care in the world. Eden was used to this deceptive pose. Noah at his most relaxed-looking was deadly. In an even, unemotional voice, he outlined his investigation. "We've identified five areas where the victims are kept, but we don't have definite locations yet. Mrs. Beard was correct. If ransoms aren't paid, the kidnapped victims are turned over to another part of the business—the one who sells to the highest bidder. Then there are those who are simply sold, without a ransom demand."

"How did we not know Larue was in the business of selling humans like cattle?" Eden asked.

"As we discussed, and from what I've gleaned from our sources, this is Alfred Larue's baby, without any of his immediate family's involvement. I'm not sure even his wife, who from my understanding can be just as cold and brutal as the rest of the family, knows about this enterprise."

Noah rubbed his temple as if he had a pain. "When we investigated the Larues, we were looking at his known illegal businesses. Those that rivaled Hector Clement's. This one never showed up. This particular venture is fairly new, maybe no more than four years old. But it's well run and, with the Larue's wealth, well funded. Larue and his bastard minions are making a shitload of money."

Eden blinked in surprise. After knowing this man for over six years and only hearing him curse a handful of times, two in one sentence was unprecedented. Something was wrong. Was it the size of the operation that bothered him, his concern for her, or something else?

Jordan apparently didn't see anything wrong with Noah's vocabulary. From what she remembered, Jordan wasn't one to hold back his curses if something disturbed him. As that thought flashed through her mind, Eden slammed the door shut on those memories.

"You got any intel on these bastard minions?" Jordan asked.

Noah shrugged. "Not enough. I've got three of my best investigators on it. In the meantime, I'd like for you and Eden to get to know each other a little. If you're going to be partners on this operation, you'll need to be able to trust each other implicitly."

Every molecule and cell inside Eden clanged a silent alarm. They were being thrown together. The explanation of getting to know each other was a crock. She'd worked with several different operatives and had only known their first names . . . probably not their real ones. She sent Noah a narrowed-eyed stare. Why was he doing this?

Though she wanted nothing more than to say they didn't need to know each other, she didn't want Jordan suspicious. If he guessed she didn't want to be within a thousand miles of him, he'd wonder. He might even see it as a challenge.

The last thing she wanted to do was intrigue or challenge Jordan Montgomery or arouse his interest.

"That's a fine idea," Eden lied smoothly.

A wicked, appreciative gleam sparkled in Jordan's eyes as he nodded his agreement. "We could have lunch together, if that's not a problem for your husband."

Before Eden could answer, Noah frowned and asked, "Husband?"

She forced a small smile. "When I met Mr. Montgomery previously, he asked to see me. Since I'd just had lunch with Georges, I was forced to lie and decline due to my being married."

Noah stood, apparently eager for them to get started. "Well, enjoy your lunch. I'll—"

"I'm afraid I must decline again. I have several issues related to my last assignment I need to review with Noah." She turned to Jordan. "Perhaps we could have dinner tonight. Say six o'clock at Le Mirage."

Jordan gave her a brief, searching look before nodding. "I'll see you there." After shaking Noah's hand, he strode out the door.

Noah stood at the opened door watching Jordan disappear into the elevator. He clicked it closed and then turned toward Eden. "Well, I think that went well. I—"

Her fist shot out. The blow, fast and furious, slammed into his jaw. Noah crashed into the closed door with a hard thud.

"You bastard," she hissed.

Leaning against the door, he worked his jaw back and forth. "Good shot."

She shook her head in confused denial at the amusement in his voice. After trusting him for all of these years, how could he? He'd betrayed her . . . in the worst way possible. "How dare you interfere. You don't know what—"

"No, *you* don't know. Sit down and I'll explain."

Fury zigzagged through her like a pinball. Her voice

quivered with hurt and betrayal. "Like hell I'll sit down. I'm through with you, through with LCR. You've—"

"I said sit down!" Noah roared.

Momentarily startled into silence, she found herself doing exactly what she'd been told, though she continued to glare her anger. Nothing he could say or do would ever make this right.

Noah sat on the edge of his desk. "Think rationally. Do you know the real reason he's here?"

"Yes, because you're an interfering, heartless bastard, and I—"

"He's looking for you."

"What?"

"He came here a week or so ago and asked if LCR could help find you."

"You expect me to believe that after seven years, Jordan has decided to start looking for me?"

Noah lifted his shoulder in a small shrug. "Apparently he's been looking for you since you disappeared."

"That's bullshit. My mother told me—"

"Exactly . . . your mother. You know what a liar she is."

Eden shook her head, denial squealing and pounding like a banshee. "No. I don't want to hear this."

"Why? Because it's easier to believe no one cared about you? Just because your mother is a heartless bitch, doesn't mean other people didn't care."

"Jordan doesn't care about me. I remember his words well. Even if he truly didn't know where I was, it's his curiosity and nothing more. He's too late . . . seven years too late."

"The man's been searching for you since he first discovered you were missing. He's spent thousands trying to find you." He held out his hand as if he actually might care. "It's time you faced your past, Devon."

Shrinking back from his touch, she snarled, "Don't you damned well tell me what it's time for me to do. That girl doesn't exist anymore. If Jordan is wondering if Devon Winters is dead, then he can wonder no more. She is dead."

"Then you're going to be the one to tell him."

"What?"

"You heard me. If that's what you want Montgomery to think, then you're going to have come up with that on your own. He's asking LCR to find you. I'll respect your right to stay Eden St. Claire, but it's up to you to deliver the sad news of Devon's demise and how it happened."

"You bastard."

"You're repeating yourself, my dear. You know I deal in facts. My job . . . our job is to rescue people, and if they can't be found or they're dead, we give a detailed report. So there's your new assignment. If you want him to believe Devon is dead, then create the proof and give it to him. I'm out of it."

Eden shot to her feet and jerked her purse and jacket up. "Fine. After today, Devon Winters will be officially dead."

"Just be sure it's what you want."

She didn't bother looking back as she stalked jerkily from the room. "Like you really give a damn."

Eden slammed the door behind her, her body trembling as Noah's betrayal warred with the astounding possibility that Jordan had actually cared about what happened to her. No. God no, don't go there. Devon Winters died seven years ago and that broken child could never be resurrected.

Devon would remain dead. Eden would see to that. And now she would find a way to deliver that news to Jordan.

nine

Soft music and muffled conversation barely penetrated Jordan's thoughts as he waited at their table for Eden to appear. He took a long swallow of his Glenlivet on ice, reflecting on the meeting earlier today. So the lovely Ms. St. Claire was an LCR operative. No wonder she'd been upset with him when they first met. He'd interrupted her while she was on a job, possibly putting her identity in jeopardy. When undercover, having your identity come into question could be dangerous. Upsetting the delicate balance of trust often put the wary on alert.

One thing he refused to give any consideration to was his attraction to Eden. Though she intrigued him more than any woman he'd met in years, he couldn't act on that attraction. Asking her for lunch at their first meeting had been uncharacteristic and stupid. An impulsive act he wouldn't repeat. He might not love Samara the way she deserved, but he could damn well make sure she never had reason to question his faithfulness.

His attention was caught by the slender vision in a scarlet red pantsuit gliding toward him. Jordan ignored the usual gut punch and rose to greet her.

Her mouth curved into a slight smile as she settled into her seat. He sensed her dislike and couldn't help wonder why. Without conceit, he knew he was attractive to women and he'd done nothing to offend her. Well, other than unintentionally putting an assignment in jeopardy and then later implying she was cheating on her husband . . . her fake husband. Okay, maybe he deserved a little hostility.

If they were going to work together and watch each other's backs, it would help if she actually cared what happened to his back. He could be as charming as the next guy; he was just somewhat rusty with the technique. "Since we're going to be working together, perhaps we should know something about each other."

There was that tiny flicker again in her expression. Jordan didn't know what it was, but it disturbed him on some level. "Do you not agree, Ms. St. Claire?"

"Please, call me Eden. And I shall call you Jordan."

Jordan nodded. "Eden it is. So, do you want to go first or shall I?"

"Go first?" Her smooth forehead wrinkled.

"With your life story, of course."

The cool smile that curved her lips and the blasé way she settled back into her chair told him she disagreed. Her words confirmed it. "My life story would bore you to tears."

"I doubt that seriously." He looked up as the waiter approached. "Why don't we order and then let's see if I get bored."

The look she flashed him seemed innocuous enough, but Jordan got the distinct idea he made her uncomfortable.

After their waiter left, he gave her what he hoped was a friendly, nonconfrontational look. "Why don't I go first?"

Her eyes flickered down at the table as she took a sip of her wine. Perhaps she thought she was the one who would be bored to tears. Hell, maybe he really did need to work on his charm.

"I grew up in Virginia. I think I mentioned that when we first met. Graduated from the University of Virginia. Just before I graduated, a stranger approached me and asked me to consider working for a government agency I'd never heard of."

Despite every instinct warning her against it, Eden settled back into her chair, fascinated. She hadn't wanted to come here, didn't want to work with Jordan. Wanted no contact with him ever again. But that choice had been taken out of her hands and she had to deal with it. For some reason Noah thought Jordan could help with their new project and she'd resigned herself to that. She had expected to hear a somewhat boring account of his work as a CIA analyst and how he could assist LCR.

Now, as he talked, she realized she was being given a remarkable opportunity. Years ago, she imagined herself in love with this man, but had known almost nothing about him, other than what she'd cooked up in her childhood fantasies. That stupid infatuation was gone, but she realized she still wanted to know Jordan Montgomery and what made him tick.

Just the knowledge he'd worked for someone other than the CIA astounded her. What other mysterious things could she learn?

"An American agency?"

"Yes, but not one that existed on paper. Still doesn't. Just a small group of people with a hell of a lot of power, quite a bit of money, and some high, if sometimes ruthless, ideas."

"Why did they approach you?"

"A number of items appeared on their radar. I spoke a few more languages than the norm, had a couple of black and brown belts in the martial arts, could handle a gun pretty well, and knew more than I should about certain kinds of explosives."

Feeling her head begin to shake in amazement, she froze. No way could she say what she wanted to say or even look surprised. Nonetheless, she was thunderstruck. Except for

the explosives knowledge, he could be describing the
unique skills she'd brought to LCR. One of the reasons
Noah asked her to join.

Though she knew Jordan was raised by his grandmother, not asking about his family would look strange.
"What about your parents? Didn't they want to know
who you were working for?"

"My parents died in a small plane crash when I was a
kid. I lived with my grandmother until I left for college.
She died right after my senior year. I didn't have any other
close relatives . . . probably another reason I caught their
attention."

"And you've been working for this agency ever since?"

"Yes."

"Then why have you agreed to work for LCR? Surely
it's a conflict of interest?"

"Possibly. Except I completed my last assignment last
week. I've left them for good."

"Why?"

Jordan shrugged as if it were of no consequence. "It
was time."

The waiter appeared with their meal and both were momentarily distracted. When he disappeared, Jordan
turned his attention back to her and smiled the devastating smile she remembered all too well. "So tell me how
Eden St. Claire became an operative for LCR."

This would be easy. When Eden St. Claire was born, so
had an intricate web of lies. A web so tightly knit to be
impenetrable. Briefly, she wondered how he would react if
she answered with the truth. *I was attacked, raped, cut,
and beaten so badly the paramedics lost me twice before
I made it to the hospital. Noah paid for my care, my operations, and saved my sanity.*

"Actually, it's not all that different from yours. I was
born in Los Angeles. Lost my mother to cancer when I
was ten. Since my father hadn't been in the picture since

my birth and no one knew of any relatives, I was put into foster care. A few months later, I was taken in as a foster child to a family."

Her mouth lifted into a small smile as if in fond memory. "They were highly intellectual individuals who'd waited late in life to have children and then when they decided to adopt, discovered they had little patience for young ones. Elaine and Claude took me in and allowed me to explore and develop my talents."

"And those talents are?"

I can lie in eight languages. "Much like yours. I had a good ear for languages, a gift for martial arts, and a thirst for adventure."

"What kind of adventure?"

Anything that helped me to forget. "You name it, I wanted to try it. I was fortunate that my adoptive parents were well off enough to let me try many things."

"How did Noah find you?"

He was called to the hospital on a charity case . . . me. "Actually, I found him. I was on vacation in France, backpacking with some friends. We came up on him. He'd gotten lost from his traveling companions and injured his ankle." Eden came up with that little lie on her own. Every time she told the story, Noah got a gleam in his eyes, but he never refuted her claim.

"And you impressed him with your amazing abilities?"

No, I begged him to let me work for him because he'd done so much for me and he was the only one who cared. "Nothing so dramatic. As we made our way back down the mountain, we got to know each other. After he reunited with his friends, I assumed I'd never see him again. He called me a few weeks later, said he was in L.A. on business. He invited me to dinner and made me an offer."

"One you couldn't refuse."

One that saved my life. "One that intrigued me."

"You're an American, but you've made Paris your home?"

"Not really, though I do spend a lot of time here. I have apartments in several areas of the world. My assignments often determine where I live."

"What about Elaine and Claude. They still live in L.A.? Know what you do?"

Her eyes flickered with sadness. "I lost them both, within months of each other, when I was still in college."

"So you're alone, too."

More than you'll ever know. "Yes, except for Noah, of course."

"And what is Noah to you?"

Savior, friend, betrayer. "My employer."

For a quick second, Eden thought Jordan looked relieved. Why? Did he think she and Noah were lovers? How laughable. Not because Noah wasn't an attractive man. He was possibly the most physically attractive man she'd ever known and that included Jordan. Noah as her lover was laughable because she didn't have physical relationships. Sex on occasion, but those rare events usually left her feeling even more frustrated than before. Anything besides a mild physical release was well beyond her capacity.

Or did Jordan ask this because he was attracted to her? Probably. Most men were. He'd seemed captivated when they first met. And why wouldn't he think it could be possible? She was a single female. He was a single . . . Was he single? No wedding ring, but that wasn't that unusual. "Are you married?"

"No."

She refused to acknowledge a tiny flicker of what felt like relief. "I guess your job would keep you from being able to make a permanent commitment."

"Something like that. What about you?"

Eden shook her head, regretting she'd brought their discussion down to a personal level. She needed to get things back on point. "What do you think about LCR so far?"

Though Jordan raised a questioning brow at what Eden knew was a less than smooth transition to change the subject, he answered evenly, "LCR? A formidable reputation, an impressive success record, and a somewhat disturbing but convenient ability to break the law and get away with it. Whether you can help me remains to be seen."

"Ah yes. Noah told me about your request."

"Really? Why did he tell you?"

A shrug. "I have contacts who may be able to come up with something." Her eyes widened slightly. "Does this bother you?"

"No, just surprised me. I thought he would handle this himself."

"Perhaps he will, but it would be helpful . . ." No, she didn't want to go down that path. She'd started a report this afternoon, detailing the final days of Devon Winters's life. The last thing she needed was Jordan talking about that fateful day. Devon was dead. Nothing could be done about that. Whatever Jordan had or hadn't done to find her wasn't important. As it stood right now, he needed resolution and very soon Eden would provide it. End of story.

"Helpful . . . ?"

Eden started, realizing Jordan was waiting for her to finish her sentence. She rarely made mistakes like this and cursed herself for this one. "Helpful to wait until I hear back from my contacts before you assume we can't help you." She gestured at his plate. "How is your steak?"

She refused to flinch at Jordan's questioning expression. Yes, she'd changed the subject and again had done a poor job of it. The realization that when it came to Jordan, she couldn't depend on herself to be the cool professional played havoc with her equilibrium. She needed to regroup and could only do that by heading in a completely different direction.

"My steak is fine. And your chicken?" Mocking amusement glittered in his eyes, curved his sensuous mouth.

Feeling like a teenager on her first date, Eden bent her head and took a bite. Though it tasted like wet cement, she nodded and smiled with an air of appreciation. It had been years since she'd felt so inept and unpolished. They needed to get this assignment over with and allow Jordan to get back to his life. Then and only then would she be comfortable once more.

Comfortable? What an odd, disturbing word. Was comfort what she felt in her current position? Was LCR an escape and refuge? Eden shut those thoughts down. Having a philosophical inner discussion on her life right now was beyond stupid. Jordan Montgomery sat across from her. She had more than enough to occupy her thoughts.

She focused on the present and what else she could learn. "So you no doubt have had some dangerous assignments with your secret government work. No?"

Jordan's sensuous mouth tilted up, his amusement at her attempt to control the conversation no longer concealed. An unexpected surge of sensual heat flooded her body and she almost gasped aloud at the astonishing and unwelcome emotion. Why had her long-absent libido suddenly reappeared after all these years and for the one man she'd forced herself to feel nothing for? Eden never considered herself a masochist, but was beginning to rethink that. Working with Jordan was bad enough. Actually wanting to be in his company . . . wanting him, was emotional suicide.

More than aware that he detected her nervousness and was humoring her, she couldn't help but be thankful Jordan accommodated her question. She sat in rapt silence, her admiration growing with each story he told. While the descriptions of what he called his more interesting assignments were vague and brief, Eden was experienced enough to know the man had lived a life more dangerous and exciting than any television superhero's. A part of her was astounded at learning exactly what Jordan Montgomery had been doing his entire adult life, while another part backed away from the hero worship she could already feel sprouting up again.

Eden no longer had heroes. She damn well needed to remember that.

"Eden, would you care for dessert?" Jordan asked in such a way she had a feeling it wasn't the first time the question had been posed.

She arched a haughty brow. "Thank you, but no, I have an early appointment, so I must leave." She rose to her feet and looked down. "But you stay and enjoy yours, Mr. Montgomery. I'll be in touch."

Knowing those watchful, too perceptive eyes were on her, Eden crossed the entire restaurant before she allowed herself a breath. Finally, outside the door and waiting for a taxi, she inhaled deeply, not caring that exhaust fumes and other noxious odors filled the air. For the first time in hours, she finally felt a small relief.

When a hand landed on her shoulder, breath left her body again.

"Are you all right?"

Eden looked behind her into dark, questioning eyes.

"Of course, I'm fine."

"Then would you care to tell me why you feel the need to run away from me whenever we're together?"

"I don't know what you mean."

His stare was hard and unrelenting for several seconds, then he expelled a long sigh. "Of course you don't. But think about this. If we're going to be working together, at some point we're going to have to spend more than a few minutes together in the same room." With those enigmatic words, he turned and stalked away from her.

Eden stared at him until he rounded a corner. Ridiculously she wanted to call him back, because as silly as it seemed, she thought she might have hurt his feelings. What an absolutely asinine idea. Jordan Montgomery couldn't care less what she thought of him or how he was treated. These feelings were just remnants from those long-forgotten emotions. Ones she thought were long gone.

How in the hell was she going to work with him?

The instant Jordan cracked opened the door to his hotel room, he knew it was occupied. Gun in hand, he shoved open the door, slamming it against the wall. Recognizing the man across the room, he lowered his gun and glowered. "You in the habit of breaking into hotel rooms or did I just get lucky?"

Slouched in a chair across the room, Noah McCall managed to look arrogant and relaxed at the same time. His steady gaze studied Jordan like he was an interesting, newly discovered species. "How was dinner?"

Pulling off his jacket, Jordan folded it over the back of a chair and then sat across from his uninvited guest. Ankle crossed over his knee, he raised a questioning brow. "This little visit is to discuss my dinner with the lovely Ms. St. Claire?" He offered his most mocking smile. "Is this another service of LCR . . . a little after-dinner wrap-up?"

"Just like to make sure my people will work well together."

Bullshit. "That so? You might want to discuss that with my new partner, then. Seems she has a problem with being in the same room with me for any length of time. It may not bode well for our future working relationship."

"You and Eden not getting along?"

Jordan's eyes narrowed in on the man sitting across from him. "What's this cat-and-mouse shit really about?"

"What do you mean?"

"You know exactly what I mean. You partner me with a woman who seems to hate men. Then you show up, unannounced, wanting to know how we're getting along. Obviously you knew there would be problems or you wouldn't be asking. I don't like games, McCall. Either you fill me in on what kind of shit you're playing or I'm out of here."

"You seem a bit touchy, Mr. Montgomery."

"Only when I'm being jerked around."

McCall raised a conciliatory hand. "Sorry, no games. I rarely partner Eden with anyone but myself and wanted to check and make sure you thought it was going to work. Eden can sometimes come across as a little tough."

"Tough?" Jordan shook his head. "That's not what I'd call it. More like nervous, evasive, and downright frightened."

Something flickered in McCall's eyes. Concern for the lovely Ms. St. Claire? What was the real relationship between Eden St. Claire and her boss. She denied anything personal, but Jordan's instincts told him they were more than employer/employee, as she claimed.

Noah McCall leaned forward. "Eden's tired. Her last operation took a lot out of her. I can see her being evasive. That's part of her makeup. But frightened and nervous aren't really her style. Give her a couple of days, she'll come round."

He stared hard at McCall. The man was damned hard to read. "I can make it work, but I'm beginning to wonder just how good Ms. St. Claire really is."

"Eden's the best there is, something you'll find out soon enough. Perhaps you just need to be more charming."

Exactly what he'd been telling himself earlier. Perhaps he could practice a bit. The lovely and elusive Ms. St. Claire would be an excellent target. "Charm has never been a requirement before. Or my forte."

McCall pulled himself to his feet; stretching, he gave a gigantic yawn. "Well, work on your charm and I'll make sure Eden makes herself more agreeable." He squinted at his watch. "I'm headed home. I'll be in touch in the next day or two. Should have some solid intel by then."

Jordan shut the door behind the mysterious Noah McCall. There was something he didn't trust about the man. Not that there were a lot of people he did trust.

Opening the top button of his collar, he shoved the heavy drapery aside and looked out the window, but his mind saw only the otherworldly beauty of Eden St. Claire. Their dinner tonight had him restless and unsettled . . . two feelings he wasn't used to and didn't care for. He hadn't lied to McCall. Eden did seem unusually nervous with him. He was exceptional at reading people, or, he amended, normally he was exceptional at reading people. Devon being one of the few who'd gotten past his radar.

Eden St. Claire intrigued him and that was a rarity in itself. That he was attracted to her he accepted as fact, but he had no plans to take that attraction further. Even if he were a free man, he doubted she would appreciate his advances. From what he could tell, he either made her nervous as hell or repelled her. Neither one made for anything promising.

He wasn't here for anything other than the hope of finding information on Devon. In the interim, he looked forward to helping with a job that sounded worthwhile and dangerous enough to work up some adrenaline, something he'd missed over the last year or so. After it was over, he'd go home and Eden St. Claire would be nothing but a memory.

In the meantime, they needed to learn to work together. After their dinner tonight, he had serious doubts about that happening. What was it that made her so nervous? She didn't seem the type to be intimidated by any man. But something was off. What?

Eden slammed the door to her apartment so hard a photo of the Louvre she'd taken when she'd first come to Paris crashed to the floor. The sound was only a distant thud in her frenzied mind as she raced to the bedroom.

Going to her knees, she dragged her luggage out from under the bed and threw it open.

Marching to her closet, she paid little attention to the expensive items of clothing as she wrapped her arms around them, ripped them from their hangers, and hauled them to the suitcase. In three trips, she emptied her closet. Muttering curses and fragmented sentences, she went to her dresser and jerked the drawers open. With the haphazardness of sheer panic, she emptied the drawers, pulling out lingerie, nylons, and sweaters without any of her usual care.

The suitcase overflowing, she slammed it shut. Grabbing a smaller bag, she dashed to the bathroom and threw bottles and jars into the bottom.

Catching her image in the mirror, she froze. The face staring back was hers but not. Her skin gleamed ghostly pale beneath a flush of hectic red. Eyes sparkled, wild with panic, beads of sweat dimpled her brow and upper lip. Dear God in heaven, who was this woman?

Eden gripped the sides of the sink as her legs threatened collapse. Turning her head, she stared at her bedroom. A small whimper left her mouth. Clothing scattered across the bedroom floor, her suitcase looked as though it had exploded. She'd panicked . . . lost control. Had wanted to run, flee from Jordan, and anything to do with her past.

What happened to Eden, the invincible? The strong, brave woman she'd become? Emotions were always locked up, hidden from view, but after one brief conversation with Jordan she had returned to the spineless, stupid idiot she'd been years ago.

Eyes closed, head bent, Eden took a long, furious breath of renewal. She would not do this. She would stay and fight. She was better than this. A powerful, strong-willed woman with more fight in her than Jordan and Noah put together. Neither of them would defeat her.

With almost terrifying calm, she turned, took the bottles

from the small bag, and placed them on the shelf where they belonged. When she had finished, she returned to the bedroom and in the same controlled fashion did the same with her clothes and shoes.

Once things were in order, she stripped naked and slid into her workout clothes. Before she entered her gym, Eden stopped to make a call, setting into motion the absolute end to Devon Winters. Within a week, two at the most, young Devon would finally be laid to rest.

Having no patience to stretch before she began her workout, Eden forced herself to at least take a semi-slow run on the treadmill. She set the speed for a seven-minute mile, telling herself that was slow enough. Her mind snarled at the memory of her physical therapist who warned her to always stretch prior to a workout. Her body would just damn well have to adjust tonight.

As her feet pounded against the cushioned surface, memories ran like a horror movie through her mind. That fateful moment when everything she'd ever thought about herself, about life and about Jordan, came tumbling down around her.

Her mother had performed the preliminary work. Jordan's disgust and contempt had almost completely destroyed her. The attack minutes later completed the destruction.

The jarring ring of her wall telephone wrenched her back to reality. Since only a handful of people knew her number and only one person ever called it, she knew not to pick it up. *Noah*. He would leave a message. Jordan might be the last person she wanted to talk to right now, but Noah ran a close second.

Perspiration blurred her vision. Sweat, she assured herself, not tears. She should be grateful Noah called. If not, she might still be inside her torturous thoughts. She'd gladly walk barefoot through broken glass to prevent those memories.

Grabbing a towel from the stack she kept by the small fridge, Eden wiped her face clean, wishing she could wipe clean her thoughts. A small bitter smile curved her lips. Odd how the mind works. While the memories of her brutal assault were mostly scattered and distant, Jordan's contempt and revulsion were as crystal clear as if the event had happened yesterday.

But it hadn't happened yesterday, and she was seven years and a lifetime away from the fragile, broken young girl she'd once been. When she saw Jordan again, she would make sure he had no doubts of Eden St. Claire's cool, sophisticated professionalism.

Stripping off her clothes, Eden headed toward her shower. A bite of curiosity made her listen to Noah's message before she went any further.

His deep voice sounded weary but determined. "I know you're ignoring my call. I don't blame you, but you need to remember who and what you are." He blew out a ragged sigh. "I'll give you a day to recover. Be here the day after tomorrow at nine." His voice softened. "Remember your priorities. Nothing else matters."

He was right. Her personal issues could not interfere with her job. What she did was too important.

Trained to overcome any adversity, she reminded herself that working with Jordan wasn't any worse than anything else she'd conquered. This was just another test of courage. One she had every intention of passing.

ten

"We hit pay dirt. Identified the five holding houses. One in Spain, two in the United States, one in Mexico, and one in Brazil. Apparently the victims are shipped all over the world, so we're not necessarily looking at just these areas."

McCall's wording struck Jordan as odd. "What do you mean, not just these areas?"

"We've known from the beginning that saving the victims won't be enough. Larue has more money coming into this operation than an ice-cream vendor in hell. We're not only going to get the victims out, we're shutting him down completely. Which means we'll not only be going after Larue and his people, we'll be raiding and closing down all of the houses.

"We've determined that though Larue's operation is quite large, Alfred Larue and one other man—a family member, no less—are ultimately responsible for it."

He looked down at the paper in his hand. "Thomas Bennett was once your everyday, average scum-sucking parasite . . . drugs, armed robbery, attempted rape . . . small potatoes, really. He got locked up early but made an influential contact in prison. An acquaintance of Larue. After Bennett's release, he started working for Larue. He married a Larue cousin and impressed cousin-in-law Alfred so much, he became a partner with him in his human trafficking ring.

"Larue's been at this awhile, but it wasn't until Bennett came on board that the business really got going. Bennett's taken it to new heights. In a relatively short amount of time, they've gone from a small side business to an efficient and well-run human trafficking and kidnapping enterprise."

"So we're going after not only the victims, but Larue, Bennett, and all of their employees, too. That's a little different for us, isn't it?"

Jordan eyed Eden with intense curiosity. This woman possessed more faces than Washington had opinions. Every time he thought he had her pegged, the more he realized he didn't. Today she was dressed in a sleek, body-hugging dress of shocking blue. With her white-blond hair, the contrast was almost painful but so damned alluring, he'd gotten a hard-on the moment she'd walked in the door.

Her demeanor was different, too. At dinner the other night, she'd been nervous, but almost approachable. Today, though she seemed calm and serene . . . something in her face told him it was an act.

Jordan whipped his attention back when Noah answered her question. "Different, but ultimately needed. If we don't shut them down, it's only going to grow."

"So what's our part? Do we get to take down Larue or are we going after Bennett?"

"Neither. You'll be handling one of the houses."

The woman to his left stiffened in her chair. "Who's going after Larue and Bennett?"

"Your cover with Larue is shot. I've assigned another team to him. I'll be going after Bennett."

Fascinated, Jordan watched as Eden, who'd showed almost no expression since she entered the room, let out a small gasp and snapped, "What the hell are you talking about?"

Noah leaned back into his chair in a lazy sprawl, his mouth twisted in a wry smile. "Are you suggesting I can't handle it?"

He was surprised even more when Eden rose to her feet and put her hands on her hips. "That's exactly what I'm suggesting." She glared at McCall for a second before turning to Jordan. "Noah shouldn't do this. You and I are more qualified. We'll do it."

"That's enough, Eden. I'll thank you to let me make the decisions about my involvement on my own. You work for me, not the other way around. Remember?"

"I know who I work for and you know damn well that I'm more qualified to do this than you are. What are you thinking?"

"It's something I need to do."

Eden glared at him for several more seconds. Jordan could see her mouth trembling with words she obviously wanted to hurl at McCall. Why was she holding back? Did she fear McCall's anger? Was there more to their relationship than what she'd admitted the other night? And why couldn't McCall handle this part of the mission? Was he disabled in some way Jordan hadn't detected?

With a sigh loud enough to be heard on the street ten stories down, Eden dropped back into her chair. This was the most animated he'd ever seen her. If he wasn't so interested in knowing why she didn't want McCall to be involved with this project, he would have enjoyed just sitting back and watching her. Damn, but she was beautiful.

"Now that we have that settled, let's discuss the particulars of your roles."

Eden glared at Noah as he began to outline the cover for Jordan and herself. Part of her mind was on what he said, while another part dealt with her fear for Noah.

She knew Jordan looked at her from time to time, but no way in hell would she explain why this concerned her. First, it wasn't any of his business. This secret, as well as so many others, was hers and Noah's. Second, Jordan needed to have full confidence in Noah's abilities. If he knew the truth of her concerns, he might question the project and that wasn't something they could afford.

Eden had forced herself to face a lot of things over the

last two days and one of the most important was that LCR needed Jordan. After hearing about his experience and expertise, she knew he was perfect for this job. In the past, she'd always been able to put the mission above anything else in her life and this should be no different. This wasn't a permanent thing. Jordan would help with this project, he would learn the *truth* about Devon, he would leave, and life would return to normal.

The mission could not be compromised . . . no matter what.

She dared a glance at Jordan as he listened to Noah. After everything she'd been through, how could she still find him so attractive? It defied logic, because after hearing his life story the other night, she found him even more appealing. Years ago, she'd fallen in love with a dream, a knight in shining armor, a hero she'd built up in her mind into almost mystical proportion . . . a man who hadn't existed. Now, though that dream was long dead, the man who inspired the fantasy sat only a few feet from her and seemed even more fascinating than before.

She hadn't known back then that Jordan was a real-life American hero. Today she accepted the new knowledge and would deal with it. Just because he was so much more than she'd ever imagined him to be meant nothing, other than that she would have to control this new and ultimately more dangerous temptation. No good would come of it, other than destroy her life again.

"Isn't that right, *Eden*?"

Noah's voice jerked her back to the present. His emphasis on her name indicated he knew she hadn't been paying attention. Fury engulfed her . . . fury at herself. Eden St. Claire was the consummate professional. Allowing the past to take over her thoughts and destroy what she had created was something she could not permit.

Fortunately her brain functioned on different levels, so she pulled in the words Noah had said prior to his question.

He'd been talking about her gift for creating a deep, effective cover.

"Yes, I have extensive knowledge and a large network to pull from." She raised a brow. "I'm assuming you used Frank for our documents."

Noah's smug smile told her she hadn't fooled him for a minute. "Yes, he sent the papers over this morning." Noah rose, sauntered to his desk, and pulled a large manila envelope from his top drawer. Opening the packet, he slid the documents onto a low table that separated Eden and Jordan.

"Eden, you are Maggie Johnson. You've been married to Barry Johnson for three years. You're twenty-three years old. . . . Barry is years older than you. . . . You're his third wife.

"Jordan, Barry Johnson is a fifty-year-old successful businessman from Atlanta, Georgia. You spent most of your years in the plastics industry. Emma, your first wife, died in childbirth. . . . The baby didn't survive, either. Your second wife, Leigh, left you after a year of marriage. She now lives in Montana with her husband and two kids.

"You met Maggie at a department store counter. . . . You were buying perfume for your mistress. You asked her out and three weeks later were married in Vegas. You love her, but treat her like a child.

"Eden, Maggie grew up in an unstable background. Mother and father both abusive and alcoholics. She's never really had anyone to love her, poor girl. Maggie sees Barry as her white knight. She allows him to control her life."

He looked at Jordan. "Barry's got everything he wants except one thing. He's got the money and the trophy wife. Can you guess what he wants but is afraid to let Maggie have?"

"A child." Jordan and Eden answered simultaneously.

"Exactly."

Eden glanced over the documents in her hands. "So Jordan and I will go in as a semi-happy couple. He wants a child, she wants to please him. Why can't they just adopt in the normal way?"

Noah smiled. "Good question. It appears that not all of Barry's business dealings are on the up-and-up. He's afraid of the scrutiny he'd come under if the normal route were taken. And he doesn't want to wait for what he wants. A white male baby, preferably no more than a month or two old."

Her stomach clenched. "They're stealing them that young?"

"Yes, but there aren't many, so the price is quite high, as well as the caution. This cover will need to be airtight. There can be no doubt this is a legitimate purchase, with nothing other than the desire to get a baby quickly. If they suspect any kind of subterfuge, I don't have to tell you what would happen."

She didn't bother to answer, nor did Jordan. They both knew what was at stake.

Eden looked up from the documents she held. "So when do we need to be ready and where are we going?"

"You'll be headed to West Palm Beach, Florida, probably within the next week or so. I've already sent an inquiry through their channels of what Barry and Maggie are searching for. I've not heard back from them, so I'm assuming they're checking out your backgrounds. I don't know how long that'll take. You'll need to be ready when the call comes. Once we get the go-ahead, I'll contact you and you can make the necessary arrangements.

"From the information I've gleaned, you'll be expected to stay for several days so you can be checked out. They'll give the excuse that they want to make sure you'll be appropriate parents. A ruse, of course. You'll be questioned, probed, and observed to the nth degree to make sure you're not going to blow the whistle on their little operation.

"Jordan, I'm sure I don't have to tell you that you'll be the go-to person here. Since Maggie is basically Barry's doll, it'll be you they'll come to. I'll leave it up to you to decide how much you want it to appear that Maggie knows."

Noah's eyes held a teasing glint. "Eden, I know this will be hard for you, but you'll need to become the subservient little woman Barry adores." His mouth trembled as if he struggled not to laugh. "Think you can handle that?"

Determined not to let him rile her, she stared him down in disdain. "I can be anything or anyone, Noah. You should know that by now."

His expression flickered with something like regret before he nodded and said, "Take a look at your profiles, as well as each other's. Learn them. Practice them. I'll contact you as soon as I get the call to move forward." He glanced first at Eden, then Jordan. "Any questions?"

While Jordan was looking down at the paperwork Noah had handed him, Eden took the opportunity to mouth, "I need to talk to you."

Noah jerked his head in a quick nod. He knew she wouldn't let their previous conversation go regarding his decision to go after Bennett. She had to talk some sense into him.

It was surprisingly easy to get Jordan out of the office. She had to agree to meet with him later to discuss their cover, but had known she'd have to do that anyway. She waited until he'd had enough time to get inside the elevator before she whirled toward Noah.

"Let me take care of Bennett. There's no need for you to do this."

Noah shook his head. Affection gleamed in his eyes, something he rarely showed. His words, however, didn't indicate anything but fierce determination. "You insist on acting like a big sister, and while that's nice, you're *not* my sister, nor my protector. I'm the boss here and what I say goes. I trained you to become who you are, or have you somehow forgotten?"

"Don't give me that, Noah. I know what you're capable of, but I also know it could destroy you if you do it. Let me take care of this. There's no reason to—"

"There's every reason, Eden. Some you know . . . some I'd rather not get into. But suffice to say, if Bennett has to be taken out, I'll be the one to do it. While it might not be something I'll particularly enjoy, it's something I need to handle myself."

"Why?" She couldn't comprehend why Noah, after all this time, had suddenly decided he needed to involve himself in something they both knew could very well destroy any of the humanity left in him.

He shrugged, clearly not willing to open up with her. "Maybe I'm tired of others having all the fun, while I sit at my desk and manipulate everyone's life."

"Bullshit. There's not an ounce of envy in you. But for some reason you've decided, after all these years, you're willing to kill. What's changed your mind?"

"Maybe I've decided there are some people who need killing."

"Don't give me that, either. You and I have had numerous conversations about this. You don't blink an eye if one of your operatives has to take anyone down."

"Then if it's something I've approved, what's the difference in doing the actual killing?"

"You know there's a difference, Noah. You don't kill people. Period."

"How can I ask my operatives to do something I'm not willing to do myself? Besides, this could all be a moot point. There's no reason to believe it'll come down to having to take anyone out." He gave her a look that told her the subject was closed. "Now tell me, how are things going with Jordan?"

Eden stared hard, hoping to guilt or intimidate him into spilling his guts. It would do no good. Noah wasn't a gut spiller, nor could he be intimidated. The only reason she knew he had never killed anyone and had an extreme aversion to it was because while working on a case together, Noah almost got himself killed, refusing to take a shot to defend himself. Fortunately Eden had been there.

After the excitement passed, she'd tried to delve into his reasons. Noah refused to give details other than his admission he could do almost anything but take a life. He'd thanked Eden for saving his worthless hide, helped her clean up the mess, and when they'd returned home, he'd disappeared for almost a week. When he appeared at her apartment, he seemed to be the same Noah as always.

Eden never mentioned it to him again. Until now.

Seeing she would get no answers, Eden gave a brief account of her dinner meeting with Jordan. At the end, she confessed something she didn't really want to admit. "I can see why you brought Jordan on board. With his experience, he'll be an asset."

"You going to be able to set aside the past?"

"Does it really matter?"

"Yes, it matters. I saw Jordan after your meeting and spent considerable time convincing him you were the professional I told him you were as opposed to . . ."

"As opposed to what?"

He sat for a few seconds, apparently trying to find words that wouldn't make her explode. "Well, it seems Jordan is concerned that you're scared of him."

Eden tapped down her anger, more than aware that Jordan had a perfectly legitimate reason for thinking this. That was then, she was fine . . . more than fine, now.

"I hope you were able to persuade him he was wrong."

"I did my best. However, it's going to be up to you in the next few days to prove him wrong. You both need to trust each other or this will blow up in our faces."

With practiced grace, Eden pulled herself to her feet. "Don't worry about me. It won't happen again. From now on, Jordan Montgomery will only see Eden St. Claire as she's always been. Professional, experienced, and easy to get along with."

Eden shut the door on Noah's snort of laughter.

Eden gripped the doorjamb and stared at the man at her apartment door. Either Noah had given him her address or he'd followed her from LCR. Either way, she'd didn't want him here. Her brave words to Noah earlier now mocked her. Handling Jordan in a public place was one thing. Alone, in her apartment, without any escape, was quite different. Especially this Jordan.

Dressed in a black T-shirt that emphasized his sculptured chest and broad shoulders and black jeans that encased his long, muscular legs and slender hips, this casual, sexy Jordan threatened a part of her she no longer acknowledged existed. It was also a reminder of what a superbly fine-looking man Jordan Montgomery still was. Something she truly didn't want to remember.

His eyes glittered with something dark and dangerous, and Eden knew she wouldn't be able to put him off as easily as she had before. Though they needed to talk about the assignment, she'd planned to arrange a meeting with him someplace safe and open. Suddenly her roomy apartment seemed closed in and much too warm.

"Have you had dinner?"

His question startled her into realizing she'd been standing at the door, staring at him. No wonder the man questioned her professionalism.

"Dinner? No."

Jordan stepped forward, causing Eden to move hastily back or be in danger of having him touch her. That she couldn't bear.

"Good. I brought dinner with me." He held up a large

basket and the fragrance emanating from it reminded her that breakfast had been hours ago and she'd skipped lunch.

"Since our dinner was cut short the other night, I thought we might get to know each other in more comfortable surroundings tonight."

She felt like an awkward teen who'd just opened the door to the town's bad boy. Jordan made her nervous, jittery, and excited all at once. She could almost hear Noah's amused chuckle in her mind.

"Were you working out?"

She glanced down at her workout clothes, forgetting she had donned them not five minutes before. Hell and damnation. That would have worked as an excuse . . . maybe a lame one, but it would have been something. Was it too late? It was worth a try. "Why yes, I usually work out around this time . . . usually at least a couple of hours. Why don't we—?" Her eyes widened as she watched him place the basket on the coffee table and kick off his shoes.

"Mind if I join you?"

Her heartbeat went into overdrive and then zoomed toward Mach one. Mouth, brain, and body went numb. No words or even a thought of words showed up on her mental radar.

As if silence was her acquiescence, Jordan began to strip.

Without remembering how she got there, Eden found herself on her sofa. She could only watch, mouth dry and heart pounding, as the man she'd once been in love with stripped down to a pair of navy blue boxers. He removed his clothes with casual ease as if he stripped in front of strange women for a living.

And there he stood . . . six feet plus of prime male masculinity. She thought about pretending to ignore his body, as though watching gorgeous men take their clothes off in her living room happened every day. But with him only a few feet away and almost completely nude, pretense was impossible.

Since he didn't seem to mind being almost nude, she could be just as blatant. Her gaze started at his lean, chiseled face and went lower. Seven-year-old memories couldn't compete with the reality standing before her. My God. Had he been as beautiful then as he was today?

Broad, tanned shoulders and torso tapered down to a washboard flat stomach. In the deepest recesses of her mind, Eden always found men with hairy chests a huge turn-on. Jordan's chest made her mouth water. He was furred with just the right amount of coal-black hair. Her nose twitched at the thought of burying her face against his chest and rubbing against that mat of fur.

Her gaze lowered to take in his slender hips and muscular thighs. He obviously worked out a lot. Those kinds of muscles only came with intensive training.

Her gaze traveled back up . . . and stopped abruptly. Blood rushed from her head, her eyes widened, and a hot rhythm of heat began to pulse in some surprising areas of her body. While Eden had been eyeing him as if he were tonight's dessert, he'd let her. And that created a result she wasn't prepared for.

The modest blue boxers were modest no more. Her hungry perusal had produced an enormous erection.

Eden forced herself to her feet. Knowing and unable to deal with the fact that she was blushing—something she hadn't done in years—she dared a glance at Jordan's face and felt her face flame even hotter.

His mouth quirked up in amusement, but his eyes blazed with something she refused to even contemplate. No way would she allow him to get that close again.

"Well . . . uh." She swallowed hard. Embarrassment turned to anger. Just what did he expect? Stripping in front of her as if he were Mr. January. She was a woman and he was . . . he was . . . Jordan. *Shit!*

She gritted words between her teeth. "My workout room is in here." Knowing she was almost stomping in her anger didn't slow her down. She needed to get all of this frustrated energy out of her. Working out to one degree past exhaustion was usually her answer.

And the man causing all of this frustration followed behind her with a slow, steady look and an erection that made certain body parts throb and scream for immediate attention.

Eden flung the door of her gym wide open. Ignoring the man behind her as if he didn't exist, she marched over to the treadmill. Not caring if she appeared rude, Eden pressed the starting speed, placed her feet on the treadmill, and began a slow jog. He'd invited himself, let him figure out what to do.

It took all of Jordan's willpower not to grab her and kiss her senseless. Who did she think she was fooling? The woman was seriously attracted to him. Admittedly he'd egged her on with his little striptease, but if she hadn't been interested, she wouldn't have gawked at him like she was a sugar addict and he was crème brûlée.

Watching her watch him had been one of the biggest turn-ons in his life. If he didn't know better, he'd guess she was inexperienced. There had been wonder and shyness in her expression and the blush on her face and shoulders had him wanting to strip her bare and see how far the pretty pink flush went.

His erection had startled her and he couldn't help but wonder why. Surely she couldn't have expected any different results after she'd almost eaten him with her eyes. He continued to throb in hopeful anticipation . . . pointless though it was.

He'd never in his life forgotten an obligation, but he'd been within seconds of forgetting about Samara. Jordan knew he had a multitude of faults, but cheating wasn't one of them. His desire for Eden St. Claire would go nowhere and he reminded himself he'd better get his mind where it belonged before he broke a cardinal rule.

Forcing his mind off a temptation that couldn't happen, Jordan glanced around the room, impressed with the assortment of machinery Eden possessed. He had a gym at home, but used mostly free weights for his lifting. Eden's collection told him she'd spent thousands on the most modern and scientifically advanced equipment. Her slender body pounding out the miles on her treadmill assured him it wasn't just for looks. The woman was in excellent shape.

Determined to ignore the enticing picture of a sweating and lightly panting Eden, Jordan sat down on a bench, placed the pin in the weight he normally used, and began to lift. Unfortunately, unless he closed his eyes, there was no way to not see her. He told himself he wouldn't touch her and it wasn't being unfaithful to appreciate a beautiful body in peak condition moving with fluid grace. His hard-on raged on.

Her body was sleek and slender without being thin. Her black tights and tank top slid over the hills and curves of her body.

She'd tied her white-blond hair into a ponytail, a little-girl look that seemed incongruent with her usual sophistication. The light from the ceiling glowed down on her, revealing a light sheen of perspiration on her creamy skin. As she ran, the muscles in her arms flexed, indicating that after her run, she would most likely lift weights. Jordan forced his eyes away from her to complete his workout.

Eden felt her body give a slight slump when she realized he'd finally stopped watching her. She'd never had an orgasm while running, but had come close to one today. Which was insane, since she hadn't experienced an orgasm because of a man since . . . *Don't go there. Please, don't go there.*

A quick look at her monitor had her wanting to turn around and snarl at him. Three miles . . . at eight minutes a mile. But it'd been the best she could do knowing those sexy brown eyes were roaming over her, watching, examining. She'd have to do better tomorrow, when hopefully she'd be alone.

Pressing the button to stop the machine, Eden stepped down and stalked to the shelf where she kept her towels. Ignoring the man who continued to lift weights behind her, she wiped her face and torso, then grabbed a bottle of water from the small fridge. She gulped half of it with one swallow, replaced the cap, and took a deep breath.

The noise behind her stopped. Jordan had finished his set. She forced herself to turn and face him.

He surprised her again. His easygoing expression in no way indicated that less than half an hour ago he'd been one very aroused man.

She told herself she was glad. She didn't need the complication of avoiding his advances. Especially not while they worked together. Eden breathed out a long, relieved sigh and continued her workout, convinced Jordan felt the same.

They finished their workouts at the same time, since as soon as she thought he was ready to quit, Eden quit, too. She couldn't handle having him watch her anymore.

She gestured toward a door leading to her guest bath. "There's a shower in there, if you'd like to use it."

Throwing her a slow smile she felt to the tips of her toes, Jordan disappeared behind the door and closed it.

She stood frozen, staring at the closed door as her thoughts went wild with things she had no business thinking. Without conscious permission, her mind pulled off the last piece of Jordan's clothing and she pictured him completely nude. . . . Hot water beat against his masculine body, beaded, and slid down taut, hard muscles . . . his big hands glided over solid velvet steel.

Heaven help her! Eden grabbed another bottle of water from the fridge and chugged it like a dehydrated stevedore. Muttering curses at her stupidity, she headed to her shower, hoping that there was truth in what a cold shower could do for arousal.

Under the cool blast of water, Eden forced herself to face some facts. Long ago, she'd determined that a weakness acknowledged could never defeat her. She was still attracted to Jordan. There. She admitted it. It was out in the open where it could no longer fester. And really, shouldn't she be glad about this? How long had she doubted that she still possessed normal feelings of sexual attraction? She'd thought they had been brutalized out of her. Nice to know there was still normalcy left in her.

She stepped out of the shower and dried off, continuing her rationalization. Jordan was a handsome, charismatic man. Any woman would be attracted to him. Yes, many men she'd known over the years were just as attractive, including Noah, but her past with Jordan made her more aware of his sexuality. She knew how hot his kisses could be. Had full knowledge of his taste, his scent, and how wonderful his mouth felt on her breasts, her sex. She knew . . . *Holy hell!*

Strange and unfamiliar sensations were pulsing through her body. Eden looked down. Nipples peaked and hard had nothing to do with her cold shower and the throb of her sex had everything to do with the man in the next room. Just thinking about Jordan had turned her on.

Furious with her body's betrayal, she finished drying and jerked on her clothes, determined to put her mind back where it belonged. Now that she had acknowledged the attraction, recognized the problem, she could deal with it. Jordan would work for LCR for a short period of time, she would provide proof of Devon's death, and then he would leave. Until then, he would never have to call her professionalism into question again. Eden St. Claire could not be defeated!

Mind and body back on the same page once again, Eden opened the door and stepped into the living room. She stopped in the middle of the room when she caught sight of Jordan. His hair, wet and gleaming, glowed blue-black under her dining room light. His slow, easy smile erased every word of her self-lecture.

"I emptied the basket and set the table. Hope you don't mind."

Frozen, she didn't say word.

"Eden, you okay?"

Giving herself a mental lecture and a subsequent kick in the ass, Eden nodded and forced her legs to move toward him. "Yes, I'm fine. Just trying to remember if I got coffee at the store yesterday."

Okay, it was an idiotic excuse. Thankfully it worked, because he grinned and said, "Hope so. Coffee'll go great with the dessert I brought."

"I'll check." She practically ran to the pantry door, flung it open, and stared at the contents. Knowing he would become suspicious any minute, she grabbed the coffee canister and turned away.

Could she do this?

She had to!

eleven

Alfred held his head in his hands. Though darkness had fallen hours ago, he didn't bother switching on the lamp beside him. The grand desk he'd had built years ago gave him no sense of satisfaction. The comfortable leather chair Inez had given him after they'd made their first million offered no respite for his weary body. His heart was ravaged, his will almost broken. His oldest son was dead and his youngest son was responsible.

Georges had brought that vile woman into their home. She'd eaten their food, slept underneath their roof, been treated with the utmost respect. They'd intended to welcome her into their loving, close-knit family. She not only betrayed them, she had come close to destroying them and made a mockery of their kindness and generosity.

Snatching Clement's daughter from beneath their noses had been an additional insult. The girl would have eventually been returned to her family. Having her stolen from them put him at a severe disadvantage, giving them no leverage over their rival. Now business would be even more difficult and hazardous.

In reprisal for her abduction, Hector had killed his precious Marcus.

Taking Hector Clement apart with his bare hands was something Alfred longed to do, but he wouldn't. Hector had made a statement by taking Marc's life. He'd avenged his daughter's loss of innocence.

Alfred hated what had happened, but he understood it.

A life for a life. Their feud was at an end. Each of them had lost something precious. Alfred wouldn't punish Clement.

Claire Marchand, on the other hand, was a totally different entity.

Not only had she caused Marc's death, she'd broken poor Georges's heart. And though it pained him to do so, he had banned his young son from the family. Georges's careless actions could not go unpunished.

He and Inez had lost two sons and it was all due to Claire Marchand's vile, devious acts of betrayal. His poor Inez had been hysterical when she'd gone to Georges's room and found him unconscious. She had thought him dead at first. While they'd been dealing with that crisis, they'd heard gunshots.

Alfred almost had a heart attack when he'd learned what had happened. His men had carried a bloodied and emotionally distraught Marc inside the house. While their family doctor tended his wounds, he'd brokenly explained how Claire Marchand and an army of men had accosted him. At that point, his darling Inez had completely collapsed, unable to comprehend how they'd allowed such a viperous woman into their midst.

Since that night, his wife had been inconsolable. When Marc was murdered two days later, Alfred had fallen onto their bed with her and they sobbed their heartache out together in each other's arms.

This Claire Marchand had been a professional. His people were working night and day to determine who she was and where they could find her. The men sent to put Jacques Marchand out of his misery never returned. He assumed they were dead. When her identity and location were uncovered, he would send his own army to retrieve her. Until then, he had a business to run and a family to keep together . . . what was left of it.

Fury, fueled by grief and exhaustion, pounded through him. When he found this Claire Marchand, or whoever the hell she was, he would personally tear her from limb to limb. Then he would let Inez finish her off. No, on second thought, he might let Inez have her first. His wife could be a ferocious tiger when it involved her family.

Yes, seeing his Inez tear apart Claire's beautiful face would be his fantasy until he could make it a reality.

Eden followed Jordan into the large, elegant bedroom. Maggie and Barry Johnson had arrived in Florida less than an hour ago. A slender, middle-aged man who'd introduced himself as Garrett Mahoney met them at the airport. He'd been friendly but vague about his role in their *adoption* plans.

When they arrived at the ostentatious brick and rock mansion, Peter Lawson, a heavyset man with an unfortunate bulbous nose and cold, watery eyes, greeted them. He invited them in and explained he would be handling their transaction. Eden was grateful that as Maggie she didn't have to pretend to like anyone but her husband. She had been around enough bad people to recognize the wickedness in Peter Lawson.

After spending almost two weeks together, she and Jordan had perfected their roles as the Johnsons. Because of this, Eden was able to sit back and observe. Maggie Johnson was a somewhat shy person, allowing her overprotective and overbearing husband to handle all details related to . . . well, everything.

Though not a comfortable role for Eden, she found herself almost enjoying playing Maggie's subservient character, because of the opportunity it gave her to observe Jordan. Maggie would be expected to fawn over him and hang on to his every word. Eden could do this and not feel as though she revealed anything.

"Nice digs. Right, babe?"

The last few days, knowing they'd be soon in their new roles, she and Jordan started speaking to each other as

Maggie and Barry. She was glad they had, since his oil slick voice now seemed natural instead of the creepy feeling she got when he'd first tried it on her.

"Oh, Barry," she gushed in a breathless, little girl voice, "it is nice. And that Mr. Mahoney said there was a pool here, too. Do you think I could take a swim a little later?"

"Sure, kitten." He reached over and ruffled her hair as if she were five. "I can't wait to see you in that new suit I got you last week."

Eden bit the inside of her cheek. The suit he referred to had been a major bone of contention between them. He'd brought it over to her apartment a few days before they left and told her to get used to wearing it. *It* was basically red dental floss sewn together, barely covering her nipples and pubic area.

The suit had provoked their first argument. Jordan insisted Barry would want to show off his trophy wife. Eden had countered with the argument that Barry would be the jealous type and resentful of anyone ogling what was his. Jordan refused to budge, saying he was more qualified to know what a man thought than Eden. She hadn't been able to come up with a better argument.

If he hadn't behaved as though she hardly existed other than a business partner over the last two weeks, she'd almost think he was looking forward to seeing her in it. However, whatever madness possessed him the first night they'd worked out together no longer seemed to plague him.

She told herself she was glad. At some point, she planned to start believing it.

Yesterday, she spent hours in a spa, getting an agonizing wax. Something she vowed never to do again. It was hard to believe women willingly put themselves through that kind of torture.

Now she faced another torture. Showing her body to him. She wasn't a modest person. Her experiences over the years called for various forms of nudity and she'd learned to ignore lust-filled eyes. Her job came before anything else. When necessary, she could strip off her clothes and think nothing of it.

But this was different and she couldn't deny it, though she wished she could. Being nude with a man you were wildly attracted to was different than being naked in front of someone you couldn't care less about. Would he find her attractive? She hated this new insecurity that only cropped up with Jordan.

Another worry hammered at her. Jordan had seen her naked before. Admittedly she'd been younger and much more rounded, but what if he recognized something?

The damned tattoo she'd kept as a badge of courage was another concern. What if he put two and two together and came up with the correct answer?

Before she left, in between preparing for their mission, Eden spent considerable time and her own money preparing and purchasing documents showing the last few weeks of Devon Winters's life. Police reports, eyewitness statements, newspaper clippings, and a coroner report all detailed how she died. On her return, everything should be ready to present to Jordan.

Eden no longer looked forward to giving the information to him, though in the beginning she had, just to be able to say it was over and done with. The last two weeks showed a side of Jordan she hadn't known existed. He wasn't a cold, heartless bastard only wanting to clear up loose ends. He actually cared about what happened to Devon.

That wouldn't stop her from giving him the file. It had to be done, no matter what. But she no longer anticipated seeing his reaction. Shamefully, she had envisioned turning the screw and giving him some vile facts . . . actual details of what had happened . . . and then the false information that Devon eventually died from her injuries. She wouldn't do that now. Devon's death would be much less dramatic . . . an unfortunate incident and nothing more.

"What'cha thinking, bunny rabbit."

Eden barely refrained from rolling her eyes at some of the ridiculous names that he insisted Barry call Maggie.

She turned from the window she'd been sightlessly looking through. They agreed to keep up pretenses no matter where they were. The chances of a camera being in their rooms were high. Neither one of them planned to blow this mission by taking the risk they weren't on display at all times.

Her smile the innocent and pouty one she'd perfected over the last couple of days, she said, "I still don't understand why you won't let me give you a baby. You know I'd do anything for you."

Eden braced herself, knowing Jordan was about to implement one of his tender touches he'd warned her about. They'd tried over the last few days to get her used to them, but she always stiffened up. She refused to do that again.

"Now, bunny." Jordan's hand tenderly stroked her hair from her face. "We've talked about this over and over. We'll love Barry Jr., just like he was our very own and you won't have to go through any kind of pain. Just thinking about that beautiful body of yours swelling up and hurting . . . Well, I just won't put you through it."

"Okay, if you're sure."

He leaned down and gave her a soft, sweet kiss, something she hadn't expected. She gasped into his mouth and Jordan grabbed her shoulders to hold her still. He trailed his lips across her face and whispered into her ear. "Steady."

Arousal, bigger than what the kiss should have evoked, shuddered through her. Eden made herself put her hands on Jordan's shoulders as he pressed kisses down her neck to the V of her dress.

Shivering, she stifled a groan as Jordan's mouth moved over her breast. Darts of fire shot through her when he tugged on a nipple with his lips. Without conscious thought, her hands cupped his head and held him to her breast.

Jordan released her slowly and stepped back. His eyes held the same shock she felt spiriting through her. This wasn't something they'd rehearsed. The last couple of minutes had been Jordan and Eden, not Barry and Maggie.

Jordan released a ragged sigh. "Let's change out of these clothes and walk around."

Eden nodded dully, unable to give him a verbal reply.

She was startled to see a tender look enter his eyes as he swept his hand down her face again. "It'll be okay. Trust me."

Trust him? As Jordan or Barry? She forced another nod.

Jordan turned away and went into the adjoining bathroom. Eden finally allowed herself to let out another shaky breath. How in the world were they going to pull this off if she got turned on that easily?

Jordan stared at the mirror. How the hell had he allowed that to happen? He'd known he'd have to kiss and fondle Eden while they were here. They'd both been prepared for that. What just happened had been unexpected and unwelcome.

He wished he could blame it on Eden. God knew she'd been provoking him to lose his control since they'd met. But he'd bet his last penny she'd never anticipated what just occurred. She'd been as shocked and turned on as he had. Her nipple had hardened sweetly in his mouth and the groan she uttered was full of arousal.

Unable to let loose the long string of curses surging inside, Jordan stripped off his clothes and stepped into the shower. Since he had to assume there were cameras in the bathroom, he maintained his slump and hurried through his shower. He didn't want to be nude any longer than necessary. Maggie Johnson was supposed to be in peak condition. Barry Johnson wasn't.

He towel-dried quickly, pulled on a robe, and returned to the bedroom. Eden had put on a short, silky robe and was sitting on the edge of the bed, apparently waiting for him.

"I thought . . . that is, if you don't mind . . . that I could shower, too."

He felt a wave of gratitude at her return to the meek Maggie. She knew what was at stake and she was a professional. He was the one who'd lost his professionalism. He couldn't afford that to happen again.

"Absolutely, darling. I'll just put something out for you to wear."

She flashed him a bright smile, but he saw the spark in her eyes. She didn't like being treated like a child. What woman would? Especially one as strong and independent as Eden? But Barry controlled every aspect of Maggie's life, including what she wore. It was only natural for him to dress her. After all, she was his doll.

He dressed quickly in chinos and a black silk shirt and then went to Eden's closet. He surveyed the clothes a maid had hung for them while they'd chatted with Lawson, selecting a light blue, sleeveless sweater and a short, multicolored skirt. The outfit was understated and sexy. It was also something a young woman would wear if she liked to show off her body, or something a man would want his lover to wear if he wanted to show her off.

Eden returned, wrapped once more in her robe, her hair covered with a white towel. He figured it would be hard enough for her to be naked with the knowledge that countless cameras probably surrounded them. He didn't intend to make it harder for her by staying and watching her, too. He could at least give her that.

"Darling, I'm going to go on downstairs. I'll meet you in the front room in, say, twenty minutes."

She flashed him a look of such appreciation, Jordan felt that momentary tug again. Before he allowed it to become something else, he turned swiftly and stalked out of the room.

He heard a loud sigh of relief just before the door clicked shut.

Jordan knew he'd only be able to wander around a little before he was encouraged to go downstairs. But while he was here, he might as well take the opportunity to see if he could find anything interesting. He doubted he would. The children weren't kept in this facility. He and Eden would be taken to another location, probably blindfolded, to pick out their new bundle of joy.

Though his stomach twisted with the knowledge that even now, parents of infant boys were suffering because of the request made by Barry and Maggie Johnson, he planned for a good outcome. Not only would those children be returned, the scum responsible for taking them would be punished.

He heard a slight noise behind him and smiled inwardly. He'd been discovered.

"Sir, is there something I can help you with?"

Barry turned and gave a broad, practiced smile to the young man who'd caught him. "No, just looking around, waiting for my wife to get ready." Standing on the second-floor landing, he gestured broadly with his hands. "My, this is a nice house."

"Yes, Mr. Peter is quite fond of it. Why don't I take you to him now?"

"Why thank you, son. Let me go get the little woman and see if she's ready to come down, too."

"I'm here, Barry."

Jordan whirled around at the soft, little-girl voice and almost forgot his role. The self-assured, beautiful woman he'd come to admire had disappeared. In her place was a meek young sex kitten. Long, honey blond hair—she'd changed the color right before they left—pulled back with barrettes gave her a schoolgirl look. The sleeveless sweater and short skirt reminded him of a school uniform. However, it covered a body that in no way, shape, or form looked like a child's.

"Do I look okay?" Anxious eyes gazed up at him with adoration.

Returning to his role as husband and father figure, he replied with just the right amount of condescension. "You look good enough to eat, baby. Come over here and let me see you better."

With a childlike giggle, Eden floated toward him, her soft blue eyes glowing with love. "Is this close enough?"

Jordan pulled her closer and smacked her bottom with a loving pat as he gave her a loud, obnoxious kiss on her mouth. He was aware of the young man waiting patiently for them to remember he was there, a sneer of disdain barely concealed.

Jordan drew his head back and winked at the man. "Can't resist temptation, boy."

The man smiled coolly and then turned toward the stairway. "If you'll follow me, I believe Mr. Peter is waiting for you in the front parlor with some refreshments."

Taking Eden's hand, Jordan gave it a light squeeze and held on as they followed their watchdog.

Peter Lawson met them at the bottom of the stairs. Eden barely controlled the shiver of revulsion as she watched the creep eye her up and down as if wondering how much she could go for on the market. The man dealt in human misery and suffering and the cold, mean look in his eyes told her he thoroughly enjoyed his occupation.

"I trust your accommodations are to your liking?"

Wrapping an arm around Maggie's shoulders, Barry Johnson nodded enthusiastically. "It's just fine." He tightened his arm around Eden and asked, "I heard there's some snacks ready for us?"

Lawson flashed a slick, weasel-like smile. "We have refreshments set up for you in the parlor. If you'll follow me, we can sit down and chat awhile."

With Jordan's arm wrapped around her as if afraid a tornado would come at any moment and spirit her away, Eden walked beside him as they followed Lawson into another beautifully decorated room.

As they snacked on finger sandwiches, cookies, and tea, an oddly incongruent meal considering their subject matter, Eden listened to Jordan answer questions related to why they didn't have children of their own and why purchasing a child seemed to be their best bet.

"I lost my first wife, Emma, in childbirth. The baby was born premature and died a few days later. My second wife, well, let's just say I didn't want her to be a mama to any of my offspring. When I met Maggie, I knew she was the one for me, but I didn't want to put her through the dangers of childbirth . . . besides ruining what no one can deny is a damn fine-looking body."

Maggie giggled and blushed appropriately, silently seething as she watched Peter Lawson give her what she was sure was meant to be a complimentary once-over. Wouldn't he be surprised to learn that his look made her want to throw up the two sandwiches she'd managed to force down?

As Peter continued to make suitably interested and sympathetic sounds, Eden sat back and let Jordan Montgomery amaze her. He looked so different from the Jordan she'd come to know.

Aware they would be observed no matter where they went, including their bedroom and bathroom, Jordan had been limited in his ability to disguise himself. Still, what he'd managed with streaks of gray in his hair, a full beard with more streaks of gray, strategically placed age spots, and the somewhat slumped posture of an older man amazed her.

He looked twenty years older. Even though she'd seen

him almost nude and knew he was in peak physical condition, the slump in his stance and the slight hesitation in his step made him appear out of shape and decades older.

"I'm sure you and your lovely wife will make wonderful parents. And we'll do our very best to find you that perfect child." Lawson leaned forward. Eden was sure he meant it to make him appear sincere, but it only made him look slimier. "I do have to ask you, though. . . . You mentioned in our earlier conversation the reason you couldn't go through normal channels to obtain a child was some unfortunate legal problems. You must understand, of course, our concern regarding any investigation you're involved with. We must make sure our privacy and names are kept strictly confidential."

Barry Johnson nodded in complete understanding. "You have my word no one will ever know how we obtained little Barry Jr. My little old business problems aren't really that bad . . . but if those damned social service people started investigating . . . well, they might just turn me down and my little Maggie just couldn't take that heartbreak."

Lawson clucked in sympathy. "I totally understand, but I hope you'll understand that due to the larger risk we'd be taking, your fee might be a little higher than what we originally discussed."

This had been something she and Jordan expected. They'd actually argued about how to play it out, but eventually agreed to wait and see how the interview went before making the decision on how to handle it.

She watched Jordan to see what his take was. She hoped he played it the way she thought it should be played.

Barry Johnson reared back into his seat and looked as though he would explode at the insult. A deliberate whimper of distress from Maggie drew Barry's attention. She watched as Barry completely deflated when he saw the distress on his wife's face.

Good. Jordan read the situation correctly. Lawson was completely taken in by Barry's overwhelming need to please his young wife. Barry might balk at additional money, but he wanted to keep his wife happy, so he would pay whatever it cost . . . within reason.

"You got me stuck between a rock and hard place, son. I'll agree to an additional ten percent, but no more." He glared at Lawson to make sure he knew he wasn't just dealing with a man who wanted to please his wife, but also a shrewd businessman.

Peter nodded as he held out a well-manicured hand. "You've got yourself a deal and soon you'll have a baby boy."

Jordan's large, age-spotted hand engulfed Lawson's. Seeing Peter wince slightly, Eden figured Jordan was letting him know he wouldn't get any more concessions from him.

Eden mentally shook her head. Jordan Montgomery was as talented as she was when it came to being someone else. For a brief moment, she allowed herself the fantasy of keeping him as her partner. With his experience, there was an enormous amount of good he could do for LCR.

For the first time since seeing him again, Eden began to wonder if they perhaps could have a real relationship. He'd indicated that after this was over, he'd return to the States. But he had quit his job. What would he do? He was much too young to retire. Why shouldn't he become an LCR operative? Why couldn't Eden and Jordan have a real partnership?

She refused to listen to the small voice inside her that whispered she wasn't really Eden St. Claire. Jordan didn't know that. What was stopping them?

twelve

"Everything okay?"

Clutching the pillow she'd been abusing to her chest, Eden stared at the man lying in bed, waiting for her. "Of course. Why?"

A shrug of his broad shoulders called attention to a well-defined chest and taut, muscular biceps. The navy blue T-shirt he wore did little to hide his overt masculinity. If anything, the material stretched across his chest only enhanced it. Her mouth watered and her fingers literally tingled to touch him.

"You've fluffed that pillow at least ten times. I just wondered if something was wrong . . . with it?"

Meaning, was there something wrong with her? If she weren't pretty damn sure their every word was being listened to and weighed, she'd say yes, there was definitely something wrong and that she wanted to sleep in another room, without him.

She was about to lie down next to a man who at one time meant the world to her. A man who'd made love to her with an all-consuming passion. How could it be that after years of not even thinking about sex, it was suddenly at the forefront of her mind? Sensual, sexual feelings she'd successfully repressed for years were suddenly springing to life, unwanted and unprovoked.

She'd known this was coming. Had known she'd have to lie beside him, sleep with him. They'd discussed this. The cameras would most certainly be in the bedroom. She knew they'd have to kiss, cuddle, perhaps even fake sex to maintain their cover.

When they talked about it, she'd been sure she could do this. She was used to playing a role. It was what she did. She was good at this, dammit.

Now, with Jordan's hard, masculine body waiting for her under the covers, she was suddenly unsure and awkward. Eden St. Claire morphing back to a young, immature schoolgirl with a crush on her hero. *No. Hell no.* That was not going to happen. Setting her chin determinedly, Eden got into bed, resolved to ignore the gorgeous man beside her.

For several long moments, Jordan held her gaze, curiosity and barely veiled concern in his expression. Eden returned his look with an arrogant arch of her brow, almost challenging him to comment.

Breathing out a long, low sigh, he turned away to flip the lamp switch beside the bed.

Darkness washed over the room, shielding their bodies. Blankets created a cocoon of intimacy. Eden told herself she could sleep like this. The king-sized bed gave her ample room. The big body beside her was no one of importance or consequence. She blew out a long, exhausted breath, forcing her body and mind to relax . . . let go.

Jordan heard the moment when she finally allowed herself to drift into slumber. What an extraordinary blend . . . cool, sophisticated beauty and an oddly insecure vulnerability. The more he knew Eden St. Claire, the more she intrigued him.

The giggly sex kitten she'd displayed earlier had him convinced she could play any role with ease. Then, tonight, she walked out of the bathroom wearing a sexy, almost nonexistent nightgown and his radar had shot up, along with a part of his anatomy he fiercely ignored. A normal male reaction to a beautiful female form, nothing more.

He'd watched with interest as she flitted around the

bedroom, putting clothes away, straightening the newspapers he'd read earlier, stacking and restacking the three magazines she'd brought with her. Hell, he wouldn't have been surprised if she'd started dusting the furniture. Then, as if she knew she was behaving oddly, she strode to the bed and began to beat the hell out of her pillow.

Watching her parade in front of him, beautiful skin glowing, long hair flowing down her almost naked back, hadn't erased his arousal. The nervous, worried expression on her face had done that. What the hell was she afraid of?

Ignoring the soft breathing and delicate fragrance of the woman beside him wasn't easy. The attraction he felt for Eden had grown stronger. McCall was right. Eden was very good at what she did. The professionalism she'd exhibited over the last two weeks was nothing short of impeccable. Quite different from what he'd perceived when he first met her as an LCR operative.

Perhaps McCall's theory that the job she'd been on had taken a lot out of her had been correct. Since then, he'd seen nothing other than a professional, undercover operative with a quick, intelligent mind and a beauty that defied description. A beauty he was doing his dead level best to ignore.

As he had for years, Jordan forced sleep. Spending years on missions when functioning on almost zero sleep was the norm; he'd trained himself to take sleep when he could. His mind drifted, his body relaxed, he slept.

A scream pierced the night.

Reaching for his gun with one hand, he grabbed for Eden with the other. Empty space met his fingers searching for his gun. Dammit, he didn't have one. Eden jerked and twitched beside him.

Uncaring about cameras or prying eyes, Jordan quickly switched on the bedside lamp. His gaze swept the room for danger, finding it empty of threats. The woman beside him seemed to think otherwise. Caught in the throes of a nightmare, Eden thrashed on the bed, moaning and whimpering, as if in pain.

Leaning forward, he whispered, "Wake up, sweetheart." The crying continued, almost heartbreaking in its ferocity. Her eyes closed, the tortured expression on her face revealed a horror only she could see.

Touching her shoulder gently, not wanting to startle her, he was unprepared for the stark cry of a wounded animal.

To hell with cameras. Grabbing her shoulders, Jordan pulled her into his arms, unable to listen to her pain without trying to help. Instead of fighting him, as he thought she would, she buried her head and sobbed against his chest.

Whispering soft, soothing words of comfort, Jordan wrapped his arms around her, cradled her to his chest, and rocked. Her sobs quieted. He felt the moment when she became fully awake and aware of where she was. Her spine stiffened, breath hitched, and then stopped for several seconds.

She pulled away and looked up at him. Beautiful eyes drenched from her tears, remnants of the nightmare still lingered. Breath shuddered through her. "What happened?"

"You had a nightmare."

Horror swept across her face. "What kind of . . . Did I . . ." Her throat jerked convulsively as she struggled for words. "What did I say?"

"Nothing. You screamed, and then you cried."

"I don't cry."

The words were said with such indignation, Jordan struggled not to smile. She acted as if he'd accused her of an outrageous crime.

Allowing her the lie, he shrugged. "I must have misunderstood."

She looked around the room as if just realizing where they were. "My God, I forgot . . . I didn't . . ."

"No, everything is fine." He shook her shoulders slightly. "Okay?"

Her body going limp with relief, Jordan released her, letting her settle back on the pillow.

"Want to talk about it?"

"Oh, Barry," she breathed, "you know I always have bad dreams this time of year. Remember, my mama passed away two years ago this coming Saturday."

And just like that, Maggie Johnson had returned.

Jordan was momentarily stunned into speechlessness. How the hell did she do that? Not only did her expression change to a naïve young woman, her entire body shifted in some way he couldn't easily identify. Somehow, she just was Maggie.

He put on Barry with a little more difficulty. "I'm sorry, sweetcakes, I forgot all about that. Come over here and let me hold you."

Alarm flared in her eyes, but she quickly doused it. Instead, her luscious lips tilted up in a smile guaranteed to make an aging Barry Johnson feel like a young buck. "Turn off the light."

In the darkness, the cameras wouldn't pick up the fact that he wasn't holding her. Refusing to acknowledge the disappointment of not being able to hold her against him again, Jordan gave her a greasy Barry smile and switched off the light.

As they settled down next to each other, he barely felt the soft whisper of her mouth on his ear as she leaned over him. "I'm sorry. That won't happen again."

Since he really didn't know what had happened, other than an awful nightmare that he doubted she'd ever explain, he merely whispered back, "No problem."

And that was that. Soon Eden's soft, even breaths were the only sounds in the room. Jordan told himself to force sleep again. He would need to be on his toes over the next few days. He needed every advantage. But somehow sleep wouldn't come as easily as before. The woman beside him continued to amaze and confuse him. She was certainly one of the most talented women he'd ever met, but the story she'd told him about her life now seemed almost too simplistic. What could have triggered the nightmare she'd suffered? Had something happened to her while she was on a mission?

Whatever had happened, it was obvious the experience still affected her, if only subconsciously. If he asked what brought on the nightmare, he was sure she'd tell him it was none of his damn business. And she'd be right.

Still, he wondered.

As if she didn't have a care in the world, Eden lay face-down on the rubber raft and floated lazily in the giant swimming pool. The sun beat down upon her almost naked back, heating her skin, but did nothing to ease the tension inside her. What would be expected of them the rest of the week, and when would they get this show on the road?

Though Lawson said it would take days to find the perfect child for them, they knew they were still under observation. They'd been *invited* to stay until it was time to choose.

So far, they'd been treated as honored and well-fed guest prisoners, allowed to roam around the estate, but not leave it. They relinquished their cellphones when they first arrived and weren't allowed contact with the outside world. This lack of action, and not knowing when they'd be able to move, drove Eden crazy. She wanted to get this over with and get these slimeballs behind bars.

"Make sure you don't burn that beautiful ass of yours."

She jerked her head up. Wishing she could glare, but knowing what was expected of her, she giggled instead. "Now, Barry, you know you'd just kiss it and make it better."

He grinned like a sleazy wolf as he stepped out of his

sandals and dropped his robe. Eden stifled what would have been a real giggle when she saw his ridiculous swim trunks. She purchased them, having assured him that someone with Barry's overbearing personality would also have deplorable taste in his clothing. He'd drawn the line at wearing flowered shirts and flashy jewelry, but reluctantly agreed with her choice of swimming attire.

The bright yellow trunks with orange stripes would be funny enough, but the giant peacock covering his groin created all sorts of hilarious images regarding his manhood. The orange T-shirt she'd bought to complement it had drawn as big a frown as the trunks had. But when she'd reminded him that he'd need to wear the T-shirt since he needed to feign a slight paunch, he hadn't been able to argue.

Her laughter disintegrated when she saw he intended to join her in the pool. The last couple of days had been relatively calm . . . no more electric caresses and looks. They'd been playing Barry and Maggie to the hilt.

The humiliating nightmare the first night had been an anomaly. Nothing remotely similar had happened since. Even sleeping side by side night after night in the king-sized bed hadn't created any kind of problem. She'd even defeated those odd, unwanted sensual thoughts.

For some reason, perhaps her own sense of self-preservation, Eden knew that was about to change.

She heard, rather than saw, Jordan slide in the water and swim toward her. Lying on a float in the middle of the pool, she felt at a disadvantage. Could it be because she was wearing her own ridiculous bathing suit, the one he insisted she wear?

"Enjoying yourself?" Where had Barry's slightly nasal, good old boy voice gone? Jordan's sexy, gravelly tone sent shivers through her. Despite the sun glaring down on her, goose bumps covered her body.

A hand, rough and tender at the same time, glided down her arm. "You cold?"

Eden knew no one could hear them. They were surrounded by water, but the chance they were being observed was great. It would be too risky to ignore or snap at him. But the greater risk was what she longed to do, which was to turn, wrap her arms and legs around him, and give him the deep, delicious, heart-stopping kiss she'd been dreaming about for days.

"Hey, you okay?" Jordan's concerned tone told her she wasn't acting normally.

Remembering her role with difficulty, Eden turned her head and smiled brightly. "I'm fine. Guess I was almost asleep and didn't hear you."

His eyes narrowed. She waited to see if he would challenge her. Instead he gave her a tender smile and softly kissed her cheek. Oh hell. There went her erotic sensors, blaring full blast at the top of their nonexistent lungs.

Repressing another shiver, she slid from the float into the water, hoping he'd get the hint and allow her to escape. His hand grabbed her as she tried to swim away and brought her flush up to his body.

"What the hell are you doing?" Hissing through a bright, adoring smile was somewhat difficult, but she managed to convey her displeasure.

A growl in her ear. "Lawson is standing at the window, watching us. I figured he'd wonder why I wasn't feeling up my gorgeous wife."

Eden closed her eyes, hoping that it looked, at least to Lawson, as though she was feeling ecstasy, when she felt nothing but the agony of not being able to act out what she wanted. She stilled at that thought. Why shouldn't she act it out? Lawson expected them to act like besotted lovebirds. She could give him the show he expected and take what she wanted for herself.

With that delightful thought, Eden relaxed into Jordan's arms and then groaned as she rubbed herself against him. He felt so good.

Warm water caressing them with a silken promise, they floated together, holding each other tight. She could hear his breath in her ear, faster than normal. Without conscious thought, she pushed him forward until he was pressed up against the edge of the pool.

When she realized Jordan had taken it no further than to simply hold her, Eden leaned back to look at him. His eyes, usually so cool, often amused, looked down at her with a dark, almost desperate fire.

Unable to let this moment go by, Eden put her hand behind his head and pulled his face toward her . . . slowly. Again he didn't stop her, but neither did he participate.

He wanted her. Desire blazed in his eyes. The thin shield of his swim trunks couldn't mask the hard evidence of that desire. Why wasn't he taking this any further?

Eden lifted up on her toes and pressed her mouth against his. With that first touch, something seemed to break loose inside him. He groaned against her mouth.

Eden opened her mouth under his, inviting him in. He took full advantage and thrust his tongue inside. His taste, familiar, yet not, plunged her into a spiraling vortex of need. She wrapped her arms around his shoulders, then her legs around his waist.

Jordan whirled her around, pressed her against the edge of the pool, and proceeded to show her what a real kiss could be.

Sucking on his tongue, giving him hers, her body undulated, mimicking the lovemaking she suddenly craved above all things.

When his hands grasped her bottom, she groaned against his mouth, thinking he meant to stop her. She soon found out differently when those large, beautiful hands began to caress and knead her ass with firm but tender strokes.

Realizing she was on the verge of climax, Eden pulled away abruptly, suddenly afraid. She opened her eyes to see Jordan's smoldering gaze. The obvious desire she saw there gave her the courage to continue. Her eyes locked with his, she untied her swim top, pulled one of his hands from her bottom, and placed it over a breast. Her nipple, hard and aching, pulsed with need as his warm hand covered the mound. When his fingers pinched the tip hard, she gasped, startled at the hot spear of arousal.

"You're even more beautiful than I imagined." He lowered his head and took the nipple into his mouth, sucking hard and then laving it with his tongue.

Eden's neck would no longer hold her head up and she rested it against the edge of the pool as Jordan suckled and devoured her as if she were the sweetest of candy. The edge of the orgasm she'd temporarily held off was back in full force, pounding, pulsing away at her sex . . . screaming for release. On the verge . . . about to drop off the edge . . . nanoseconds from climax, Jordan pulled away.

She was so into the moment, it took several seconds to realize Jordan no longer suckled her breast and was, in fact, holding her away from him. His erection, hard and throbbing, still pressed against her. But the look on his face, the dark, sexy, "I want to slide inside you and stay there forever" expression, had disappeared.

"Jordan?" she whispered in confusion and a want so bad that she literally ached.

"We can't do this. . . . *I* can't do this."

"But . . . but . . . why . . . ?" Oh God, she was sputtering like a schoolgirl. Eden froze. *Schoolgirl.* No. God, no. She couldn't . . . wouldn't go back to that feeling.

With a small, soft sob, she shoved him hard. He was three times stronger and twice as big, but he moved abruptly, allowing her to swim away from him. She swam deep, shutting out all thought but the terrifying certainty that if she didn't get away from him, she would scream.

When she finally surfaced, he was gone. With careful, calm movements, she replaced the minuscule cloth that covered her breasts, ignoring the slight sting as the fabric abraded her sensitive nipple.

Knowing she was being observed . . . Hell, they'd seen a peep show of her almost naked, a near sexual intercourse, and what probably looked to them like a little tiff between lovers. She refused to give them anything else. Her main purpose and goal was to get to her room and hide until she regained her composure. And if Jordan was in the room? She'd throw him out the window.

thirteen

Jordan didn't stop until he reached the other side of the estate. Since he was supposed to look a bit out of shape and much older, he'd had to refrain from running full speed. With every footfall, he cursed himself. How unprofessional could he be? He'd almost taken her in the pool, in front of an audience.

What the bloody hell had he been thinking? Nothing. That's what. At least nothing to do with his brain. The minute he saw her lying on that raft in the pool, that luscious bare body glistening under the sun, he'd lost all sense of time, his reasons for being there, and that at least four pairs of eyes bored into his back. His only thought was to get to her and touch her. He'd told himself he could remain in his role and still touch her. It would be expected of him and damned if he didn't want to suddenly play the role of a man who had every right to caress and kiss every inch of that sexy, beautiful body.

She'd been on the verge of climax. He'd felt her sex throbbing against his. When she'd given him her breast, he'd lost it, had come within a second of pulling that scrap of material out of the way and plunging into her, riding her until they both shouted with release. Witnesses be damned.

But he'd come to his senses in the nick of time and hurt her in the process. What excuse could he give? That they had an audience? They had, but that wasn't why he'd stopped. He wasn't a totally free man. He had a woman waiting on his return . . . counting on him to be faithful.

Since he'd been with Samara, he hadn't slept with another woman . . . hadn't even really wanted one, though he'd had many opportunities. Why was this different? Why was Eden different? Yes, she was a beautiful woman, but so was Samara.

It wasn't Eden's beauty, or her sexuality, which she wore as comfortably as a second skin, that made him want her. It was . . . hell, what did it matter the reason? He couldn't let what just happened ever happen again. When this project ended, he would return home. That was the way he wanted it. Though he longed to find Devon, he also longed to settle down with a nice, normal woman and have a simple, quiet life.

Damned if Eden was either nice or normal. Life with her would be an endless adventure. He'd had enough adventure to last several lifetimes.

Jordan turned to go back, his mind once again on the mission and his role. He ignored the ache in his groin and the even more painful one in his gut.

Eden held her head under the shower, her face down. It was the only place she could hide. They had no proof of cameras in the bathroom. Having decided early that to check for any kind of bug or camera would give them away, they lived as Maggie and Barry. Until today.

How had they allowed it to get so out of control? And where did *we* come from? She was the one who instigated that little drama. She'd kissed him, uncovered her breasts, taken his hand and put it on her chest. He just responded the way any normal man would . . . only he had stopped it. He'd been the one with control. If it had been up to Eden, they would have made love in the pool, within sight of who knows how many people.

How could she be so reckless? So abandoned? In the years since the attack, her training, her entire life had been built around control. It had been the only way she survived. Had it disappeared?

As Eden twisted the handle to turn the shower off, the answer resounded in her head. No, it hadn't disappeared. Her control was still in perfect working order . . . except with Jordan.

She toweled off, still keeping her head down, afraid what her expression might reveal as she contemplated what Jordan did to her. How could he have so much power over her . . . after all this time?

Wrapping her wet hair in a towel, she pulled on a short terry robe and headed back to the bedroom. She stopped at the door, startled to see him standing in the middle of the room. An expression she'd never seen before flickered in his eyes. Regret?

"You okay?" His voice sounded gruff, rougher than usual.

Eden flashed a girlish Maggie smile. "Of course, I'm fine. Why wouldn't I be?"

Relief and admiration flashed in his expression as he made his way over to where she stood.

Eden held her ground, determined to react the way an adoring, young wife would.

Jordan pressed a soft kiss to her forehead and then her cheek. His voice, barely audible, sounded in her ear. "Sorry about that. It won't happen again."

She ground her teeth to keep from retorting that she'd make sure it didn't, while another part of her wanted to scream at him, "Why not?" Pulling away slowly, Eden beamed up at him like the simpleton she was supposed to be. So what if her lips wobbled a little and her breath held tiny gasps; the camera couldn't pick them up.

Jordan's eyes narrowed slightly as if he realized how

hard she was working at her control. He turned from her and headed toward the door, allowing her to regain the composure she'd once again come close to losing.

"I'm going to go talk with Peter to see how much longer our wait will be. I'll be back in a minute."

"Barry . . . do you think that's a good idea . . . rushing him . . . I mean?"

"Don't you worry your pretty little head, sweetheart. Peter's a businessman." With those vague words, Jordan walked out the door.

The tone had been Maggie's, but the words were Eden's. The last thing they wanted to do was rush this and make a mistake. She'd already made enough. If Peter Lawson took Jordan's words the wrong way, he might call off the exchange. They couldn't afford to let that happen. Being taken to the facility where the children were held hinged upon them being able to go as a couple and choose a child from their lineup.

If Lawson called it off, LCR would have to start all over again with another couple. That would take time—time those children didn't have.

Knowing she couldn't do anything to hurry it along— Jordan being the one Lawson would listen to—Eden turned back to the bathroom to finish getting ready.

Jordan was a professional. He knew how to deal with scum such as Lawson. There was no need for her to worry.

Jordan pressed his thumb against the other man's windpipe. Lawson's bright purple shade was the only thing that forced him to ease the stranglehold.

Lawson wheezed and squeaked, "You'll pay for that, Johnson. Nobody treats a—"

Jordan cut off his air again. He spoke in a slow, deliberate way so Lawson could understand him beneath the rushing roar in the choking man's ears. "I'm telling you for the last time. We came here for a child and by God, not you or anyone else is going to try to extort money from me. Do I make myself clear?"

Lawson's eyes were bugging out of his head, but he managed to give a jerky nod of understanding.

Jordan eased his grip again. "Now, when will we be going to choose our son?"

"I . . . I'll try to set it up for tomorrow, but I told you about the—" He closed his mouth as Jordan pressed again and then let up. His head jerking in a nervous nod, Lawson added, "I'll set it up for tomorrow."

Releasing Lawson, he gave him a glare that might have some men questioning his sanity and stalked out of the room. He wanted—needed—to be by himself for a while, but he wouldn't leave Eden alone with these bastards. Besides, she had a right and a need to hear what had happened.

Just as he started up the stairs, Eden was descending.

"Everything okay, Barry? You look—"

He held out his hand and Eden took it. Pulling her along with him, he stalked out the front door and across the exquisitely manicured lawn. Not until they were standing in the middle of a large grassy area did he stop.

Eden tugged on his hand and whirled around to stare at him. "What's happened?"

Jordan ran his hand through his hair and turned away from her. The rigidity of his shoulders and the grim set of his mouth told her something catastrophic had occurred.

"Dammit, Jordan . . . tell me."

"I approached Lawson about hurrying up the process. He hemmed and hawed for several minutes, then when he saw I was getting pissed, he admitted there had been what he called 'a slight glitch.' "

"What kind of a glitch?"

When Jordan turned back to her, she was astounded to see sorrow in his expression.

"Talk to me, Jordan. What?"

"There was an unfortunate incident while they were trying to nab a baby. . . . The mother was stabbed . . . killed."

Eden closed her eyes. Dear God, what kind of world did they live in? Her eyes popped open as horror hit. "It's our fault."

Jordan shook his head. "It was a baby girl. Though it could have been just as easily the boy we are supposed to buy." His voice hardened. "Lawson now understands, in no uncertain terms, that we want to get this over with."

"Uh-oh, what'd you do?"

"The fool had the audacity to ask for more money—called it the cost of doing business. Since there was a death, he feels the chances they're taking are worth more than the three hundred thousand we're paying."

"Bastard."

"I told him we wanted to go tomorrow. Can Noah get his teams ready that soon?"

"I think so. He's been waiting for us to give the go-ahead. Everyone else is pretty much in place." She pulled the tiny transmitter off her wrist, then the small stick from around her neck . . . an odd-looking piece of jewelry, but very useful when entering the information into the transmitter. Both items had gotten past the monitors and screening in the airport as well as the mansion.

Eden entered the information, trying to ignore the heat of the man standing beside her. They were getting ready to execute their mission; she couldn't allow herself the distraction he created. She refused to acknowledge the voice inside her telling her that once this was over, he'd leave. Now was not the time.

Within seconds, the tiny display screen revealed Noah's message. She shot a glance at Jordan. "Ten in the morning doable, do you think?"

Determination gleamed in his eyes. "We'll damn well make it doable."

The squawk of a bird flying overhead caught her attention, making her abruptly aware they'd been talking freely, out in the open. Eden couldn't believe she'd forgotten. Finding out what was wrong with Jordan had been her primary concern. Now she couldn't help but wonder if their carelessness would cost them.

Guessing her concern, Jordan touched her arm in reassurance. "Don't worry about it. We're out in the middle of nothing." He gestured around him. "See, not even a palm tree to hang a camera from."

Eden flashed him a grateful smile, glad he'd been on the lookout, because she certainly hadn't. For the first time in her years with LCR, Eden began to question her abilities and focus. Admittedly, working with the man she'd once thought herself in love with might be one of the reasons, but was it the only one?

"Hey, you okay?"

"Yeah, just thinking about tomorrow."

"Since we're out here, relatively alone, I want to apologize again for what happened in the pool. I was totally out of line."

Eden couldn't believe he was taking the blame for something that was most definitely her fault. "Jordan, I'm the one who instigated it."

"But I'm the one who—"

An unusual gurgle of laughter burst from her. "Let's just agree we were both less than discreet and leave it at that, shall we?"

He held out his hand and Eden placed hers in his, thinking he'd shake it and let her go. Instead he brought it to his mouth and pressed a kiss to the back of her hand. "You're a hell of a woman, Eden St. Claire."

Resisting the urge to pull her hand away and the even greater urge to fling herself into his arms, Eden stayed put and forced a jaunty smile. "So I've been told."

When her hand returned to her side, she breathed a

little sigh and looked around again. "Are there any details we need to go over before tomorrow? Anything we need to change from our original plan?"

"No, we'll implement as planned. As soon as we're in, we separate. I'll take care of whoever is with us, while you make sure the rest of the team gets in."

Eden nodded. Come what may, tomorrow at this time, Alfred Larue's business of abducting children and selling them off like cattle would be destroyed.

Jordan checked his watch. "I'll go back to Lawson. Make sure he understands the transaction will be made tomorrow morning."

Eden watched him walk away. His body language switched with ease to the older, less fit Barry Johnson. What would tomorrow bring? And how long would it be before Jordan left her life forever?

As they pulled up in their limo, Lawson, his voice unusually gruff, said, "Take the blindfolds off. We're here."

Eden smiled appreciatively as Jordan pulled the cloth from her eyes. Her demeanor of barely contained excitement wasn't an act. The time had come to rescue these children and put some very bad people where they couldn't hurt innocent people ever again.

They entered the large facility that from the outside looked like one of many vanilla-colored buildings lining the street. Eden was used to the façade of a building looking like one thing and being something different on the inside. However, a baby-selling building . . . She never would have been able to come up with what one would look like.

Jordan held her hand, both of them looking anxiously around as if they were excited parents eager to meet their child for the first time. Peter Lawson followed behind them. Eden politely ignored the bruises surrounding the man's neck, though more than anything, she would love to laugh at him and then knock the hell out of him. She reminded herself that either she or Jordan would get to do both, but all in good time.

Lawson led them into a small office, nothing attractive or even particularly clean-looking. Her stomach leaped and then took a queasy turn. This was the place of purchase, the place where human life was sold like . . . now she knew what this place reminded her of . . . a pet store. On the way to the office, she'd spotted a glass enclosure, similar to what a pet store would have so people could hold a puppy or kitten and play with it before deciding on the purchase. God, these people had to be stopped.

The cheap chair Lawson plopped into squeaked under his weight. A beat-up metal desk held a shiny, expensive computer. Lawson turned to the monitor, his fingers clicking quickly over the keyboard. His eyes on the screen in front of him, he growled, "You wired the money?" The oily, boyish charm Lawson met them with had disappeared. He was now a cold-minded businessman, making sure he was being paid for the service he was about to provide.

"Yes, all of it should be in the account, based upon the account number and name you gave me."

Lawson stared at the screen for several seconds and then turned to them with a superficial smile. "Let's go meet your son."

Eden and Jordan exchanged smiles and rose. Lawson strode to the door. Before he could put his hand on the doorknob, Jordan was there to stop him. Lawson turned with a frown. His eyes widened in comprehension just as Jordan's hand came down on the side of his head. Jordan caught him before he reached the floor.

"Open that door over there . . . looks like some kind of closet. We'll keep him there till we're through."

Eden opened the door and watched while Jordan, using a phone cord, trussed him up like a Thanksgiving turkey

and covered his mouth with duct tape he found in the
desk. He then dragged Lawson's body, dumping him on
the floor of the tiny closet. With a great sense of satisfaction, she closed the door.

Jordan handed her another roll of tape and winked.
"Let's go kick some ass."

Flashing him a delighted grin, she ran from the room to
the front door and waved her arm. Six LCR operatives
who had followed them from the mansion marched up the
steps. Eyes glinting with anticipation, they wore bullet-
proof vests and carried just enough weapons to do the job.
No way in hell were any kids getting hurt on her watch.

Baker, one of her favorite men to work with, handed
her a gun. "You ready to play?" His rich Georgia drawl
was laced with amusement.

"You bet." Eden took the gun and whirled around. "I'll
take the upstairs." She glanced over at a tall, imposing
man sporting a ponytail, earrings, and multiple tattoos.
"Sam, find Jordan and give him some firepower. We've
got one bastard locked up in a closet. Everybody else is
still at large."

Eden ran toward the stairs, Baker on her heels. Noah's
people were the most highly trained in the world. They
knew what to do.

At the top of the stairs, she turned right while Baker
went left. Hearing voices, she made her way down the
long landing, the worn carpet muffling her steps. Eden
checked each door she passed. They were unlocked, and
other than empty, unmade beds, they were vacant.

She stopped at the third door on her right and opened it
a tiny crack. Amazement widened her eyes. The room
looked just like a small hospital nursery, filled with cribs,
baby beds, and, dear Lord, even an incubator. Three
women stood in the middle of the room chatting. Two
were frumpy and middle-aged, the other one looked to be
in her late teens.

Easing the door open, Eden looked left and right to make sure they were the only adults in the room. Satisfied, she kept her voice low so she wouldn't wake any children. "Okay, ladies. Hands up, nice and easy."

All three whirled around. One covered her mouth with a gasp, another squealed, while another reached into her pocket. Eden pointed her gun at her. "I said hands up . . . not in your pocket." Making the wise decision, the woman raised her hands along with her companions. "Good girl. Now, why don't you all have a seat?" Eden pointed toward three rocking chairs close to the wall. She waved her gun at them. "Ladies."

The woman who'd gone for her pocket snarled, "You're making a mistake. We don't have any money."

Eden pulled the duct tape from her pocket and motioned to the young girl, who seemed the most frightened. "Come here."

With tentative steps, the terrified teen moved forward. Handing her the tape, Eden ordered, "Wrap this around their wrists and ankles."

The girl turned and Eden instructed her as she wrapped the strong, gray tape around their wrists and ankles and then the legs of the chairs.

"Good job. Now, sit down." Eden then proceeded to do the same to her. After they were secure, she pressed tape over their mouths.

After everyone was wrapped up tight, Eden went through the pockets of each. While they grunted and moaned as if they were being molested, she ignored them. Her discoveries were mostly harmless. A pack of cigarettes, some nasty-looking tissue, a piece of gum. The one who had put her hand in her pocket had the most interesting item: a tiny derringer.

Holding the small firearm up, she glared at the woman. "Don't you know better than to have a gun around children?"

Eyes flashing fire, the woman grunted what Eden figured was an obscenity. "You shouldn't swear around them, either. Did they not teach you that in baby kidnapping school?"

Eden double-checked to make sure the tape was secure on all three women and then turned to the cribs. *Babies.* Dear God, some of them were only a few weeks old. A couple of them looked to be almost one. They were still, thankfully, all sleeping. She hoped they continued to sleep for a little while longer. She didn't need six infants screaming, attracting attention.

Eden turned to the outraged women, whispered, "Don't go anywhere," and scurried out the door.

Jordan jogged through the house, searching for Eden. There'd been three people on the first floor to neutralize. He and Noah's people had handled them with almost no resistance. No bullets or blood . . . a nice change of pace.

Two frightened toddlers were found on the first floor, locked in a large bedroom. He hoped Eden had found more and that she was okay.

Though he knew she could take care of herself better than any woman or man he'd ever met, it didn't stop him from worrying. Over the last couple of weeks, he'd come to admire her. She wasn't an easy person to know, since she held a lot of herself back, but he'd seen her commitment to her cause, her heart and courage.

A slight muffled sound caught his attention. Gun in hand, Jordan broke into a run down the long hallway. Hearing a curse, then a groan, Jordan skidded to a halt at the entrance to a room. His mouth lifted in a slow smile of admiration.

Eden stood over two men. The short yellow sundress she wore, along with her dainty sandals, made her look like a sexy, innocent angel. The steady way she held the gun pointed at the men on the floor told a different story. One man lay facedown on the floor, the second lay crisscrossed over the first one's back. Hands over their heads, they were cursing a blue streak.

"Need some help?"

Eden's head jerked up and the triumphant grin she flashed went straight to his gut. The woman was in her element. Without a hint of warning, his heart—the one he was sure couldn't be moved—flipped over.

fourteen

"Well, look what the dogs dragged in." Years and thousands of miles from his Mississippi roots, Noah could still sound like a good old southern boy when the mood struck him.

Eden came through the door, followed by Jordan. Since they'd returned two days ago, they'd gone everywhere together. She was thrilled he seemed to want to be with her as much as she wanted to be with him, but she was also terrified. At some point, possibly very soon, Jordan would turn to her, give her that sexy grin that seemed to come so easy to him, and say, "Well, it's been fun," and leave. And once again she'd be alone.

The door slammed shut on her poor-pitiful-me thoughts. They'd done good work—damn good work. They all should be happy with their efforts. She and Jordan, along with six of Noah's finest, had brought down eleven very bad people, but most important, they'd saved eight children.

The authorities had been called, having been warned by Noah what was going down, and had agreed to stand back and wait. At no cost or risk to themselves, the police brought in a horde of human traffickers and took full credit for the entire job.

That was LCR's preferred way. Yes, some laws were bent or broken. Those transgressions were generally overlooked. In a case like this, where everyone but the bad guys won, it was a no-brainer.

Now she and Jordan were here to debrief, but not before Eden found out about the other houses that had been raided the same time their operation was going down.

Swift steps carried her to her favorite chair. She perched on the edge and waited. Both men knew she was anxious. Jordan had heard nothing from her for the last two days other than her need to know that all operations went as smoothly as theirs.

To torture her, she was sure, Noah went to the bar, offering them coffee. Jordan, with a small smile on his face, accepted. Eden flashed him a glare, but he just grinned and waited as Noah poured a cup for himself and Jordan.

Noah turned toward Eden, all innocence. "Sure you don't want any? You know what a mean cup of coffee I make."

"Stop torturing me, Noah, and tell me what happened. I've seen bits and pieces on the news, but nothing about Larue or Bennett. Don't tell me they got away."

He handed Jordan a cup of coffee and then slumped down in his chair with a long sigh. Eden saw something she'd never seen before. Noah looked not only exhausted but defeated as well.

"What happened?"

"Four of the projects went off without a hitch. All totaled, eighty-five people were rounded up and taken to the hoosegow."

Eden glanced over to Jordan. "He means jail."

Jordan's mouth quirked up. "I know what a hoosegow is, sweetheart."

Ignoring the gallop of her heart at his endearment, and Noah's slight frown, she returned to the subject. "So how many people were rescued?"

"Sixty-eight . . . mostly women and children."

Eden surged to her feet. "But that's wonderful, Noah, why do you . . . ?" She slumped back into her chair. "You said four went off without a hitch. What happened with the other one?"

Noah spoke in a hard, grim tone. "We had a traitor."

"LCR had a traitor? But who?"

"Stephan. You never met him. He'd only been on a few months . . . was still on probation. That's why I put him with our most experienced man." He leaned forward and Eden knew that whatever he had to tell her didn't come easy. "Milo was killed."

Her heart clenched. "Milo?"

A mixture of burning rage and grief blazed in Noah's eyes before he quickly doused it. "Yes. By one of Bennett's men."

Without realizing Jordan had risen, she felt his comforting hand on her shoulder. His voice rumbled above her. "So this Milo. He was one of your best?"

Eden shook her head, answering before Noah could. "He was *the* best. He's been with Noah since the beginning of LCR . . . helped him put it together."

"Both Bennett and Larue have disappeared off our radar, thanks to Stephan and my own poor judgment. Now Milo's dead, so stopping them is even more important. It's personal . . . very personal." His eyes seared her. "You realize that, don't you, Eden?"

Eden stiffened at his tone. He was trying to tell her something and she wasn't sure what he meant. But evidently it involved something he thought might upset her. She'd already argued with him and lost regarding his decision to be the one to go after Bennett. What else was he saying?

"So Stephan ratted us out?" Treading softly wasn't her usual style, but Eden wanted to make sure she understood where Noah was going. Besides, the man just lost a dear friend. He didn't need her jumping down his throat. She made a silent promise to hold her temper, no matter what Noah had planned.

"Yes, from what we got out of him before he clammed

up, he contacted them within hours of getting his assignment. Fortunately, since he was new, he was on a need-to-know basis only. Therefore, the Brazil op was the only one he knew about."

Jordan blew out a silent whistle. "That's why all the other ones went so smoothly. Larue and Bennett were only aware of that particular one."

Noah nodded and let a small, grim smile lighten his features for a moment. "The one smart thing I did."

"Don't beat yourself up. You saved a hell of a lot of people."

Eden flashed an appreciative glance at Jordan for his gruff but encouraging words. "Jordan's right, Noah. You did good. . . . We all did good. Milo didn't see Stephan's deceit and he worked with him."

"Nevertheless, it's going to be tougher to get to the bastards than what I'd planned. The team I assigned to Larue believes they're still in France. I think Bennett's holed up somewhere in Brazil. I've got to get down there, which means I need a project manager while I'm away."

Eden was already shaking her head, knowing where Noah was headed. They'd had this discussion on numerous occasions. She was comfortable in the field. It was where she worked the best. The assignment of projects needed to be done by a person with better people skills than she. Eden knew her strengths. Diplomacy and patience were not even in the top twenty.

"Noah, we've had this conversation before. You know I—"

Noah held up his hand to stop her. "I know . . . I know. That's why I'm going to make an alternate suggestion. That is, if Jordan would be willing to stay on in Paris and help out?"

Eden's head began to shake again, for a whole other reason. What was Noah thinking?

"Jordan, Eden's one of my finest and most experienced

operatives, but she's at her best in the field. I know you've done fieldwork most of your career, but if I'm not mistaken, you've also been a project manager. Is that correct?"

Eden dared a look at Jordan's face. She wished she could read him better. His expressionless face told her nothing. Part of her wanted him to jump up and tell Noah no, absolutely not. Another part—the unwise, wholly feminine side of her—jumped for joy, hoping he'd agree to stay.

Finally, after staring hard at Noah for endless seconds, Jordan said, "I know very little about the day-to-day activities of LCR. Don't you have anyone else who could do this?"

"Only a few, and those people are already on other projects I don't dare pull them from. With your experience and background, it would be a natural fit for you. It'll only be for a few weeks . . . a month at the most." Noah turned to Eden. "Eden knows the workings of LCR as well as I do. She just doesn't have the . . . how shall I put this . . . ?"

"She doesn't put up with a bunch of bullshit," Eden cut in, finishing Noah's stumbling explanation.

Noah smiled. "That's one way of putting it. I sometimes have to use finesse and diplomacy to get what I want. Eden prefers the more direct method, which tends to create some animosity between our partners."

"Your partners being?" Jordan asked.

"The police, the mayor, local government, the president." Eden once again finished Noah's sentence.

Jordan's mouth twitched as if he were hiding a huge grin. "So basically anyone who might get in your way."

She shrugged. "Again, I'm not big on bullshit." She grinned at Noah. "Noah, however, is a master."

"Why thank you, my dear. The perfumery of your words never fails to astound me."

Eden shot her eyes over to Jordan. His expression held the faraway look of deep thought. He was seriously considering Noah's request. In the few weeks she'd spent with Jordan, she knew without a doubt he enjoyed working with LCR. Why he'd decided to stop working for the American government she didn't know. They didn't talk personal things. She couldn't, because of obvious reasons. But neither did he and suddenly she wondered why. She had secrets. What were Jordan's?

"I'll have to make a few calls, check on a few things, before I can accept."

Noah nodded. "Understandable. If you could let me know by tomorrow, though, it'd be helpful. If you can't do the job, I'll need to call someone. Milo would have been my first choice, but . . ."

Eden swallowed a lump. Milo had been a dear, sweet man. He'd taken her side on so many things against Noah. When she'd first come to LCR, Noah pushed her to the point of collapse several times. Milo had been her shoulder to lean on. She could pour out all of her frustrations about Noah to Milo and he'd let her.

It wasn't until years later she realized Noah had planned it that way. Eden needed a support system. He couldn't be it since he was her trainer, so he'd asked Milo to fill that role. Milo had been perfect for the job. A former minister, his steady, no-nonsense advice and compassion had made him a favorite of all operatives. His death was a tremendous loss not only for LCR, but for the world.

Jordan stood. "I'll let you know something tomorrow morning."

Noah stood and shook Jordan's hand. "Whatever you decide, I just want you to know how grateful LCR is for your excellent work."

Jordan nodded and then looked over at Eden. "I'll call you later."

As he disappeared out the door, Eden had to dig her fingers into the arms of her chair to prevent herself from following him. She didn't want to lose sight of him. What if he decided not to take Noah's offer? Would this be the last time she saw him? What if he called and told her he was leaving? What if he didn't even call? What if he just left? What if—

"Eden, you okay?"

She shook herself out of her unwelcome and unexpected needy moment. Where the hell had that come from? She was a strong, independent woman . . . needing no man. Jordan least of all.

"I'm fine."

"And you're okay with continuing to work with Jordan, if he decides to stay?"

She gave a small smile and shrugged. "More than I would have expected. Though if you'd asked me that several weeks ago, I'd have punched you out again."

"Tsk-tsk. You're definitely one of the most bloodthirsty ladies I've ever had the pleasure of knowing."

"Noah, you will be careful, won't you? I know Milo's death was harder on you than anyone, but you're not going to go all crazy, are you?"

He shook his head. "Not a crazy bone in this good old boy's body."

"Can't you tell me why you targeted Bennett for yourself? Do you know the man in some way?"

Noah lifted a shoulder in a lazy, slow-motion shrug. "Just need to stay sharp . . . clean out my cobwebs."

Evading the question—something he did if he didn't want to answer. Noah was scrupulously honest. Eden thought he must have been a Boy Scout in another life. But if he didn't want to answer a question, he had ways around it.

"How was it working with Jordan?"

He was also excellent at changing the subject. Eden allowed him to since no matter what kind of coercion she used, Noah would never tell her something he didn't want her to know. She only hoped he kept his head straight if there was an underlying reason he was taking on the project.

"Better than I thought it would be. He's definitely a professional. Has the charm, intelligence, and the experience to be one of LCR's best. As much as I hate to give you a compliment, since I know your ego is quite inflated already, you were right about Jordan."

A gleam of something like pride sparkled in his eyes. "I'm glad you feel that way. I didn't like going behind your back, but I knew if I told you what I was going to do, you would have pitched a fit."

"I don't pitch fits . . . I . . ."

"You what?"

"I just express my feelings somewhat loudly."

He rubbed his jaw where she'd hit him several weeks before. "Or sometimes physically."

She shrugged, not one bit repentant. "You deserved it."

Noah nodded, knowing full well she was right. "Have you decided what you're going to do?"

He didn't need to explain what he was talking about. She'd thought of little else the last couple of days. Would she tell him Devon died or tell him the truth?

"Not yet."

"I'm not pushing you. In fact, it would probably be best if you waited. If he takes my place for a while, the last thing he needs is you telling him . . . whatever you decide to tell him."

With no small amount of remorse, Eden realized Noah's words gave her time. An excuse to delay the inevitable. She hated continuing to lie to him, but more than that, she hated to ruin what was fast becoming an exciting and unique friendship. Would putting it off a little longer make that much difference?

"You know, whatever you decide to do, I'll support it."

A rush of affection for the man who'd given her so much swept through her. There was no telling where she'd be if it weren't for Noah. Eden stood and, surprising both of them, gave him an unexpected hug. The number of times she'd shown physical affection in the last seven years could be counted on less than one hand.

Thankfully Noah didn't question the unusual gesture. He returned the hug and then led her to the door. "I'll be in touch as soon as Jordan notifies me of his decision."

With a nod and wave, Eden left. Not until she was on the street, hailing a cab, did she wonder who it was that Jordan needed to check with.

Jordan stared at the phone for several minutes before he made the call . . . contemplating what he would say . . . how he would say it.

Samara had been a big part of his life for almost a year. He admired and liked her immensely. Had thought they could be happy together. He didn't like or admire many people. That she was beautiful and kind didn't hurt, either. Spending his life with her seemed to make such sense. What more could a man want?

But that was before he met Eden.

Not that he was thinking of anything permanent with Eden. He still wasn't sure he even liked her. But he admired her and she turned him on faster than any woman he'd ever met. If he hadn't come to his senses a few days ago, they would have made love in the pool. Thankfully he realized the mistake, but it made him face some things he'd avoided for too long.

Liking and admiring the woman you were to marry was important. But if someone else attracted you like none other, how fair was that to your future spouse? He could say it was just lust and would pass, but Jordan knew himself. Lust didn't stir him like this—hell, lust hadn't stirred him since that debacle with Devon. He'd learned a long, hard lesson from that and vowed never again.

Odd that when he'd first seen Eden's shoulder he'd

thought she was Devon. Now it was hard to think of them as being even the same species. They were such polar opposites.

Eden stirred something inside him he'd never felt. Whatever it was, he wanted to pursue it. If it turned out to be nothing more than mere attraction, a possible short affair, so be it. But he would never know until he tried. Which meant he had to end his relationship with Samara. She deserved to know the truth, she deserved his faithfulness, and Jordan knew he could no longer keep that promise.

He would break it off with Samara and then he would be free to pursue Eden. An added bonus to working in Noah's place at LCR was finding out about Devon. When he questioned Eden about it yesterday, she apologized, admitting she hadn't had time to work on the case as much as she would have liked. She promised to focus on Devon now that she was back.

Until another project came along, perhaps they could work the case together. His insight into Devon's thoughts at that time would be important information for Eden to have.

fifteen

Three days later, Eden entered Noah's office. Her footsteps faltered at the door. Even knowing Noah had left the night before for South America, it was still a shock to see Jordan sitting in his chair. She hadn't seen him since that day in Noah's office. He'd called her several times, but for some reason, he seemed to need some distance.

At first she'd been concerned. Now that he was essentially in charge, did he intend not to see her other than for business purposes? She told herself that's what she should want, but for the life of her she couldn't mean it. Getting to know Jordan—really getting to know him—was heaven and hell.

At some point she was either going to have to come clean about her real identity or finally have the courage to pull the fake file she'd prepared. Either one would destroy something inside her. But something else had become apparent: No matter how much it hurt her, she wanted to hurt Jordan even less.

Noah had given her a small reprieve, but Eden still wasn't sure she'd use it.

"You just going to stand in the door and stare? Do I look that strange in this chair?"

Eden mentally rolled her eyes. She was rarely an introspective person, but with Jordan it seemed she was constantly thinking inside herself, measuring every step and every word. She gave herself a short and sweet lecture as she glided inside and sat across from him. *Get your head out of your ass, Eden!*

Jordan's eyes darkened as he watched her legs cross, and hot zings of sexual awareness shot through her. She forced herself to concentrate on business. "How does the chair feel? Like you were born to it?"

"Hell no. Noah's slouch has ruined this chair. I'll probably have a bad back by the time he returns."

"Have you heard from him?"

"No . . . don't really expect to, unless he needs some backup. This is his deal, his baby. He may call you, though. He mentioned you had a way with deep cover. He thought he might need some help later on."

Eden nodded, not wanting to go into detail about just how good she was at deep cover. Another day, another time.

"So, anything on our agenda or the radar I need to know about?"

Jordan turned to look at Noah's computer monitors. He was logged into links all over the world, showing missing persons and suspected kidnap victims.

"Nothing we've been called in on." He looked up at Eden in wonder. "How hard is it for Noah to not go after every one of these people, especially the kids?"

"I think he still struggles with it from time to time, but he learned his lesson. Usually within minutes of the abduction, the local police and other officials get involved. Noah tried numerous times to offer a helping hand, but it wasn't appreciated.

"Now he mostly just waits until LCR is contacted and that's usually after all other avenues are exhausted. We're known worldwide, but we don't necessarily get appreciated by certain agencies." She shrugged delicately. "Our actions aren't always legal or ethical, but they're effective."

"And I'm assuming by the time LCR is contacted, most

people have given up on all other avenues and don't give a damn about legalities."

"Exactly. Or sometimes, the person abducted isn't known to the police."

"You mean it's not reported?"

"Yes, as was the case with Christina Clement. Her family is heavily involved in a variety of illegal businesses. When their daughter was kidnapped, they knew it was the Larues, who are one of their main rivals. They assumed the case would either not get the same attention as other kidnap victims, or they would have to give up something. They came to LCR, and we were able to help them."

"That doesn't bother you . . . knowing you're helping the scum of the earth?"

"The children we rescue are innocent. What their parents do or don't do is up to them and their maker. And it's a lucrative practice for us. They pay highly to get their children returned to them."

"Drug money."

"Drug money that would be spent on many other things if they kept it to themselves. Because of such money, we've never had to turn anyone away because they couldn't afford our services. We've helped innumerable people with that money, no matter where it comes from." Her brow furrowed. "Did Noah not explain all of this to you?"

He grinned like a precocious kid caught stealing a cookie. "Yeah, I just wanted to get your take on it."

"So do you think the end doesn't justify the means?"

Jordan gave an emphatic shake of his head. "When I worked for the government, I dealt with some of the lowest people in the universe, often catered to them. I've paid millions of dollars to the sickos, using money that I have no idea where it came from. It didn't matter to me. I saved lives and prevented a lot of damage. You don't have to like or admire someone to do business with them. If it serves the purpose—a good purpose—I'm all for it."

"That's good, because chances are, before Noah returns, you'll get another opportunity to work with these people."

"Does it bother you to work with such scum?"

"As you said, for the greater good. I'll admit I do much better if I'm undercover. If I can be a completely different person, then it's much easier for me to forget and just do what needs to be done."

"You were undercover when I first met you. With one of the Larues. Tell me about that case."

As afternoon flowed into early evening, Eden found herself describing how she grew her cover as Claire Marchand. She explained the despicable things Georges's brother, Marc, was responsible for and how, as much as she wanted, she couldn't get to Marc because she wasn't a teenager.

"So you went after his brother instead."

"Yes, Georges wasn't the perverted sick bastard Marc was, though to say he was a good person would be incorrect. From what I can tell, the Larues have little goodness in them. Georges's intense love of beautiful women was a weakness we discovered and could exploit. My cover was of a young woman, married to a much older and wealthy man who was an invalid. I arranged to meet Georges at a party. He took me out for a drink and from there we established a friendship."

"How long did you have to do this before you were able to act?"

"Almost a month. I knew I had to be careful. Alfred, Georges's father, had everyone his family got involved with investigated. My cover was tight, but Georges wasn't as easy as I thought he would be. He enjoys the wordplay and seduction almost as much as the sex act. I couldn't push him."

"Did you have to have sex with him?"

Eden raised her brow at the growling tone of his voice. Was he jealous? Surely not.

"No, thankfully it never came to that. That was the biggest reason I posed as a married woman. Georges has few ethics, but one of them was his aversion to sleeping with married women. Even so, near the end, his one decent belief weakened considerably under some stronger desires."

"Getting you in bed?"

"Yes."

"Would you have done it?"

They were getting into a realm that wasn't exactly business-related. She and Noah had an agreement: She did what she deemed necessary. If she wanted to talk about it afterward, he was available. If not, then no questions were asked.

Not only was Jordan's question inappropriate, he had a look in his eyes that told her if she said yes, it would upset him. Yet she wasn't going to lie to him about this. If her answer bothered him, it was something he needed to deal with. It wasn't her problem.

A small amount of prudence might be wise, though. "I had a few tricks in my makeup case." She saw no reason to explain just how far she'd had to go to subdue Georges.

Those too-intelligent eyes told her he couldn't be taken in and sidetracked. "And if those hadn't worked, would you have slept with him?"

Eden took a breath and answered proudly, "To save a child from rape, or worse? Yes, I would have slept with him."

Other than his jaw working slightly, Jordan revealed no sign that her answer bothered him. "I'm assuming by that answer, it's something you've done before?"

Eden blew out an exasperated sigh. She'd been exceedingly nice to answer the questions he'd asked so far . . . something she wouldn't have done with any other man. But she was coming to the end of her slight patience.

"I work for an organization whose main purpose—often

its only purpose—is to rescue victims. As an operative, this means I come second. If I have to screw the entire French army to save a child, it's worth it. Does that answer your question?"

Jordan knew he was being unfair and Eden had every right to her indignant anger. She had her priorities straight and he was beginning to realize that where she was concerned, his were seriously skewed.

He bit the inside of his jaw to keep from saying something he didn't mean. No way in hell could he sound sincere and tell her he totally agreed with her. If they were talking in generalities about someone else, perhaps he could. But this was Eden, saying she had slept and would sleep with a man or men to accomplish her goal. Hell, he'd had sex a couple of times to attain something he needed. Why was this different?

Because this is Eden and she is different.

"Jordan?"

She looked at him questioningly, and if he wasn't mistaken—though she was almost impossible to read—he saw hurt in her eyes. He was the last person to be passing judgment on anyone.

"I'm sorry, Eden. I had no right to ask that question."

A small, tight smile was her answer. His words had done nothing other than make her more uncomfortable. They needed to move on to something she'd be more comfortable with.

"Since there's not anything urgent pending, I'm assuming you'll be working on Devon's case?"

Though her face remained impassive, her hands, which rested on the arm of her chair, clenched slightly. Was she angry with him? He'd have to figure out a way to assure her he hadn't intended to hurt her and in no way judged her. If he continued talking about it, though, he would probably only make it worse.

"Since I was the last person to see Devon before she

disappeared, I thought you might have some questions for me. We never really got to talk about her in as much depth as I would have liked."

"Didn't you give Noah all the information you had?"

"Yes, but I'm not sure he would have been able to explain to you the sense of desperation and hurt she might have been feeling at the time she disappeared."

"And you feel you know what was going on in her head?"

He shrugged. "Probably as well as anyone. You see, Devon's mother—"

Eden shot to her feet. "Jordan, I do apologize, but I just realized it's after five and I have an appointment with a friend for dinner at six. Would you mind if I returned tomorrow and we got started then?"

Jordan stood. "Of course not. I didn't realize how late it was, either." Only to himself would he admit disappointment. He'd hoped that after their discussion they could go to dinner. He'd missed her the last couple of days, but after breaking it off with Samara, he had needed some time to himself.

Now he was ready to pursue something with Eden and he, Jordan Montgomery, who rarely felt uncertain in any situation, was suddenly unsure of a woman.

Eden clutched her purse as she hurried toward the door. "I'll see you tomorrow then."

"Wait. I was hoping, if you're not too busy, to have dinner with you tomorrow night."

He watched Eden stop in her tracks and turn around. Her eyes gleamed, but he couldn't tell if she was excited or angry. Would he ever know this woman?

"About business?"

"What?"

"This dinner you want to share. Is it a business meeting?"

"No."

A small, satisfied smile, one he almost missed, it was so fleeting, crossed her face. "Then yes, I'd like to have dinner with you." She closed the door behind her.

Jordan's mouth lifted in his own satisfied smile. She'd just told him something important. She wanted more than a business relationship with him and that was very good news.

Eden ignored the worried glances of the taxi driver as she muttered curses under her breath. She couldn't believe how she'd handled his request that they begin work on Devon's case. She should have been prepared. It was foolish and unprofessional of her to not be ready with an answer . . . with several answers.

Stupidly, she'd allowed the last few weeks with Jordan to lull her into a sense of, not security, but almost lassitude. She'd just enjoyed being with him, getting to know him. She hadn't forgotten why he'd come to LCR, but she'd allowed it to go to the back of her mind.

Now she had to shift gears swiftly. Days before they left for Florida, she'd set things into motion and it would only take a few hours to complete the fully prepared report. She just wasn't sure she would have the courage to give it to him.

Rushing through the door of her apartment, Eden stripped off her clothes on the way to the bedroom. As was her usual course of action when something upset her, she slid on her workout clothes and went to her gym.

Pummeling her boxing bag, she weighed her options, none of them pleasing. Tell Jordan the truth, let him feel sorry for her . . . possibly hate her for once again lying to him, deceiving him. Or, tell him the lies she'd developed and let him put the past to rest.

How easy it would be to just give him the file. The way Jordan looked at her when she left Noah's office told her he was thinking of her as more than an LCR operative.

He wanted her. The experience at the pool had proved that. If she let Jordan believe Devon was dead, then could there actually be a future for them?

God, she was just kidding herself. She wasn't the person she'd once been. That person wouldn't have kept Jordan's interest. She was wise enough, mature enough, to know that now. But was Eden St. Claire any better for him? A woman who'd seen and done things few people had or would ever consider doing?

Jordan was interested right now because she intrigued him. She was an enigma . . . something different. When he realized what she was capable of, would disgust or disdain replace his attraction? She'd barely survived his contempt once. She didn't think she could do it again.

By the time she'd finished her grueling workout, she was exhausted and aching all over. And still hadn't come to a decision.

Under the hot spray of the shower, she allowed herself the choice she'd subconsciously wanted all along. It wasn't smart or noble, but something she wanted with a desperate urgency. Even after all these years, she still had strong feelings for Jordan. Could it be called love? Was she even capable of love? After closing herself off to any tender emotions, could she open up and allow herself to be vulnerable again?

She had no answer. But she wanted to take this time with him. To get to know him. Spend time with him. Relive the magic she'd experienced in his arms all those years ago.

It wasn't wise, and Eden prided herself on being wise. But it was what she wanted most in the world and she was going for it, come what may.

sixteen

Graceful and composed, Eden glided into Noah's office the next day, prepared to do what she needed to do. She wasn't sure how long she could hold out making the decision about what she would tell him, but she would stall for as long as she could.

Today wouldn't be easy. Hearing from Jordan's own mouth what he thought of Devon, what his opinion of their night together was . . . well, she expected to exist in a silent hell for several hours.

She would do it, though. She'd sit and allow him to dissect everything to the bare bones and then that would be that. There would be no reason to discuss Devon any further. She would tell him she was working on the case and in the meantime, they'd have the time together she wanted.

Eden refused to feel guilty for the sheer selfishness of that decision. She'd given up a lot over the years, why shouldn't she have these days of happiness?

"Good morning, Eden. You look well rested."

A genuine smile, one she rarely showed, spread across her face. "Thank you. I had a good night's sleep." She gestured widely with her hand. "And you're beginning to look like a natural in that chair."

He shook his head. "I don't think I could get used to sitting behind a desk all day."

"It is hard to imagine you doing that. You seem too much a man of action."

Though she hadn't intended anything sexual in the remark, a sensual gleam darkened Jordan's eyes and his mouth lifted in that sexy grin. Pinpoints of heat immediately swept through her, settling between her legs to create a slow, deep throb.

With one look, he'd turned her on.

Forcing her shaking legs to the chair in front of the desk, she plopped down with an embarrassing inelegance.

Jordan had stood when she walked in, and instead of sitting again, he came around the desk and stood in front of her.

"Eden?"

She looked up at him and swallowed hard. She who seduced men to get what she needed was suddenly stunned to find herself dry-mouthed and speechless. Not only that, but she found herself feeling overwhelmed. He stood so close to her, she felt closed in . . . almost claustrophobic. Something she hadn't felt in years. After a couple of tries, she managed a raspy "Yes?"

Evidently sensing her need for space, Jordan backed up and sat in the chair beside her. "I know this meeting today is for us to discuss Devon. And I intend to do that . . . help in any way I can to find out what happened to her. But I think we need to get something out of the way before we begin."

"We do?" Was that wobbly, insecure voice hers?

Jordan leaned forward and touched her hands. She looked down, surprised to see her hands clenched together. What was happening to Eden, the sexually confident woman? She was beginning to act more like Devon, the fragile, innocent young girl.

Eden took a deep, controlled breath. Damned if she'd let that happen.

She unclenched her hands and took Jordan's hand in hers. Forcing confidence back into her voice, she glided a finger down the back of his hand. "What exactly do you want to 'get out of the way'?"

"This." Standing, Jordan moved quickly, leaned down, and put his mouth on hers. So surprised was she at this move, Eden's mouth had been half open in shock. Jordan took advantage and swept his tongue deep inside. Pressed back against the chair, Eden could only respond the way her body screamed for her to. His deep growl of approval vibrated against her lips when she opened her mouth wider, allowing him even greater access.

Before she could pull him to her and respond the way she really wanted, Jordan pulled away just as swiftly. She was gratified that though his smile was of a satisfied predator who'd just captured his prize, he was also breathing heavily.

Leaning over her, his mouth hovering within inches of hers, he growled, "You know I want you?"

"Yes." Though it sounded breathless, she was proud to be able to utter even a single word.

"I usually get what I want."

A slight smile tickled at her lips. "Do I have a say in the matter?"

"Sweetheart, you have all the say. I just want you to know that I'm going to pursue you until you say yes."

"And do you think you'll have to do a lot of pursuing?"

"That's up to you."

Without waiting for a reply, Jordan turned away and went to the minibar. "Would you care for something to drink?"

What she'd like to have was good stiff drink to settle her nerves. But since it was just past ten o'clock in the morning and that would no doubt make Jordan aware of just how rattled she was, she answered, "Water, please."

As he poured bottled water into a glass, she watched his profile. A smile, satisfied and sensuous, played around his mouth. He knew he'd already won. Her pride told her she shouldn't make it so easy for him. But her pride with this man disappeared a long time ago. She didn't want to play games with him. He wanted her . . . at last . . . Jordan Montgomery really wanted her. And she, despite all the obstacles and warnings inside her head, was going to take this opportunity for a second chance.

She accepted the water with a silent nod of thanks. Sipping the cold liquid, she forced rational thought back into her head. Jordan was ready to talk about Devon. She'd been prepared when she arrived, but he'd taken her off guard. She needed to settle down and get back to the place and the person who could handle what was about to take place.

Pulling courage from deep within, Eden set her glass down and took a notebook and pen from her slender briefcase. She would pretend they were talking about a stranger . . . someone she had no emotional investment in. This was a case, nothing more.

Jordan evidently felt the same need to compartmentalize. The sexy seducer disappeared. In his place was a man with a mission. "Let's start with what you do know about Devon . . . what Noah told you."

Eden was glad she'd written down earlier what Noah had told her. If she hadn't, she might have told Jordan a lot more than what she should know. That would be very difficult to explain.

She glanced down at her notes, thankful she didn't have to face him right now. "I know that Devon Winters was last seen April 6, seven years ago. That you believe you were the last known person to see her before her disappearance." She didn't look up for his confirmation. "She'd suffered an emotional trauma that night."

"Yes . . . and not that you're interested, but I take full responsibility. She was a young, idealistic girl. I should have seen through that façade."

"Why didn't you?" She asked the question before she realized it was out of her mouth.

Jordan rubbed his forehead and blew out a sigh. "I

wanted her. . . . It was as simple as that. I'd just come back from a soured mission. . . . Some good men died. I hadn't slept in almost two days. The drinks I had went straight to my head. I shouldn't have gone at all, but couldn't face being alone. Stupid, I know. And she was . . ."

He closed his eyes briefly, and when he reopened them, Eden saw bitter self-recrimination. "Those are just excuses. The bottom line was, she was beautiful. I made the stupid assumption that because she was at this certain event, looked at me like I was her favorite brand of ice cream, and was dressed in a barely there see-through dress, that she was experienced." His sigh was one of deep regret. "It was a stupid, selfish assumption. One I realized almost immediately."

Eden frowned. "Immediately? So you stopped when you realized . . ."

Jordan leaned back in his chair and looked out above Eden's head as if seeing that night all those years ago. "No. That's the god-awful part of it. I won't go into detail, because I don't think it would serve any purpose, but suffice to say that within a few minutes after we were alone, I knew she wasn't as experienced as she was presenting herself to be."

Though she wanted to ask how he knew that, it wasn't something Eden, the investigator, needed to know.

"What happened next?"

"We made love. . . . I went to the bathroom for a warm washcloth. When I returned, she was gone."

An aching tenderness filled her. She thought he'd been angry with her, instead he'd wanted to soothe her. Clearing her throat of the developing lump of emotion, Eden looked down at her notes again. "Noah mentioned that she told you her name was Mary, but that you actually knew her and her family, but hadn't seen her for several years?"

"Yes, she'd changed so much. Even if she'd told me

who she was, I might have doubted her. She'd made a complete and total transformation."

"Would that have made a difference?"

"What? If she'd told me she was Devon?"

"Yes."

"Hell yes. No matter how beautiful she'd become, I never would have touched her. I practically watched her grow up."

That information only confirmed what she'd known all along. Not that it made her feel any better to know she'd been right about that . . . since she'd been so wrong about everything else.

"So, she was gone. What did you do then?"

"I went looking for her."

Now, *that* surprised her. She'd just assumed he'd gone back to bed. A rush of warmth filled her at the thought of him wanting to find her.

"And there was no sign of her?"

"No. By the time I made it out to the street, I saw a taxi round a corner. I assumed it was Devon. I planned to wait until daylight and call the cab company to find out where she was taken."

Another rush of warmth flooded her. "Why go to all that trouble?" A question that had nothing to do with the case, but one she desperately hoped he'd answer.

He shrugged. "I had questions . . . lots of questions."

Well, that hadn't been what she'd hoped for, but pursuing it any further might make him wonder.

"So after she left, what did you do?"

"I took a shower and got dressed. Then I checked my messages. I was expecting a call from headquarters about another job. I got that message but there were several more . . . all from Alise Stevens."

Eden forced herself to not stiffen at that name. Her mother and her cruelty could no longer touch her. Jordan's information that Alise called him verified what she'd suspected.

She glanced down at her notebook and then up at Jordan. "That's Devon's mother, right? What did she have to say?"

"She kept insisting I call her . . . that there was something urgent I needed to know."

His look of intense distaste surprised her. "You don't look like you care for the woman very much."

"I've never met a more devious or self-serving woman in all my life."

So surprised at this information, Eden leaned forward with a fascinated interest. "Really? Why do you say that?"

Jordan shrugged. "It might help you to understand Devon's mind, so I'll explain a little. Henry, Devon's stepfather, was my godfather. My parents were his best friends. When I first met Alise, I was somewhat surprised he'd been able to capture such a young, beautiful wife. It didn't take long to figure out that Alise married Henry for one reason only and it had nothing to do with love. She wanted the prestige of being married to a well-respected man in the government. Henry had contacts she'd never be able to get as a single mother whose only asset was her outward beauty. From the moment she married the man, she made his life a living hell."

"Why didn't he leave her?" It was something she'd wondered for a long time.

"Because of Devon."

Eden forced a cough to cover the gasp that caught in her throat. Swallowing hard, she winced slightly at how shaky her voice sounded. "What do you mean?"

"Henry knew what kind of mother Alise was. She refused to let him legally adopt Devon, so he stayed to protect her . . . even insisted she go to boarding school and college, hundreds, sometimes thousands of miles away, hoping to keep them separated as much as possible."

Eden dropped her gaze down to her notes again, surprised to see them somewhat blurry. How many times had she considered calling Henry? Millions . . . but she'd never been able to make the call. She blinked back tears. How in the hell would she explain that to Jordan?

Swallowing hard, she forced strength into her voice. "So, Devon's mother was evil, her stepfather a good man. What does this have to do with Alise calling you?"

"Alise had been trying to get me into bed for years. I don't know how many times she'd cook up schemes to get me to come over when Henry was out of town."

Holy crap. Was there no end to the surprises today? She'd thought this would be information she'd have to listen to to appease Jordan. She hadn't imagined to finding out things she'd never guessed.

"I only called her because she sounded so furious in her messages."

"What did she say?"

"She told me some people called and told her I'd left the party with Devon. At first I denied it, but when she explained how Devon had changed, I knew she was telling the truth.

"Since Devon got home very late, she put two and two together and came up with the right answer . . . that we'd slept together. She said Devon made improper advances to several other of their friends . . . that she was under the care of a psychiatrist." His voice hardened with bitterness. "Then she threatened to have me arrested for statutory rape."

All this new information slammed into her gut with the force of an out-of-control freight train carrying dynamite. Her heart wanted to leap from her throat. "But . . . but." She couldn't get the words out. What could she say? Jordan had thought she was underage? No wonder he was furious. And her devious bitch of a mother had lied about the reasons she was seeing a psychiatrist. Alise had done her best to destroy her daughter . . . and she'd almost succeeded.

She cleared her throat. "Of course, from what Noah has told me, that was a lie since Devon was twenty-one."

Thankfully Jordan seemed to think she was shocked only because Noah had given her age as twenty-one. He had no way of knowing that she now understood his fury when she'd appeared at his house.

Something hit her. "I thought you'd known the family for a long time. Did you not know Devon's age?"

"Stupid, I know. Devon had been a child to me for so long . . . I lost count of the years . . . hadn't seen her for so long. When I thought of her, I only saw the child she'd been."

"What happened next? I believe you told Noah that Devon came to see you?"

"Yes, it wasn't long after I talked with Alise. She came to explain why she'd deceived me. Only I was so furious with her, so disgusted at myself, I said a lot of things I didn't mean."

Eden concentrated on scribbling her notes, knowing it was the only way to get through the next few minutes. The retelling of this particular episode was the one she'd dreaded the most. The shattering of dreams and the loss of innocence. A fitting prequel to what lay ahead a few minutes after she left his house.

"Do you need something else to drink?"

She jerked her head up. "No . . . why?"

"I don't know. . . . You're looking a little pale. You feel okay?"

"Yes, of course . . . probably just my late night." Of course this belied her earlier claim that she'd gotten a refreshing night's sleep. She didn't care. They just needed to move beyond this.

"So, anyway, you said some . . . cruel things and then she left."

"Don't you want to know what I said?"

No, God, no. "I don't really think it would help the case, unless you thought of something you didn't tell Noah?"

"No, I told him everything. Actually, I'm glad not to have to repeat what I said. I'm certainly not proud of it."

Eden nodded quickly. "So we'll go on. After Devon left your house, what happened next?"

"I waited maybe all of ten seconds before I went after her. The hurt I saw in her face . . . hell, I'd never seen pain like that. I didn't know what I was going to say to her, but I didn't want her out on the streets in that kind of condition."

It was only by digging into deep reserves of control and determination that she didn't reveal her absolute dismay. Jordan *had* come after her. He might have been walking the very street she'd been dragged from. Since she'd been unconscious seconds after the attack, she had no idea how far she'd been taken. When she'd come to, everything was a blur . . . the pain . . . the blood. . . . *Don't go there.*

To think Jordan had been only seconds from her. He could have prevented the attack. He could have saved her.

Dear God, she was going to be sick.

Eden jumped up. "Excuse me, Jordan. I'm suddenly a bit queasy." She dashed to the adjoining bathroom. Slamming the door on his concerned face, she made it to the toilet with no time to spare.

It was an unfortunate fact that there was no way to throw up quietly. At least, none she'd ever discovered. Eden gagged and coughed her way loudly through her bout of sickness, while humiliation and fear danced with gleeful malice inside her mind.

How in the world was she going to explain this?

"Eden . . . you all right?" The jiggle of the handle gave her barely a second to prepare for Jordan's entrance. She should have known he'd have a key.

Hurriedly flushing the toilet, Eden rushed to the sink.

Refusing to look in his eyes, she murmured her apology. "I'm so sorry, Jordan. I must have eaten something last night that didn't agree with me."

As she rinsed her mouth, she was startled to feel a warm, gentle hand on her cheek, in a soft caress. Then, surprising her still, he held her hair up, away from her face, to keep it from getting wet.

"Don't apologize." His voice was gruff with concern. "Do you need to go to the hospital?"

She turned the water off, grabbed a nearby towel, and wiped her mouth. "No, I'll be fine. I'm sure it's out of my system."

Willing herself more courage, she turned around and tried to smile. Based upon his frown, the smile hadn't been very convincing.

"I'm fine . . . really. Shall we continue?"

"You're as white as a ghost. Go home and we can pick this up later."

Go through this again? Not in this lifetime or any other. She would get through this if it killed her. The fact that Jordan had never considered there was another reason for her to be sick only showed her how much he trusted her. Her stomach twisted again.

"No . . . the sooner I get all the information, the sooner we'll find out the truth." She took a step to walk around him and was stopped by his hand on her upper arm.

"You're sure?"

"Absolutely."

Seated once more, Jordan eyed her for several nerve-racking seconds. She knew he was just trying to determine if she was truly all right, but that intense stare didn't help her nerves.

Glancing down at her notes, Eden took a breath. "Now, you said you went after Devon, only seconds after she left the house, but saw no sign of her."

"Yes, I walked up and down a couple of the streets. It

was early morning and few people were out. I asked the ones I saw. No one had seen her. I assumed she'd caught a taxi as she had earlier."

A natural assumption. If only she had. Stupidly, she'd been trying to save money and was headed to a bus stop. "And then what?"

"I went back to my house. I had a new assignment, one that would take me out of the country for a while. I thought it best to get some perspective. When I returned, Devon and I could talk . . . a bit more rationally.

"It was almost two months later. I'd had a lot of time to think about what happened. To see Devon's side of things. I stopped to see if she was in or ask Henry how I could get in touch with her. That's when I found out she'd been missing since that night."

"I'm surprised her stepfather didn't contact you . . . or perhaps the police."

Jordan shook his head. "I was deep cover. No one, other than a couple of people, knew where I was, and they wouldn't have told anyone. No one even knew she was missing until her college roommate called to see why she hadn't returned to school. That's when they called the police."

It had been years since she'd thought about Mindi Simpson, her college roommate, and one of the few friends the painfully shy Devon had ever made.

"That's also when I learned her real age and why she hadn't denied seeing a psychiatrist, though it certainly wasn't for the reason Alise claimed."

Since it would look strange if she didn't ask the reason Devon was getting therapy, her numb lips mumbled, "What was the reason?"

Jordan suddenly surged to his feet, as if unable to remain still with his memories. "When Devon was five or six—Henry couldn't remember her exact age—Alise punished her for spilling grape juice on Alise's dress just before she went out to a party. She canceled the babysitter, locked Devon in the closet, and left. She was apparently gone all night. Henry returned from a business trip the next afternoon and found her almost unconscious, still in the closet. After that, Devon suffered from claustrophobia and achluophobia—that's a fear of darkness."

Oh, she knew exactly what that term was. Hearing Jordan describe her mother's cruelty was actually somewhat cathartic. Alise Stevens truly was an evil person.

Jordan's voice jerked her back to the present.

"I went to the police station and talked with the detective in charge. Devon's photo had been put up everywhere. Henry had posted a large cash reward. The police had interviewed all of the people who knew her, had done everything they could to find her. She became another statistic. I think they decided, based upon what she'd gone through, that she was a runaway and didn't want to be found."

This fit in perfectly with the file she'd prepared. So why didn't she feel any relief at how easy it <u>was</u> going to be to convince Jordan?

"I couldn't accept that. The Devon I knew—not the one I slept with, but the young girl—she was a fighter. I just couldn't see her running away. She was hurt when she left my house, but I saw fire in her eyes. I don't base this on anything other than a gut feeling, but I thought she'd give me some time to cool off and then come back."

Eden kept her face down as a small smile tickled at the corner of her mouth. He'd read her well.

"So then what?"

"I took a leave of absence from work."

She couldn't squelch her startled gasp. "You did?"

Jordan nodded, his dark eyes grim. "I thought, with all my experience and contacts, I could do what the police hadn't been able to do. I retraced every step they took. My contacts in the government gave me access to files no ordinary citizen would have. Not that it did any good. She'd just vanished into thin air. After six months, I gave up and went back to work."

He'd looked for her for six months. Eden couldn't believe what she was hearing. Noah had hinted at what he'd done, but she hadn't really paid attention. She'd been so upset at Noah's betrayal, everything else had been lost.

"Is there a reason to think you missed something . . . or the police missed something?"

"Hell if I know. I contacted LCR in D.C. a few months later. I was getting nowhere and hoped they could help. They did some checking and told me they couldn't."

Eden sat in dismay, realizing that Noah more than likely halted their investigation. He'd done it to protect her. She'd still been in therapy, hadn't even begun the numerous surgeries to repair her face. Still, she was surprised he'd never told her. Not that it would have made a difference. There was no way she could have returned to her old life.

"Why did you decide to come to LCR again?"

He lifted his shoulder in a small shrug. "Just in passing, an acquaintance of mine mentioned that since I was coming to Paris, I should contact the founder of LCR. I thought, what the hell, and the rest you know."

Noah. There was no way to prove it, and he'd dance around it, but Eden felt certain that Noah had somehow planted that little seed. Someday Noah would find a person he was unable to manipulate or an event he couldn't fix. Eden hoped to be around when that happened.

She looked down at her notes, suddenly so exhausted she wasn't sure she was going to be able to get to her feet without his help.

"Dammit, Eden, you look like you're about to fall out of that chair."

She managed a wan smile. "I am feeling a little tired."

"Do you need help getting home?"

The last thing she needed was for him to go with her. She needed to be alone . . . just for a little while.

"Of course not. I'll catch a cab. You know I don't live far from here. I'll be fine by tonight."

"Let's cancel tonight. You need to stay—"

"Don't be ridiculous, I'll be fine. Come by my place at seven."

"You're sure?"

Eden stood, gratified and relieved that her legs held her. "Absolutely sure."

Jordan took her hand and kissed it softly. "I'll see you tonight then."

Eden managed a quick smile as her unsteady legs carried her out the door. Didn't she feel the fool? She'd gone into the meeting confident she could handle hearing his side of the story, but never would she have guessed what she would learn.

He had cared and searched for her . . . extensively. He still searched.

With startling clarity, Eden knew what she had to do. She had to tell him the truth. No one deserved the truth more than Jordan. When she'd thought he hadn't cared, that he just wanted to get to the bottom of a mystery, she'd been prepared to give him the fake file. But now there was no way.

She would come clean. Tell him everything. But not yet. When she told him, she fully expected he'd be furious at her deception and most likely would never want to see her again. She had to tell him the truth, but she would wait. She would take the days she had with him . . . enjoy and treasure them.

She told herself she deserved them and so did Jordan. She told herself she believed that lie.

seventeen

Jordan watched Eden leave the office, more than a little concerned for her. Yes, she looked better than she had earlier, but she still looked ill . . . almost shell-shocked. Did she judge him for the way he'd treated Devon? God knew he had nothing to be proud of there, but dammit, he was doing his best to correct that, in the only way he knew how. Finding the truth.

Standing, he turned to look out the window. It was late afternoon, and Paris traffic was in its full frenzy. Not that it slowed down very much at any time of the day or night.

He had a sudden and unusual longing for his boyhood home. Living with his grandmother hadn't been the easiest upbringing in the world. Somewhat abrasive, always opinionated, and at other times downright mean, Hannah Montgomery had been quite the character. Showing affection was synonymous with vulnerability to Hannah, but she'd made sure he got the basics and he had to be grateful for that. Looking back on it, he'd had it better than most kids. Plenty of food, green hills and valleys to roam and play in, and someone who, in her own way, cared for him.

It was amazing how similar Eden's background was to his. With so much in common, no wonder he felt this incredible draw toward her. And it was mutual. The look she'd given him yesterday and the kiss they'd exchanged today told him that very soon, he'd have her in his bed. He hardened at the thought.

He'd ended things with Samara. A phone call was a piss-poor way to end a relationship. If he hadn't needed to stay in Paris and help Noah out, he would have gone back home and ended things face to face. She'd deserved that much . . . hell, she deserved a whole lot more. But she also deserved a man who loved her more than anyone else in the world. Jordan knew he couldn't be that man. She'd told him she understood, and he knew he had hurt her deeply, but he'd had no other choice.

Never in his time with Samara had he felt this fierce surge of desire as he had for Eden. He had tremendous admiration for both women, but they were so different, it was hard to even believe he'd been attracted to both of them.

Samara was goodness and light. An open book. If she had something to say, she said it. She was rarely in a bad mood, with an energy and contagious enthusiasm he'd always found delightful.

Eden was shadow and mystery, enclosed in a cloud of earthy sexuality. He'd never met anyone quite like her. Yes, he wanted to get her in bed . . . she could turn him on with a look. He had every intention of getting her there and keeping her there for hours . . . maybe days.

But it was more than that. She had an incredible depth of character, steel-hard determination, and performed a job few women or men could do. She was also passionate, courageous, and, he strongly suspected, deadly when necessary. He knew that much about her and wanted to know a hell of a lot more.

Jordan checked his watch. He had a few more calls to make, to check in with operatives, then he would head home. He'd found a nice flat not far from Eden and it wasn't far from his favorite restaurant . . . the one in which they'd met.

He'd have a meal delivered from there; the staff knew him well. Maybe he'd pick up a bouquet of flowers on his way home.

Tonight, as long as Eden was feeling well, he'd make sure they both got to know each other much better.

After a long hot bath and a cup of tea, Eden felt much improved. Stronger and refreshed, she dressed with care. This was her first date with Jordan and she wanted to look spectacular. One thing she'd learned in all the years she'd worked for LCR was the supreme confidence of a woman comfortable with her body and her beauty.

Though she knew herself to be outwardly beautiful, she took no credit for it. The plastic surgeons Noah hired were responsible for her looks. They'd worked endless hours, repairing broken bones, removing scars, and reconstructing her features into something almost otherworldly.

Noah told her they'd done that at his request. She could have been repaired and still have been passably pretty. Since they'd agreed she would work for LCR, he'd asked the surgeons for stunning and his request, according to him, had been exceeded.

She carefully made up her face, paying special attention to her eyes, one of the few features the surgeons hadn't tried to improve. She wished she didn't have to wear colored contacts. Her real eye color was a pretty shade of light gray, but she couldn't take the chance of Jordan seeing them. Though she doubted he'd remember after all this time, she still wouldn't risk it.

Tonight, she chose a clear aqua blue and enhanced them by outlining her lids with a smoky blue liner. She'd changed her hair color back to her preferred white-blond, which only made her eyes more appealing.

She slipped into an ice-blue, almost nonexistent thong and a sexy lace bra with a front clasp. Opening her closet, she perused her multitude of dresses. Her eyes fell on a purchase she'd made last year in Milan but had never had a chance to wear. Made of blue silk, it draped over her body like melted wax over porcelain.

Eden stepped into it and turned to the full-length mirror behind her. The dress, seductive and provocative, reflected her mood. Exactly what she needed for tonight.

Today, in the office, Jordan's kiss told her he wanted her, and if she wasn't mistaken, he planned to try to seduce her. Though she didn't intend to immediately fall into his arms and make it easy for him—what was the fun in that?—she planned to make sure he knew she wanted him just as much and he could have her.

Playing coy was usually a game she played with men she wanted information from. Tonight, she'd do it for a different reason. She wanted to have fun with Jordan. To have what she'd never had . . . a real love affair. With genuine emotion and caring.

Eden cautioned herself from slipping into that silly romantic mode she'd had years ago. She would never be that stupid again, but that didn't mean she couldn't have romance.

The doorbell rang, and with one last glance to make sure the seductress was in place, she went to open the door.

Damned if she didn't keep surprising him. Every time he saw her, her beauty astounded him. Tonight, if possible, she'd outdone herself.

Feeling like a geeky teenager picking up the prom queen, he practically shoved the bouquet of violets in her face.

Eden apparently didn't see anything strange in his presentation. A delighted smile covered her face, causing his heart to kick up toward a galloping speed.

"They're lovely. Come in while I put them in water."

He closed the door behind him, then leaned against it. The way she looked, he was pretty sure if he advanced further inside, he'd try to convince her to skip dinner and go straight to bed. Not because he thought she'd be that easy, but because he wanted her that much.

He wanted her, but he also wanted to take her out and just enjoy her company. The dinner he ordered would be delivered around nine. That gave them almost two hours to sit down and talk. Not about business, not about Devon. He wanted to know Eden, the woman.

Eden returned and stood in the middle of the room. "Would you like a drink?"

He shook his head slowly. "I thought we'd go out for drinks and then dinner at my place. That okay with you?"

He could see the acknowledgment in her eyes. Dinner at his place meant something more than dinner.

She gave him a slow, sensuous smile. "Sounds perfect."

His hand at her waist, Jordan ushered her to a table overlooking some of the most beautiful lights of a Paris night. As he pulled the chair out for her, he pressed a soft kiss on her bare shoulder as soon as she was seated. A shiver of extreme desire swept through her. Jordan was trying to seduce her and doing a damned fine job.

The expression on his face as he sat across from her told her he knew exactly what kind of effect the small caress had on her.

"Are you feeling better?"

"Yes, thank you. I took a nap and a long hot bath. A cure for almost anything."

The waiter appeared and they ordered their drinks. Eden could have ordered for Jordan. She remembered he favored scotch. He'd been drinking it the night they made love.

"So, what do you do when LCR gives you some time off? I'm assuming you do get some vacation?"

"There's no set time or even amount of time for vacation. We pretty much set our own hours. If we feel the need for time off, we take it. I think one of Noah's requirements is to hire people who need to work almost constantly."

"So no three-day cruises or weekend trips to the country?"

She tilted her head in a flirtatious, teasing slant. "Are you asking me to join you on something like that?"

"If I did, would you?"

"I believe I might be able to make room on my schedule."

He leaned forward. "I don't want to deter you in your investigation of Devon."

"Much of my work will be done through others. Since she was last seen in Washington, many of my investigators will work from there."

"I wish you luck with that. Every step I took forward, I seemed to take three steps back. No one saw or heard anything."

She reached for his hand, wanting to comfort him. Stupid really, since she was responsible for this. She would come clean, though. She just needed some time.

"We'll do our very best . . . I promise."

He returned the squeeze on her hand. "I know you will."

As their conversation turned to other topics—politics, religion, global warming—Eden gloried in what she considered a gift: to be with Jordan, having him not only attracted to her, but treating her with respect and admiration, listening to her answers and views as if they mattered to him.

Her ego had never been tied to a man before and it wasn't now. But even after all this time, Jordan's opinion meant something to her. It wasn't a childish crush from a long-ago yesterday, but the want and need of approval from a man she respected and admired.

In the few weeks she'd known him, that respect had increased enormously. She wasn't ready to call it love. That was too dangerous, even if she was still capable of that emotion. But whatever it was, she wanted to savor the feeling for as long as she was able.

"I'm having dinner delivered to my apartment at nine. Are you ready to leave?"

Eden nodded and stood. As he draped her wrap around her shoulders, he whispered in her ear. "You hungry?"

And just like that, any desire for food disappeared as a new hunger took control.

She shivered, this time wanting him to know how he affected her. Tilting her head back, and flashing a look that told him exactly what she hungered for, she whispered, "Famished."

Jordan's eyes widened slightly before they narrowed into a hooded, hot gaze. "Do you enjoying eating in bed?"

"It's one of my favorite places to dine."

He gently nudged her toward the door. "Good, because I don't have any other furniture."

A surprised giggle escaped her as he hustled her out of the bar and into the elevator.

Ten minutes later, Jordan opened his apartment door, and allowed Eden to enter first. She'd taken it in stride when he assured her he hadn't been lying. He'd barely had time to find an apartment and buy a bed. All the other furnishings he figured he'd pick up at some point.

Though he'd been halfway teasing about having dinner on the bed, he had thought they could dine on the floor, like a picnic. The bed sounded like a much better idea.

Her beautiful mouth curved with an enigmatic tilt, she gazed around the spacious and empty living room before turning back to him. "You weren't kidding."

He wondered if she was rethinking their dinner plans, but the doorbell rang before he could ask if she'd rather go out. Dinner had arrived. He turned to open the door and heard her footsteps as she wandered through the apartment.

Food bags in hand, Jordan closed the door and turned.

No Eden. He headed to the bedroom and stopped at the door. Again that curious flip to his heart. One that only she had ever been able to make happen.

The comforter had been pulled down and pillows were placed at strategic spots on the king-sized bed. Eden sat, barefoot, her legs curled under her, in the middle of the bed, with a teasing glint in her eyes. "The table is set."

"So I see." Jordan took the three large sacks, set them between the two of them, and unloaded everything on the bed. If Giorgio, the kindhearted but temperamental chef, saw where they were eating his elegant meal, he'd probably keel over.

Jordan couldn't imagine a better place.

As they dined on smoked salmon, roasted chicken, fresh spinach, and mashed potatoes, Jordan couldn't help but be fascinated at the change in Eden's attitude. She acted younger, almost carefree, and damned if he didn't find her even more attractive, if that was even possible.

They talked little during dinner, but the hot looks she sent him had Jordan thinking of a different kind of dessert than the one he'd ordered with the meal.

He opened a box of pastries and held a small piece to Eden's mouth. Full, sensuous lips opened and closed over his fingers. A surge of lust hit him like a tsunami. Before she could realize his intent, he came over her and pressed her back against a pillow.

She swallowed the small bite of pastry and then, with an even more sensuous smile, wrapped her hands around the bedposts and wiggled her body in a blatant sexual move.

Jordan propped himself above her on his forearms, his eyes roaming the delectable offering. "You are the sexiest, most enticing creature I've ever met."

She responded by lifting her body and rubbing against him.

Jordan couldn't stop looking at her. Her eyes glittered

with desire, those luscious "suck on me" lips beckoned, and her beautiful, "do wicked things to me" body threatened his control unlike anything ever had.

He wanted to ravage her. He wanted to take his time with her. He wanted to fuck her hard until she screamed in release over and over again. To slowly uncover and savor every inch of her body . . . swallow each gasp, breathe in each sigh.

"You know, touching is allowed." Her sultry voice held a tinge of amusement.

"Anywhere in particular?"

"Anywhere you like."

Leaning down, he moved his mouth softly against her velvet skin, breathing in the fragrance of woman . . . Eden . . . his woman.

Unable to wait any longer, he rose up to straddle her hips, unbuttoned his shirt, pulled it from his pants, and threw it on the floor. Pulling her hands from the bedposts, he placed them on his chest. "You know, it goes both ways."

"Jordan." She gave a whispered sigh as her hands roamed over his chest and shoulders.

Gritting his teeth at the surge of arousal from her touch, Jordan pulled her hands away so he could slip the straps of her dress off her creamy shoulders. The small lace bra covering her breasts almost disintegrated in his hands.

He swooped down, his tongue circling the beautiful, plump nipple, before he closed his mouth over it, sucking hard. His cock grew harder as she arched into him, a gasp of longing leaving her lips. Moving to the other breast, he gave the tender mound the same treatment. His tongue lapped and swirled, then settled into a strong, hard suckle.

He felt Eden's hands move from his chest to his fly. He thrust his hips forward, telling her without words what he wanted . . . needed.

When she released him, her soft hands held him, stroking firmly from the base of his erection to the tip. Fluid leaked from him and she used it to rub harder.

With a strangled gasp, Jordan grabbed her hands and held them still. "Wait . . . let me get out of these clothes and get you out of yours. Then you can play all you want."

It took tremendous control to get off the bed and drop his pants and underwear. Instead of taking her own clothes off, Eden raised up on an elbow and watched him, seemingly fascinated.

"Like what you see?"

Her nod was a languid movement. "Come down here and I'll show you just how much."

"In a second. Let me make room." Jordan wrapped his arms around plates, dishes, and sacks and practically threw them onto the floor, ignoring the clatter and the mess, but enjoying Eden's soft laughter at his urgency.

Finally, at last, only Eden, in all her wonderful, disheveled sexiness, remained on the bed.

Jordan, naked and so aroused his erection and heart raced to see which would explode first, crawled slowly onto the bed. But instead of helping Eden off with her dress, he slid it up over her hips until it bunched at her waist.

Jordan gazed down at what he'd uncovered. He knew she had the longest, silkiest legs he'd ever seen. Seeing them again, imagining them wrapped around him, almost undid him. But he wanted, needed to do something else. Something he'd thought about . . . dreamed about almost from the moment he'd met her.

Smoothing his hands up her legs, he pulled her thong down and then spread her legs wide, until she was fully exposed. A reverent curse escaped as he gazed down at her feminine beauty.

Before they'd left for Florida, she'd gone to a spa and complained vehemently about the wax treatment she'd endured. Since then, he had dreams of seeing her—he liked what he saw—completely nude, with the exception of a small tuft of golden blond hair covering the top of her sex. He'd wondered what her real hair color was. She'd changed it at least three times since he met her. Now he knew she was a natural blonde.

"Jordan . . . please . . . I can't stand not having you touch me. Please."

Her husky, pleading voice, filled with wanton need, penetrated his haze of lust. Jordan bent his head, inhaled the womanly scent of arousal, then rubbed his cheeks against her bare mons.

Eden bit back a cry of need. How much longer could he torture her like this? She was almost to the point of begging him to take her when he rubbed his face against her. The rasp of his beard stubble against her bare, sensitive skin increased the throbbing to an almost orgasmic level.

"Jordan, please, oh please."

"Shh."

A puff of hot breath gave her a small warning and then his mouth was there . . . at first, a light stab of his tongue on her clit, causing Eden to arch toward him. Placing his hands on her hips, he held her still. Then, with slow, exquisite torture, he lapped, licked, and sucked . . . long, slow strokes, followed by deep plunges of his tongue and then light, playful licks.

Bright electric shock waves zinged through her, warm flashes of heat wrapped her in a cocoon of sensual pleasure. Ecstasy zoomed, speeding her toward mindless oblivion. Eden shrieked and grabbed his head, pushing him deeper between her legs. Hot sparks of electricity—the universe exploded—her body imploded. Screaming his name, she fell into a deep, dark velvet cloud of beauty.

Before she could recover, Jordan was settling between her legs. She vaguely realized he'd put a condom on. Now was not the time to tell him it didn't matter. The most important thing was to get him inside her.

As his penis pressed into her, Eden arched to make it easier for him. It had been so long and he was very large. She willed her body to open, relax, and accommodate this man she so desired. This man she'd never been able to forget . . . would never forget.

Jordan pressed halfway in and halted. "Sweetheart, you're tight." His voice, tense with need, rasped out a gentle command, "Bend your legs up just a little more, baby . . . that's right. Yeah . . . that's good. God, you feel amazing."

Eden heard whimpering, gasping, sobbing. She knew it came from her but couldn't stop it. The need, desire, and sheer lust of this moment consumed every thought, every fiber.

Finally, barely aware that Jordan had lifted her legs so the back of her knees rested in the crooks of his arms, he slid in completely. Eden gasped at the feeling of complete and absolute rightness of having him inside her. She wrapped her arms around his shoulders, pressed her face against his chests and held him as tight as she could.

Jordan took her slowly at first, sliding in, then out, building heat, need . . . then, even more need. Finally, as if he could no longer hold out himself, his big body surged hard, and began a strong, deep thrust and retreat.

Eden met his every thrust with one of her own . . . until, yes . . . there it was again . . . higher, brighter, more fierce than before. The world ceased to exist—a sunburst of heat, hot, intense, burning—implosion and then . . . absolute ecstasy. She heard Jordan's gasping groan as she buried her face against his shoulder and together they exploded into mind-numbing pleasure.

Jordan woke to the feel of Eden's soft lips kissing his stomach. "Looking for something?" He grimaced at the gravel-rough sound of his voice.

She didn't pause in her activities as she murmured, "Mmmm."

His cock, ever eager for this woman, rose to attract her attention. "And what exactly would that be?"

"Paradise . . . have you seen it?"

A soft chuckle came from deep inside. "Yeah, about an hour ago."

She raised her head and gifted him with an adorable smile. "Me too . . . but I was hoping to find it again."

"Think it's down there somewhere?"

In unison, both looked down the length of his body. Moonlight from the window reflected on the bed and showed he'd most definitely risen to the occasion.

Eden gasped as if she'd found a hidden treasure. "There it is." With that, she trailed her mouth down farther until he could feel her hot breath right above him.

He saw her eyes widen in seeming wonder as he grew even harder under her avid gaze. "Touching is allowed there, too." And please, let it be soon.

"How about kissing . . . licking . . . sucking?" A small smile played around her mouth.

His entire body jerked. "Oh yeah . . . That's definitely allowed."

As if she'd just been waiting for his permission, Eden proceeded to kiss, lick, suck, and then take the full head into her mouth. Jordan closed his eyes and literally saw bright explosions as he surged in and out of her hot, wet mouth.

"Eden . . . oh yeah . . . I don't think . . . yes . . . just . . . like . . . that." Incoherent words, sounds, and groans accompanied the soft slurping of the most exquisitely delicious fellatio he'd ever experienced. When he knew he wouldn't last another second, he grabbed her shoulders to pull her up. He felt the soft swish of her hair across his stomach and knew she'd shaken her head . . . refusing to stop. At the point of losing his famous control, Jordan hooked his hands under her arms and pulled hard.

Eden moaned a disappointed sound, but when he turned her over and plunged deep, she wrapped her arms and legs around him and held on tight. Jordan retreated, drove deep again and again. Lightning zipped like a bullet up his spine and he lost everything in the oblivion of her body.

Gasping like a racehorse that'd just won the Preakness, he rolled over. Pulling her so she lay sprawled on top of him, he remained inside her warm, velvet sheath as she throbbed and rode his shaft to her own release.

What he'd done, continued to do, was dangerous as hell. He'd forgotten protection for the first time in his life. But at this moment, it seemed to be the most right thing in the world. What that meant, he didn't know . . . didn't want to delve too far into his psyche to find out.

He just allowed himself the sheer magic of being connected to her in the most elemental and natural way possible. Everything else he'd worry about later.

His breath slowed to almost normal, he rolled over and gathered her to his side. Eden's beautiful face held a supremely satisfied expression of absolute contentment.

Jordan knew, probably had known all along and refused to acknowledge it, that he was in deep water with her, so deep he might never emerge. Something settled inside him as he accepted that it didn't bother him in the least.

As she snuggled more securely into his arms, he brought up the obvious, unwilling not to face and discuss what had happened.

"I didn't use protection that last time."

Though she stiffened briefly, she relaxed almost immediately and blew out a long sigh. "It's not an issue with me. . . . I can't get pregnant."

The bald statement bothered him. Not that he had any real desire to father children of his own. He'd even considered a vasectomy several times, but when he started a relationship with Samara, he'd changed his mind. She had wanted children.

After traveling all over the world, he was more than aware of the millions of children who desperately needed a home and someone to love them. Before Samara, he'd always figured that if and when he settled down, that's the route he would go.

What disturbed him was that Eden, a young woman who appeared to be in peak condition, believed herself to be sterile. Why? Based upon the stillness of her body, he suspected it was something that bothered her a great deal . . . though, knowing Eden, she'd deny it to her death.

"Why do you think you can't get pregnant?"

Eden blew out another long sigh. She didn't want to get into this so early in their relationship. Long ago, she'd come to terms with what happened and the physical consequences. However, she'd never had a relationship where anything of such a personal nature was discussed. Therefore, she had never had to explain the reasons for her sterility.

Since she couldn't tell him the truth, Eden used the lie she'd thought up when she'd first been told of her condition. "When I was a teenager, I was diagnosed with a rare form of cancer. The only alternative at that time was a complete hysterectomy."

Jordan squeezed her tighter against him, his arms giving her comfort, though not for the reason he thought. The knowledge that this was just one more lie in her already mountain of them tore into her, decreasing the joy of his embrace.

"I'm sorry, sweetheart. That must have been devastating for you to go through at such a young age."

She shrugged, wanting more than anything to get away from the subject and go on to something she could actually talk about without having to lie.

Jordan must have sensed her need, because he drew away from her, allowing her head to fall softly onto the pillow. Leaning over her, he kissed her softly, sweetly on her lips.

Eden sighed in appreciation at his consideration and kindness.

He murmured against her mouth. "There's some wine left . . . want some?"

Eden moaned "Mmmm" against his lips but wrapped her arms around him, refusing to let go.

Chuckling, Jordan returned her kiss, the wine forgotten as a much more pleasurable activity commenced.

eighteen

"I think we should both go after Honeycutt," Jordan said, glowering his displeasure at her insistence that it was a one-person job.

"Don't be ridiculous, Jordan. I've done these kinds of rescues in my sleep. The jerk who took Honeycutt is not only an amateur, he's an idiot. There's no need for you to get involved. I'll probably be back in time for a late dinner."

"Then let me take care of it. I've not had a chance to do one of these."

Eden sat up straight in her chair. "What's going on here?" She knew the answer, she just wondered if he would tell her the truth—if he even realized what he was doing.

Another glower, darker than before. "What are you talking about?"

"This is the third assignment you thought someone else could handle. Since you've been working Noah's desk, I haven't been on anything requiring more than a slight frown and a verbal threat."

He shrugged. "There's not been that many. Besides, we had the manpower—excuse me, people power. What was the point of putting our best operative on them?"

"Don't try to butter me up. You're not assigning projects to me because you're afraid I'll get hurt."

Instead of looking indignant or evasive, he shrugged again. "Is that so bad?"

Laughing softly, she leaned forward and kissed his cheek.

"No, it's actually quite sweet. But this is what I'm trained for. It's what I do. I don't take unnecessary risks. I have too much self-preservation for that. You can't keep coddling me. It's sweet but not necessary. Okay?"

With a disgusted sigh, Jordan stood, picked up the file from his desk, and handed it to her. "Okay, take it. But if anything happens to you, I'm going to be very pissed."

Standing beside him, she leaned forward and pressed a tender kiss to his mouth, showing him without words how much she appreciated his caring enough to want to protect her. She pulled away before she got carried away, as she tended to do with him. "Leave the light on for me." At the door, she turned to blow him a kiss and then breezed out.

Jordan shook his head as he watched Eden close the door behind her. She'd seen through his ruse from the very beginning, but allowed him to get his way. His overprotectiveness was unfair to the other operatives and he knew it. Eden was right. She was a trained professional. This is what she did for a living. He'd better get used to it.

Get used to it? That sounded damn permanent, but he couldn't deny that that was the way he was feeling. It had been over two weeks since they'd first made love. They saw each other almost every day, spent every night together. Their relationship—intense, passionate, and wild —had all the elements of a fling that should expend itself in a few weeks from exhaustion. And Jordan knew to his soul that it wouldn't happen.

He wasn't to the point he was ready to declare his feelings . . . wasn't sure what they were yet. Eden wasn't ready, either. Oh, she wanted him. She liked spending time with him and even admitted he made her laugh like no one ever had before. But she was skittish. He didn't know if it was just a natural part of her, because of her training, or if there was something else.

He was willing to let things develop in their own time. Last night, he'd had a lengthy conversation with Noah.

Bennett had gone so deep, he was having a hell of a time finding any trace of the man. He'd indicated it would probably be at least another couple of weeks before he returned to Paris. That gave Jordan time to discover Eden's fears, answer them, and gain her trust.

Eden was still working on Devon's case. She hadn't told him anything yet, saying she preferred to give him all the information at one time. That was fine with him. If he'd learned anything about her, it was that she was thorough, forthright, and very good at her job. If and when she solved Devon's case, Eden would make every effort to give him everything she learned.

He trusted her unconditionally.

Twenty minutes after leaving the office, her cellphone rang. Knowing instinctively it was Jordan, she answered with a teasing "Miss me already?"

"Get back to the office," Jordan said. "I'm sending someone else after Honeycutt."

Really, this protection thing was going way too far. "Don't be ridiculous."

Jordan's chuckle told her he knew exactly what she was thinking. "Just got a call from the team tracking the Larues. Looks like Larue and Bennett are having a little get-together in Nantes. They found a talkative mole inside Larue's household. We're running a scenario in the office before we head out. Figured you'd want to be involved."

Fingers gripped the steering wheel as adrenaline zoomed. "We're going in after them? What about the authorities?"

"They agreed to hold back."

In other words, Jordan's charm and negotiation skills had bought them some time.

For barely an instant, Eden was torn. She'd been assigned the Honeycutt project and was loath to hand it over, even if it was a simple snatch-and-grab. She always finished what she started. But going after the people responsible for Milo's death? Hell, who was she kidding? There was no contest.

"Give me half an hour." Throwing the phone on the seat beside her, Eden checked the rearview mirror. Ignoring the blaring horns and screeching brakes, she made a U-turn and headed back to the city.

Twenty-six minutes later, she pushed open the door to Noah's office to find Jordan, leaning against the desk, arms crossed, obviously waiting for her. "Where is everyone?"

He pressed a kiss to her forehead. "The big conference room. This office was too small."

Curious, Eden turned to go out the door. How many were on the case? LCR rarely sent in more than absolutely necessary. She halted when she saw the number of people standing in the hallway peering into the conference room. The room could accommodate twenty, but it was filled to overflowing.

She shot a questioning glance at Jordan. "What's going on?"

A wry smile curved his mouth. "Word got out that we're going after Milo's killers. Looks like everyone who knew him wants to be in on the raid."

That was because Milo had touched every life at LCR. A lump developed in her throat. It made sense that the people he'd helped the most would want to avenge his death. Unfortunately, unless the Larues or Bennett traveled with an army, that couldn't happen. The fewer people on the job, the greater their ability for stealth and success.

Jordan murmured something to the people blocking the door. They moved, allowing Eden and Jordan through. Gabe Maddox and Ethan Bishop stood at the front of the room.

Blue-eyed and grim-faced, Gabe was known for his cold, emotionless analysis of an op. The man's expression rarely changed, no matter what was going on.

Hotheaded Ethan, with his wild mane of golden hair

and peridot eyes, had the reputation of having a death wish, often defying orders to get the job done. The jagged scar etched down the left side of his face was an indication of the hell he battled inside his soul.

Eden had worked with both men on several jobs and was glad to have them on this one. They were two of LCR's most experienced people.

The men were studying a giant map of Nantes on the wall. Gabe acknowledged Eden with a nod. "Jordan wouldn't let us get started without you."

A rush of emotion swept through her at Jordan's thoughtfulness. She bit her lip to keep from saying something inappropriate in front of so many people. Determined to show him her appreciation later in private, Eden nodded and said, "Thanks for waiting."

Jordan turned and addressed the group. "Okay, let's get started."

Hours later, Jordan, Eden, and Ethan Bishop arrived in Nantes. Larue and Bennett had rented a small villa along the Erdre River. Why they'd decided to come together for a meeting was a puzzle, but it worked to LCR's benefit. Having them together under one roof was a gift.

Only three would go in for the takedown. Gabe and his team had traveled with them and would wait just outside the main gate in case of unexpected problems.

Warm wind whipped around them, stirring up dust and the hint of fish from the river close by. Jordan watched Eden shove strands of hair from her face. Dressed in black from head to toe, her slender body practically vibrated with excitement. This assignment probably meant more to her than any other she'd been on. Apprehending the people responsible for Milo's death was top priority for all LCR, but the determination in Eden's eyes told the story. She might be almost impossible to read most of the time, but when she talked about Milo, there was genuine affection. This mission was very personal.

The brick wall surrounding the villa was daunting, but breachable. Based upon the lack of activity outside the perimeter, all security was posted inside. According to Gabe's informant, the Larues traveled with only three guards. The operation should be easy.

On the other side of the estate, Ethan Bishop was perched in a tree overlooking the mansion. He'd already confirmed there were only three guards, which reassured the team that their informant had told the truth.

Three clicks in his earpiece . . . their go signal. Eden threw her rope over, getting ready to scale the wall. His heart lurched. Jordan forced himself to ignore it, once again reminding himself that this was her job and she was damn good at it.

Jordan's rope soared over. With a sharp tug, he secured the line and scaled the wall half a second behind Eden's descent. Landing lightly, he watched as she unhooked her harness and took off toward the back of the estate, gun in hand. She gave him a quick wink as she passed him.

Their planned scenario fell into place. From photos downloaded from the Internet, they knew the small mansion had two doors in the back, leading to a patio and pool. Eden would block those exits. Jordan loped to the side yard, where moss-covered cement steps led to the wine cellar. The outside door was to be conveniently left unlocked. Bishop would go through a door at the kitchen, also left unlocked.

At the entrance to the cellar door, Jordan checked his watch. They would go in three . . . two . . . one.

Pushing open the door, Jordan ran into darkness.

Alfred frowned with worry as Inez's sharp fingernails practically dug into her arms. The poor woman was wound up tighter than a drum. They needed to get their business settled as quickly as possible. Over the last few weeks, Inez had become so much more fragile and brittle.

Her golden blond head turned to him, she whined, "Alfred, I can't handle this any longer. Why am I even here? Why can't I leave, and then you can follow after you finish up?"

Weariness and depression shrouded every step as Alfred trudged across the room to comfort his wife. Putting his arms around her slender shoulders, he soothed her as best he could. "We will leave, my love, but not yet. There are still many issues to resolve. That's why we must concentrate on the business at hand while we are with Thomas."

"But why do I need to be here?" Her eyes filled with tears. "I could be setting up our lovely home while you handle the details."

Alfred fought back impatience at her petulant tone and a slight hurt at her insensitivity. Yes, he could have handled these matters himself, but they'd shared everything in their marriage. He counted on her savvy business sense as well as her love and support. The seed of doubt he'd had since that terrible night when their holding houses had been raided and almost all of their hard work had been destroyed began to grow. Since that horrific day, Inez had been distant and uncommunicative, not the loving, supportive spouse he'd come to depend upon.

Feeling guilty for his disloyal thoughts, he pressed a kiss to her brow. They'd both been under a tremendous amount of emotional strain. Unable to see family and friends, hunted down like animals. No wonder she was so emotionally fragile.

"We will leave soon and set up our new home together. I promise."

Though she smiled, her eyes told him she hadn't liked his

answer. Alfred drew in a sigh, determined to finish their business so they could indeed begin their new life.

"Let's get started."

Alfred lifted his gaze to a smug-looking Thomas Bennett. Though furious that he had to let go of his profitable and thriving business, Alfred valued his family even more. Selling his companies would allow him and Inez to retire quite comfortably. Years ago, they'd purchased a lovely island in the South Pacific. Though neither of them had been prepared to retire at such a young age, in a way it was a relief. After losing his sons, much of his youthful fire had disappeared. Now he just wanted to live out his life in comfort, with his loving wife at his side.

Papers shuffled, reminding him that Thomas waited for his signature on the multitude of documents that would transfer his interests in offshore businesses and stocks, as well as ownership of various warehouses all over the world. Selling at a loss pained him, but couldn't be helped. Cousin Thomas didn't have the funds to pay what the businesses were worth, but another buyer could take years to find—years he'd rather be enjoying, instead of spending them in hiding.

Returning to the small table they'd set up to sign the documents, Thomas handed him a stack. "These transfer your warehouses in Rio, Madrid, and the two in Thailand to me. I've marked the pages where you need to sign."

Nodding, Alfred scrawled his signature on page after page. A long, drawn-out sigh brought his head up. Inez sat on the couch, facing a window. Her body stiff, she stared out into the dark night, an expression of longing on her delicate face. Poor dear. She hated being cooped up even more than he did. Unfortunately, she couldn't go outside for fresh air. They'd traveled with a minimum of security, not wanting to attract attention.

"Inez, my sweet, why don't you go up to our room and

rest. You didn't sleep well last night. These contracts only require my signature."

With a surprising spring in her step, Inez gave him a relieved smile and scurried across the room toward the foyer.

"Stop right there," a masculine voice thundered.

Eden grinned at Jordan's unusually dramatic slant. They'd been watching this procession for almost five minutes without anyone noticing them. Eden stood just inside one of the sliding glass doors. Jordan stood at the entrance of the living room, and Bishop had placed himself just inside the room, to the left of Jordan.

Inez Larue screamed. Alfred shouted an obscenity and jumped to his feet. Bennett's hand stretched toward his pocket.

"Don't even think about it, Bennett," Jordan growled.

His thin face almost purple with fury, Thomas Bennett held his hands up, apparently seeing the benefit of following orders.

Jordan pointed his gun at Inez. "Why don't you join your husband. Everyone, get on the floor, hands out in front of you."

Looking more furious than frightened, Inez Larue glared at Jordan, then turned and marched toward her husband.

Eden relaxed against the edge of the door. This was going to be easier than she thought. The guard she'd handled had gone down with a minimum of fuss: a clunk on his head. Eden had tied him up and left him lying on the patio.

When Jordan and Ethan had radioed they'd each taken down a guard, she'd headed toward the room with voices. Now they just needed to—

Events elapsed in a surreal, slow-motion quality. Bennett pulled a gun from underneath the table and shot at Jordan. Jordan ducked, rolled for cover behind a couch, and fired at Bennett. Dropping to his knees, Bennett fired randomly at Jordan and then Ethan.

Staying low to the ground, Alfred Larue took advantage of the commotion and ran toward an alcove.

Jordan sprang to his feet and shouted, "I'll take Larue." Dashing across the room after Alfred Larue, he fired shots toward Bennett. Larue disappeared from view. Jordan followed.

Her anxious eyes fixed momentarily on Jordan, Eden almost missed seeing Inez Larue go through an open window and jump. Holy hell, if they weren't careful, everyone but the guards would get away. Cursing her lazy inattention, Eden ran outside after Mrs. Larue.

Ignoring the gunshots coming from the house wasn't easy, but this was her job and she'd almost blown it. Her soft-soled shoes barely made a sound as she ran across the brick patio. The back floodlights were on, allowing her to catch a glimpse of blond hair as Mrs. Larue headed toward a small, seedy-looking boathouse.

Eyes on her target, Eden picked up speed. At the entrance to the building, she stopped and peered inside. The room was pitch dark. Her small flashlight glowed with a minimum of light, showing no sign of the older woman. Locating a light switch on the wall beside her, Eden flicked it on and slammed the door behind her. If Mrs. Larue tried to run, she'd have to go through Eden.

The single low-wattage bulb glowed dimly. Eden saw paddles, skiing equipment, and a small, dilapidated boat, but no sign of Inez Larue. The rolling boards on the floor and cobwebs indicated the boathouse hadn't been used in years. Eden moved cautiously forward. Water gently lapped and sloshed underneath the building. Uneven gasps coming from deeper inside the building told her the exhausted older woman lurked in the shadows. From what she'd observed about Mrs. Larue when she'd first met her, the woman posed little threat.

"Come on out, Mrs. Larue, and I won't hurt you."

"Stop—don't come any closer."

Eden jerked to a surprised halt as Inez Larue stepped out from behind a post. Eyes gleaming with a cold determined light, her steady hand pointed a gun at Eden. *Well hell.* She shook her head at the older woman. "My gun's bigger and I'm a better shot. I'd advise you to drop your gun while you still have a choice."

The gun clutched in Inez's hand didn't waver as she walked toward Eden. Okay, perhaps thinking she'd drop the gun had been a bit unrealistic. Still, Eden hadn't expected her to come closer.

Inez's eyes widened with recognition. "You! You're that Claire bitch . . . the one who caused all our problems . . . destroyed my family."

Eden snorted with disbelief. "I think you've got things somewhat reversed. If you and your sleazy family weren't bent on kidnapping and selling people like cattle, we would have left you alone."

The older woman's body jerked with the insult. "It is a business. If we didn't provide the goods, someone else would. A simple case of supply and demand."

The Larues' skewed morals no longer surprised her. "No wonder your son turned out to be a pervert."

"You bitch!"

A killing rage swept across Inez's face. Uh-oh, wrong thing to say to a crazy woman with a gun. Guessing her intent, Eden jumped sideways, dodging the bullet. Her foot landed on an uneven board, her ankle twisted. Unable to catch herself, Eden fell backward, slamming onto the rotting wood floor. A second later, she sprang to her feet. The stabbing pain in the back of her upper left arm barely registered. After she took care of the crazy woman with the gun, she'd check it out.

Angry now, Eden lunged toward Inez with a low growl. The woman's eyes widened. She raised her gun to shoot again. Eden swung an arm out, knocking the gun across the floor where it skidded out of reach.

With an ear-popping shriek, hands extended like claws, Inez sprang toward Eden like a rabid hyena.

Eden's fist shot out, landing a punch to Inez's jaw. The woman plopped down on her ass, her addled expression almost comical.

Panting slightly, Eden stood over Inez Larue. "Give it up, lady."

Shaking her head as if to clear it, she looked up at Eden. "You have to let me go."

Despite the increasing pain in her arm, Eden couldn't help but sputter with laughter. "Now why would I let you go?"

"Because I helped you . . . that's why."

Eden blinked. "You did? How?"

Her eyes swimming with tears, she muttered between pitiful little sobs, "This . . . this wasn't the way it was supposed to be. . . . I'm not even supposed to be here. Alfred should be taking care of things. I shouldn't be the one. . . ."

Eden stared down in amazement as Inez Larue's words began to make sense. "My God, you're the mole."

An odd, cold flicker in Inez's eyes told Eden she'd guessed correctly.

"You set up your husband and Bennett to get caught."

"It should have worked, too, only Alfred can barely tie his shoelaces without me. He insisted I had to come along. I should be setting up our home, holding the family together. If one of us had to pay the price, it should have been him." She covered her face with her hands as she cried piteously. "It's all his fault."

Eden knew she shouldn't be surprised. All of the Larues had shown a serious deficiency in decency and integrity. Having Inez betray her husband of forty years should be no big shocker. Somehow it was, though.

Tired of the woman's pathetic sniffling, Eden waved her gun at her. "Get up before I knock the hell out of you just for the fun of it."

Getting to her feet, Inez lowered her head and rushed her. Eden's fist swung up, knocking Inez in the temple. With a slight whimper, the woman crumpled at her feet. Stooping down, Eden rolled Inez over, pleased to see she wasn't faking her unconsciousness.

Eden stood, and was stunned to find herself almost tipping over. Stiffening her legs, she gingerly touched her left arm. Pain bloomed . . . abrupt and acute. Her fingers met warm wetness. She looked down at her hand covered in blood. Vision wavering, she gripped a splintery post and blinked back unconsciousness. Gazing around, she saw a large nail protruding from the floor close to where she'd fallen. The wet gleam of blood on the floor told the story. Hell, no wonder it hurt. Biting her lip to stay upright, she grabbed a ski rope from a wall. Her arm fast becoming useless, she used the last of her strength to tie the unconscious woman's hands together, then to a post.

As Eden rose, the room swirled and whirled. She gazed longingly at the door. At the rate she was losing blood, she'd pass out before she got halfway to the house.

Eden squatted and pressed against a wall. She'd really like to sit all the way down, but figured she wouldn't be able to rise again if she did. Nausea rolled through her while a steady gush of blood flowed down her arm. If she didn't get it bound soon, she would either throw up or pass out. Neither one appealed to her.

Her left arm almost useless, she used her teeth to rip off the bottom of her shirt and wound it around her arm as tight as she could.

"Eden?"

Jordan's urgent voice in her earpiece startled her. Relief that he was alive and well almost did her in. She hadn't realized how desperately she needed to know that.

"Eden, dammit . . . where the hell are you?" The voice was a mixture of anger and worry.

"Boathouse."

"How bad are you hurt?"

"How'd you know I was hurt?"

"I can hear it in your voice. Now, tell me, how bad is it?"

"Come on in the front door. Mrs. Larue won't mind."

"Answer me, dammit. How bad?"

"Need a couple of stitches, nothing major."

His grunt told her he didn't believe her. Deciding that sitting down might now be a good idea, since she was about to keel over, Eden plopped down on her bottom. She groaned softly at the jar to her arm.

"What's wrong? You still there? Talk to me, sweetheart."

"I'm fine . . . just needed to sit down for a little while."

"Hang on. I had to chase Larue halfway down the drive. For a chubby, middle-aged man, he gave me a run for my money."

Despite the pain, Eden couldn't help but chuckle. "Damn, I wished I'd seen that."

Jordan snorted. "It wasn't a pretty sight."

She tried to move to a more comfortable position and couldn't stop the groan.

"Hang on, babe. I'm almost there."

"I will . . . I . . . Jordan?" She blinked as her vision blurred. "I think I might need to take a nap, okay?"

"No, you will not take a nap. You stay awake. Do you hear me? Tell me what happened."

Eden shook her head to clear it. Rationally she knew she shouldn't let herself lose consciousness, but it was becoming increasingly hard to keep her eyes open.

"Eden, talk to me . . . tell me how you fucked up so bad."

Her eyes popped open at this obvious insult. "Who said I fucked up?"

"Well, you tell me who's been hurt and then I'll tell you."

"The stringy-haired bitch lying in front of me doesn't

look too healthy, either." Her voice sounded as petulant as a four-year-old's. Jordan's husky chuckle soothed her. She closed her eyes.

"Eden, you still there?"

Eden jerked awake. "Of course I'm still here. Where do you think I'm going?"

"Knowing you, there's no telling."

"You don't know me, Jordan. Don't you know that?" Her voice sounded slurred to her own ears and some kind of unconscious self-preservation molecule was telling her to shut up, but she couldn't figure out why. She ignored it as she mumbled on, "If you really knew me . . . you wouldn't like me."

"Now, why do you say that?"

Eyes closed again, she listened to the rumble of his deep baritone voice. No one had ever touched her with his voice alone.

"Why, thank you, sweetheart, I like your voice, too."

"Huh?"

"You said you like my voice."

"Really? Who said?"

"Hey, you're not about to conk out on me, are you?"

"Don't . . . conk . . . don't know how."

"Okay, babe, I'm here."

The front door smashed opened, slamming against the wall—*the man didn't know how to turn a knob?* A tall, dark silhouette loomed in front of her and she breathed a sigh of deep thankfulness. "I'm over here."

Jordan whirled at the whispered sound, his heart turning over. Rushing to the crumpled figure, he touched her face first . . . just wanting to feel the heat of life. God, she was ice-cold.

"Eden, I'm going to lay you on your back and then take a look at your arm."

"Germs . . . everywhere."

Her whispered protest didn't stop him from lowering her

body to the floor. He checked her pulse. It was a little thready. Pulling her bloodied hand away, he looked with approval at the makeshift bandage, but blood continued to stream down her arm. He took his knife and sliced the material. She had a good-sized hole and jagged cut in her upper arm.

"What caused this, sweetheart?"

"Fell on a nail."

He grunted in sympathy, knowing that had to hurt. Pulling his T-shirt off, he wrapped it around her arm. "Come on, let's get you out of here."

"Mrs. Larue . . ."

"Gabe's team is coming. They'll take care of Mrs. Larue. I need to get you to Dr. Arnot."

Jordan scooped her into his arms. Adrenaline surging through him like an erupting volcano, he ran from the boathouse to the front of the estate. Gabe and his team were just getting out of their cars.

Jordan stalked to the closest vehicle and pulled the back door open. He deposited Eden in the backseat and covered her with a blanket.

"How bad is she?" Gabe stood behind him, peering in at Eden.

"Upper arm's messed up. Call Dr. Arnot's office and let him know I'm coming." He jerked his head at the mansion. "Mr. Larue's tied to a chair in the kitchen. His wife's in the boathouse. Bennett escaped on wheels, Ethan went after him."

Gabe nodded and turned toward his people to give directions.

Jordan jumped into the driver's seat. He blew out a ragged breath as he spun out of the driveway. Things had gotten out of control fast.

As he'd set out after Alfred Larue, Jordan seen Eden go after the wife. That hadn't worried him since the real danger would most likely come from Alfred or Bennett. Turned out, once he caught up with Mr. Larue, the breathless, out-of-shape man had gone down with no resistance. As he'd pushed the wheezing man back to the house, Bennett had sped past them in a truck, barely glancing at his cousin-in-law and business partner. Seconds later, Ethan Bishop zoomed past in pursuit.

Worry set in on his way back to the mansion with Mr. Larue. Why hadn't he heard from Eden? As soon as he heard her voice, he'd known something was wrong. Pain had throbbed in her every word. Pure panic bubbled inside him. He'd tied Larue up and ran toward the boathouse—the longest run of his life.

Twisting his head, Jordan glanced back at Eden. She hadn't moved since she'd lost consciousness in the boathouse. That concerned him as much as her injury. Was it blood loss and shock or some other problem he hadn't detected?

He checked the navigation screen. He should be coming up on . . . there it was. Dr. Arnot's house was a medium-sized older home miles from any others. Since the man often treated LCR operatives, living far away from nosy neighbors was a must. Jordan drove up behind Arnot's house. A young man wearing a white lab coat stood at the back door.

"Dr. Arnot?"

"No, I'm his assistant. He's inside, waiting for Eden. Do you need any help getting her out?"

Jordan shook his head and opened the car door. He lifted Eden, wincing as he noticed the shirt he'd wrapped around her arm was soaked with blood. He stalked into the house, the young man behind him.

"Go through the door there."

Jordan carried Eden into a room that looked just like an operating room in a well-equipped hospital. A gray-haired man wearing wire-rimmed glasses entered from another door. He gave Jordan a kind smile and a wink. "What's our Eden gotten herself into now?" With a wave of his hand, he indicated Jordan should place Eden on the examination table in the middle of the room

"She fell on a rusted nail. It's her upper left arm."

Jordan watched the doctor and his assistant remove the bloody shirt. Dr. Arnot made a tsking noise in the back of his throat. "Not sure she'd want a scar from this one . . . hate to think of her having to go through more surgery, though."

As if just realizing Jordan still stood beside the table, he smiled again and pointed to the door. "Go on out and pour yourself a cup of tea, young man. This young lady will be right as rain in just a jiffy."

Despite his worry, Jordan couldn't help but be amused at the doctor's homespun words and mannerisms. He felt as if he'd walked into a doctor's office in small-town middle America.

Jordan didn't want to leave her, but figured since his legs felt like jelly, he'd better find a place to light. He walked into another room, this time a cozy living room, filled with books. A steaming pot of tea sat on a high table beside a chair. Jordan poured himself a cup, laced it liberally with sugar, and then slumped down into the chair.

He took a long swallow of the hot, sweet concoction. He wasn't fond of tea but found the warm sugary liquid surprisingly soothing.

As he waited for word on Eden, he examined the unsettling feelings that had erupted over the last hour. If he'd doubted he was in deep with Eden, he doubted no more. When he'd known she was hurt . . . hell, he never wanted to go through anything like that again.

But how was he going to prevent it? This was Eden's job. He'd seen her file. She had one of the highest rates of recoveries for LCR. The events today, getting hurt, had been a fluke, but what if one day another fluke happened and it was more than a slice in her arm? How would he deal with that?

An answer still hadn't come to him when an hour later Dr. Arnot stood at the door, his wrinkled face beaming. Jordan pushed to his feet.

"She's going to be fine, son. I cleaned out the wound, fixed her up right as rain. Gave her a couple of shots, tetanus and an antibiotic. The nail nicked a vein, but we got the bleeding stopped. Missed most of the muscle, too." He winked. "Tell her it went through the fatty part of her arm. That'll get her riled."

Jordan chuckled as the doctor meant for him to.

"Don't think it'll leave much of a scar, either. If she wakes and is in pain"—he took a small pill bottle out of the pocket of his lab coat—"give her one of these." He shook his head. "Doubt she'll take them, though. Eden's not much for taking pills."

"You've treated her before?"

Something flickered in the doctor's eyes, but only briefly. Then he smiled and continued as if Jordan had never asked a question. "I'll come by in the late morning to check on her."

"It's a couple hours' drive home. She okay to travel?"

"Bundle her up in the backseat. Knowing Eden, she'd prefer to wake up in her own bed. She woke up when we were cleaning the wound, so I gave her a sedative. She's out cold. Probably will be till morning."

Jordan followed the doctor back to the treatment room. Eden lay on the table, her face still pale. She looked small and vulnerable, so different from the smart-mouthed, spirited woman he'd come to know the last few weeks.

Jordan gingerly picked her up, being careful not to jostle her left arm. With a nod of thanks to the doctor and his assistant, he carried her to the car. Easing her into the backseat, he pressed a light kiss to her forehead, then covered her with the blanket he'd used earlier.

Fortunately, traffic was light as he drove back to Paris, the unconscious woman in the back oblivious of the man driving her home and grappling with incredibly powerful emotions. He'd protected people all of his adult life, but he'd never felt so strongly about one person. Now he was bound and determined to protect this one small individual and he had a feeling she was going to be as difficult as all the other people he'd protected put together.

nineteen

"What do you mean I can't go back to work for a week?"

Eden knew she was being rude and grumpy. Dr. Arnot, one of the sweetest people she'd ever known, didn't deserve her sour attitude. But not work for an entire week? What was she supposed to do?

"Now, Eden, when's the last time you took off to rest?"

"I'm twenty-eight, Dr. Arnot, not eighty. I don't need to rest."

"She's quite stubborn, isn't she?"

Eden turned her head quickly, then winced at the pull on her sore arm. She hadn't even known Jordan was in the room. Maybe the doctor was right. Maybe she did need a rest. It was becoming more and more apparent that her instincts and reflexes were way off.

Dr. Arnot smiled at the man at the door. "Do you have any control over this young woman?"

Jordan chuckled. "A loaded question I dare not answer."

The doctor stood, patted her head as if she were a toddler, and then pointed a finger at her. "Get some rest. That's an order. You're at least ten pounds lighter than you were this time last year."

Since the last thing she wanted was to have him ask, in front of Jordan, if she was under more stress than usual, Eden managed a somewhat sincere smile. "I'll do better . . . I promise."

Dr. Arnot gave her his "I mean business" frown. Eden

bit her lip to keep from grinning at him. He was going for his most intimidating expression, but it was like trying to make Santa Claus look mean. It couldn't be done.

"You see that you do." He looked toward Jordan. "Young man, I'm holding you personally responsible if this girl's cheeks aren't rosier and her weight's not up by at least three pounds by the end of the month."

Jordan nodded solemnly, but Eden could tell he was fighting a smile, too.

As the doctor walked out of her bedroom, Jordan turned back to her and pointed a finger. Now this man could teach a class on intimidating looks. "Don't move a muscle till I get back."

Deciding she'd already acted childish enough, Eden resisted the urge to stick out her tongue and just smiled innocently.

Jordan's eyebrows rose at such an unusual submissive look.

When the door closed behind him, Eden sank into her pillows and allowed herself a groan. She'd forgotten how painful it was to be cut and how weak it made her. Though this wasn't anything nearly as serious as other injuries she'd had since working for LCR—and didn't even compare to what happened seven years ago—she still hated the vulnerable and weak feeling. Battling vulnerability came much easier to her than accepting it as part of being human.

Jordan came back into the room. One look at him told her he didn't plan to discuss whether she would be returning to work soon. Since she didn't think she'd win an argument with a mouse at this point, Eden blinked up at him and smiled.

There went his brows again, and she struggled not to laugh. She was really throwing him off with those looks.

"How are you feeling?"

"Like someone backhanded me all the way to Spain."

Jordan gave a sympathetic grimace and sat down gingerly on her bed. Taking her hand, he kissed it gently. "Feel like eating something?"

Now it was Eden's turn to raise a brow. "I just finished breakfast less than an hour ago. Are you trying to get me to gain all three pounds today?"

Instead of smiling at her teasing, Jordan swept his eyes over her body. "I hadn't realized until he pointed it out that you have lost weight in the last few weeks."

Great, just what she needed. "My weight fluctuates. I'm just one of those people who have trouble keeping weight on. I'll eat a few more meals and I'll be fine."

"You're sure that's all?"

"What else would it be?"

"You're not worried, perhaps about Noah?"

Eden swallowed a relieved sigh. When he'd begun probing, she'd been concerned he suspected something, even though she was reasonably certain he didn't. But to think he thought she wasn't eating because of her worry for Noah . . . That never crossed her mind.

"Why would I be worried about Noah?"

"It's just when he first announced he was going after Bennett, you didn't seem to think he could handle it. Now that Bennett's disappeared again, I just wondered . . ." He broke off with a questioning look.

If she told Jordan the truth about why she'd been concerned for Noah he would be surprised. She also knew he would never tell a soul, nor would he judge him. However, she and Noah made a pact, years before, and it wasn't something she was willing to break, not even for Jordan.

Noah's secrets were his own and if he wanted Jordan to know, he'd tell him. Eden had more than enough secrets of her own; she didn't want or need to be responsible for anyone else's.

"Noah's a trained professional. He trained me and countless others. He knows how to take care of himself."

Jordan's jaw twitched as if he were holding back words. Eden brought his hand to her mouth. "I promise you, I'm not worrying about Noah. Okay?"

Evidently seeing he would get nothing further from her, he released her hand and rose to his feet. "Since you're not going to be able to work for at least a week, why don't we take a short trip. Before he left, Noah told me if anything came up, Gabe could handle things for a few days. Since Bennett's disappeared off his radar again, it looks like he won't be back anytime soon, we can take—"

Eden held up her hand. "Wait . . . wait . . . wait. Who said I wasn't going to work for a week?"

"The doctor just said—"

"Dr. Arnot has been telling me to take time off since I started working for LCR. He does that to everybody. I'll be up and about tomorrow. I may not be able to do any fieldwork, but I can at least—"

"Eden, I don't think you understood me. Not only did the doctor make that recommendation, I'm *ordering* you to take a week off."

"You can't order me."

"Oh yes I can. As interim director of LCR, I'm in charge of you. You either do it willingly or . . ."

"Or what?"

Jordan leaned over her, inches from her face. "Or you'll pay the consequences."

Snuggling deeper into her pillow, Eden couldn't resist a sensuous groan. "Oh yeah? That sounds interesting. What kind of consequences?"

"Get that sexy little smile off your face. Those kinds of consequences will have to wait until you're better."

Shifting on the pillow, she hid a grimace. She hated feeling like an invalid and hated being treated like one even more. Before she could utter the sex-filled innuendo she planned, a giant yawn came on. After she recovered, she eyed him from half-closed lids. "Let me take a little rest and I'll show you just how well I am."

"We'll see." Jordan kissed her forehead. "Get some sleep. I'll be in the living room if you need me."

"You don't have to stay. I'll be fine."

"I know I don't . . . and I won't be able to stay long. But I'll stay till you wake up. Okay?"

Jordan watched her nod sleepily and close her eyes. She was asleep within seconds. He slipped quietly from the room. Rubbing his gritty eyes, he slumped onto the sofa in the living room. He'd sat in the chair beside Eden's bed all night, watching her sleep and trying to figure out how he was going to deal with the fact that a woman he was becoming very fond of put herself in harm's way on a daily basis.

The decision to get involved with Samara had been an easy one. Though she sometimes dealt with dangerous people as a social worker, she rarely put herself into a position where her life might be endangered.

With Eden, it was what she was all about. The thrill of it . . . the intricacies of going undercover, the constant danger . . . the rush of adrenaline . . . It was a game to her.

Jordan well understood that mentality. He'd lived and thrived on it for years. But he'd made a decision last year to leave all that behind and settle down with a nice, normal woman. Eden didn't come close to fitting that description.

Was she a good person? Absolutely. She saved lives, rescued innocents, and often brought justice to people who might not get it otherwise. She had a good heart and a strong spirit. He admired her immensely. But she was far from normal. She'd much rather be up to her neck in kicking some bad guy's ass than she would, well . . . doing normal things. Whatever normal things were.

Jordan knew he was far from normal himself. He'd lived

too long in the shadows and undercover to be completely at ease in a cozy, comfortable relationship.

Eden knew what he'd been through, because she'd been there herself. She saw him as he was . . . not what he appeared to be. She knew what a dangerous, sometimes cruel person he could be and it didn't bother her in the least. In fact, he'd bet it attracted her to him even more.

They were so alike, they just made sense.

But how was he going to learn to live with the danger she put herself in? Because two things were becoming apparent. Eden needed the danger she faced every day to thrive and Jordan greatly feared he needed Eden simply to survive.

twenty

"You never said where you were taking me," Eden said.

Taking his eyes from the road for a second, he glanced over at her. "No, I didn't. Did I?"

Eden swallowed a laugh at the sexy, unrepentant grin. "Jordan, that's not fair. You practically kidnap me, forcing me to miss work, and now you won't even tell me where we're going."

"That's right."

"What about LCR? We can't just—"

"Noah is fully aware of the situation and in total support. I told him the only way I was going to keep you from working was to cart you off somewhere. Gabe's taking care of things at LCR. You've got nothing on your agenda other than to rest and relax." He picked up her hand and kissed it softly. "Why don't you lie back in your seat like a good girl? Take a nap, if you like. It'll be at least a couple of hours before we get there."

Eden tried for a glare, though she was pretty sure it wouldn't do any good.

She still couldn't believe he'd actually abducted her. She'd gotten up this morning, fully intending to head to the office. It had been three days since she'd been hurt. Yes, her arm still ached, but she was far from being incapacitated. When Jordan offered to drive her in, she'd jumped at the chance instead of grabbing a cab. She should have known he had something up his sleeve. Silly her, she assumed that since he hadn't mentioned again that she needed to take the entire week off, he'd changed his mind.

Eden knew from experience she should never underestimate a man like Jordan Montgomery.

She'd gotten into the car. He'd told her to buckle up and then they'd been on their way. She'd been looking out the window, daydreaming about Jordan and how she planned to seduce him tonight. It wasn't until they were almost out of the city that she realized they were miles past where they should have turned off.

After alternately laughing, yelling, silently pouting, then spewing what she'd thought were some pretty vile threats, she'd exhausted herself and Jordan hadn't relented.

Now, though she would never tell him, she was beginning to look forward to whatever he had planned. It was true she'd rarely taken a day off. She had no family and no real friends other than Noah . . . who also rarely took time off.

So she lay back onto her seat, watched the lush green countryside flash by, and reflected on the amazing things that had happened in the last month. After all these years of pretending she didn't care about Jordan, that he was a shadow in her past best left in the past, he had reappeared and thrown her life into turmoil. At first, she'd been so fearful he'd find out who she was, but when that fear passed, she'd just wanted to pretend any feelings for him disappeared long ago.

But then, like a blast of a furnace, she'd realized the attraction was still there and hotter than ever. She had never intended to start up a relationship with him, never intended it to go this far. And now that it had, she couldn't regret it.

The time had come to tell him the truth. She didn't know how he would take the news. Anger—that was a given. But would he be able to overcome that anger and realize what they'd created together the last few weeks?

Eden never anticipated she'd ever be able to have this kind of relationship with a man. And it wasn't just the physical, though that in itself was a miracle. A person doesn't go through the trauma she endured without having deep-seated emotional scars. While she was fortunate that she'd never been able to recall many of the things that had happened to her, she still remembered enough. Being vulnerable and intimate with a man was just something she'd come to accept as not being possible. Until Jordan, it hadn't even been desirable.

The physical pain she'd endured created almost as many emotional scars as if she'd remembered her attack. Going through numerous surgeries, counseling, physical therapy, and then months of recuperation can change a person enormously.

Eden always assumed she'd never be able to trust another person as she had before. Noah had come close, but there were still things she'd held back from him . . . feelings, emotions, fears.

With Jordan, she wanted to experience and share everything. She didn't . . . couldn't compare the feelings she'd had for him years ago to the ones she had today. That was a lifetime away and she was a different person.

So the time had come to spill her secrets. Could she tell him while they were here? Wherever they were going? She could wait till the time was right, maybe after they'd made love and were holding each other.

Surely she could make him understand. Surely to God he would forgive her deception.

He thought she was working on Devon's case, and she had been. But that file had been ready days ago. It clearly explained what happened to Devon, and detailed the last days of her life. After she admitted the truth, she would also tell him about the file and what she had planned to do. And ask for another sin to be forgiven.

"We're here."
Eden jerked awake, startled that she'd fallen asleep. She

blinked and then blinked again. She shook herself slightly, deciding she must still be woozy. What she saw through the window just didn't seem possible.

A castle . . . a fairy-tale castle . . . complete with turrets, balconies, and oh my, even a moat.

"Jordan, where in the world are we?"

"Fleurelle." He grinned as if he knew he had surprised the daylights out of her and was delighted to have done so. "The chateau belongs to the Rousseau family. I asked a few people, did some research on the Internet."

"But this can't be where we're staying."

"It most certainly is . . . all eighty rooms and ten servants."

Eden could feel her face flushing and her heart pounding. Pressure in the bridge of her nose and tiny prickles in her eyes told her she was in deep trouble. She bit the inside of her jaw to keep herself together. What this man had done—actually brought her to a castle. It astounded her, overwhelmed her.

A tender smile lifted his lips. He knew how touched she was and also knew her well enough to know she was embarrassed at such an emotional response. "Come on. Let's go explore."

He jumped out of the car and walked around to open her door. Eden stepped out onto the graveled drive stunned, disoriented . . . and completely and wholly in love with the wonderful, handsome man in front of her.

She leaned against the car, the castle forgotten. So there . . . she admitted it. She loved him, had never stopped loving him. Yes, she'd known her feelings were deep . . . but love . . . the everlasting, till-the-day-I-die kind . . . she hadn't expected.

"Hey, you need to sit down? You look like you could pass out any minute."

Eden blinked, bringing the present into focus. Jordan stood in front of her, concern furrowing his brow.

"No, I'm fine . . . just so surprised." She glanced over her shoulder at the huge hulking castle behind him, then leaned forward and kissed him softly. "This is the sweetest thing anyone's ever done for me."

His mouth kicking up into an "I've got a secret" grin, he held out his hand. "Just you wait. I plan to surprise you all weekend."

Lighthearted and so in love she could barely contain herself, she let him lead her to the entrance of the castle. "I can hardly wait."

A sigh of pure joy left her lips as Jordan led her inside the ancient, beautiful castle. All the old romantic dreams of yesterday were returning with jubilant glee. A fairy princess could never feel such enchantment.

"Do you like it?" Jordan's warm breath caressed her neck.

Eden whirled around to kiss him softly. "It's absolutely perfect."

An odd tenderness darkened his eyes and Eden knew a curious, fleeting moment of unreality. Her heart leaped like a jester giving the performance of his life at the knowledge before her. *He's in love with me.* The look disappeared as quickly as it came, but couldn't erase the knowing. And in that instant, she knew everything would be all right. Later today, maybe tonight, she would tell him the truth. She would withstand his anger and she would do all she could to soothe his hurt and disappointment in her. But ultimately, things would work out.

He loved her . . . she loved him. That was the way it was meant to be.

Everything was beginning to make sense. Jordan had come back into her life when the time was right for both of them. She'd felt years ago they were meant to be together, but after the horrific events of that day, she had forced herself to accept that her dreams had been a fantasy, made up by a romantic fool. Today, here and now, that romantic fool had returned and Eden embraced her with a wondrous welcome.

"Eden?"

Jordan stood before her, grasping her forearm. Concern once again darkened his face. And no wonder. She'd been standing, gazing around her like a zombie on Valium. "I'm fine . . . just in awe."

Eden caught a glimpse of Mrs. Hopkins, the middle-aged caretaker, who'd answered the door. Though her black dress and white apron looked somber and businesslike, the twinkle in her eyes told Eden she was enjoying their romantic moment.

"Could we look around a little?" Eden asked.

Mrs. Hopkins nodded. "Of course. I'll have your bags carried to your room. It's on the third floor, second door to the left." She smiled up at Jordan and no doubt took pleasure in the view, as any sane woman would. "You're welcome to wander around on your own or I can have one of the servants take you round."

Jordan grabbed Eden's hand and pulled her across the giant hallway toward an enormous double door. "I think we'll just wander at our own pace." He flashed a grin Eden knew would turn Mrs. Hopkins's heart over. Lord knows it did hers. "If we get lost, we'll give a shout-out."

Without waiting for a reply, Jordan led her inside the door and clicked it shut. Eden barely had a second to notice the room was a huge library, filled from floor to ceiling with books. Before she could speak, Jordan pulled her into his arms and slammed his mouth down on hers.

He swallowed her moan of delight, his tongue plunging in over and over as if he couldn't stop, and Eden didn't want him to stop. Cupping her hands over his head, her fingers weaved into his thick hair. When she felt him pulling her dress up over her hips and kneading her ass, she pulled slightly away. Gasping against his mouth, she whispered, "What are you doing?"

Jordan dropped his hands and though Eden knew a moment of disappointment, she knew they couldn't make love here. There was no telling who might walk in the door. Her pounding heart was slowly heading toward normal when she noticed Jordan hadn't answered her question.

Incredulous and so much in love she could hardly speak, she watched as he unbuttoned his shirt and pulled it off. "What—Jordan, what are you doing?"

Eyes glittering hot with desire and need, Jordan reached for the hem of her dress and with magician-like speed, lifted it over her head. "I rented the entire castle, sweetheart. All eighty rooms. No one, without being asked to, will interrupt us."

Standing in heels, lavender thong, and barely there bra, in the middle of an unfamiliar location, might not be the norm for her, but Eden recovered quickly and got into the spirit of the moment. Slipping off her shoes, she shimmied out of her panties and then dropped her bra on the floor. She stood before him, proud of the dark, powerful hunger flashing in his eyes and prouder still of the incredible lust that swept through her body.

Going to her knees, Eden gazed adoringly up at the man who'd stolen her heart twice in a lifetime. "We've got seventy-nine rooms left. . . . We'd better get started." Slowly and with delicious intent, she unzipped his pants.

Curled up on a cushioned window seat, Eden gazed out over the lush green pasture below and watched a family of squirrels chase one another. She didn't want to move from this spot. The last two days had been the most glorious and fulfilling of her life. Though they hadn't made love in all eighty rooms and were due to leave tomorrow, Eden thought they'd definitely made a decent showing— or indecent, as the case may be.

They'd woken late this morning and had a leisurely

breakfast. Jordan went out for a quick run, but she'd pleaded laziness. She just wanted to stay inside and pretend the world didn't exist . . . just for a little longer.

The days had been so idyllic, her determination that Jordan should know the truth had wavered under the incredible bubble of happiness she'd cocooned herself within. Every moment she whispered to herself, "Just one more moment." Tomorrow, they would leave and that time would arrive no matter how much she wanted to hold it off. Jordan had done nothing to deserve the lies she'd told him. Whether he would want to still be with her after he learned the truth was up in the air, but if they were to have any kind of future together, she had to tell him.

Her cellphone jingled beside her and Eden didn't bother to look at the display as she held it to her ear.

"You all better now?"

Her mouth lifted up in a small smile at Noah's gruff concern. "Much better, thank you. Any luck on Bennett?"

"A little, but no location yet."

"You'll find him, Noah."

"I know it." His hard tone indicated cold determination.

"I appreciate you letting Jordan take me away. It was exactly what I needed."

"About damn time you took some time off. Too bad you had to get hurt to do it, though."

"Yeah, that wasn't fun, but the rest has been marvelous." Despite her reluctance to share her rediscovered love for Jordan with the world, Eden couldn't keep the truth from the man who'd made it all possible. "Thank you for bringing him back into my life. I owe you so much."

There was a long pause before Noah's somewhat cautious voice asked, "So you've settled your differences?"

"If you mean, have I told him the truth yet, then no, not yet. I'm going to tell him before we leave. I've put it off far too long. If there's any hope for a future for us, I've got to come clean."

"What do you mean, a future?"

Eden laughed softly. "Don't worry. You're not losing me as an employee. I'm almost certain Jordan will want to stay on and work for you. And I'm sure you—"

"Eden, are you—? Shit. Are you involved with Jordan?"

She jerked at the snarl in his voice. Why would he be upset about her and Jordan getting together? Hell, he was the one who'd brought him back into her life.

"What's wrong with that?"

Noah blew out a long sigh. "I need to talk to Jordan. I tried calling his cell and didn't get an answer. Is he there?"

The amusing incident from yesterday flashed into her mind. She and Jordan had gone for a canoe ride. In the middle of the lake, she'd said something that had caused him to kiss her. Before she knew it, they were both standing, locked in a passionate embrace, and then, somehow, the boat tipped. Eden had managed to hang on, but Jordan had fallen, submerging himself and his cellphone into the murky water. Eden had laughed until she cried, watching the man she loved curse a blue streak with green algae hanging from his hair. Suddenly that image no longer made her smile.

"No, he's not here and his cellphone isn't working. Now, tell me why you don't think it's a good idea that Jordan and I are together."

"I'd rather talk to Jordan first."

Her anger rose. "Well, you've got me instead, so deal with it. Why aren't Jordan and I a good idea?"

"Has he given you any indication that he's thinking anything permanent with you?"

"No, but . . ." Eden closed her eyes and took in a calming breath. Just because he hadn't said he loved her didn't mean it wasn't so. After all, she hadn't said the words, either. They'd both been hurt in the past. It was only normal they would be reticent to share their feelings. But there was obviously a reason for Noah's concern and she'd damn well dig it out of him.

"No, he hasn't. Stop being so damn evasive and tell me what's wrong."

Another long sigh, this time sounding very ragged. "When Jordan first came to see me, he told me one of the reasons he wanted to finally come to a resolution about Devon was because he'd quit his job and was getting married. He wanted to start fresh . . . with nothing hanging over his head." Noah's voice softened though his words barely registered. "I wanted you to be able to put your past behind you, not start an affair with him."

Eden closed the phone, ending the call, uncaring that Noah continued to speak. The phone rang immediately. She ignored it. What he said couldn't be true. Jordan would have told her. He wouldn't have lied to her . . . led her on.

Why not? You've lied and led him on. Why shouldn't he do the same to you?

Because he's a better person than I am, her heart screamed. He wouldn't do this to me. He wouldn't. . . . I know he wouldn't.

What promises had he made? None. They'd made love for hours, held each other, fell asleep in each other's arms. He'd had numerous opportunities to tell her he loved her, that he wanted a future with her. He'd done neither of those things. Given her no indication that his feelings went deeper than desire and maybe affection.

And Noah wouldn't lie to her. Perhaps not always the kindest person, still, he wasn't maliciously cruel.

She suddenly remembered Jordan's response when Noah asked him to take his place for a while. He said he needed to check with some people. Eden remembered wondering at the time who he would check with. Now she knew. He'd checked with his fiancée.

And he'd been passing time with her. He had a job to do here, why not make it more fun by having a fuck partner, too.

How stupid could one woman be in a lifetime?

In a flurry of mindless horror, Eden jumped up from the window seat and began to pack. They had planned on leaving tomorrow . . . she'd make sure they left today. She would scream at him, demand he tell her why he'd led her on. Demand to know why he didn't love her. . . . What was wrong with her?

She was halfway through stuffing her bags, unaware that tears poured down her face, when she stopped, pulled to a standstill by a sudden thought. Did Jordan have to know how he had hurt her . . . humiliated her . . . destroyed her again?

Did she want to live that agony of seven years ago all over again? Every organ and cell within her body screamed a resounding "No!" She wouldn't survive it this time . . . the pain . . . the anguish. . . . She wouldn't be able to live through it again.

With a calm finality, Eden unpacked what she'd packed. She'd been acting a role for most of her adult life, pretending to be someone else. She would do that with Jordan, as she had when he'd first arrived at LCR. But she would do it even more now. Nothing would make her lose her poise. She could be the cool, self-confident sophisticate he seemed to think she was. Sex for the sake of sex—yes, she could do that.

Tomorrow, when they returned to Paris, she would present Devon's file to him. Had she lied to herself that he'd ever cared what happened to Devon? Was it what she'd suspected in the beginning? Devon Winters's disappearance was a mystery to be solved and nothing more? Had she given Jordan attributes he didn't possess simply because, romantic fool that she was, she wanted to believe the very best of him? Was he, quite simply, just a man . . .

and not even a particularly good man? Once again she'd turned him into a hero; once again he'd disappointed her.

Fine. She'd learned her lesson—her final lesson. Tomorrow the mystery would be solved. Jordan could at last put Devon's disappearance behind him and move on.

Noah would be returning soon. Jordan could be on his way, could get back to his fiancée and his nice, normal life.

And Eden would return to the insulated, isolated world she had created for herself.

twenty-one

"You sure you're feeling okay tonight?"

An odd little frown cracked the cool marble of an unnaturally composed face. "Of course, I'm fine."

Well, there he had it. Three fines, one distinctly fake laugh, and a kiss that would freeze the ass off a penguin. What the hell was wrong with her? He'd always put Eden in a category by herself. One that didn't include being temperamental or moody. When she was angry, she let it show.

When he'd first met her, he had to dig deep to see beyond the beautiful mask she showed the world, but in the last few weeks, that mask had disappeared. She'd been open, loving, tender . . . everything a man could want in a woman.

Tonight, she was just as beautiful, but something was missing. Vitality . . . life. Had he done or said something earlier?

At that thought, Jordan stopped himself in disgust. This had been another reason he'd avoided serious relationships. Women. Who could understand them?

"Do you want more wine?"

She shook her head and offered him another cool smile. "Honestly, if you don't mind, I think I'll call it a night." With those words and no explanation, she rose to her feet and walked away.

Jordan stood and threw his napkin on the table in disgust. This night sure as hell hadn't turned out the way he'd planned. When had anything with Eden gone the way he planned?

He'd brought her here for rest . . . but also seduction. Instead, he'd been the one seduced . . . spellbound, mesmerized, and ready for a commitment.

Using the excuse of taking a run this morning, he had gone to a nearby jewelry store one of the servants told him about. He'd found the perfect two-carat diamond ring. It would look beautiful on Eden's slender hand . . . her left hand.

Now, for whatever reason, she was treating him as though he had the plague.

Jordan's long legs ate up the stairway three steps at a time. He wanted an explanation. Maybe her arm was hurting her. Whatever it was, they needed to get it settled because he had every intention of proposing tonight.

Eden whirled around when Jordan stomped into the room. She knew he was angry and confused. She'd done a lousy job of hiding her feelings. All of her training had deserted her. There was no poise, no calm, no self-confidence. She was a woman betrayed by the man she loved, and she couldn't seem to get past that and be anything else.

"Okay Eden, out with it."

She blinked up at him warily. He was ready to fight and she wasn't sure she could win against a gnat in her overemotional condition. She tried for a cool look. "I beg your pardon?"

"Don't play games with me. What the hell's wrong with you? Ever since this morning, when I came back from my run, you've acted as if I had a disease you didn't want to catch."

Knowing if she continued to look at him, she'd spill her guts, she turned her back on him. "Don't be ridiculous. I just—"

A hard hand grasped her upper arm and pulled her around to face him. Without meaning to, Eden cried out. Her arm was healing, but still sore. Jordan inadvertently grabbed the most sensitive part.

"Shit . . . Are you okay?"

She burst into tears. Of all the stupid, asinine, completely unpredictable things she could do, Eden found herself blubbering like a two-year-old.

Warm arms wrapped around her. "Shh. It's okay. I'm sorry I hurt you." He continued his soft monologue, though Eden only heard parts of it. Her loud sobs overwhelmed his voice.

She was dimly aware that Jordan had picked her up and was laying her on the bed. Eden tried to turn away from him, but he held both her shoulders, giving her no opportunity to escape.

"Let me take a look at your arm. Then we're going to talk."

She kept her eyes closed, to ward off tears, but mostly because she had humiliated herself. She didn't break down like that, and had always been somewhat disdainful of women who allowed their emotions to bubble up and explode. Now she had joined those ranks of overemotional women, and on top of everything else, she probably looked like crap.

She felt fingers probing gently at her tender flesh. It hurt a little, but Eden refused to show any more weakness. Besides, the fault had been hers as much as his. She knew not to turn her back on a tiger. She'd reacted with pure panic.

"The skin's not broken. I must have hit a tender spot. I'm sorry."

Eden shook her head and forced herself to open her eyes. He looked so gentle, so concerned, so incredibly loving. How could he be a cheater? How could he dishonor his promise to his fiancée?

Oh God, how can I bear to let him go?

"Eden, talk to me. Tell me what's happened. . . . What's wrong?"

"Devon's dead." The words sprang from her mouth without will or purpose. They were just there.

Jordan's eyes widened and blinked as if not quite believing what he heard. "How do you know?" His hoarse whisper grated across her heart.

Eden struggled to sit up, feeling too vulnerable to talk while on her back. Jordan pulled away from her and watched as she sat up in bed. Crossing her legs in front of her and hugging her arms tight around them, Eden did what she'd done so well for the past seven years. She lied.

"While you were gone, I got a call from my source in D.C. He was able to track down the last town she went to. After she left D.C., she lived in at least three different small towns we know of. The last one, she was working as a waitress. There was a robbery. . . . She was killed."

While she'd been talking, Jordan moved away from her and was now slumped in a chair several feet away. Eden breathed deeply, finally feeling a small semblance of control. When he was close, she never knew what she would say, how she would react. That was one of the reasons she'd blurted out the news. Another reason had been much simpler but even more selfish. She simply wanted to take his attention off her and put it somewhere else.

It worked, but not the way she'd hoped. Jordan's tanned, healthy complexion was pale, his eyes empty, tortured, like a man who'd just received devastating news. And she'd delivered that news with all the sensitivity of a short-order cook announcing the daily specials at a diner.

"I'm sorry, Jordan. I know you'd hoped for a better outcome. I wish—"

"Where is she buried?"

"Wha . . . what?"

"I want to see where she's buried . . . talk to the people who were with her the last hours of her life. Who were they, did they know her well, was she lonely? I have to see for myself what her last days were like."

"Jordan, I'm not sure . . . the people who spoke to my source . . . they wanted to keep their privacy . . . I'm not sure I'll—"

He stood and jerked open the closet door. "Then I'll go there myself and convince them to talk to me."

Panic and guilt zoomed through her. "What are you doing?"

"I'm packing. I need to get back to the States."

"Wait . . . it's late. We'll leave early in the morning. There's no need to leave tonight. The drive's too long."

Jordan threw his duffel bag on the floor with a disgusted sigh. "You're right." He glanced at his watch. "I'll go call the airlines and book my flight for tomorrow night. That way I'll be able to get you back home, take a look at your files, and then take off."

The door slammed behind him before she knew he was even leaving the room.

Eden almost fell off the bed, in complete shock at what had just occurred. Jordan hadn't acted the way she'd anticipated. He acted as if he really cared . . . as she'd thought before Noah delivered the devastating news that Jordan was engaged.

God, what had she done?

The answer twisted her stomach with acidic truth. She'd let her hurt and betrayal overcome her common sense, and her decency.

And now what was she going to do? He wanted to talk to the people she'd talked with. She hadn't really talked with anyone. Oh, she had some sources she could put together quickly if she needed to, but nothing to the magnitude of producing a burial site and people who'd worked with her and known her. She had names of eyewitnesses, but they weren't real people. Even when she'd thought

Jordan cared, she never thought he'd want to go so far as to talk to anyone. She stupidly believed he would take it at face value and let it go.

What was she going to do? If she told him she'd lied and Devon wasn't dead, he would hate her. If she went even further and confessed that she was Devon, he would hate her even more.

And if she just let him believe the lie, he'd go to the States and realize she lied. It would take days to come up with the tangible proof Jordan insisted he needed to see.

No matter what she did, she was caught in a lie . . . and had no one to blame but herself.

Eden had never known a self-loathing as she did right now.

Wearier than she'd ever been before, she shuffled to the bathroom. After her bout of tears, her eyes stung as if filled with sand. She needed to get her contacts out and give her eyes a rest. Avoiding her reflection, she removed her lenses. Her shame was so immense, she couldn't bear to see the guilt and ridicule in her face.

After brushing her teeth, she slipped into a nightgown and fell into bed. How funny that this night started with her hating Jordan for deceiving her about being engaged. And now, only hours later, that particular sin no longer seemed like such a terrible crime. He'd never promised her anything, had given no real indication he wanted anything but a good time and mind blowing sex. She was the one who'd created this fairy-tale world . . . just as she had once before.

No matter what Jordan had or hadn't done, he didn't deserve what she'd done to him.

Something stilled inside her. There was no hope for her and Jordan—that much was evident. But there was still time to redeem herself . . . still time to be a better person. Though it would be like filleting the skin from her bones, she vowed that when he returned, she would tell him everything.

Minutes or hours passed. Eden didn't know how long. She felt a slight bounce to the bed, then a hand swept up her thigh, caressing her hip . . . her stomach.

"Mmm. Jordan," she whispered in a sleep-fogged voice.

Hot breath caressed her as his lips trailed down the side of her face, before coming to rest on her mouth. "Let me love you, Eden."

Shutting down her conscience, Eden went with her emotions. She opened her mouth, inviting his kiss. This was her last chance, her only chance to have him . . . one last chance to show him how much he meant to her. One last chance to be his.

Jordan groaned when her hand swept down his chest. She felt his stomach clench when she caressed his abdomen, seeking the hot male part of him she craved. Wrapping her hand around as much as she could, she pumped him lovingly.

"Eden, baby . . . I have to be inside you right now."

No thought of denying him entered her mind. Eden spread her legs wide, allowing Jordan to settle between them. He gave her no warning, but surged inside her fully. Though she wasn't quite ready for him, she shifted and squirmed, working to allow him deeper, wanting him inside her, as deep as he could go and to stay forever.

Jordan gave her a few seconds to get more comfortable and then began a long hard ride. She met every thrust with an upward surge . . . allowing him to pound into her . . . rejoicing in the heat . . . the sensation . . . the sheer power of his body working over hers.

He rose to his knees and spread her legs even wider; hooking her legs over his arms, he thrust deeper, harder. Eden opened her eyes . . . startled that the room was so bright. Jordan must have turned on a light. She could see his face . . . his beautiful, wholly masculine face staring down at her with the darkly intent expression of supreme male conquering his female. Feral, wild, and delicious.

They stared at each other for endless seconds. Both seemingly mesmerized by the intensity of the moment, the amazing primal connection . . . male to female . . . mate to mate.

Surge, plunge, retreat . . . over and then over again.

Her climax near, Jordan pressed down harder, giving her the freedom of riding his shaft . . . milking him and allowing the sweet, sweet promise of release all the way to the culmination of a fiery, explosive end.

Jordan reached his climax seconds later, pounding into her forcefully . . . wonderfully and completely.

At last, both breathing with heavy pants, they lay in each other's arms. Though she wanted to wait, to savor and exploit every second, she couldn't. Trembling for a new reason, she whispered hoarsely, "Jordan, I—"

The deep, even breaths in her ear told her he was already asleep.

She lay there till dawn, not wanting to sleep and miss a moment. Unchecked tears fell down her face as she savored this last time in the arms of the man she had loved forever . . . would always love.

Hours later, Eden woke . . . surprised she'd slept . . . angry she'd slept.

The sound of the shower running in the bathroom alerted her that Jordan was up, already getting ready. For endless seconds she lay there, sadness and regret pressing deep. When the water stopped, she forced her body to move. There was another bathroom just down the hallway, and she'd made use of it a couple of times. If she could get cleaned up, feel refreshed and halfway human, she would face Jordan with much more self-assurance than she felt right now.

As water beat down upon her, she rehearsed what she would say. The reasons for her lies at the beginning were valid. Hopefully she could make him understand that. But later, when she had numerous opportunities, there were no excuses. And last night, blurting out Devon was dead. Nausea stirred in her gut.

Stepping out of the shower, she dried quickly and threw on her clothes. The need to get the words out was suddenly a compulsion. She opened the door to their bedroom to see Jordan zipping her suitcase.

Eyes solemn and searching, his expression was impossible to read. "I figured since I packed them for you, you wouldn't mind if I repacked."

She shook her head and offered him a tight smile, so tongue-tied she couldn't form a coherent word, much less the full and complicated truth of her deception.

He jerked his head over to the small table in the corner where they'd shared so many of their meals the last few days. "Coffee and croissants." He picked up the bags. "I'll be back in a minute."

He walked out the door and she didn't try to stop him. *I'll tell him in the car. We have a three-hour drive ahead of us . . . surely by the time we reach the city, I'll be able to come up with the right words to make him understand.*

Four hours later, Eden opened the door to her apartment, Jordan following her. They'd said almost nothing to each other on the way home. She'd tried—honestly she had. But Jordan cut her off so many times with "Not now . . . later" or "I don't feel like talking right now," she'd given up.

Eden knew she could have blurted it out as she had last night, but she couldn't do that to him again. One thing was certain. They were here now and she wouldn't let him leave until she told him the full truth.

"Jordan, we really need to talk."

"Get me the file."

"Wait . . . please."

"The file. Now."

She'd never heard his voice so hard, almost cruel. A chill rushed through her veins, freezing everything in its path. Yes she had. Seven years ago, Jordan had sounded just like that.

Her movements jerky and uncoordinated, she went to her desk and pulled the file she'd prepared weeks ago. Feeling as though wet cement pulled at her feet, she crossed the room and handed it to him.

"Before you read it, I need to tell you—" Eden stood frozen in place as she watched him turn and stalk out the door without a word.

Fool me once, shame on you. Fool me twice, shame on me. And what a shame he was such a stupid fool. Things started clicking into place almost immediately and he'd ignored every damn one of them.

Jordan took one last look at the file Eden had given him and flung it across the room. He didn't care what happened to it. All of it, every word was a lie. He'd gone through it twice. It was good . . . damn good. A damn good fake.

How the hell had he let it happen again? A man who'd relied on subterfuge his entire life had been screwed twice by the same woman. It'd be damn funny if he didn't feel like such an idiot.

He shouldn't be angry with her. She'd seen her mark . . . saw a chance to get back at him and she had . . . with a vengeance.

She was good, he had to give her that. Noah, too. He had known all along . . . went along with it. For all he knew, they called each other and laughed about what a supreme sucker he was.

Clues that should have been apparent sprang to his mind one by evil one. The tattoo on her shoulder. How many people had a vibrant blue hummingbird on their right shoulder? He'd asked her about it once and she lied convincingly that she'd done it in a fit of whimsy a couple of years ago after seeing a documentary on hummingbirds.

Her animosity when he first met her, when she'd had no reason to dislike him. The conversation he'd heard between Dr. Arnot and his assistant that she didn't need to have more surgeries. Just how many had she had to make her look like a completely different person?

Then later, when the doctor came to see her, she admitted she was twenty-eight, Devon's age.

Last night, the final piece fit into place. He'd walked into the bedroom, ready to make love to her. Needing solace and support. For whatever reason, something . . . maybe his subconscious since his conscious mind sure as shit hadn't been working right . . . told him to turn on the light. When he'd been deep inside her, he looked down, and there were her eyes . . . Devon's eyes. He'd stared at pictures of them for seven years. He knew them better than he knew his own.

He had waited to say anything to her. Waited to see just how far she would go with her lies. The fake file she'd given him told him—she had gone all the way.

Now the question was, what was he going to do about it? She had committed no crime that he knew of. She'd just deceived and lied to him as easily as some people walk across the street. Lying was her job. She'd been a liar seven years ago. Nothing had changed except that she'd gotten much better at it.

He could just leave, take the flight back tonight as he planned. He didn't owe LCR a thing. In fact, Noah owed him . . . several thousand dollars, in fact.

Jordan poured another drink. The more he drank, the angrier he became. It was one thing to be lied to once, but to do it again . . . for months? Why? For what purpose? Revenge? The sheer fun of fucking someone over?

Well, there was only one way to find out. He slammed his drink down on the table, grabbed his keys, and the file of lies from the floor.

This time, no matter what he had to do, he would get the truth.

twenty-two

Sweat poured from every pore as Eden increased the speed of the treadmill, raising the incline to its highest level. She couldn't outrun her demons, but was going to do her damnedest. With every pound of her foot, *liar* throbbed inside her head. She'd lied about everything. That's all she was . . . all she was good for . . . lying.

Why couldn't she have just said the words? She'd had no problems last night blurting out that Devon was dead. Truth should be even more simple. But it wasn't. Once Jordan knew everything, he would hate her. The respect and affection she'd seen in his eyes would disappear.

When had she become such a coward?

Gasping and heaving with exertion, she looked at the display board. Seventy-five minutes at full speed. If she didn't stop now, she would pass out. Not that she would really mind . . . Oblivion sounded like heaven. But as much as she would have liked that, she refused to even allow herself that sweet, temporary release.

Her trembling hand punched the stop button. The treadmill made an abrupt halt, almost knocking her off her feet. Weak legs wobbling, she grabbed the handle to steady herself.

Stepping from treadmill, she turned to the bar, where she'd put her water bottle. Her pounding heart jumped toward her throat. A small, shocked scream left her mouth. Jordan stood beside the bar, holding the water in one hand . . . Devon's file in the other.

"You startled me. I didn't hear you come in. I—"

"Hard workout?"

Alarm flashed through her. A dangerous light burned in his eyes. His face held a dark mercilessness she'd never seen in him before. Heart pounding with an uneasy fear, she held out her hand for her water bottle. After such an intensive workout she was dehydrated, desperate for water.

Without changing his expression, Jordan held the bottle over his head, out of her reach.

"What are you doing? I'm dying of thirst."

"Oh, I don't think so. In fact, I'd call that a lie. Wouldn't you?"

"What the hell are you talking about?"

"I think you know." Without a hint of warning, Jordan lunged, twisted her around, and slammed her down on the mat.

In the past few weeks, she and Jordan had wrestled several times, practicing self-defense moves or just in sexual play. He had never intentionally hurt her. Now, with him pressing down hard, her cheek flat against the mat, what breath she'd been able to catch completely left her body.

When he heard her choking, he eased up slightly. "Breathe. I don't want this to be over so soon." His tone sounded flat, bored, as if he really didn't care if she died . . . but would rather not be bothered by the inconvenience.

He knew . . . of course he knew. When he'd left this afternoon, she'd seen something in his eyes. She tried to tell herself there was no way he could have figured it out, but deep down, she'd known.

Wheezing like an asthmatic, Eden gratefully drew in deep breaths. She'd depleted most of her energy with her workout. Her arms and legs felt like wet noodles, but she was a trained professional. She'd been in tighter spots before. She could handle Jordan.

Jordan twisted her arms behind her back. "Get up. You smell like a dead cat."

A bitter smile twisted her lips. "Sorry. If you'd warned me you were going to attack, I would have showered first."

Jordan chuckled as he pulled her to her feet, her arms still held in a tight, harsh grip. Eden stooped low and bucked up to throw him off, but he wouldn't budge. His hands pulled tighter. She bit back a cry. God, would he actually break her arm?

"Okay, I'm up. What is it you want?"

"Just a nice chat. That's all. Come on over here and sit where I can see you."

He pushed her toward a chair against the wall. Thinking he would let her go so she could sit down, he surprised her when she heard the click of handcuffs.

"What the hell are you doing?"

"Just making sure I have your undivided attention. You did say you wanted to talk to me earlier, didn't you? Well, here I am." He shoved her to the chair, turned her around, and pushed her down in it.

Hands shackled behind her, she jumped to her feet and rushed him. With the insulting effortlessness of the truly fit, Jordan shoved her back down. Once again surprising her, he pulled plastic ties from his back pocket and bound her legs to the chair.

"There darling . . . all comfy?"

"Jordan, please . . . you don't have to do this. I'll talk to you. I *want* to talk to you."

"Really?" He pulled up another chair, straddled it, and leaned his forearms on the top. Dark eyes glittering with pure fury, his mouth twisted in a sneer. "Then let's chat. What was it you wanted to talk about?"

Eden struggled against her restraints. She couldn't believe it had come to this. After all her agonizing about telling him the truth, and her decision to do just that,

Jordan had literally tied her up and was making her talk. If not so close to breaking down, she would be laughing.

He raised a mocking hand to his ear. "I don't hear anything."

Eden drew a shuddering breath, determined to keep it together. "I'm sorry. I was going to tell you . . . really I was. But . . ."

"But what? Did it slip your mind? Were you waiting till you got tired of screwing me? Was this just a sick joke you and Noah cooked up?"

"No! It wasn't anything like that. Noah didn't . . . He said . . ."

God, how could she explain? Eden blinked as Jordan's features blurred. Her heart pounded hard against her chest, roaring sounded in her head. She was losing control again, just like before. Only this time, it was worse . . . so much worse. Because not only did she deserve his censure and wrath—she loved him a thousand times more.

"Jordan . . . please believe me. I didn't mean to—"

"What Eden? Oops. Now that the cat's out of the bag, shouldn't I just call you Devon?" He shook his head slowly as a humorless laugh burst from him. "You know, you are quite the piece of work. It wasn't enough you lied seven years ago. Disappear for years, not caring that hundreds of people are looking for you, spending enormous amounts of time and money to find you. You obviously landed on your feet since you were able to achieve an entirely new face. Though I do think that's carrying lying just a bit too far.

"But Eden—oops, I mean Devon—the sheer beauty of it all is, you landed in a job tailor-made for you. You lie for a living. How fucking great is that? Alise would be proud she raised a lying, deceitful bitch in her own image."

Trussed up like a game animal, she had no control over her body as it began to shake. "Shut up . . . just shut up. You don't know anything. You know nothing about—"

"You got that right. I don't know anything. Because you were too busy enjoying your lies. But this . . ." He raised the file in his hand. "Gotta hand it to you, babe. This is priceless. You really ought to write fiction for a living. I especially loved the dramatic climax when Devon jumped in front of a bullet to protect a pregnant mother. Such a sad end for a scheming little liar."

She closed her eyes. That actually happened to her a few years back. How stupid to put truth in fiction.

"I'm only glad Henry is dead so he can't see what you've become."

Oh God . . . Henry. It took every ounce of willpower not to just topple over. She'd never kept tabs on her mother or Henry after she'd recovered. That one run-in with her mother had been enough to convince her to leave everything behind. Even the man she loved as a father. And now she would never get the chance to tell him how grateful she was, how much she'd loved him for protecting her, loving her as a real father.

"How . . . how did Henry die?"

"Don't pretend you care, Devon. You haven't cared for seven years."

Everything stilled. Hearing about Henry damaged something inside her . . . maybe even killed it for good. Maybe she realized this was it. After taking blow after blow, she just couldn't hurt any more than this. At some point, the pain just stopped. Nothing remained but a mindless, numbing void, impervious to any kind of feeling. Yes, this was much better.

"Come on, Devon, you can do better than that. Let me hear how you loved Henry, how you missed him. Let me hear that every second you were lying to your family, you hated it.

"Devon?" She felt a small slap on her face, but it couldn't penetrate the numbness. "Come on, Devon. . . . Snap out of it. You said you wanted to talk. Let's talk."

Though she knew Jordan's words continued, she stopped listening. She knew he taunted her for a few minutes and then, as if he knew she was at her limit, she felt the loosening of the restraints on her legs . . . then he unlocked the cuffs on her hands.

She remained seated, staring at nothing. Jordan stood in front of her, but for some reason she didn't really see him. What an odd, dreamy, almost pleasant feeling. The water bottle pressed against her lips. She took a small sip, and then another.

"Okay, Devon. You've convinced me you didn't know about Henry. Now, let's cut the crap and get to the rest of the story. Where did you go? Did you even care—"

"Shut up." Eden surged to her feet, knocking the chair out of the way. She backed up against the wall, her fingers pressed against the surface so hard, they went numb. On the verge of everything within her collapsing at his feet, she had just enough fire left to convince him to leave. Then she would fall apart . . . but not before then. By God, Jordan Montgomery had seen the very worst of her for the last time.

And he had seen her for the last time.

Jordan chuckled as if he'd been expecting her response. "That's my girl. Now—"

"Leave. There's nothing else to say to you. You know who I am. You know Devon's not dead. What more do you need to know?"

"How about why?"

Her mouth moved up into a bitter, twisted smile. He wanted to believe she was a cold, heartless bitch who cared about no one but herself and could lie without any kind of remorse? That's exactly what he was going to get.

"Because I could, Jordan. I'm a good liar and I've made a boatload of money doing it. So there's your truth. Happy now?"

"That's all you are . . . all you've ever been . . . a liar. Getting paid for it just makes you a whore."

Refusing to utter another word, in her defense or otherwise, she pushed off the wall and forced her wobbly legs to walk around him. Head high, she marched through her apartment into her bedroom and closed the door. A few seconds later, she heard a door slam. He was gone.

Cold shivers attacked. Shock, probably. She blinked in confusion. What did you do for shock? Should know the answer . . . warmth. She needed to get warm. Shaking so hard she could barely function, she ripped and tore at her clothes. Nude, she stumbled to the bathroom, turned the shower to the hottest setting, sat down on the shower floor, and allowed herself hot, steamy comfort and oblivion.

Sometime later, she awoke, still on the floor of the shower, and found herself looking up into Noah's furious face.

"What happened?"

"What are you doing here?" She winced at the rough, raspy sound of her voice.

"You're soaking wet. You're going to catch pneumonia."

Using curse words she didn't even know he knew, Noah wrapped a thick towel around her and carried her to the bed. He sat her down and, while Eden sat shivering, dried her hair and body. In another life, another time, she'd be at least a little embarrassed. As long as she and Noah had known each other, he had never seen her nude. Now she really didn't care. Nothing mattered. Nothing. No one.

She must have fallen asleep, because Noah was shaking her again. "Eden. Dammit . . . Wake up and tell me what the hell happened."

She blinked up at Noah. "You really need to stop cursing." Then she collapsed in his arms.

Noah held her as harsh, dry sobs tore through her body with the force of a cyclone. He whispered soothing words she didn't really hear but found comfort in anyway. Finally, when she was exhausted and unable to move a muscle from fatigue, Noah pulled back the covers and put her in bed.

When she felt an unexpected kiss to her forehead, her eyes flickered open. What she saw frightened her. His eyes raging with a dark purpose, he stood and started for the door.

"Leave him alone, Noah. It's not his fault."

"Stop protecting him, Eden. Jordan's a big boy. I'm not going to give him anything he doesn't deserve."

"Don't hurt him."

Noah shook his head sadly. "You're hopeless." And with those words he walked out, leaving Eden to wonder what exactly he would do to Jordan. Noah and Jordan were about the same size . . . well matched in skill also.

Her eyes drifted shut. Noah wouldn't hurt Jordan, and Jordan wouldn't hurt Noah, not really. Other than that, she just couldn't think about it anymore. With a soft sigh, she once again found the sweet oblivion she so desperately wanted.

Feet propped up on Noah's shiny desk, Jordan glared as McCall stormed into the office. "Welcome home," he growled sarcastically.

McCall shot a glare of fury at him, as though royally pissed. What the hell right did he have to be angry? Jordan was the one who'd been lied to and deceived.

Bypassing him with barely a glance, McCall growled, "Follow me."

Jordan watched as the other man pushed aside a large potted plant. He pressed a button beneath it and the wall in front of him slid open. When McCall walked inside, Jordan got to his feet and followed him. What was the prick up to now?

Surveying the large room filled with free weights, machines, and exercise mats, Jordan blew out a low whistle. "And I thought Eden or should I say Devon's gym was nice. You don't have as much equipment, but—" He stopped abruptly when he observed that the other man appeared to be stripping. "Uh, you want to tell me why you're taking your shirt off? I don't want to offend your sensitive ego, but you're really not my type. Besides, I think I've been screwed enough by you and Devon for a lifetime."

"Trust me, that's the last thing I'd want."

Jordan snorted. "Trust you? Man, you gotta be kidding."

Jordan stood at the door, his arms crossed in a deceptively nonchalant pose, and watched McCall take off his shirt, then his shoes and socks.

"If you're not feeling amorous . . . I'm assuming you're stripping for another good reason?"

"I don't want to get *your* blood on my shirt."

Jordan straightened slowly. Now that sounded like an enticing proposition. "That's one offer I simply can't refuse." With those words, Jordan slipped off his own shoes and socks and removed his shirt.

Noah strode over to the mat and turned toward him. Fury engulfed Jordan at the glint of cold amusement in McCall's eyes. He fully intended to wipe that smug expression off his face and, while he was at it, looked forward to knocking out a few of his perfect teeth.

The men circled each other warily, both looking for weak, vulnerable spots to target first.

Jordan struck first. Catching his opponent off guard, he slammed a hard fist into his jaw. McCall gave a quick shake of his head and grinned. "Now I'm awake."

On the next punch Jordan threw, Noah blocked him, then shot an upper cut to Jordan's chin. The pain startled him as blood spurted from his mouth. The evil grin on

McCall's face forced the pain away as Jordan slammed a fist into his nose.

Over the next fifteen minutes, each man threw blow after blow, kick after kick. The sounds of grunts, curses, and the occasional harsh laugh were the only sounds in the room.

Blood and sweat ran in streams down Jordan's face. He was sure he had a broken nose; one of his eyes was already closed and his mouth was filled with blood.

McCall looked no better, with his lip split in two places, several interesting bruises on his face, two nasty-looking bruises already showing on his rib cage, and, if he wasn't mistaken, a broken nose.

Breathing hard, Jordan circled his opponent warily, looking for the right time and place to land a blow to end this thing. He didn't really care why Noah wanted to fight but couldn't help but be pleased. The release was much needed, and damned if McCall didn't look like he could pass out any minute. In an effort to throw him off, Jordan remarked casually, "So were you and Devon in on this from the beginning or did you jump on later?"

The mean smile Noah flashed him gave Jordan no choice. He had to go for those teeth. He whirled and made a wide sweep with his leg. Noah dodged him at the last second, but Jordan managed to clip him on the temple. A look of stunned surprise crossed McCall's face before he slammed face-first onto the floor.

The bastard wasn't dead, but Jordan bent down and checked his pulse, just in case. No, just unconscious. As he straightened, every muscle in his body protested. With one last contemptuous look at the man on the floor, Jordan grabbed his clothes and headed toward the door, wincing with every painful step.

"Wait."

Jordan stopped in midstride, somewhat surprised the man had regained consciousness. "What?" he mocked.

"You ready for another beating? I doubt you'll survive the next one."

McCall rose to his knees, swaying. Swollen eyes blinked heavily, as if having problems focusing. "The cabinet over in the corner . . . There's a file in it. You wanted the truth about Devon Winters . . . then take it."

Jordan eyed him warily. Now what was the catch?

"You'll find this file to be less of a fairy-tale version. More along the lines of a horror movie, as opposed to what I'm assuming was the G-rated version Eden so kindly gave you."

Like he was going to believe anything Noah McCall ever told him again. Jordan shook his head but went over to the filing cabinet anyway. He pulled it open to find it full of files. Since he didn't care about any of the others, he quickly located Eden St. Claire's.

This one was much thicker than the one Eden had given him, somewhat battered-looking. As if it could actually be authentic. Anticipation lightened the darkness burning inside him. Maybe the bastard was actually telling the truth this time. Not that it mattered. Nothing or no one could ever justify the lies he'd been told.

File in hand, he trudged out of Noah's office. He'd go home and take a shower, grab a large glass of scotch, and read the truth at last.

After he did, he would have no real plans other than to never see Devon/Eden again. Once he found out the entire truth, he could finally put all of this in the past where it belonged.

In a distant place in her mind, Eden heard groaning and then small, soft sobs. This person, whoever it was, was in pain. Why didn't someone help them? Couldn't anyone else hear the sounds?

With Herculean effort, Eden blinked her rock-heavy

eyelids open. She needed to help, had to get to them. Not until she was completely awake did she realize the sounds came from her.

She blinked. Her lids had to weigh ten pounds apiece. Why did she feel as though someone had stuffed her head with cotton? Her mouth felt as if she'd been chewing sand and her throat hurt as if she'd swallowed glass. She twisted to sit up and bit back another groan. The rest of her just felt like shit.

Forcing herself to move, Eden shuffled to the bathroom. Before she did anything else, she had to get something to drink. Why was she so thirsty?

A scene from last night flashed in her mind. She'd worked out for hours, sweated profusely, and then Jordan appeared. He'd tied her up and denied her water.

She gulped down three glasses before she felt the slightest relief. Other needs taken care of, Eden shuffled back to her bedroom. Uncertainty stopped her in the middle of the room. What was she supposed to do now? For almost seven years, she'd had purpose . . . a reason to exist. Now, after last night, she wasn't sure that reason was even valid anymore.

Jordan had discovered the truth, in the worst way possible. He'd figured it out for himself instead of her being courageous enough to give it to him . . . the way he deserved.

Silly, weak tears flooded her scratchy eyes and she battled them back. No, her crying days were over. She didn't deserve the relief of tears. Besides, tears were for others, not for people like her. When you've walked through fire and come out singed but alive, tears are a way of going backward. The last few weeks she'd allowed herself to go backward, but no longer.

With little thought, Eden dressed in a warm sweater and jeans. She didn't bother with makeup and took care of her hair by pulling it back into a ponytail. Before she left her bedroom, she caught a glimpse of herself in the full-length mirror and blinked in surprised horror.

Devon Winters stood before her. Yes, there were still differences to her facial structure, but Devon was there, too. It was the first time in years Eden had seen the young girl she'd tried so hard to forget. Why now? And then it hit her. It wasn't the reconstruction from the dozens of surgeries that changed Devon into Eden, it had been the "I can survive anything" attitude Eden had adopted. Now that lost, little girl was back. Those clear gray eyes she'd taken such pains to disguise stared at her with bewilderment and sorrow. She looked like the broken spirit she'd once been.

At that thought, a transformation took place before her eyes, as if someone touched her with a magical wand. Eden St. Claire had overcome too much, suffered untold pain and trauma, and, dammit, done too much good in her life to allow herself to become broken again.

Yes, she'd lost the man she loved, and yes, she had made some major mistakes, but she refused—*refused*—to allow it to overwhelm what she had accomplished.

For the first time in a very long time, Eden gave herself a break.

Feeling more in control and much more like herself, she headed to the kitchen. It had been more than twenty-four hours since she had eaten. Not being hungry was no excuse for not taking care of herself.

She'd just poured herself a fortifying cup of coffee and was about to begin breakfast when her doorbell rang. Refusing to consider for a second that it might actually be Jordan allowing her one more chance to make it right, Eden pulled the door open wide and could only stare in surprise at the face she'd never thought to see again.

"Hello, darling. Did you miss me?"

Trauma from the last few days slowed her reaction time.

She threw a hand out to ward him off. Before she made contact, a small cylinder pressed against her neck. Her muscles locked up and then collapsed. Eden felt herself falling to the floor. Her last conscious thought was the ridiculous wondering of how she'd ever thought this man was attractive or harmless.

twenty-three

Grim, dark silence hung in the air. Jordan's heart . . . soul . . . his very being ached. A half-empty glass of scotch sat on the table beside him, a taunting reminder that he'd fully intended to get good and drunk and then read Devon's file. He'd taken one sip, opened the file, and plunged into hell.

Now, as dawn made a wide sweep of soft light across his living room, Jordan's sleep-deprived eyes stared at the document as if it were loaded with poisonous snakes.

Snatches of doctor's reports slithered their way into his mind.

Patient's Name: Jane Doe

Injuries: Severe concussion. Deep facial lacerations, both jaws and nose broken, left wrist fractured, left ankle fractured, cracked pelvis. Vaginal and anal bleeding and bruising indicate repetitive and brutal rapes.

Facial lacerations will require extensive reconstructive surgery.

Suffering from exposure and blood loss.

No identification or distinguishing marks found other than small tattoo of hummingbird on victim's right shoulder.

According to the report, she'd been found the night of April 6 in an alley two blocks from his house. It had to have happened right after she ran out his door. After he'd hurled those vile, hideous things at her, she'd plummeted into an even more horrific nightmare. She hadn't just been

RESCUE ME   313

attacked, she'd been brutally beaten and sexually violated for hours . . . tortured.

How she must have hated him. If he'd listened to her, let her stay and explain. If he'd just called a cab, none of this would have happened.

No wonder she hadn't told him the truth. He was only surprised she hadn't shot him the moment she saw him. She'd spent seven years trying to forget everything that happened and he'd waltzed in and put her life in turmoil all over again.

He couldn't blame her for her deceit and manipulations. She played him for the fool and he could only wonder why she hadn't tried to destroy him completely. It was no less than he deserved.

Elbows propped on the table, he rubbed his hands over his face. Last night . . . the way he'd treated her . . . the things he'd said. It was seven years ago, all over again, but so much worse. Jordan shook his head, quite sure there could be no forgiveness from her. But he had to see her anyway.

He pulled himself to his feet, the pain from his fight with Noah a dull throb compared to the pain in his heart. She wouldn't want to see him. Probably even figured he was on his way back to the States.

Well, he wouldn't take no for an answer. He thoroughly intended to do some major groveling. Olympic-style begging, if necessary. And he still had some questions. He didn't want to hurt her any further, but he had to know everything. It was time—way past time—for all of it to come out in the open.

He headed toward his bedroom, figuring a shower would clear his mind somewhat. Then he'd go to Eden. Unless she'd changed the locks this morning, he still had a key. If she refused to see him, he'd get in and wouldn't leave until they'd both had their say.

A knock on the door stopped him. Jordan stalked to the

door, hope rising that somehow Eden had come here to kick his ass. If so, he'd gladly bend over and let her have at him.

He pulled the door open and then immediately tried to slam it shut. Noah's big hand stopped the forward progress.

"I know you don't want to see me, and buddy, let me promise you, I couldn't care less about seeing you again. However, I figure you still have questions and there're only two people who know the answers. I won't have you going back to Eden and destroying her any more than you already have."

Jordan had been ready to blast him back to the bowels of hell, but his words took the wind right out of him. Wasn't that exactly what he'd done? Seven years ago, and then again last night?

Jordan turned around and slumped into the chair he'd just left. He indicated with a wave for Noah to sit, too.

Noah wrinkled his nose at the booze on the table. "What'd you do, drown your sorrows?"

"I intended to, but got distracted."

Noah nodded with solemn understanding. The bruises on his face stood in stark relief to the pale green pallor of his complexion. "I tried to do the same. Unfortunately, I never could stand the stuff. Ended up puking my guts up."

"Want some coffee?"

"No. I just want to get this over with so I can go see Eden and clear my conscience. She'll be furious I told you, but all of this has gone too far. You deserve to know and God knows Eden doesn't need to relive it . . . what she remembers of it, anyway."

"What do you mean?"

Noah gave a slight shrug and then grimaced as if the movement cost him. "Just that . . . she remembers very little of the attack. A blessing really."

"How much of it?"

"Oh, she remembers the pain . . . the fear. Said she remembers brief glimpses, but not the entire event. Good for her, because at least she was spared that. Bad for the police because the punks could never be identified."

"Why weren't Devon's mother and stepfather notified? I know she was found without identification, but when they reported her missing, Devon would've still been in the hospital. Surely a connection could be—" Jordan jerked at the odd look on Noah's face. "What?"

Noah snorted a small laugh and shook his head. "Devon's mother *was* contacted. She came to the hospital, took one look at Devon, and denied it was her daughter."

Jordan shot from his chair. "No way . . . no fucking way!"

"Afraid so. Gave the police all sorts of reasons why this woman couldn't be Devon. She was too short, too thin, wrong color hair, and of course, Devon would never have something as common as a tattoo."

He couldn't believe a mother, even one as vile as Alise, could deny her daughter when she was in such need. "Maybe she really didn't think it was Devon. The tattoo was on her shoulder. Maybe Alise had never seen it."

"I can't believe you're making excuses for her."

"I'm not making excuses for the bitch. I just can't believe that even the monster I know her to be could do that to her own daughter."

"Well, believe it, because a few months later, Devon called Alise."

Jordan was still standing from his reaction to the previous bombshell. At this news, he dropped back into his seat, once again in disbelief.

"The police . . . they never said . . ."

"The police didn't know. Took a lot of courage for her to do it, but she called Alise and told her what happened. She didn't know then and still doesn't that Alise already knew about it and denied her daughter while she was still unconscious."

"What did Alise say?"

"Pretty much what you'd expect from the spawn of Satan. 'You brought these troubles on yourself. . . . You live with the consequences.' Then she hung up on her."

"Bitch."

"Can't argue with that." Noah rubbed his hand across his face and then winced. "By that time, a lot of Devon's major injuries were healed, but she was still going to need months of medical care and counseling."

"Did she . . . why didn't she . . . ?" His dry mouth grew even drier. "Did she try to contact me?"

Noah's smile was gentle, almost pitying. "Did you really expect her to?"

He hadn't expected her to, but he'd had to ask. "So how did you get involved? Did you even know Devon?"

"No, but LCR has far-reaching contacts. When Devon began to recover, one of the doctors discovered her gift for languages. This particular doctor kept an eye out for cases such as hers. People LCR could help and then, at some point, train them to work for us.

"I first met Devon about a week after her attack, just briefly. She was still heavily sedated, but I wanted to make a contact . . . see what she was up against, physically and emotionally. After that, I met with her a couple of hours each day."

"Did you tell her who you were, what you wanted?"

"Not at first. I posed as a staff psychologist."

"And you got away with that?"

Noah shrugged, as if impersonating a doctor was a commonplace, ordinary activity. "As I said, I have some contacts. Anyway, after a few visits, I began to see her potential. But it was going to have to be up to her to decide. She was in for a hell of a rough road, but I could tell she was a fighter.

"After she was released from the hospital, one of the nurses was kind enough to invite her to stay with her, but she needed extensive plastic surgery, as well as ongoing physical therapy."

"Because of her ankle?"

"Ankles, pelvis, wrist . . . She even had a dislocated shoulder, though the doctors thought that was inconsistent with her injuries and suspected it didn't happen during the attack."

A memory flashed through him of seven years earlier. Devon's small hiss of pain when he grabbed her arm, the stiff way she held herself when she'd walked into his study . . . her request for aspirin. She'd been hurt before and he'd been so focused on himself, he hadn't seen it.

Jordan hadn't thought he could feel any worse than he already did; he'd been wrong. He didn't know how she'd been injured, but could only guess how that injury might have facilitated what happened later. Would she have been able to fight off her attackers if she hadn't been hurt?

"Jordan . . . You still with me?"

Shaking his head to clear it, Jordan answered with another question. "So when did you tell her who you were?"

Noah's eyes had a faraway, shadowed look for a second, then a small smile kicked up his lips. "About a month after we met. Gotta tell you, seeing the fire in her eyes when she realized I'd lied to her did me good. She was one pissed woman. But then, when I told her what I did, what LCR was all about . . ." His voice filled with admiration. "When I first met her, I'd never met anyone more broken. Then, getting to know her, I realized how courageous she really was and what she could bring to LCR. When I told her I wanted her to come work for me, I saw excitement and hope, but also despair."

Though Jordan figured he knew, he had to ask, "Why despair?"

"She was so scarred . . . about as bad as I'd ever seen.

But I talked to the doctors. As young as she was, they had great hope that with extensive surgery, she could be put back together.

"I brought her here to Paris and flew the best plastic surgeons in to assess her. We interviewed them and then Eden—Devon chose the one she felt the most comfortable with. I think the surgeon and his team looked at her as a challenge. Thank God they met that challenge and then some.

"In between surgeries and recovery, we trained. She was fluent in six languages already and had a good start on self-defense training. She was a perfect fit for LCR. She just needed extra training and some focus."

The more Jordan learned, the greater his realization that Eden St. Claire was perhaps the most admirable person he'd ever met. How many people who had gone through the trauma she endured could not only overcome that trauma but risk their life and perhaps their sanity to help others? Jordan had never believed in heroes as much as he believed in ordinary humans who sometimes performed extraordinary deeds. There was nothing remotely ordinary about Eden St. Claire.

A haunting memory of her last words to him seven years before flashed in his mind. She told him she wished she could have been his hero. And now that wish had come true, but he was no longer her hero. Hell, she probably hated him beyond anything he could imagine.

A thought pounded on him, information Eden shared with him when they'd first become lovers. It was either ask Noah now and get it out of the way or find out from her later on. Right now, the most important thing was to get all the information he could. Then he'd find a way to deal with her pain.

"Eden told me she can't have children."

Noah raised a brow, but answered quietly, "The damage to her female organs from the rapes was too severe. She had to have a hysterectomy."

Jordan nodded as sadness pervaded his entire being. What this woman had gone through because of one small lie was a travesty, and what he had done to her was criminal.

Noah interrupted his tortured thoughts. "Something's been bothering me. I would have asked Eden last night, but she was in no condition to talk."

"What do you mean?"

"What do you think I mean, Jordan? I don't know what you said to her but . . ." He shook his head. "You'll just have to go over there and see for yourself. But what I don't understand is, why were you leading her on in the first place?"

"What the hell are you talking about?"

"When you first came here, you told me you were getting married. Why would you start something up with Eden if you—" He stopped at Jordan's head shake.

"I was never officially engaged. We'd just talk about it. I broke it off with Samara the day you asked me to help you out. By that time, I knew there was something between me and Eden and it wasn't fair to—"

"That's why Eden didn't tell you the truth."

"What are you talking about?"

"I talked to her a couple of days ago, when she told me you were involved. I told her you were engaged."

Jordan closed his eyes. "If I hadn't already beaten the hell out of you, I'd do it again."

"Hey, you're the one who told me."

Jordan nodded, grimly aware he was trying to place the blame on Noah's shoulders when it should fall directly on his own. "Eden was going to tell me the truth?"

"Yes."

And once again his memory demons rose up, reminding

him of the numerous occasions over the last couple of days when Eden told him she had something to tell him . . . and he pushed her away, his anger overriding everything.

Noah stood. "Well, since I think I've made you look even worse than you did before, I'd say my job is done."

"One more thing."

"Yeah?"

"Thank you."

Noah jerked at the unexpected words. "For what?"

"For saving her life . . . giving her a job. Being there for her when no one else was." Jordan held out his hand. Grasping Noah's firmly, he gave it a hard shake.

Noah laughed softly. "Man, I don't envy you. The next few days are going to be rough, but I hope you and Eden can work things out."

"I hope so, too." Jordan twisted his wrist for a quick glance at his watch. "I'm headed over there as soon as I get a shower. Do you mind not going to see her until I at least give it a try?"

Noah shrugged. "Fine with me. I don't expect I'll be her favorite person for a long time, either."

Jordan heard the door close and knew Noah had gone. Now, with renewed purpose in his step, Jordan headed to take a short shower. The longer he waited, the more time Eden would be able to shore up her defenses. He needed to get to her before she decided to totally cut him out of her life.

He'd do a lot of things for the woman he loved, but that was one thing he absolutely could not bear.

Eden woke to the sound of dripping water and complete darkness. She lifted a head that felt watermelon-sized and filled with thunder. Her shoulders protested the movement. Why did they ache so much? She shook her head slightly to clear it and then realized her wrists were bound and held over her head.

A morbid kind of amusement hit her. For the second time in two days she was in handcuffs. She'd never been into kinky, but damned if she didn't think she should have at least enjoyed one of those times.

Her fuzzy brain tried to comprehend why she was here. She remembered drinking a cup of coffee and then . . . nothing. That worried her almost as much as being locked up in some kind of dungeon. Having her memories stolen from her was not one of her favorite things. No matter what her counselors told her, having memory loss was like losing a part of your identity.

Worry about that later, Eden. Get the hell out of here and then pout about a few minutes of lost time.

Pep talk over, Eden ignored the throbbing in her head as she pushed it back, hoping to find something behind her, like a wall, she could lean against. A soft groan escaped when her head flopped back like a dead daisy.

Her feet were firmly planted on the ground, so at least she was spared the agony of actually hanging from something. She lifted a foot and felt around her, grimacing at the cold wet mud that met her bare feet.

Bare feet? Another worry popped into her head. She brought her now filthy foot back and lifted her other foot to feel her leg. Well, there was another relief. She still had her clothes on.

So, what did she know? An unknown assailant or assailants had abducted her. She was in some kind of tunnel or maybe a dirt basement, with dripping water. Her clothes were still on and other than a slight memory loss, a huge headache, and an increasing cramp in her shoulders, she was basically okay.

She tugged on the handcuffs, hoping to feel some kind of loosening to give her shoulders a rest, but no such luck.

Unwilling to believe there was no way of escape, she lifted her foot again and felt behind her. A wall of some sort stood maybe a foot behind her. It felt like brick or mortar. So probably not a tunnel. Most likely some smelly old damp basement.

A quiver of a long-forgotten fear tingled up her spine. *Great, what a wonderful time to remember all your phobias.* Her timing sucked, as usual. Eden gritted her teeth and then forced long, deep breaths through her body. She'd conquered those fears along with a multitude of others years ago. She refused to allow them back into her life.

A slight, muffled sound caught her attention. Her breath held. Yes, there it was again. And getting louder. Within seconds, she recognized the noise as the shuffle of someone's feet.

Muscles tensed in anticipation. At least she was about to find out just who her captor was and possibly figure out a way to overpower them. Light flooded the room. Her eyes briefly snapped shut in a protest of pain.

"Ah, you're awake. I was kind of hoping you'd still be out of it. I've been dreaming a long time about getting you tied up and unconscious. Oh well, I'm sure I'll figure out another way to have fun."

Now, there was a face from the past she would have been glad to never see again. "Well hello, Georges."

Jordan jerked the door open to Noah's grim face. After arriving at Eden's apartment ten minutes ago, he'd known immediately something was wrong. Eden's favorite mug lay just inside the door. There were coffee splatters on the carpet and wall. His only comfort was it hadn't dried, so it couldn't have been that long since she'd been taken.

He had called Noah immediately, knowing the man would have a better idea who might have her.

Noah looked around. "Any sign of a struggle?"

"No, just the coffee mug and spilled coffee. I'm guessing they took her at the door."

He cast a glance over to her desk. "Any indication she'd

been talking with someone? Any messages on her machine?"

"No, I checked all that while I was waiting for you. All her clothes are here. Wallet, purse, cellphone. There's no doubt in my mind she's been kidnapped," Jordan said.

"I agree. Only problem is, who and why?"

"Ransom or revenge?"

"Revenge, most likely. Few know our connection. Somehow, someone's found out her identity."

"Any idea who would—"

"Yeah, I do." Noah pulled his cellphone from his pocket and hit a couple of keys. "It's McCall . . . put Stephan on. Yeah, I know . . . but I've got a situation here."

Jordan watched Noah's face. A tick in his jaw was the only indication of his concern. Whereas Jordan felt everything within him was surging toward explosion. He would not lose Eden. No matter what he had to do to get her back, he would not lose her.

"Hey Stephan, they treating you well over there?" Noah waited a few seconds and then added, "Poor Stephan, everybody's deserted you, haven't they? Well, what if I could make your time there a little easier?" His eyes blazed with fire. "Don't push it, man. I'd just as soon cut your measly little dick off and stuff it into your big mouth till you choke to death." His voice softened. "But I won't do that if you're willing to give me a little info."

Jordan listened to every word, understanding that this was the man who'd sold LCR out several weeks ago. The man responsible for Milo's death. They just hadn't known how much info he'd sold.

After several more grunts and one more threat, Noah closed his phone. "It's the Larues. Most likely Georges. I think you met him at the restaurant."

Yeah, he remembered the tall, sandy-haired Frenchman with a fake smile and cold eyes. The one Eden double-crossed, the one who'd wanted to sleep with her, despite the fact that he thought she was married. His family was all but gone and he would hold Eden accountable for all of it. What would he do to accomplish that revenge? Jordan refused to let himself speculate. First he'd get Eden back, then panic.

"Any idea where he would have taken her?"

"Stephan mumbled something about an old estate at the edge of the city. I think I know where it is."

Jordan opened the door. "Let's go."

An hour later, Noah parked in a small field not far from the entrance to a dilapidated estate. Grass and weeds intertwined and grew several feet high, hiding most of the first floor of the small mansion.

As both men checked their weapons, they discussed the best options. Jordan listened as long as he could without interrupting. Finally unable to wait any longer, he stuck his sunglasses in his shirt pocket. "I'll go around back. You distract him. I'll give you five minutes."

Noah arched an eyebrow.

"What?"

Shrugging, Noah tucked his gun into his pocket. "Nothing. It's just been a long time since someone has given me orders."

He'd never figured McCall to be a prima donna. "You got a problem with that?"

A brief flicker of delighted surprise flashed in his eyes and then he grinned like a kid who'd just been given an extra piece of candy. "Actually, I don't."

Shaking his head at this odd behavior, Jordan took off around the back of the estate. Fortunately the weeds gave him good coverage. He was dressed in tan shirt and pants, blending well with the overgrowth. He kept low, almost crawling, as he approached the back of the building.

Though the mansion had probably been nice at one time, now it was an eyesore. Vines ran with haphazard abandon, covering the crumbling brick façade. Even some of the top windows had growth around them; the bottom windows were boarded up.

As he waited for the agreed time, Jordan forced himself to not think about what Eden might be going through. If he did, he wouldn't be able to do what needed to be done. When this was all over and he held her safe in his arms, then he would let his emotions go. But right now the situation called for cold, rational reasoning.

Jordan crouched lower and approached the house. He tried peeking inside the windows, between the boards, but saw only darkness. The windows were painted on the inside—a good clue that whoever painted them had something to hide.

Pulling out a couple of tools, Jordan set to work on the door lock. It'd been a while since he'd done any breaking and entering, but it was kind of like riding a bike . . . never forgotten. Just as one lock clicked and he started on another, he heard a sound that sent shivers of dread down his spine.

A woman's scream.

Fuck stealth and silence. Jordan threw his tools on the ground, raised his foot, and kicked the door open.

twenty-four

Eden glared her most intimidating look. If this bastard didn't let her go soon, she was going to get really pissed. He'd taunted and threatened her for what seemed an eternity . . . never touching her. He walked around the perimeter of where she stood, alternating between shouting curses and threatening torture. As if hearing him scream like a five-year-old with the mouth of a crusty old sailor wasn't torture enough.

As Georges continued his circling tirade, Eden realized one thing. He was afraid of her. That was why he wouldn't come closer. Those wild eyes of his kept glancing down at her legs. Georges knew he'd made a mistake in not tying her legs down. Though she'd never choked a man to death with her legs, she wasn't opposed to trying. Especially with this maniac.

Why hadn't she seen how crazy he was before? Or had her betrayal, Marc's death, and his parents' incarceration pushed him over the edge? If it had, he must have been teetering there already. She just hadn't seen the signs.

Growing bored with the entire situation, Eden forced herself to listen. Maybe in the middle of a rant, she'd be able to make some sense out of his words.

"You think you're so fucking smart . . . so beautiful . . . but you're like all the rest . . . ugly on the inside. My mama is the only truly beautiful woman."

"Why Georges, I never figured you for a mama's boy." Yes, she knew she shouldn't taunt him, but she needed some action here. The way this was going, the loon would wear a trench in the ground where he circled her and they'd still be no further along than they were now.

"Come on, Georges. Be a nice guy and let me down."

His eyes grew wilder. "You think I'm going to let you go? After what you did to me? You knocked me out. My mama saw me naked. My brother is dead and now Mama and Papa are going to prison.

"Damn, Georges. If you tell me you wrecked your pickup truck, you got yourself a country music hit."

"Huh?"

Cultural differences obviously prevented the understanding of her humor.

His confusion only lasted a second and he was off again. "My papa kicked me out of the family. My mama won't let me come see her. They even cut off my allowance. When they find out I captured you, they'll forgive me. I know they will."

So at least she knew why he might have gone off the deep end. His mama didn't want to see him, he'd been kicked out on his ass, and now the poor, rich playboy was no longer rich.

"You should thank me, Georges. At least now you don't have to watch your pedophile brother rape children or watch your parents sell them to the highest bidder."

That stopped him in his tracks and Eden watched in fascination as his face turned a deep crimson red. Holy hell, what if he had a heart attack or stroke? She didn't want to die hanging from a ceiling with a dead man at her feet. *Yuck.*

"Come on, Georges," she wheedled, not unkindly, "calm down and let's talk rationally."

"Rationally! Rationally!" he squeaked—literally squeaked. And then he did something so unexpected, Eden had no time to dodge. He picked up a rock and threw it at her.

The stone hit her face, right above her right eyebrow. Blood began to pour. *Damn. That really hurt.* "Dammit, Georges, that better not cause a scar or I'll have your balls for breakfast. And what are you, a twelve-year-old? Come over here and fight like a man instead of a little boy."

Obviously forgetting his concerns about her legs, Georges let out an inhuman grunt and lunged. Though blood blurred her right eye, she could still see him clearly enough to be ready. Just as he reached her, Eden wrapped her hands around her restraints and lifted her legs. With the grace of a ballet dancer and the dexterity of a monkey, she brought her feet to his crotch. To her amazement and his horror, she managed to grab him by the balls, twist, and squeeze—hard.

Grunting like a crazed pig, Georges clawed at her feet, pushed at her legs. Gritting her teeth, Eden held on. Tears poured from his eyes, and she knew a brief moment of triumph. The jerk had definitely earned this.

With an agonized sob, Georges leaned forward and punched her on the side of her head with his fist. Without her consent, her legs loosened and dropped to the ground. She blinked at him blurrily, unconsciousness a jagged edge away.

With one last bit of strength, Eden willed a leg back up again. Georges, who held his entire manhood in his hands as if offering a gift, was caught off guard as she aimed her foot at the gift and kicked like it was a football and she was scoring the game-winning field goal.

Her last conscious thought was to wonder if Georges knew he could scream like a girl.

Jordan smashed through the door into what appeared to have been a washroom. Gun at the ready, he ran through the rooms, seeing nothing but dust and cobwebs. He met Noah in the middle of the foyer.

"Could you tell where the scream came from?"

Noah shook his head. "No, tried breaking the door down, but didn't have any luck. I found a window with a cracked board and was able to break it and crawl through."

Jordan pointed to the stairs. "You take the next floor. I'll check this one."

Nodding, Noah ran for the stairs and Jordan searched throughout the first floor, noting that fast-food wrappers and soda cans littered the place. Someone had been living here, but he saw no signs of life. He started looking for a door that might lead to a basement. The only sounds he could hear were his own footsteps and the distant sound of Noah's. The ominous silence worried him more than the scream. At least with a scream, he knew there was still life. In silence—who the hell knew?

After a five-minute search, which seemed interminable, he finally opened a door with a stairway leading down-stairs. A single dim lightbulb hung from a string, giving him just enough light to keep from breaking his neck, but not much more.

Jordan stepped silently down into the dark, dank space. He thought he heard crying or sniffling, but he couldn't be sure. The sound was gruff and oddly muted.

He reached the bottom and rounded a corner to find only more darkness. Following the slight noise, he moved farther into the pitch darkness. With only his hands and his senses, Jordan kept moving until he hit a wall. Feeling with his hands, he found the edge and made his way around it.

Turning a corner, he saw light in the distance. Panic setting in, he ran toward the light and then came to an un-steady halt. His heart plunged. Eden, handcuffed, hung from the ceiling. Her head drooped to one side, and blood covered her face.

Without any thought, other than to get to her as quickly as possible, Jordan dropped his gun and grabbed her body. His shaking fingers pressed against the pulse in her neck, and his knees almost buckled at the reassuringly strong beat. Reaching up, he checked the cuffs. Standard issue. He pulled a key from his pocket and was about to insert it in the hole when he heard the ominous click of a gun.

"You can't have her. I'm not through with her yet."

Eden's lids flickered. She was awake. He pressed the key into her palm and felt her take it. Then, hands held high, Jordan turned around.

Three things registered at once. Georges Larue's wild-eyed stare indicated he wasn't quite sane. Based on the fact that while one hand held a gun, his other hand covered his crotch, Eden had been able to inflict some kind of damage to the bastard. Worst of all . . . the gun? Jordan's. *Of all the unprofessional, stupid things . . .*

Keeping his body planted firmly in front of Eden, Jordan went for a friendly "I'm not here to hurt you" demeanor. He figured since the guy had a gun on him, he wouldn't be too worried about that. "Let's talk about it."

Georges shook his head and offered Jordan a sly smile. "I don't think so. I'm the one in charge. I tell *you* what to do." He jerked his head toward the wall. "Get over there and sit down. Claire and I still have some things to talk about."

Jordan shook his head and offered him an empathetic smile. "Georges, she's hurt. She needs a doctor. You can talk with her when she's better."

Wild eyes flickered to Eden for a brief second before settling back on Jordan. A chilling, eerie expression spread across his face, turning him from a half-insane idiot to something much more evil. "I made her bleed." And then he smiled.

Jordan went cold. In that instant, he knew Georges intended to kill Eden. That may have not been his initial plan, but now, with a gun in his hand, he felt powerful, omnipotent. He had authority and strength he'd never felt before.

Jordan wouldn't let that happen. This woman had suffered tremendous anguish already for his stupid mistakes. He'd be damned if he was once again the cause of her pain.

Eden must have read his mind or body language. She whispered, so softly that only he could hear, "Don't do it, Jordan. Please . . . he'll kill you."

Without bothering to whisper, Jordan answered, "Better me than you, sweetheart."

Georges's crazed eyes blinked his confusion. "What?"

"I'm begging you, Jordan. Please don't."

Hands still in the air, Jordan reached back and gently caressed her cheek. Dying for this woman would be no hardship. He'd die a thousand times over if it would take away her pain.

Since he had every intention of living a long and healthy life with Eden at his side, he sincerely hoped Noah was on his way and dying wouldn't be necessary.

"What are you mumbling about?" Georges glanced up at Eden. "You awake, bitch? Want to watch me kill your lover boy?"

"Georges, this has gone on long enough. Put the gun down before you hurt someone."

While Georges grew angrier and spewed obscenities at Eden, Jordan's eyes searched the darkness. Sure enough, there was Noah. Resisting the urge to blow out a sigh of relief, Jordan held up a hand to stop Georges's rant.

"Come on, Georges. Let's all sit down and—"

Georges raised the gun higher, pointing it at Eden's head. "I'll shoot her if you don't move."

Jordan moved forward, wanting to get Georges's attention off Eden. If Noah shot Georges, there was every chance the gun would go off and hit her.

Georges pointed the gun at Jordan. "Get back!"

"Be careful. That things got a hair—"

A bullet tore into Jordan's chest. Eden screamed. Another gun fired. He heard a squeal and then a distant thud.

For a second, Jordan stood stock-still . . . shocked into immobility. Dammit, he'd been shot. Then, with the force of a wrecking ball, pain slammed into him. He fell to his knees and then face-first into the dirt.

Slumped in a threadbare chair in the intensive care waiting room, Eden held her head in her hands. In a dim part of her brain, she knew it pounded like a jackhammer. That pain was easy, compared to the pain in her heart.

Jordan was still in surgery, five hours so far. The bullet had lodged near his heart, and had nicked an artery. They'd been trying to stop the bleeding but so far had been unsuccessful.

Noah had been beside her for a while, but left to deal with the police and endless rounds of questions. They'd had no choice but to call an ambulance for Jordan. Georges had a bullet in his leg and would probably be released in a couple of days—to jail. Noah hadn't killed him, and though Georges's death would have been no great loss to mankind, she was glad he hadn't. Not for Georges's sake, but for Noah's. He didn't need that on his conscience.

Noah would handle the authorities and keep them away from her. All her energy, all of her focus, had to be on Jordan.

He'd saved her life. She sensed, just as he had, that Georges was prepared to kill her. Though she didn't think that had been his original intent when he'd kidnapped her, opportunity and motive had changed.

Fiery streaks of guilt pumped through her. She shouldn't have taunted Georges. When she'd had the chance to completely incapacitate him, she'd opted for the pleasure of his pain. If he'd been unconscious when Jordan arrived, none of this would have happened.

Jordan shouldn't even be in Paris in the first place. If she'd been honest with him that first day, told him who she was, explained what happened, he would have left and that would have been that. But instead she'd selfishly and cowardly kept the truth from him, lied with every breath, hurt him, and now he might die because of her.

"Here."

Noah stood in front of her with a steaming cup of coffee. His battered and bruised face looked as tired and sad as she'd ever seen it.

Taking the proffered cup, she wrapped her fingers around it, needing the warmth on her hands more than anything. She couldn't remember when she'd felt so chilled.

Noah sipped from his cup and grimaced. "Tastes like mud." He cast a look over at the wall clock, and then at Eden. "Anybody come out lately?"

She shook her head, her throat so tight she couldn't utter a sound. Almost every hour, a nurse had thoughtfully come into the waiting room and given them an update. Usually it was just that they were still trying to stop the bleeding, but at least she knew he was still alive.

It had been an hour and a half since anyone had come out. Eden didn't know if that was a good or bad sign. Fear kept her frozen to her seat. She was so afraid to get up and ask. If Jordan was gone, she really, truly, did not want to know. If she stayed here, not knowing . . . at least there was still hope.

A slight sound signaled activity. A middle-aged man in green scrubs, weary exhaustion etched on his face, shuffled toward them.

Eden gripped the arms of the chair and forced herself to stand. Her legs wobbled briefly and then, by sheer force of will, she stiffened them.

"Are you Mr. Montgomery's family?"

Eden managed a nod, grateful Noah was there to answer for her.

"Yes, we are."

The doctor began a long, involved explanation of how hard they'd worked to repair Jordan's heart. She caught only pieces . . . lost him once . . . still touch-and-go . . . might still have to go back for more surgery . . . wait and see.

She couldn't seem to stop nodding, as if she were one of those toy dogs with the wobbly heads. Only when Noah wrapped an arm around her did she realize the doctor had left.

"He's alive?" she whispered, still uncertain she'd heard correctly.

"Yes, he is. And you know what a fighter he is. The most tenacious bastard I've ever met."

A crooked smile trembled at her lips. "He is stubborn."

Noah leaned back and peered down at her. "What'd the doctor say about your head?"

"He patched it up, and said I was fine."

Noah's eagle eyes took in her pallor, dilated eyes, and shaking body. "He also said you have a slight concussion and need to be in bed."

"If you already knew, why'd you ask?"

"I wanted to see if you would tell the truth."

Tears sprang to her eyes and Eden fought them back, increasing the pounding in her sore head. "I don't think I know how to tell the truth anymore. Jordan was right. All I'm good at is lying."

Noah pulled her into his arms. "Jordan's a bastard."

Eden buried her face against his chest. "He is not. . . . He's wonderful," came her muffled reply.

"Okay, he's a wonderful bastard." Noah gave her another tight squeeze. "I told him everything."

Eden wasn't sure how he thought she was going to react to this news, but the push against his chest and the slap on his face seemed to surprise him. "How could you? That wasn't your place, Noah McCall. Just because you helped me gives you no right to tell anyone . . . especially Jordan. How could you?"

"Eden, I'm sorry, but he had a right to know."

"Yes, he did, but it was my right to tell him, not yours."

Her gaze swung wildly around the room. Oh God, he knew. . . . Jordan knew everything. That she'd been raped, sodomized, beaten, carved up beyond recognition.

She wanted to ask Noah how he reacted, but she was so furious, she didn't want him to know she wanted to know. How could he have betrayed her like that?

"Noah, you play God with people's lives because you can't face living your own. Well, this is the last time you manipulate mine." She whirled away from him and ran to the door.

"I didn't mean to hurt you. It was just time."

Eden pointed a finger at him, her voice shaking with fury. "It's my life. It should have been my choice when and what to tell him—not yours." She turned and stalked out.

Less than an hour later, Eden was back at the hospital. She'd gone home long enough to shower and change out of her bloody clothes. Hoping to appease her headache, she allowed herself two aspirin and forced down a piece of toast and a cup of hot, sweet tea. It had been almost forty-eight hours since she'd eaten and her legs were about to give out on her.

Noah was no longer at the hospital. Though she was still furious with him, a part of her grieved for the loss of his friendship. He'd been her mainstay for so long, she wasn't quite sure what she was going to do without him.

But all of that would have to wait. The most important thing was making sure Jordan was okay. After checking at the front desk, she was relieved to discover that though he was still in intensive care, he hadn't had to go back for more surgery.

Eden found a semi-comfortable couch and forced herself to lie down. The doctors and nurses knew she was here. If she didn't get some rest soon, she would end up in the hospital, too.

She closed her eyes. Using an old trick from years ago, when things got out of control at home, she forced all of her fears and doubts into a small corner of her mind and pictured the one person who always made her feel safe and happy. *Jordan.*

She wasn't sure how long she lay there, drifting in a sea of semiconscious bliss, before a hand shook her shoulder. "Mademoiselle St. Claire?"

Fear surging through her, she sprang from the sofa. "What? What's wrong?"

A smiling young nurse stood beside her. "Nothing at all. I just wanted to let you know that the doctor says it's okay for you to see Monsieur Montgomery. You can only stay a couple of minutes."

"Really?" Eden stood and smoothed her hair and clothes. She probably looked like the wrath of hell, but she didn't care. Jordan was alive, well enough for a visitor. Suddenly nothing else seemed important.

Her heart tripped over as she ran to the room. The door stood open. Tubes and machines surrounded the man on the bed. He looked so pale . . . lifeless. Eden gripped the doorjamb. This was not the time to break down.

As she approached the bed, his eyes flickered open. With a tentative, trembling hand, she touched his hair, then his face. Tears blurred her vision, but she thought he looked like he was trying to smile.

There were so many things she wanted to say, so much to explain, apologize for. Where did she start?

"Eden?" It was a barely a whisper, but she heard it.

Smiling through her tears, Eden leaned forward and

kissed his forehead gently. "There's so much to say . . . I don't . . ." Why couldn't she speak . . . say how sorry she was . . . that she loved him?

"I wanted—" He stopped and swallowed.

Whatever he had to say seemed vitally important. Leaning closer, she asked, "What?"

"All those years ago . . . I couldn't rescue you . . . should have. Wanted to make it up to . . . you."

He closed his eyes, unconscious again. Through a haze of tears, she saw the nurse at the door, signaling her to leave. Allowing herself one small gift, she leaned down and kissed his cheek. "I love you, Jordan. I always have . . . I always will."

Eden shuffled out the door, emotions bubbling to the surface so fast, her heart pounded to keep up with them. She headed back to the waiting room, determined to continue her vigil. A woman's voice, soft and distinctly American, caught her attention.

"I'm here to see Jordan Montgomery."

"Your name and relationship to the patient?" a bored voice asked.

"Samara Lyons. You called me as Mr. Montgomery's emergency contact. I'm his . . . his fiancée."

And with those words, Eden's world crumbled again. How could she have forgotten? Jordan was engaged . . . belonged to another woman. The words he'd whispered only seconds ago took on a new meaning. He'd felt responsible for not being able to help her before and had come to her rescue this time to make up for the last time. That's all it had been. Not a promise of forever, certainly not a declaration of love. An obligation, nothing more.

Ignoring the curious and sympathetic eyes of the nurse who'd heard the young woman's words, Eden walked past them to the open door of the elevator. She pressed the first-floor button and made it all the way to the lobby without allowing herself to breathe. Finally outside, she took in deep, cleansing breaths. She would survive. She was a survivor. Besides lying, it was what she did best.

She hailed a cab, and as she made her way back to her apartment, she realized with an odd sense of detachment that another phase of her life had ended. Devon Winters had been found alive and well, and Jordan finally knew the truth. There were no loose ends, nothing to wrap up. For the first time in years, the past was finally in the past.

A little voice inside taunted her. If the past was truly in the past, why were tears pouring from her eyes and why did her heart feel ripped to shreds?

Eden had no answer.

twenty-five

Noah pushed the door open, his gaze zooming to the man in the hospital bed. So pale, he rivaled the sheets covering him for whiteness. Just hours ago, a cold, emotionless Eden had left the country on assignment. Noah couldn't decide who looked worse, an unconscious Jordan with a bullet hole in his chest or the woman who swore she'd kill Noah if he ever interfered in her life again.

Feeling lower than sludge under a snake's belly for his part in this, Noah entered the room as quietly as possible. If Jordan didn't wake soon, he'd leave. There wasn't much he could do but go back to LCR and put his ass to work. Rescuing was his business, his life. Solving relationship problems was not his forte, though he sure seemed to have a knack for creating them.

"Who are you?"

Noah whirled around. A petite young woman stood at the entrance to the bathroom, a vase of white daisies in her hand. "Who are you?"

Holding the vase with both hands as if she might use it as a weapon, she advanced into the room. "I believe I asked first."

Despite his dismal thoughts, Noah had the urge to smile. Whoever the woman was, she posed no threat. Barely over five feet tall, with long, wavy black hair, vivid ice-blue eyes, and creamy magnolia skin, she looked more like a beautiful fairy sprite than anything else.

Noah surprised himself by answering with the truth. "Noah McCall. And you are?"

"Samara Lyons. I'm a friend of Jordan's."

"The former fiancée?"

Her eyes flickering toward the unconscious man on the bed, she shook her head. "No . . . he called . . ." Stopping, she cleared her throat, then continued, "We never . . ." One more throat clearing, then, "We called it off." Her smooth brow wrinkled. "Jordan told you we were engaged?"

No way was he going to get pulled into that discussion. He jerked his head toward Jordan. "How's he doing?"

Looking somewhat irritated that he hadn't answered her question, she said, "About the same."

"Well, let me know if he needs anything." He turned to the door and opened it.

"Wait."

Noah twisted back. "Yes?"

"He woke up a few minutes ago, mumbling something about Eden and then asked where Devon is. I thought he was hallucinating, but now I'm not so sure. Did he find Devon?"

"He'll explain everything, I'm sure."

"Excuse me?"

Again Noah fought a smile. There was just something about this woman that made him want to annoy her. Not that he would tell her about Eden and Devon . . . that was Jordan's job. But for some strange reason, seeing her irritation gave an odd lift to his mood.

Jordan hadn't told him anything about his former fiancée, but Noah found himself surprised they'd even dated, much less considered marriage. Sure she was beautiful. Hell, just looking at her made him think of things he hadn't thought about in years. But she was obviously the wrong woman for Montgomery. He couldn't really say why he felt that way. A gut feeling and nothing more.

"If you know something about Devon's whereabouts, then I believe you should tell me."

Unable to hold it back this time, a grin lifted his mouth. "You do, huh?"

Sparks shot from those remarkable eyes of hers. He'd thought her beautiful; he now amended that to breathtaking. A vision of what this woman would look like in the throes of passion slammed into his brain. Flushed cheeks, passion-glazed eyes, small breasts covered by his hands, his mouth. His gut clenched. Where the hell had that come from?

"Jordan is my friend. If there's something you know about Devon, then I should know so I can help him."

A curious tenderness hit him. Even though Jordan had most likely broken her heart, she still cared about him. "Jordan's a lucky man to have such a good friend." Resisting the ridiculous urge to chuck her under the chin for being so brave, he nodded toward Jordan. "Tell him to call me if he needs anything."

Ignoring her startled expression, Noah went through the door, closing it behind him. He needed to get back to his office where he could do the most good. Fantasizing about a woman he didn't even know was pointless and certainly not the most productive use of his time. He'd given up his fantasies a long time ago.

"You mean Devon and this LCR person Eden are one and the same?"

Jordan nodded, fighting a grimace. Hell, even a mere head movement hurt. He'd been in this bed for almost two weeks now and it still felt as if a meteor had landed on his chest. Today was the first day he'd been halfway coherent and immediately asked for Eden, only to be told by Samara that so far, Noah had been his only visitor. Where the hell was Eden?

Eyes wide with surprise, Samara shook her head. "How is that even possible?"

"LCR saved her life years ago. She became an operative for them."

"When did you find out?"

"Right before I got shot." He saw no reason to explain how incredibly stupid he'd been. The most important thing right now was finding Eden and making sure she was all right.

"But didn't you recognize her?"

"It's a long story, but she had plastic surgery . . . looks completely different."

"She's the reason we broke up, isn't she?"

A pang, having nothing to do with his wound, clawed at him. Lovely and fresh, Samara stood bravely in front of him. She'd come here because the hospital had called her. Months ago, he'd put her name on his emergency contact card and had forgotten to change it. Without any hint of anger, she'd sat by his bed for two weeks. Her presence had nothing to do with her hope that they'd somehow get back together, and everything to do with the character and heart of Samara Lyons.

"I fell in love with her. I'm sorry, Samara."

Though her mouth trembled slightly, she managed a smile. "Falling in love isn't something someone plans. It just happens."

"I never meant to hurt you."

"I'm glad you found her again. I don't think you could have ever been truly happy until you did."

"You're right, but now, where the hell is she?"

"Is there anyone I can call and ask? Do you want me to go to her house or apartment?"

"Noah knows. I called him earlier. He wouldn't tell me anything."

Her entire body stiffened. "Is there *anyone* else I can call?"

"You don't like Noah?"

"He's a jerk."

"Can't argue with that."

With a deep, resigned breath, Samara said, "What's Eden's address? I'll go there first and see if I can find her. If I can't, tell me where I can find Noah McCall, but don't expect me to be nice to him. He doesn't inspire niceness."

Jordan grinned. "Can't argue with that, either."

Noah glared at the screen. He was no closer to finding Bennett than he had been a month ago. It was like the creep had dropped off the face of the earth. And the bastard who worked for him had gone with him. He had to find them. Not completing this particular mission was not only unacceptable, it was incomprehensible.

The buzzer on his desk sounded, telling him he had company on the way up. He had no appointments until tonight, but Angela would only allow LCR people inside. He clicked off the screen he'd been staring at for hours. Pushing back his frustration, Noah stood and waited for his visitor.

Samara Lyons entered without knocking. Wearing a pale blue dress and a determined look, she was even lovelier than the last time he saw her.

"How the hell did you get past Angela?"

With a shrug of her slender shoulders, and an easy, feminine grace, she glided into the room as if she belonged there. "I told her I had a message from Jordan I needed to deliver in person. She showed me how to get in, and here I am."

Thousands of dollars worth of security and all she'd had to say was one sentence? And he thought he was good at manipulating people.

"Ever heard of a phone? Whatever Jordan has to say, he could have called."

"He did. You wouldn't tell him anything."

"And I'll tell you the same thing in person. I'm not getting involved in his and Eden's business. When he gets out of the hospital, he can go after her. I'm out of it."

Hands on her hips, Samara advanced toward him like a mother bear protecting her cub. "According to Jordan, you're the one who brought them together again. Seems pretty damn convenient for you to stay out now that it's gotten messy."

"Darlin', you don't know what messy is. I'm just trying to keep a promise to Eden. No more interfering. She told me to stay the hell out of her life. That's what I'm doing."

Luscious lips trembled and tears misted her eyes. Noah took half a step toward her and stopped, fighting the bizarre urge to wrap his arms around her in comfort. What the hell was he thinking?

"I don't think Jordan's going to get better until Eden can be found."

"Why do you care so much? He stomped on your heart."

She flinched at his bluntness but tilted her chin bravely. "Because I care enough about him to want him to be happy, no matter what."

"Jordan's a lucky man to have two women who care so much for him."

"If Eden cares about him so much, then why isn't she with him?"

"That's something she'll have to explain herself . . . to Jordan." Noah went past her and headed to the door. "Now, if you'll excuse me, I have a receptionist to fire."

Hands on her hips, Samara whirled around and glared. "Don't you dare fire Angela. She's got a little brother and sister to support. Her mother's in poor health, and her father just lost his job. She needs this work."

"Now, how the hell do you know so much about Angela?"

"I had a little chat with her before I came up. She's a sweet young woman and you'd be an ass to fire her."

He shot her a cocky smile, figuring it would irritate her even more. "Wouldn't be the first time."

"That's about the first thing I've heard you say that I actually believe."

"Smart girl." He opened the door. "I really do have some work to do."

She didn't move. "You're not going to fire her, are you?"

"No, I won't fire her. Happy now?"

A brief flicker of devastation swept across her expressive face, and Noah saw what she'd been desperately trying to hide. This poor girl had a broken heart and instead of going back home to nurture her crushed feelings, she'd stayed here, doing her best to help the man she loved find the woman he loved. That took a hell of a lot of courage.

Since he couldn't tell her where Eden was, he did the next best thing. "Tell Jordan that Eden is on assignment. I'll let him know as soon as she comes back."

As if she knew she'd allowed him to see a part of her she wanted to keep hidden, she nodded and walked out the door. Halfway to the elevator, she stopped. Her slender body tense as if expecting a blow, she asked without turning, "Does she love him, Mr. McCall?"

"Yes, she loves him very much."

"Thank you," she whispered before disappearing into the elevator.

Noah stared at the closed elevator for the longest time, the unfathomable longing to go after her and offer comfort almost a compulsion. Finally coming to his senses, he shook his head and returned to his office, determined to put the woman and her heartache out of his mind.

An hour later, he had no explanation for staring at a

blank screen, his mind still on the spirited and beautiful Samara Lyons.

"Dammit, Noah, tell me where the hell she is." Taut fingers dug into the leather as Jordan gripped the edge of the chair. It was all he could do to stand up, he was so damned weak. But if Noah didn't spill his guts soon, he planned to find enough energy to beat the information out of him.

Noah sat slumped in his chair, once again in control of other people's destiny. Jordan was determined his and Eden's destiny escaped his interference. First he had to find her.

"Eden told me to stay out of her life and that's what I'm trying to do, which includes telling people her location. She's on a job. When she comes back, go see her at her apartment." He pushed his chair back and glared at Jordan, as if he had a right to be angry. "I'm out of it."

"It's been a month. I'm not going to wait any longer."

"She'll be back in a few days. You can wait that long."

Jordan played his trump card. "If you don't tell me where she is, I'll see if Samara can get it out of you."

The man actually looked horrified, as Jordan figured he would. It was a lie, of course. Samara had left several days ago at his insistence. Nevertheless, it was damned funny to see his threat provoke such a strong response. Noah McCall had finally run across someone he couldn't manipulate.

When Samara returned from confronting Noah in his office, she'd announced that the head of LCR had to be the biggest SOB she'd ever come across.

Jordan had never seen this side of Samara, hadn't known it existed. He'd always seen her as a sweet, uncomplicated woman. How intriguing that Noah brought out these hidden depths.

The thought that Noah McCall had finally found his nemesis in Jordan's former girlfriend was damned funny. But the humor he'd found in that hadn't lasted long. As days passed, Jordan knew Eden wasn't coming back.

Noah shook his head. "I can't risk it, man. Even if you sic that fiery little virago on me—which, by the way, I'd never forgive you for—Eden's in a delicate situation right now. Having her distracted . . ."

"Eden's a professional and you know it. She wouldn't—"

"She's not the same as she was."

The blunt statement put a fresh stab of pain in his heart. "What do you mean?"

"I mean I thought she had ice in her veins before . . . well, until you came here and rattled her. But now, it's like she's on automatic . . . no emotion, no fire. She's just there."

Jordan forced his shaky legs to move around to the front of the chair. Slumping into the soft cushion, he breathed out a ragged sigh. He'd gotten out of the hospital two hours ago, against doctor's orders, but he couldn't wait any longer. Every day he'd hoped to see her face, had hoped that whatever reason had made her leave had been resolved and she would reappear. That had never happened.

Noah's frequent visits to the hospital had been no help, other than to confirm she'd left town on assignment and she'd told him to never interfere in her life again.

"You picked a damn convenient time to develop scruples about playing God. You know I could just come over there and kick your ass."

"Man, you don't look like you could kick the ass of a baby flea."

Jordan leaned back and closed his eyes. He was right about that. After two operations, and then a setback of pneumonia, he was lucky to be alive. But, he'd never be truly alive until he was with Eden again.

Noah let out an explosive sigh. "I'm going to regret this, I know. In fact, since you can't do it, Eden'll probably come and kick my ass for you."

Jordan sat up. Now he was talking.

"She's in Las Vegas."

"What's she doing there?"

"Domestic dispute turned nasty, then nastier. Billionaire husband kidnapped the kids . . . basically holding them for ransom till the wife signs divorce papers, giving her less than she wants. Wife didn't want any press, so she called us."

Jordan stared at him in disbelief. "You're telling me it's taken a month to get this done?"

"Not at all. This'll be Eden's third assignment in four weeks."

"Hell, Noah, she's going to burn out with that kind of schedule."

"I know. So what're you going to do about it?"

Jordan relaxed into his chair, feeling for the first time as though something was finally happening. "That depends. You got room for another LCR operative?"

A genuine smile spread across McCall's face. "Yeah, I think we can accommodate one more. You got anyone in mind?"

Jordan pushed himself up to stand. "Yeah, Eden St. Claire's husband . . . but only after an extensive honeymoon break . . . say about a month?"

"A month! You want to spend a month alone with Eden? Man, you must be in love with her."

Figuring that was pretty damn obvious, Jordan didn't bother to comment. "Tell me about this assignment. Is Eden getting the kids back for the mother?"

"Yeah, but neither of them deserves the kids. He's mean, the wife's meaner."

"You said it was a delicate situation. What's so delicate about it?"

Amusement sparkling in his eyes, he turned a monitor around so Jordan could read the screen. It was an email from Eden to Noah, with today's date.

Noah, neither parent deserves these kids. I'm keeping them.

Jordan looked at Noah. They both burst out laughing.

twenty-six

Eden meandered through the casino, the musical clang of slot machines intermingling with the din of desperate and excited voices created a cacophony of blurred noise. Smoke stung her eyes; the stench of alcohol, unwashed bodies, and too much perfume blended into a nauseating odor. She ignored it. Though she could have gone through the lobby to get to her room and skipped this mass of people, she didn't really want to reach her room so soon. All that waited for her was an empty bed and another lonely night.

She'd just delivered two beautiful children back to the greedy clutches of their mother, against her better judgment. What she'd emailed Noah had been correct, neither parent deserved those precious children. But they legally belonged to the Baxters. So she'd returned them, but not without a stern lecture to both parents about allowing their children to become pawns. Though they'd had the grace to look ashamed, Eden figured that shame would only last until the next time one of them wanted something from the other.

She had a flight back to Paris tomorrow, but was seriously considering rescheduling it. Not that Vegas held that much appeal to her, but she had no real desire to return home.

Jordan would be leaving the hospital any day now, according to Noah's last report. She knew he'd had a tough time and though she desperately wanted to be there with him, it wasn't her place. Jordan had someone to hold and comfort him. He certainly didn't need her around to complicate things.

When she'd left the hospital after seeing Jordan's fiancée, she'd gone home and packed. She'd called Noah on the way to the office and told him she wanted an assignment. He'd been full of questions, of course. She'd refused to discuss anything with him other than assignments, demanding once and for all that he stay out of her life.

She'd met him at the office, grabbed the information, and stalked out. No words had been exchanged. He'd tried without success to talk with her. She ignored him. At some point, she'd have to forgive him. After all, he was her best—make that, only—friend. But for now, she needed distance and time. Her assignments had given her that.

Now this one was over and though she could return to Paris and get another one, for the first time ever Eden was thinking about taking time off. But did she want to stay here or find another place to lick her wounds?

Abruptly, she noticed a tall, beefy security guard eyeing her with suspicion. Since she'd just been standing in the middle of the room, staring into space, he probably thought she was either high on drugs or planning a casino heist. Who knew?

With as much excitement as one would face the guillotine, Eden pulled a twenty from her purse and stuck it into a slot machine. The mindless activity kept her busy. What was Jordan doing now? Was he out of the hospital? Was he headed back to the States? Did he wonder what happened to her, or now that he knew the truth, did he consider everything over?

Though she never got the opportunity to apologize for her deceit, she wasn't masochistic enough to contact him. Everything was over and done with. He would get on with his life and she with hers.

As the slot machine greedily swallowed the last of her

money, Eden rose. There was no reason to stay and lose more. Maybe she'd take a hot bath, or order an ice-cream sundae and watch a movie.

Sitting on a stool close to the entrance, Jordan had seen her when she first drifted into the crowded casino. Beautiful and much too slender, she wore a simple, light green sleeveless dress and stood out like a fragile swan among overblown peacocks. *Fragile.* A word he never thought he'd use to describe this beautiful, gutsy woman. His heart literally ached.

He'd watched her stand in the middle of the casino and stare at nothing for almost ten minutes, seemingly lost in thought. Then when a security guard frowned at her, she hurriedly sat down and began to play a machine.

He didn't like any of it. The lifeless look in her eyes, the slight slump of her shoulders, and he sure as hell didn't like the meek way she'd looked at the guard. The old Eden would have arched an arrogant brow or winked at him.

Noah was right. She wasn't the same. And he still didn't know what had happened, but he'd bet his last nickel he was solely responsible for it. When had he not caused this woman heartache? Had she left because of the way he treated her when he confronted her about being Devon? He'd been deliberately cruel. Said things it would take a thousand years to forgive himself for. How long would it take Eden to forgive him? *Would* she forgive him?

Why hadn't she stayed so they could talk about what happened? Why couldn't she have called him the bastard he was, bashed his head in, and then forgiven him?

Jordan followed slowly behind Eden as she headed for the bank of elevators. He waited until she got on an elevator and then took a different one. He'd already been in her room . . . had a few things prepared for her. Well aware he was taking an awful chance with her, he didn't see any other alternative. She might still be hurt about how he'd treated her. If she was, his plan might screw everything up. But he wasn't giving up on her and if this was the only way, he'd take the chance. He couldn't fix the problem until he knew what the problem was.

Admittedly, he was hanging his hat and heart on one vague memory of the day he was shot. Though his brain had been fogged with medication and the pain in his chest felt as though a herd of elephants had stampeded over it, he remembered Eden's soft lips kissing his cheek as she told him she loved him . . . had always loved him.

Tonight he would find out.

When he got off the elevator, Eden stood at her door, her head bent as she rummaged around in her purse looking for her key card. She had no awareness of her surroundings. If someone came at her from the back . . . Jordan didn't even want to contemplate what could happen. This was so unlike her, to be unfocused this way.

With very little compunction, he used her distraction to his advantage. She finally found her key and just as she slid the card in, he rushed her. Wrapping one arm around her torso, he pressed a hand against her mouth. Before she could take a breath, he whispered, "Open the door. Get inside."

She didn't relax, but he knew she recognized his voice since she didn't turn around and slug him, which she was fully capable of doing.

He'd left a lamp on in the corner, casting the room in a soft romantic glow. Keeping his arm around her, he closed the door with his foot and then released her mouth.

"What are you doing here?" Her voice sounded hoarse and deliciously familiar.

Jordan knew he shouldn't. They had so much to get through, to say to each other, but he couldn't resist the urge to wrap his other arm around her and just hold her against him. Just for a second. Burying his face against the tender spot where her neck and shoulder met, he breathed in the beauty of the fragrance that was Eden . . . spicy, sweet, and alluring.

Just by touch, he could tell she'd lost more weight than he'd thought. Between the two of them, they probably looked like refugees from a third-world country. Well, if he had his way, they'd both be happy and healthy within a few weeks.

He pressed a kiss to the nape of her neck and smiled at her shiver. "God, I missed you so much."

She relaxed into his arms, seeming to sink into him. They stayed that way for a few seconds. Absorbing the sheer joy of touching each other again.

Then her body stiffened and she tried to pull away.

His laugh, soft and low, moved tendrils of her hair against his cheek. "You're not getting away from me that easily." He pressed forward and forced her to walk into the room and then to the edge of the bed.

Her body stiffened even more when she saw what he'd attached to the bedposts.

"Jordan, you can't just waltz in here, handcuff me again and . . . and—" A gasp of air escaped her when he unzipped her dress. He loosened his arm long enough to let it slide to the floor, leaving her in shoes, panties, and bra. Jordan made quick work of the bra.

"No, you can't . . ." She swallowed a groan when his teeth bit gently on her earlobe.

"Slip out of your shoes, sweetheart."

Relief swept through him when she obeyed. At least now if she decided to kick him, he might recover. If she'd tried a kick with those stiletto heels, their honeymoon would be celibate and painful.

Left only in her panties, breath caught in her throat as his hands slid to her hips and hooked her panties on the way down. They dropped at her feet and everything within him shouted "Yes!" She was completely, totally bare.

His cock, always ready to celebrate when Eden was present, sprang up in eager anticipation. Though he'd like nothing better than to let it have its way, they had a few things to take care of first.

"Get on the bed, baby."

Her words came out in puffy breaths of air. "Jordan . . . no. We have to talk. . . . You can't just come in here and . . . and . . ."

"We will talk. I promise. This is just my insurance you won't get up and walk out on me again."

She blew out a long sigh and then got on the bed.

Swallowing hard, desire beating a throbbing tempo, Jordan watched her perfect and deliciously bare ass wiggle its way up the bed.

"Come on, sweetheart. On your back. No hiding . . . for either of us."

She rolled over and got her first look at him. "Oh, Jordan. You look terrible."

Laughing softly, Jordan went to the side of the bed, pulled her hands gently up, and encircled the handcuffs around her wrists. While she watched, her eyes growing hungry and glazed, he stripped off his clothes.

He'd lost at least twenty pounds. The scar on his chest had healed but was still damn ugly. If he'd worried about how he would look to the woman he loved, the second her eyes turned dark and dreamy, those worries vanished.

Now naked as she, Jordan crawled on the bed and straddled her. Eden looked down at his penis and the damn thing seemed to preen, growing larger and harder as if wanting to show appreciation of her perusal.

She practically purred, then whispered, "It's nice to see you haven't lost weight everywhere."

He grew harder still.

Bending lower, Jordan growled in her ear, "Behave for a few minutes and then I'll let you play as long as you want."

Raising tortured eyes, she audibly swallowed and whispered, "Jordan, you're engaged."

Hell, he was going to kill Noah McCall. Why had the man not told her the truth? "I'm not engaged." *Yet.*

"But Noah said . . . and the woman at the hospital . . . I saw her."

"You saw Samara? When?"

"When she first arrived." She closed her eyes as if the memory still hurt. "I heard her tell the nurse she was your fiancée. I knew then I had to leave."

"Open your eyes and look at me, sweetheart."

He stared down into the beautiful gray depths of eyes that had haunted him for seven years. No longer concealed by colored contact lenses, they held sadness but also a tentative hope.

"No more secrets . . . no closing your eyes, no turning away. Okay?"

She nodded.

"I didn't know you'd seen Samara. She came because the hospital contacted her. Her name was on an emergency contact card in my wallet. I don't know why she told the nurse she was my fiancée, unless she thought it would get her in to see me sooner. I never told you about her because I broke off our relationship before you and I ever got involved."

"You did?"

"Yes . . . Now, let that be a lesson. Ask me before you go running off."

"But Noah said—"

"And another thing. That man's way too nosy for his own good."

She giggled and he delighted in the rare sound.

"I told Noah I was getting married, but I was never even officially engaged. It was just something we'd discussed. That was before I met you and it ended before we became involved. Okay?"

"Okay," she answered softly.

"Now, let's get something else straight."

"What?"

"It's big."

Eyes wide, she looked down at him.

He chuckled. "Not that, silly. What I'm about to say. It's big."

"What is it?"

"You have to promise you'll never leave me."

"Okay."

Jordan grinned, delighted at her easy agreement, but that wasn't the extent of the promise he was looking for. Touching his forehead to hers, his mouth inches from the luscious lips he was dying to kiss, he said quietly, "Repeat after me. 'I, Eden St. Claire, aka Devon Winters, promise to never leave Jordan Montgomery ever again.'"

A tiny sob escaped her and everything within him wanted to hold her, comfort her, but he forced himself to wait. He held his breath until she whispered the first words.

"I, Eden St. Claire, aka Devon Winters, promise to never leave Jordan Montgomery ever again."

"'I promise to stay and fight it out with him, realizing he is often an idiot.'"

Soft laughter caressed him as she repeated the words.

"'I also promise to tell him when I'm angry, frightened, confused, or any other emotion he's too thickheaded to see.'"

Solemnly, she again repeated his words.

"'And I also promise that when he doesn't seem to get it, or acts like a complete prick, or does things to infuriate me, I will give him a warning and if he doesn't shape up, I'll whop him on the side of his head.'"

In between giggles and his help in remembering all the words, Eden repeated them.

"Now that those vows are over, I have some for you. But first, let me free your hands. You promised to never leave me. . . ." He unlocked the cuffs, his thumbs tenderly caressing the silky skin on the inside of her wrists. Locking his eyes with hers, he knew his next words might be what she needed to hear more than anything. "And I have complete and total faith in your word."

When her eyes flooded with tears, Jordan knew he'd said exactly the right thing.

Eden barely waited for her arms to be free before she threw them around Jordan's shoulders and held him as tight as she could. She couldn't believe he was here. Couldn't believe what he said, what he'd made her promise. That he trusted her after all that had happened.

Jordan held her just as tight, as if he never wanted to let her go. Finally, with a small sigh, Eden loosened her hold on him.

Jordan pulled away slightly, his eyes so full of tenderness and love, Eden could barely restrain herself from screaming with sheer happiness.

"You okay?"

She nodded, her smile brighter and more authentic than she'd had in years. "Very okay."

"Good. Now here comes my vow to you. I love you, Eden St. Claire, aka Devon Winters. You are the strongest, bravest, most beautiful person in the world. I want to spend the rest of my life with you. Hold you in my arms every night, and wake with you in my arms every morning. You're my past, present, and future. No one could ever or will ever love you as much as I love you."

He leaned down and kissed her softly . . . tenderly. Then, while she was still absorbing his amazing words, he began to make love to her as if she were a goddess and he her only worshipper.

Hands glided all over her body, stopping to caress and rub her most sensitive areas. His mouth moved down her face, to her chest, kissing, sucking, and licking her breasts until Eden was sobbing with need.

A hand rubbed between her legs and Eden parted her legs to allow him in. Fingers probed and entered gently, then thrust repeatedly, till she was on the edge of release. Then he lifted his body and settled between her legs.

Eden wrapped arms and legs around him and held tight for the sweetest, most beautiful ride of her life. Within seconds, they'd both found the release they sought.

Held in Jordan's arms, Eden knew she'd never been happier. Never would she have guessed he felt the way he did about her.

Jordan rolled over, gathered her to him, and pressed a soft kiss on her forehead, her cheek, and then her mouth. "We still have to talk about what happened."

"I know we do. I'm so sorry for not telling you in the first place. It was wrong—"

Jordan pressed a finger against her mouth. "Sweetheart, you have nothing to apologize for. I don't blame you for not telling me. I'm just surprised you didn't shoot me on sight. I caused you so much grief, you must have hated me."

"No, I never hated you. When I saw you again, I panicked. . . . I'd worked so hard to forget. I'd built this new life for myself, and suddenly, my old one was staring me in the face. I just wanted to keep it buried. But I never blamed you for any of it."

"You should have. I lost my temper, said some hideous things, and instead of allowing you to explain, I practically forced you to leave."

"No . . . please, don't apologize. What I did—deceiving you like that, letting you make love to me, without knowing who I was—it was so wrong. I was a stupid, idiotic romantic and never gave any thought to the consequences or what it might mean to you."

"That night, Eden . . . You need to know. It meant more to me than just a one-night stand. I think that's why I was so angry. Why I believed your mother's lies." Elbow propped on a pillow, Jordan gazed down at her. "But the things I said, I can't—"

Eden pressed a finger to his mouth. "It's over. We both made mistakes."

Gratitude and love gleaming in his eyes, Jordan pressed his mouth to hers in a tender kiss. Raising his head, he whispered, "I'm sorry about Henry . . . telling you about his death that way. I know you loved him. He ended up leaving your mother a few months after you disappeared. Last year he had a heart attack on the golf course. Even though it hurt him that we never found you, the last few years of his life were much happier than the time he spent with your mother."

A knot formed in her throat as she thought about the father she would never see again. "He was a good man . . . a good father. I wish I'd been able to say goodbye to him . . . let him know I was okay. I thought Alise would tell him, but since you were still looking for me, I'm assuming she told no one I contacted her."

Jordan blew out a harsh sigh. "No, she didn't tell anyone. I don't want to talk about her because when I even think about her, all I want to do is get on a plane to D.C. and—"

Eden covered his mouth with hers. He was right. Bringing Alise into their reunion would mar the perfection of the night.

Jordan pulled her under him and for several long moments, sighs and groans were the only sounds. Alise Stevens, now and forever, forgotten as the nobody she was.

Catching his breath, Jordan asked softly, "Were you attacked right after you left my house?"

Eden knew he couldn't let it go until she'd shared as much as she could. The vague memories couldn't hurt her anymore, but Jordan needed this for closure. "I think so . . . I don't really remember much about it, which is a blessing, I know. I woke up in some sort of abandoned building. I managed to crawl out into the alleyway, but I'd lost so much blood, I didn't make it much farther than that before I passed out. Someone was passing by and happened to notice a large lump. The lump turned out to be me."

"And you remember nothing about the bastards who did this?"

"Not really. I know there were two of them . . . after it happened . . . maybe for a month or two . . . I'd hear an occasional rough voice in my mind or a facial feature would suddenly flash in front of me, but nothing I could hang on to that helped the police."

Jordan gathered her in his arms as if wanting to absorb her pain into his own body. "I swear, I would have given up my life to prevent what happened."

She trailed a tender finger down his face. "I know that, and believe me, I would never wish what happened to me on anyone, but if it hadn't happened, I would never have found LCR. I'm proud of what I've accomplished for them."

"You're the most amazing woman I've ever known."

She shook her head in wonder. "I still can't believe this isn't all a dream. That I won't wake up in the morning and it won't have happened."

"Believe in me, sweetheart. Believe in us. Please."

She took deep breaths, wanting for once in her life to get something right. Her hands cupped his face. Eyes locked with his, she whispered, "I never stopped loving you."

Tension she hadn't been aware of left Jordan's body. "I promise you, I'll not mess up this time, Devon. This time, I'll get it right."

Had he realized he called her Devon? Her last worry, her last fear disappeared. Tears blurred her vision, but she didn't mistake the tears she saw in Jordan's eyes. In a voice quiet with conviction, she gave him another promise. "We'll both get it right this time."

Standing yards away from the dock, Noah watched two of his best operatives board their honeymoon yacht. Hours ago, he'd given the bride away in a small, private ceremony. He, Dr. Arnot, and Samara Lyons were the only witnesses. The bride, radiant and beautiful, had gazed at her groom as if he were the sun, moon, and stars. And the groom looked at his bride as if his life could not continue without her.

Noah had questioned himself many times on bringing Jordan Montgomery back into Eden's life, but questioned no longer. It had been the right thing to do.

Now they were headed for a monthlong cruise, and while he might be upset by such an inordinate amount of time off for an employee, the fact that Eden and her husband would be returning and continuing their work with LCR made him feel extraordinarily generous.

Noah turned away from the couple who couldn't seem to keep their hands off each other, and looked out over the bright blue water, his eyes only seeing what lay ahead for him.

When Eden and Jordan returned, Jordan would take the controls of LCR for a while. Noah had plans to go back into the field for an extended period of time. After all these years, his past had caught up with him and it was time, way past time, for Noah McCall to repay a debt . . . no matter how deadly.

Acknowledgments

Writing is often a solitary endeavor, but my path to publication involved many. I would like to express my deep appreciation to the following:

My husband, who, without his support and encouragement, I never would have been able to go the distance, and my mom, who shared with me her love of reading and continues to share her favorite books. My furry writing companions, Mae Blossom, who sleeps in my lap as I bang away on my computer, and her sister Prissy Louise, who sleeps beside my chair, forcing me to stay put and write. My sister Debra, who, years ago, stayed up all night reading my very first manuscript and swore she loved it, and my sister Denise, who read the unedited version of this book and told me this was definitely "the one." I love you both.

Kelley St. John, Jennifer Echols, Carla Swafford, Marie Campbell, and Erin McClune for guidance, a willing ear, and laughter when I needed it most. Darah Lace, brainstormer extraordinaire. Brenda White, former neighbor and forever friend, who was kind enough to read my early manuscripts. And Jill Lawrence, my very first critique partner.

Danny Agan for his kindness and willingness to answer my endless questions, and Susan Vickerstaff for her French translations. Any mistakes are entirely my own.

Laurie Schnebly Campbell and Candace Havens for the incredible online classes that put me back on the right path. The employees at Borders Books and Music in West

Lafayette, Indiana, for their kind encouragement to a bookseller who desperately wanted to become a published author. I miss you guys! And Romance Writers of America, especially my wonderful home chapter, Southern Magic, and the fantastic Kiss of Death chapter.

My talented editor, Kate Collins, for her wisdom and vision in whipping this book into shape. Also the wonderful Linda Marrow and the entire staff at Ballantine. What a fantastic group of people you are!

Special thanks to the entire team at Trident Media, especially my incredible agent, Kimberly Whalen, for her belief in this project and especially in me. Thank you for making my dreams come true.

Turn the page to catch an
exclusive sneak peek at

RETURN TO ME

the second novel in Christy Reece's
romantic suspense trilogy!

Published by Ballantine Books

Birmingham, Alabama

"I found the man I want to marry."

This announcement received mixed reactions from the three women sitting at the table with Samara Lyons. Rachel just rolled her eyes, Allie ignored the comment because of the cute guy at the bar making eyes at her, and Julie, the newest member of their Thursday night margarita-fest, leaned toward her eagerly.

"Where'd you meet him? What's his name? Have you been dating—"

"Wait . . . hold up," Rachel interrupted as she raised her hand to signal their server. "Let's call for another round and then Samara will explain to you. With your psychology degree, you can tell us the name of Samara's mental illness."

Samara grinned and stuck her tongue out at her best friend since the first grade. Rachel, the cynic, as Samara fondly called her, didn't believe in "happily ever afters." Samara, on the other hand, knew they existed. She'd seen them firsthand. Having parents who'd been happily married for over thirty-five years, not to mention five very happy brothers and sisters-in-law, reinforced her beliefs.

Rachel referred to Samara as Pollyanna for what she called her amazing belief in the goodness of humanity when all evidence showed the exact opposite. Samara never argued with that statement, because it was true. She did believe in the basic goodness of people, and so far, with only a few exceptions, she hadn't been proven wrong.

"Okay, girl." Rachel took a sip of her frozen concoction, licked the salt from her mouth, and leaned forward. "Who is it this week?"

Being humored didn't bother Samara in the least. "Did you see that new foaming bath commercial where the husband runs a hot bubble bath for his wife and then takes the kids to the park while she has the house to herself?"

"Yeah, so?"

"He's the one."

Only Julie looked startled by this statement. "Do you know the man in the commercial?"

Looking satisfied with how the conversation was going, Rachel settled back into her chair with an amused, rapt expression.

"No, I don't know him. He's just the guy I'd like to marry."

"But why?"

Ignoring Rachel's smug grin, she attempted to explain her philosophy. "I have the ideal man in my head. I've just never met him. But sometimes I'll see a guy on television or read about him and I recognize a certain characteristic I want in my future Mr. Right."

Julie nodded. "Actually, that's a very healthy attitude."

Rachel stared at Julie. "You gotta be kiddin' me. Don't encourage her lunacy. Heal it!"

"No, really. It is healthy." Julie waved a hand at the crowded bar in Mama Maria's. "Look at all these people, searching for that one special person they think they want to spend their life with, and most of them have no clue what they're looking for. At least Samara has a good idea what she does and doesn't want."

Taking a long, icy swallow of her drink, Samara couldn't help but be glad that at least someone thought knowing what she was looking for was a good idea. She also knew what she didn't want, having learned that the hard way. She took another sip, refusing to give the humiliating memory any more thought.

The sound of sizzling fajitas heading her way caught Samara's attention. Her stomach rumbled with a welcoming growl as the spicy aroma hit her senses. Samara looked around in anticipation. Behind the waiter, to her left, her gaze was caught and held by the tall, looming figure in the corner. A man she'd gladly walk barefoot across the country to avoid. Her stomach backflipped and spiraled downward. What was he doing here? And why did he have the expression of a hungry tiger on his too-perfect face? He sure as hell hadn't looked that way the last time she'd seen him.

Refusing to acknowledge him, Samara turned away. There were thousands of reasons he might be here, none of them to do with her. He'd made it painfully clear he wanted nothing to do with her, and she had every intention of showing him she felt the same way. Now, if only her pounding heart and adrenaline-filled bloodstream would cooperate. Despite herself, she dared another peek. *Dammit, he was still staring.*

Noah McCall hadn't been able to keep his eyes off Samara since he'd walked into the bar. Some people glowed with purity and light; Samara did that more than most. His jaw clenched at the reason he was here. She already hated him, and he doubted his request for help would make her like him any more.

The decision to come here hadn't been easy. Coming anywhere close to the South always set up a burning in his gut that would take him days to dispel. The air was different here. Thick and warm, it had character, life. Sucking at you, pulling you down. The warm, cloying sweetness made him want to gag.

Noah threw off his disquiet and shut down the memories. This wasn't about him. Never would be again. This was about doing the right thing, no matter the cost.

Straightening from his slouch against the wall, he sauntered slowly toward the beauty glowering at him. He plastered on his most cocky smile, quite aware it would rile her even more. And Samara had enough reason to be angry for a lifetime. A year ago, he had turned down the sweet, sexy offer of her beautiful body. He knew enough about human nature to know that kind of slight wasn't something one quickly recovered from.

Fiery sparks shot from ice-blue eyes, making them appear even more glacierlike. A genuine smile kicked up his lips. Feisty, spirited, and sexy as hell . . . Samara Lyons was just what he was looking for. Perfect for the job in every way.

"Hello, Samara."

Myriad emotions flashed across her expressive face, none of them friendly. *Good.* She would need that anger to fuel what he was going to ask of her. He'd channel the anger in the right direction, but until then he'd just enjoy the show.

She did what he expected. After giving him a glare of pure loathing, she turned her back on him. Her spine was so stiff, it looked as though it would crack at the slightest touch. Testing the theory, with his index finger Noah lightly brushed the nape of her neck . . . a tender, fragrant spot his mouth watered to taste.

As she jerked around, the glare grew hotter and Noah couldn't hold back his laugh.

"What do you want?" Her tone indicated that whatever it was, he shouldn't plan on getting it.

"I need to talk to you. Let's go."

"Excuse me? Just who the hell do you think you are?"

Ignoring the wide-eyed gazes of the three women sitting at the table with her, Noah leaned down and whispered in her ear, "I need you."

Samara jerked away from him. Bestowing her most insulting look, she started at his feet and gave him a scathing once-over. She brought her gaze back to his face, her voice dripping with disdain. "I've got nothing you want."

Something tugged at his heart . . . the one he knew he didn't have. He'd hurt and humiliated this woman and she still stung a year later. If he had a conscience, he'd leave and find someone else. But since that didn't exist and he needed her cooperation, he did the next best thing. Saluting her with a small wave of his hand, he retreated into the shadows. Having others around when he talked with her wasn't optimum anyway. He'd allow her this small reprieve.

Samara watched Noah back away and disappear out the door. Fury and hurt waltzed like buffalos throughout her body. Why should seeing him again bother her? He meant nothing to her other than a humiliating moment she'd sworn was erased from her memories. How dare he come and stir them up again. Noah McCall, devil-handsome and arrogant as sin, could piss her off faster than anyone she'd ever met.

"Good heavens, Sam," Rachel said. "You going to just sit there and stare into space, or are you going to tell us who 'Mr. Tall, Dark, and Please-Jump-My-Bones Sexy' was?"

Samara dragged herself back from the dark memory and looked at the stupefied faces of her friends. "Just someone I'd rather forget."

"Forget a man who looks like that? No way." This from Allie, who'd even stopped flirting with the cute guy at the bar to weigh in on the sexiness of Noah McCall.

Samara gave an emphatic shake of her head. "Looks aren't everything."

Allie flashed a wicked grin. "No, but they sure don't hurt."

While the girls continued chatting, Samara retreated back to her thoughts. What could Noah want to talk to her about? The last time she saw him, she'd been lying on the bed with the room whirling around her. Noah had just carried her to bed, kissed her on her forehead, and walked out the door.

Samara had wished more than once that she'd either had too much to drink so she wouldn't remember her humiliation, or that she hadn't had anything to drink at all. Unfortunately she'd been sober enough to remember Noah's refusal and just drunk enough to have issued an invitation in the first place.

In Paris for the wedding, she thought she had accepted and resigned herself to the fact that the man she'd planned to marry, Jordan Montgomery, was in love with another woman. She told herself she was happy for them. Jordan and Eden had suffered enough and deserved every happiness. But that was before Eden walked in the room for the ceremony and Samara saw Jordan's face. The tiny crack in her heart became a gaping crevice. Never had she seen a more honest, naked look of adoration.

After the wedding, they'd all gone to a small restaurant to celebrate. Since she, Noah, and a friend of Eden's were the only guests, the party broke up quickly. The happy couple headed to their honeymoon, and Dr. Arnot, Eden's friend, said goodbye and left. Barely saying a word, Noah had disappeared abruptly, leaving Samara alone at the table.

The first time she'd met Noah, she'd been instantly attracted to him—until he opened his mouth. Within seconds, the man had her fuming. He'd been arrogant, cocky, and evasive—and those were just his *good* characteristics. She'd gone to him for help and he'd practically laughed in her face.

Samara was used to people, especially men, being nice to her. Because she was just a little over five feet tall, with a slight build, creamy magnolia complexion, and large, ice-blue eyes, she was treated by most men as a fragile doll. It wasn't something she encouraged or took advantage of, just something she was accustomed to having. With five older brothers, she'd been taught how to take care of herself, but that didn't stop men from feeling that they needed to protect her.

Noah McCall hadn't even acted as though he knew she was a woman. He'd refused to give her information on Eden for Jordan, laughed at her temper, and then had practically thrown her out of his office.

So why had she found herself sitting alone at the table, fantasizing about him? Were those broad shoulders really as strong as they looked? Was his short, ebony hair as soft and silky as it seemed? Did his deliciously sensuous mouth taste of the wine they'd had with dinner?

Physically, Noah McCall was the most perfect-looking man she'd ever seen. Tall, muscular, with a swarthy complexion and the deepest, darkest brown eyes she could ever imagine. The kind of eyes a woman could lose her soul in, lose herself.

What happened next was inevitable, but also one of the most painful experiences of her life. Why couldn't she forget? And how could she now, when the cause of that pain had stood in front of her only minutes ago?

Samara took a gulp of her slushy margarita. She remembered everything as if it were just yesterday—overwhelming need, consuming heat, and then cold, frozen reality.